THE BUS STATION MUR[

Miss Julia Tyler is taking her great-niece. Julia enjo passengers, until it is time to depart. That's w... discovers that one of her fellow passengers seems to have fallen asleep. To her horror, Julia sees that the woman has been stabbed in the heart with a large knitting needle. And as it happens, the detective on the case is one of her former students, who shares that the murder victim was stabbed as the bus was emptying. So of the 16 passengers, only eight could have committed the murder. But before the murderer is discovered, two more sudden deaths occur—and Julia is pulled right into the heart of the mystery.

NO POCKETS IN SHROUDS

After her experience in Annapolis, Miss Julia finds herself fascinated with playing detective. When she reads about the mysterious and unsolved poisoning of a Louisville butler—and realizes that an old friend is related to the family—she visits her friend, and falls into a twisted family knot. It was old Breckingridge Helm's butler who had been poisoned, and now Helm himself has suffered a stroke, surrounded by his six grown grandchildren. They all expect to share in the inheritance when Helm dies, and they have just found out that there is a new will. The threat of murder is in the air. And Miss Julia finds herself right in the midst of it all, getting closer to crime than she had ever intended.

Louisa Revell Bibliography
(1910-1985)

Mysteries:
The Bus Station Murders (1949)
No Pockets in Shrouds (1949)
A Silver Spade (1950)
The Kindest Use a Knife (1953)
The Men with Three Eyes (1955)
See Rome and Die (1958)
A Party for the Shooting (1960)

Non-Fiction:
Charles Carroll of Carrollton (1942)

The Bus Station Murders
No Pockets in Shrouds
LOUISA REVELL
Introduction by Curtis Evans

Stark House Press • Eureka California

THE BUS STATION MURDERS / NO POCKETS IN SHROUDS

Published by Stark House Press
1315 H Street
Eureka, CA 95501, USA
griffinskye3@sbcglobal.net
www.starkhousepress.com

THE BUS STATION MURDERS
Originally published and copyright © 1947
by The Macmillan Company, New York.

NO POCKETS IN SHROUDS
Originally published and copyright © 1948
by The Macmillan Company, New York.

Copyright © 2024 Stark House Press. All rights reserved under
International and Pan-American Copyright Conventions.

"Louisa Revell: Sally Lunn of Mystery" © copyright 2025 by Curtis Evans

ISBN: 979-8-88601-126-5

Book design by Mark Shepard, shepgraphics.com
Cover design by Jeff Vorzimmer, ¡caliente!design, Austin, Texas
Cover art by Dennis McLoughlin
Proofreading by Bill Kelly

PUBLISHER'S NOTE
This is a work of fiction. Names, characters, places and incidents are
either the products of the author's imagination or used fictionally, and
any resemblance to actual persons, living or dead, events or locales, is
entirely coincidental.

Without limiting the rights under copyright reserved above, no part of
this publication may be reproduced, stored, or introduced into a retrieval
system or transmitted in any form or by any means (electronic,
mechanical, photocopying, recording or otherwise) without the prior
written permission of both the copyright owner and the above publisher
of the book.

First Stark House Press Edition: January 2025

7
Louisa Revell:
Sally Lunn of Mystery
by Curtis Evans

21
The Bus Station Murders
by Louisa Revell

163
No Pockets in Shrouds
by Louisa Revell

LOUISA REVELL:
SALLY LUNN OF MYSTERY

By Curtis Evans

American mystery writer Louisa Revell burst onto the literary crime scene in the spring of 1947 with her lauded debut detective novel, *The Bus Station Murders*. The story is brightly and amusingly narrated by former high school Latin teacher and avid reader of crime fiction Miss Julia Tyler, a kindly though opinionated and inquisitive sixty-seven-year-old spinster. The spinster narrator-sleuth of a certain age was quite a popular "type" in American mysteries of the Thirties and Forties, although the species had some detractors. In his notice of the novel in the *San Francisco Chronicle*, crime writer and reviewer Anthony Boucher, by no means a fanatical devotee of this singular fictional example of sleuthing womanhood, reflected amiably that "[w]ild coincidence and a solution devoid of detection do not lessen the appeal of this attractive book, which manages to blend the romantic and local-color elements of [Maryland mystery writer] Leslie Ford (Miss Julia's favorite author) with an agreeably humorous perception of its own snobbish garrulity." Although Boucher erred in one thing in his review—by her own words in *The Bus Station Murders* Agatha Christie, not Leslie Ford, is Miss Julia's favorite author (Ford was runner-up)—he concluded admiringly: "Even those allergic to spinster-narrators may want more of Miss Julia."

And, indeed, more of Miss Julia was just what mystery readers wanted. Over the next dozen years a half-dozen additional Miss Julia detective novels appeared from Louisa Revell's hand for the delectation of her appreciative public: *No Pockets in Shrouds* (1948), *A Silver Spade* (1950), *The Kindest Use a Knife* (1952), and, a bit more belatedly, *The Men with Three Eyes* (1955), *See Rome and Die* (1957) and *A Party for the Shooting* (1960). Despite the praise afforded the Louisa Revell books on both sides of the Atlantic, however, they have remained out-of-print in English for more than six decades now (*The Bus Station Murders* was republished in France in 1995); and today very little is known about their author.

So who was the woman behind Louisa Revell? Modern attention began to focus on the author in 2015, when blogger NancyO at *The Crime Segments* favorably reviewed *The Bus Station Murders*, identifying Louisa Revell as "the pseudonym of Ellen Hart Smith, who . . . also wrote a famous biography [of an American Founding Father] . . . *Charles Carroll of Carrolton.*" The next year at his *Pretty Sinister* blog John Norris lauded several Louisa Revell mysteries, singling out for praise the series' sleuth, Miss Julia Tyler, as "the epitome of what an amateur detective should be in fiction." Additionally, Revell's mystery *See Rome and Die* was reviewed in 2019 at the blogs *Clothes in Books* and *Dead Yesterday* and her mystery *A Silver Spade* at the blog *My Reader's Block* in 2021. One blogger stated that the author "lived in Maryland for most of her life and retired to Owensboro, Kentucky," but in fact Ellen Hart Smith resided for almost her entire life in the Ohio River city of Owensboro. She derived her ample knowledge of Annapolis, Maryland, the setting of her first mystery novel, from research trips which she made to the city when she was working on her Charles Carroll biography.

Born on July 16, 1910 in Owensboro, Kentucky, then merely a town of some sixteen thousand people, Ellen Hart Smith was the daughter of Edward White Smith, a tobacco manufacturer turned furniture store owner and prominent civic leader, and Susan (Hart) Smith, a schoolteacher and amateur musician who cofounded and frequently served as president of Owensboro's Saturday Musicale concert series. Tragically the much beloved Susie, as she was familiarly known, died suddenly at the age of forty-three on the last day of December 1912, when her daughter Ellen, the only child from her later-in-life marriage to native Mississippi widower Edward Smith, was merely two years old.

According to a local newspaper, Susie Smith had been "a woman of rare attractiveness of character" and "one of the leading teachers of the city," possessed of "a fine intellect, an unusual sense of humor and great sympathy." She herself was the daughter of two much admired Owensboro educators, Henry and Mary Ellen (McClarty) Hart, who for many years during the last third of the nineteenth century had conducted a private school adjoining their antebellum home at 521 Daviess Street. At her death Susie's only sibling Henry (Ellen's uncle) resided in Reading, Pennsylvania, where he recently had become engaged in the motor trade. He did not wed until he was forty and he seems to have sired no children.

Ellen Hart Smith was raised by her father Edward—who, twice

widowed after brief marriages, never wed again in the nearly four decades of life which remained to him—and a couple of older, unmarried, working women cousins on her late mother's side who boarded with them at the house on Daviess Street: Lettie Boyd and Jennie McClarty, respectively employed as a schoolteacher and a stenographer. Ellen Smith proved herself a worthy intellectual descendant of her distinguished educator forebears. Nicknamed "Tip" by her classmates (a typically masculine cognomen connoting curiosity, intelligence and resourcefulness), Ellen was chosen valedictorian of her graduating class of '27 at Owensboro High School, where she acted in and served as treasurer of the school drama group, the Rose Curtain Players.

The leading light and president of the Rose Curtain Players was then Ellen's talented classmate Samuel Yewell Tompkins, who became famous in the Fifties as stage and film star Tom Ewell. Best known for portraying Marilyn Monroe's nervous middle-aged married admirer in the hit Billy Wilder comedy *The Seven Year Itch*, Ewell lived a half mile from the Smith house at 521 Daviess Street, though he and Ellen seem never to have acted in a play together. His most praised performance with the Players was as the detective in the famed mystery play *The Thirteenth Chair*. Perhaps this play gave Ellen her lifelong taste for the fine art of murder.

During her teenage years Ellen Smith was also active with the Young Women's Christian Association, or YWCA, spending three successive Twenties summers at the organization's Kentucky camps at Mammoth Cave and Camp Daniel Boone. Further afield she attended the YWCA's Camp Maqua on Loon Lake near Poland, Maine, the basis for the setting in her third Louisa Revell detective novel, *A Silver Spade*. After high school Ellen successively enrolled in the University of Kentucky and Miami University at Miami, Ohio. She graduated from Miami University in the early 1930s (presumably having received an advanced degree in history) and returned to live in Owensboro with her father and two maiden cousins, along with a Delta Zeta sorority sister and intimate friend from Miami University, Margaret Elizabeth Evans. Margaret and Ellen would live together in Owensboro for the rest of their lives, a full half-century.

During this tumultuous Depression decade, the most noted event that took place in growing Owensboro, which was now nearing a population of thirty thousand, was the 1936 downtown hanging, in a repellent carnival atmosphere that drew thousands of excited, gawking spectators, of Rainey Bethea, a black man convicted of the robbery-rape-murder of an elderly white woman at her home in the Lower Town neighborhood, located a mile from 521 Daviess Street. Adding piquancy for the press and public was the fact that the execution was supervised by Florence Shoemaker Thompson, a woman sheriff. She had succeeded to the office after the sudden death of her sheriff husband, under the practice known as widow's succession.

This repellent event, to which Ellen Hart Smith implicitly alludes in her mystery *The Bus Station Murders*, would become the last legal public hanging in the United States, having been wrathfully condemned by newspapers across the United States, even in the South. In neighboring Virginia, for example, the *Newport News Daily Press* thundered, under the stinging banner "A Public Disgrace":

> The public hanging of a Negro in Owensboro, Ky, last Friday was one of the most sickening events of many years. It was a Roman holiday for nearly 10,000 morbid, bloodthirsty spectators from several states. There were hoots and jeers while a priest administered the last rites. And after the Negro was pronounced dead scores swarmed up to his body and stripped from it bits of clothing to carry away as souvenirs....
>
> Owensboro's public hanging was little better than a lynching. It was a disgrace not only to Kentucky, but to the entire country.

The same year as this ghoulish affair, Ellen's college friend Margaret Evans—a railroad engineer's daughter who in high school at Lima, Ohio, had excelled at math, basketball and track—took employment as an Owensboro public school science teacher. In 1942, after American entry into the Second World War, Margaret, unconventionally for her sex at the time, went to work as a processing engineer analyst with the Kentucky Radio Corporation (aka Ken-Rad), a manufacturer of radio vacuum tubes which significantly contributed to the American cause in the great global conflagration. Indeed, Ken-Rad was deemed so vitally important to the nation that when a strike threatened the company in 1944, President Roosevelt ordered its seizure by the War Department.

Being musical (like Ellen's mother), as well as scientific and athletic, Maragret also played cello with the Owensboro Symphony Orchestra. She became a fixture at the house on Daviess Street, remaining there after the death of Ellen's cousins in 1939 and 1943 and Ellen's father in 1950 and inheriting the home from Ellen after Ellen's own death at the age of seventy-four on April 28, 1985. Margaret passed away there a dozen years later at age eighty-eight.

The daughter of a well-off father, Ellen evidently eschewed regular salaried employment, instead spending much of the Thirties composing her biography *Charles Carroll of Carrollton*. Upon its publication by prestigious Harvard University Press in 1942, Ellen along with her friend Margaret made the social rounds in Annapolis, where they were entertained by Mrs. Alexander McCormick, daughter-in-law of a rear admiral, and Mrs. James A. Walton, wife of a banker. While being feted in Annapolis Ellen took the opportunity to speak out in favor of historical preservation, a cause of great importance to her. Meanwhile her biography received a stellar notice in the book pages of the *New York Times*, with the reviewer praising Ellen's "sparkling" writing and expressing the hope that she would produce many more such scholarly works. (Just last year, the most recent Charles Carroll biographer, Bradley J. Birzer, proclaimed Hart's earlier work "a wonderful read.") Yet at age thirty-seven Ellen in 1947 followed her scholarly opus not with another serious historical or biographical tome, but rather with *The Bus Station Murders*, the first of her seven mysteries, all of which were written under the high-toned, ladylike pen name of Louisa Revell. Under her own name Ellen contributed scholarly book reviews to the *New York Herald Tribune*, *New Yorker* and *Maryland Historical Quarterly*.

Throughout her life Ellen seems to have hugged her identity of "Louisa Revell" as a closely held secret, rather like the precise nature of her relationship with her friend Margaret Evans. She was hardly a shrinking violet when it came to Owensboro public life, however. In the early Thirties, as the Depression tightened its cruel grip upon the country, she and Margaret volunteered with the Daviess County chapter of the Red Cross, which her father then headed, to distribute sacks of flour to the needy. After American entry into World War Two, when Margaret was engaged in vital work with Ken-Rad, Ellen again volunteered with the local chapter of the Red Cross, at their offices on the third floor of the Federal building channeling the rising tide of tasks which the chapter faced with the assistance of only its executive secretary until March 1943, when a professional woman finally arrived upon the scene to take charge. Two decades later, in the 1960s, Ellen headed the Board of Trustees of the Owensboro Public Library. Yet all during this time she maintained a remarkably low prolife for a successful mystery writer, when all the while, one presumes, she could have queened it the locals as Owensboro's premier writing celebrity.

By my own research Owensboro's newspaper, the *Messenger-Inquirer*, has not once mentioned Louisa Revell's name to this day, although after Ellen in 1948 published her second Miss Julia Tyler detective novel, *No Pockets in Shrouds*, which she set in Louisville, Kentucky, downtown Louisville bookstore W. K. Stewart Co. ran an ad in the

Courier-Journal teasingly asking the questions *Who Is Louisa Revell?* and *A Novel of Murder In Louisville By ? ? ?* Answer came there none to these questions from Ellen, despite the fact that it would have been lucrative for her actually to have stepped briefly into the Louisville limelight to promote her book with an actual signing, like her Great Plains mystery writing contemporary Edith Howie did with her own cozy Forties crime novels in Sioux Falls, South Dakota. Did Ellen deem mystery writing too lowbrow an endeavor for the sole remaining scion of the educator Hart clan (even though it is clear from her mysteries, in which Miss Julia drops the names of real-life mystery writers with affectionate abandon, that the author herself was an inveterate enthusiast of fictional crime)? Or did she worry that her local Methodist church, of which her relations were bedrock members, would disapprove of her frequently irreverent mystery writing?

Light on the anonymity matter is shed by correspondence exchanged in 1950 between Ellen and Hilda McLeod Jacob of the Maine State Library. Jacob wrote to Louisa Revell through the author's publisher McMillan, requesting an inscribed copy of her latest mystery, *A Silver Spade*, for the library's Maine Author Collection, noting: "It is not often we have a mystery with a Maine background." Jacob hintingly added that "we have been unsuccessful in our search for biographical information about you." Upon receiving the letter, Ellen duly sent the library a copy of the novel, though she apologized in a separate missive for not inscribing it in more detail, "as I know you would prefer." She explained to Jacob that the library's "failure to find biographical information about 'Louisa Revell' was not your fault but our triumph. Other ladies leading double lives have sometimes written too much, to their own undoing." Likely Ellen had in mind Agatha Christie's public exposure the previous year as being as well "serious" novelist Mary Westmacott, a revelation which a Christie biographer has characterized as devastating to the author. Said Christie sadly of her Westmacott masquerade: "it's really all washed up." Ellen wanted to avoid getting similarly "done-in" by her more frivolous mystery writing alter ego.

Mystery writing's gain, however personally unheralded, was the teaching profession's loss. After she retired in 1942, Ellen's cousin Miss Lettie Boyd observed that it was the first time in seventy-five years [i.e., since just after that Civil War] that "some person has not gone forth from that home [at 251 Daviess Street] to teach at the city schools." Ellen personally may have foregone teaching as a career, but for her own retired schoolteacher sleuth, Miss Julia, she clearly derived inspiration from her kinswoman Miss Lettie, a graduate of Nashville's Peabody College who devotedly taught in the Owensboro public schools for forty-four years, from the ages of twenty-eight to seventy-two, stepping down only a year before her death.

When Margaret Evans died in 1997, a dozen years after her longtime companion Ellen, the old house on Daviess Street, where varied Hart and Smith relations and a single Evans had successively resided for 130 years, was cleared of its contents. These went for far more, the *Messenger-Inquirer* reported, than the four-bedroom, three-bathroom house itself, it being badly in need of repairs. Eager bidders snapped up bulky antique furniture pieces, flatware, silverware, opera glasses and vases of Venetian glass, as an enigmatic grey cat, its owner (if any) unknown, lithely wound its way between shifting legs. Naturally, there were also boxes upon boxes of books, filled with "encyclopedias or tomes on Churchill, Jefferson and other historical figures." A fancy set of weighty Dickens volumes fetched $300. An armoire of burl walnut went for $2300, while a French curio cabinet with a curved glass front took in $2850.

No mention was made in the newspaper account of any sale of those lowly yet highly collectible things, mysteries, but then no mention was made either of Ellen Hart Smith ever having been a mystery novelist. Instead she was identified worthily but vaguely as "a writer, book reviewer . . . and former chairwoman of the library board." Locals fondly recalled her companion Margaret's charming tea parties, where Margaret, a member of Trinity Episcopal Church, would "serve laughter, Sally Lunn cakes and good conversation with equal measure." Of Ellen's spirited Louisa Revell detective novels, however, nothing whatsoever was said.

Newspapers took no notice of the author either, after the publication of the final novel in the Miss Julia Tyler mystery series in 1960. Even Ellen and Margaret's historic home was torn down and replaced by a modern dwelling in 2007—the same year, ironically, that Owensboro began hosting its International Mystery Writers' Festival. Now, however, Louisa Revell's sparkling Miss Julia Tyler mysteries can be enjoyed once again, with or without Sally Lunn cakes—though the latter surely would make a fine accompaniment, provided that no one has sprinkled them with arsenic!

THE BUS STATION MURDERS

Miss Julia Tyler—a sixty-seven-year-old retired high school Latin teacher from the town of Rossville, Virginia near historic Williamsburg—made her fictional debut as the narrator of Ellen Hart

Smith's first Louisa Revell mystery, *The Bus Station Murders*, published in 1947. The novel, which is set over the Christmas season of 1944 at Annapolis, Maryland, home of the United States Naval Academy, sees Miss Julia paying a visit to the city to stay with her great-niece Anne and her naval officer husband Dick Travers. En route to the Travers' quaint little dormered frame home on Cornhill Street, the peppery spinster becomes involved in her first murder investigation when at the Annapolis bus station another passenger on the bus is found viciously slain in her seat, having been first drugged with morphia, then dispatched with a knitting needle to her heart.

The murder victim is the second Mrs. Roger Barnes, widow of the late admiral, who died from wounds sustained during the engagement at Pearl Harbor. It does not to take Miss Julia, an avid reader of mystery fiction, long to discover that the late, unlamented Mrs. Barnes was one of that odious tribe of individuals, so frequently found in Miss Julia's favorite reading matter, whom literally a busload of individuals had some sort of motive to murder. Soon the retired Latin teacher is unapologetically nosing into the mysterious affair. "I hoped people wouldn't think their aunt was an old curiosity-box," she announces, "but if they got the impression, that was, as Dick says, just too bad." Miss Julia does so love a good mystery, making a real-life murder simply too hard for her to resist.

The Bus Station Murders has an engaging mystery plot of bluff and double bluff, but, as reviewers of the day noted, where the novel truly excels is in its setting and characterization. As the author (under her actual name) of *Charles Carroll of Carrolton*, Louisa Revell knew both Maryland and Annapolis well, and she effectively portrays the social snobberies endemic to the naval city, as bemusedly described by Miss Julia, certainly no stranger herself to snobbery. An older Virginia lady from a highly respectable small-town family—she shares her surname with antebellum America president and Virginia native John Tyler—Miss Julia would have been born presumably in 1877 (about a dozen years after the end of the Civil War, or War Between the States, as she calls it), making her seven years younger than her real-life model, Revell's highly respected schoolteacher aunt, Mary Letitia Boyd, who died in 1943. In the novel Miss Julia names and details many actual Annapolis locales, and at mid-point she and Anne make a highly interesting side trip to interview a couple of suspects on Maryland's wild Eastern Shore, in the guise of shopping for handmade hooked rugs.

The former Latin teacher's unconsciously amusing narration is an undoubted high point of *The Bus Station Murders*. "No, ladies don't commit murder," she insists at one point, adding scrupulously: "Not if they're in their right minds." She and a prominent Annapolis matron take time to visit a movie house to see Bob Hope's hit comedy film *The Princess and the Pirate*, which premiered in the United States on November 17, 1944. "[I]n the end he got the beautiful princess," Mis Julia tartly divulges, "though why she wanted him I do not see." She also manages to find some moments to peruse none other than *Charles Carroll of Carrollton*, thriftily noting of the pricey volume: "It cost three dollars and seventy-five cents, so I read it with the tips of my fingers, thinking I could give it away for Christmas."

Meanwhile there are two more "bus station murders" to consider. Both of these victims were passengers on the original murder bus as well as leading suspects, until their own respective demises, in the original slaying. How are all these killings connected? Have no fear, Miss Julia is on the case, along with Detective Lieutenant Ben Kramer, a former Rossville student of Miss Julia's from the Twenties. "I never expected to see him in Annapolis or any place else outside of jail," confesses Miss Julia unsentimentally of Ben. "He was . . . into something every minute."

Part of the fun for mystery fans in *The Bus Station Murders* are Miss Julia's copious meta references to mystery fiction of the Thirties and Forties. Her great-niece and nephew-in-law are fond murder fans too, which leads to humorous exchanges among them like these:

> "We haven't made a list, and in books they always do."
> "But does it ever do them any good?" I questioned. "It seems to me that when they've finished, they always sit and look at it for a while, and then sigh, and push the paper away."

Then there is this hilariously accurate takedown of snobbish, popular Maryland mystery writer Leslie Ford, who for many years herself lived in Annapolis, where her husband was an English professor at a local college:

> I had Leslie Ford's new book propped up in front of me. She is my favorite right after Agatha Christie, though Dick says that by the time the heroine has looked in the carved and gilded Queen Anne mirror that's reflecting also the pair of sunburst tables with pale creamy tea-rose petals spilling onto them from the pair of fluted Sheffield urns that have stood there nearly as long as the Corinthian columns have stood on the wide porch overlooking the river George Washington used to travel by barge,

rowed by his liveried slaves, he's forgotten who she is and why.

In contrast with Miss Julia and Anne, Dick Travers, one will not be surprised to learn, is a fan of hard-boiled crime writers like Dashiell Hammett, who famously, according to Raymond Chandler, took mystery fiction out of the Venetian vase—or Sheffield urn—and dropped it into the alley (though Dick likes that posh, pretentious fancy pants sleuth Philo Vance too).

A complete (I think) list of Miss Julia's author and sleuth references in *The Bus Station Murders* is: Mignon Eberhart, Agatha Christie (Miss Marple, Hercule Poirot), Mary Roberts Rinehart, Rufus King (Lieutenant Valcour), Ngaio Marsh (Chief Detective-Inspector Alleyn), E. Phillips Oppenheim, Patricia Wentworth (Miss Silver), Leslie Ford, S. S. Van Dine (Philo Vance) and Frances and Richard Lockridge (Lieutenant Weigand). Even the surname Travers may allude to Christoper Bush and his posh detective Ludovic Travers. Will Miss Julia's extensive fictional sleuthing knowledge enable her to solve the "real-life" series of murders which she encounters? Is truth even stranger than fiction? Read on and see for yourselves.

NO POCKETS IN SHROUDS (1948)

"Charlotte says I read too many murder books."
—confirmed murder fancier Miss Julia Tyler

One of the unusual facets of Louisa Revell's Miss Julia Tyler series of mysteries is the chronological precision of the seven narratives. The second novel in the series, *No Pockets in Shrouds*, takes place in the May 1945, just four months after the shocking criminal events detailed in *The Bus Station Murders*. These last four months Miss Julia, now sixty-eight, has been living in Annapolis, Maryland with her beloved great-niece Anne and her husband Dick Travers, renting out, at the sum of two hundred dollars a month (about $3400 today), her historic home in Rossville, Virginia. At that rate it pays to make long visits to family and friends.

Miss Julia finally decides to depart to stay with her old friend, the widowed Mrs. Thomas Crittenden Buckner, who now resides in Louisville, Kentucky, but the journey is by no means a sentimental one for our Miss Julia. Rather the gentlelady from Virginia—who has "read murder books since the first of the Mary Roberts Rineharts" (meaning back nearly four decades ago, during the Edwardian era) and has much more recently started her own scrapbook of real-life murders—wants practically to be in on the ground of a society slaying in Louisville (famously home of the Kentucky Derby) that of late has been making the crime headlines in newspapers. Miss Charlotte had invited Miss Julia to visit her in Louisville in the aftermath of the Annapolis killing spree, fondly imaging that the mayhem must have mortified her old friend; but the stouthearted retired Latin teacher only belatedly accepted the invitation after learning of Louisville's own murder. Miss Julia had had invitations to call from other ladies in Virginia, all of them "much closer and more recent friends than Charlotte," but, as she mercenarily explains to Anne and Dick, "nobody but Charlotte could provide a murder to entertain me with." Her great-niece instantly sympathizes, like any good murder mystery fan would, declaring: "This is just exactly the kind of murder you read about in books—all those rich people and butlers and all. And you and this Charlotte Buckner can walk right in."

Miss Julia has her doubts about Miss Charlotte as a partner in crime investigation, bluntly explaining to Anne and Dick: "Well, she's just tiresome, that's all. She means well—she's a good, kind Christian woman, and a lady too, of course. But she never was what Dick calls a brain...." However, the lure of murder in Louisville is too hard to resist, even with dim Charlotte in the midst of things, so off she goes to Kentucky.

So who was it who went and got themselves murdered this time, you may well ask. Well, it seems that at the end of March someone poisoned Gus, the dignified old "Negro butler" of Charlotte's "close kin" the Breckinridge Helms, one of the richest and most socially prominent families in Louisville. (Like Charlotte's husband's "Crittenden," the name recalls, as no doubt it was meant to, famous deceased Kentuckians, this time John C. Breckinridge, an American vice president and United States senator, and John L. Helm, a two-time governor of Kentucky.) Elderly and ill family patriarch Breckinridge Helm married twice and has three grandchildren by his first marriage—Breckinridge Helm III, Mary Preston Helm and their cousin Emily Craig—as well as two step-grandchildren by his second marriage: John Todd Brown and Martina Greer, wife of Dr. Robert Greer, an Ohio dentist. (The surname Todd recalls Mary Todd, yet another prominent native Kentuckian, the wife of President Abraham Lincoln.) These individuals constitute the quintet—or sextet if Martina Greer's husband is included—of squabbling heirs of the inevitable rich, unlikeable old man who is so provokingly prone to making changes in his will; and all are suspects in the murder of Gus and, ultimately, their own

Grandfather Helm, for someone does in that ill-tempered old man too, using the very same poison that killed the butler.

Discovering the culprit (or culprits) in these crimes takes Miss Julia on an oft-perilous course, which includes even, at the climax of the tale, a midnight meeting with a self-confessed murderer! Miss Julia continues to have a keen eye for local detail—many actual places in Louisville are observed and described, including Charlotte's place at The Puritan, today a senior living center—and a delightfully tart tongue (even more so than in *The Bus Station Murders*). Local snobbishness again is much in evidence and is lightly mocked. Naively goodhearted Charlotte, bless her heart (as the characters say), comes in for a large share of gentle mockery. "Charlotte was like the husbands who never dream their wives have married them for money," Miss Julia pronounces of her old friend.

Even though Miss Julia "was brought up in a rectory and educated in a church boarding school," her religious views seem rather less orthodox than those of pious Charlotte. "The rector of Grace and St. Peter's was there too," she sharply observes at one point of an episcopal clergyman, "hovering over one decayed gentlewoman after another like a fat black buzzard." Not that less prestigious faiths escape comment either: "Emily had quite a time explaining the Primitive Baptists to Charlotte, who apparently had thought they were all primitive."

More references are made to other mystery writers, with a specific implicit nod to Mignon Eberhart's *With this Ring*, a 1941 crime thriller set in Louisiana. A couple of rings play parts in *Shrouds* and the poison employed in the murders is of note for being quite topical to the day. All in all, *Shrouds* is a delightfully told tale, more than fulfilling the promise of *The Bus Station Murders*.

On a sadder note, Louisa Revell's prominent father, Edward White Smith, would step down from public affairs in 1948, the same year in which *No Pockets in Shrouds* was published. A much-admired business and civic figure in Owensboro, Kentucky, the old man would pass away two years later at age eighty-seven. I suspect that many of the infirmities of the elder Breckinridge Helm which are detailed in *Shrouds* were drawn from real life by the author, who then lived with her father and her companion Margaret Evans at the family home in Owensboro. Consolingly, caregiving for her father did not prevent the author from publishing a third mystery the year he died. It is always gratifying again to encounter Miss Julia Tyler in print. Certainly she is not the only person who likes a good murder.

—October 2024

Curtis Evans received a PhD in American history in 1998. He is the author of *Masters of the "Humdrum" Mystery: Cecil John Charles Street, Freeman Wills Crofts, Alfred Walter Stewart and British Detective Fiction, 1920-1961* (2012), *Clues and Corpses: The Detective Fiction and Mystery Criticism of Todd Downing* (2013), *The Spectrum of English Murder: The Detective Fiction of Henry Lancelot Aubrey-Fletcher and G. D. H. and Margaret Cole* (2015) and editor of the Edgar nominated *Murder in the Closet: Essays on Queer Clues in Crime Fiction Before Stonewall* (2017). He writes about vintage crime fiction at his blog The Passing Tramp and at Crimereads.

The Bus Station Murders
LOUISA REVELL

TO
E. M.
R. A. H.
W. C. M.

CHAPTER ONE

My great-niece Anne had been pestering me to visit her ever since her husband got his commission and she started following him around. But I'd read too much about Navy boomtowns, how crowded they were, full of all kinds of trash with too much money to spend, and how expensive, and how young schoolgirls stood around on the corners speaking to sailors. So I told Anne I'd just wait till they sent Dick some place respectable.

The children wired me as soon as Dick got his orders to the Naval Academy, and when they were settled in a house I came right on. I had a high opinion of Annapolis. I'd been there before—a good many years ago, it's true—and it was a respectable town if I ever saw one.

"And it was in Annapolis, after all that," Dick loves to tell people, "that the murders happened!" I reckon he and Anne will tease me about that as long as I live.

I still think, though, that a bus station isn't really part of a town. It always seems to me more like one of those independent states set down in the middle of a country, like the Vatican in Italy. Or like the foreign embassies that really are British or French or Peruvian soil, right in the District of Columbia. Certainly the bus station in Annapolis didn't take much character from the half Academy, half colonial, wholly civilized old town I remembered. It was big and expensive and supposed to be beautiful—maybe it was beautiful, if you like modern architecture. I thought it was stark and depressing as a dentist's operating room, with the same false brightness; and how a building only ten months old, which I later found out it was, could have accumulated such a smell is beyond me. It smelled the way you'd expect a pyramid to, if you opened it.

Dick says maybe it was murder in the air, and reminds me how sinister and foreboding everybody always feels in Mignon Eberhart's books. I certainly did feel sinister, not only in the station but long before the bus got there. But I think I was just sick at my stomach. Even the biggest and finest of new buses jolt the life out of you, and they all let off that blast of nasty exhaust when they start and stop. We weren't fifteen minutes out of Baltimore before I wished I'd taken the B. & A. Bump and agony those letters may stand for, as the midshipmen say; the bus had bump and agony as well, and lacked the charm of the antique.

"But I expect some of it is my fault," I told Mrs. Barnes honestly. "I'm too old to go racketing around the country like this. I'm old and tired and cross, and that's why this road seems so rough and the passengers look as if they'd crawled out from under rocks."

Mrs. Barnes laughed. She was nice. Dick says I shouldn't talk to strange people I meet in wartime, and usually I don't. I'd come all the way from Rossville to Richmond, Richmond to Washington, Washington to Baltimore without speaking to a soul. But I believe even Dick would have approved of Mrs. Barnes. She looked more like a missionary society president than one of the desperate characters he seems to think lie in wait for me when I travel.

"Look at those two up front," Mrs. Barnes said. "They'd make anybody feel better."

Well, they did. The girl was the prettiest little thing you ever saw, perfectly radiant in a tiny cheap hat all made of flowers; he must have married her in a state where the law allows child brides. Not that he looked much older than she did, especially in that ridiculous little-boy suit they make sailors wear. As for their baby—it was incredible enough that they should have one, but she must have been sixteen or eighteen months old—Anne would have had a fit over her. She was a beautiful child, and good as gold, too—not a whimper out of her, and holding her hands out to her father as if she'd known him always. Judging from the number of campaign ribbons on his chest they were probably meeting for the first time.

I admitted grudgingly that they did seem nice. "But that girl across the aisle!" I said. "Three shades of red, not to speak of her fingernails. And wouldn't you think she could take her nose out of *True Romances* long enough to remember *she's* got a child? He's smeared his all-day sucker all over the Red Cross girl and the fat man, and now he's started crawling on that little stenographer-looking woman, and the way this bus jolts he's likely to get stabbed on her knitting needles."

"Mothers don't take their responsibilities as hard as they did in our time, certainly," Mrs. Barnes agreed. I was flattered by her saying "our time"; she must have been ten years younger than my sixty-seven. "Did you hear those two women talking up front, right after the bus started?"

I said, "Those women remind me of what— Well, who did say it? He was a smart man, anyway. 'There are many worse things than war, and war is the cause of all of them.'"

Mrs. Barnes hadn't heard that before, evidently, and she repeated it after me, slowly and under her breath. "There are many worse things than war. And war is the cause of all of them."

She didn't say anything more, just sat and looked out the window;

and after a minute or two I picked up my book. I was annoyed with myself for being so tactless. Of all the things I shouldn't have mentioned to Mrs. Barnes the war was the worst. I'd overheard her talking to the Red Cross girl on the platform, before the bus started—that was how I knew her name—and she was just coming back from visiting her son, who was in the Ashford General Hospital at White Sulphur Springs. He had lost a leg at Salerno and the sight of both eyes; but he was learning to use an artificial leg, and a little later he was going up to the place in New Jersey where they have Seeing Eye dogs. He said he was going to be all right. Mrs. Barnes nearly broke down and cried when she told that, and I expect I would have joined her, if she'd been talking to me. But the Red Cross girl knew all the right things to say.

The Red Cross girl was another of the nice ones on the bus. There really were some. But I still say that at least half the passengers were thoroughly unattractive specimens of humanity. Four of the men, that is, and the woman Mrs. Barnes and I had been talking about.

Those women! When I was a girl my dear father made me read Dickens straight through, and I resolved there and then that if I ever wrote a book there wouldn't be a single description in it. But those two women certainly needed to be touched up, as Dick says. One of them was a big fat thing in blue overalls and a red bandanna and a diamond wristwatch—just like a cartoon or a Whither-are-we-drifting? editorial. The diamond wristwatch she'd taken out of her bag after the bus left Baltimore, and while she put it on she was telling the woman next to her—and the whole bus full of people, too, for her voice wasn't what you could call low and soft—how much her husband had paid for it. It seemed he was a maintenance man, whatever that was, in a big airplane plant in Baltimore and she was a riveter there. She started in to tell about some other diamond-studded things she had at home, but she didn't get very far. She met her match in the woman next to her. This one was a good deal younger, thirty-five or forty maybe; and it turned out that she worked in a Baltimore war plant too. She was an inspector—accent on the first syllable. She was dressed to the guards, with a real alligator bag and a blond pompadour built up until it looked like the back end of a fantail pigeon. This one had a lot of fine things at home too; but, unlike the first woman, she wasn't enjoying working for them. She missed being at home with her babies, to hear her tell it. Her babies were fourteen, nine, five, and four, all girls; and the big one took care of the little ones. She left lunch on the table for the two youngest, who were too little to be in school, and they got along just fine, locked up in the house all day with their nice toys. It seemed that Sheila Fay, who was the baby, had a real Angora wool

THE BUS STATION MURDERS

lamb with electric eyes, and Sandra JoAnn, the five-year-old, had a tricycle that cost thirty-nine-fifty.

Those two women sat way up at the front of the bus, on the right, and back of them was the curly-headed private who'd slept most of the way. Nobody close enough to smell his breath wondered why. I didn't care for him—nor for the scrawny, bald-headed little man beside him. He had a pompous fat stomach in spite of his scrawniness, so his ready-made business suit didn't fit except in that one place, and he was one of those people who can strut just as well sitting down. But at least he was quiet. Somebody on the bus certainly needed to be, between the bragging women up front and the noisy, sticky little boy and the big young man—the biggest, heartiest young man I believe I've ever seen. He looked like a bull and was just about as socially presentable. I took him for a Greek or some kind of Balkan—he was black-haired, oily-faced, and very expressive with his hands; and maybe his being an unnaturalized foreigner was the reason he wasn't in uniform. He certainly didn't look 4-F. The boy beside him, now, was obviously unfit for service. He was the most nervous human being I ever saw, not leaving out Cousin Eliza Woodcock. His fingers twitched, he had a tic in one cheek, and he'd fidgeted around so in his seat that his gray overcoat looked as if he'd slept in it. I felt sorry for the child (he couldn't have been more than nineteen or twenty), but he was one of those people you can feel sorry for forever and still not like. He had one of the meanest faces I ever saw, and when he laughed it made cold chills run up and down my spine.

He laughed often, he and the big greasy young man. Unless I was very much mistaken—and, after forty years of keeping study halls, I thought not—they were telling dirty jokes. They'd get their heads together, and one of them—the young Greek, usually—would tell something in a low voice; and then they'd both roar with laughter, and the young Greek would slap his leg with a noise like a thunderclap. Then he'd begin all over. "This one will kill you," he'd say every time, by way of introduction. "Wait till you hear this one, son. This one will kill you."

This One Will Kill You. What a good title for a murder story, I thought, letting my mind wander again from the murder open in my lap. It was a very poor one, one of the hundreds on the market since people found out you can sell anything that looks like a murder, no matter how bad it is. If I'd had an Agatha Christie, now, or one of the all-too-rare Mary Roberts Rineharts, I wouldn't have known or cared how noisy and unpleasant passengers could be, or how hard the bus jolted and how bad it smelled, or how long the trip dragged on.

I shut my book up finally as we crossed the bridge over the Severn, and Mrs. Barnes and I talked about how lovely it was: the wide, gray river with gray ships riding at anchor, off at the left where the Naval Academy buildings rise up almost right out of the water. And then on the other hand the town of Annapolis spread out, one of the really charming places of this world. The streets are crooked and the sidewalks old uneven brick and the beautiful eighteenth century houses, cheek by jowl with twentieth century drugstores and ten-cent stores and slums, are all the more emphatic for it. St. Anne's spire and the lovely cupolas of the State House and McDowell Hall are lifted over everything, and there's water in sight nearly every way you look.

Then the bus pulled into the station and stopped, and we all got up and surged toward the door the way passengers do, even if they're not in a particular hurry. I was. Anne is all I've got in this world, and I hadn't seen her for seven months. There she was behind the barrier—they wouldn't let anybody but passengers in the area where the buses come. But she was as close as she could get, bless her heart, pressed up against the rail and holding on to it with both hands.

Maybe I oughtn't to say it, but it's always a pleasure to me to watch Anne in a crowd—she stands out so. It isn't just that she's pretty; she shows she's got sense and she shows she's a lady, even if she does wear too much lipstick. And of course she's pretty too, with brown hair that curls up at the ends like a twenty-dollar permanent, and brown eyes, and skin smooth as a brown eggshell in summer and a white one in winter. She can walk into a store and walk right out in a size fourteen, which means she's fairly tall, and also means it's a pleasure for her to shop. I've always thought Anne spent too much for her clothes—the new tweed suit she had on wasn't bought on Main Street by any means; but I changed my mind after I'd been in Annapolis awhile. Naval officers do look nice in their uniforms, and they take a lot of living up to. I saw too many Navy wives who were neat and clean and nicely dressed, period, as Dick says. Beside their husbands, and beside my Anne, they looked like something picked up at a rummage sale.

I don't care what Dick says about telling things to strangers, I couldn't help pointing her out to Mrs. Barnes and the Red Cross girl. We three went down the aisle more or less together, and were still talking when we got off the bus.

We were the last ones off except for the four young naval officers who'd been on the back seat: three ensigns and a lieutenant, junior grade. At least I thought we were until we got way up to the front of the bus and saw there was a gray-haired woman still sitting in the seat back of the driver's. Her coat was hunched up over her shoulders, part way over her averted face, and she seemed to be sound asleep.

"How anybody can sleep with all this going on!" Mrs. Barnes said, the last thing before we stepped off the bus. "But she's quiet and peaceful as she can be."

The reason was, of course, that the woman was dead.

I was the one who discovered it. Later the bus driver apologized, but of course he couldn't have known what he was letting me in for, as he expressed it, and I told him so. I thought he was a mighty nice young man. Some drivers wouldn't have cared how hard they shook a passenger who slept right on (apparently) after the "All out for Annapolis!" This one got in the bus and got back out again with a worried look on his face, though he was smiling a little too.

"I wonder if one of you ladies would help me," he said, coming up to Mrs. Barnes and the Red Cross girl and me. We three were still together, waiting for our bags, and Anne was waving, and I was telling them how I'd raised her since she was six years old, and they were saying how-lovely and isn't-she-lovely and of course it is and she is, too. "There's a lady still inside the bus just won't wake up," the young driver said, "and I hate to just shake her. If one of you ladies don't mind—"

"Of course," I said briskly. It's been my observation that some people are born to do things in this world, just as some others are born to sit back. "I'll be glad to wake her up," I told him. So I climbed back into the bus.

The woman was lying in the aisle seat, the one at the left just back of the driver's—well, it's at the right, of course, as you go in—with the uncomfortable wheel seat between her and the window. Her pocketbook was lying on that seat, so apparently nobody had been sitting there. The bus had been pretty full when we left Baltimore, but we'd stopped to let off passengers in a lot of little two-by-four towns along the way, so by the end of the trip there were a dozen or so vacant seats. In any case, this looked like the kind of woman who always would get an extra seat to put her bag on, who had always been able to spread her things out and be comfortable. They were luxurious things, too. That black suede bag must have cost every bit as much as the pompadoured inspector's had, and her coat was black Persian lamb. I used to hope I'd have a coat like that someday, but now I don't know. I don't believe I'll ever forget the way that fur felt under my fingers, when I took the woman by the shoulder and turned her so I could see the beautifully made-up dead face, the stain on the pale blue dress, and the heavy silver knitting needle stuck in the middle of it.

CHAPTER TWO

Normally I am a calm person. Dick always says I would be a good man to have on ship in an emergency. But this time I wasn't good at all. Maybe it was just because I was feeling sick from the bus trip, but anyway I felt sicker. I sat down, hard. Fortunately, on a bus it's easier to drop down on a seat than it is to hit the floor. I don't know how long I sat there. I do know that I didn't move until the bus driver's nice sunburned, concerned face appeared in the doorway. Then I screamed.

At least scream was what I meant to do. It came out a feeble little squeak. But I needn't have made a sound; he saw the knitting needle right away.

I thought he behaved mighty well. I learned afterward that he was addicted to reading murder mysteries too. All the most unlikely people—and I suppose I'm one of them—do read them nowadays and aren't ashamed to admit it. So of course he knew he wasn't supposed to move the woman, or touch anything, until the Annapolis police could get there.

Fortunately there was a policeman in the bus station. A redcap ran to get him—ran hard, letting out little yips like a puppy, because he'd looked inside the bus first. Served him right, of course, but you couldn't blame him. A blind man could have seen there was something wrong, the way the young driver had half carried me out. Even the crowd behind the barrier was uneasy. I could see Anne pointing at me and waving her hands around and arguing with the guard, but he wouldn't let her through.

Mrs. Barnes and the Red Cross girl took me in charge, though, and were kind as could be. I was thankful for the arm across my shoulders and for the big flat hatbox they pushed under my inglorious knees. All I could do for quite a while was sit, and let the babble of excited questions go over my head. I remember marveling that so few people could make so much noise. Only a few of the passengers were left; most of the people who'd been on the bus were daily commuters and, not needing to wait for baggage, had walked right through and out of the station before the murder was discovered. I supposed they were halfway home by then. Coming out of it a little, as Dick says, I registered the fact they'd have to be brought back for questioning.

Meantime the young driver had the situation firmly in hand. He was a credit to the books he'd read, not like me. There was more than a touch of Lieutenant Valcour about him (or maybe it was Chief Detective-

Inspector Alleyn) as he stood up and made the speech somebody always makes, with variations, toward the beginning of every detective novel.

He told us inclusively, cutting off the questions: "There's a lady been murdered. I don't know when, and I don't know why. I don't know who done it. The police'll find all that out, and they're on the way. I do know this much—things are plenty bad for all of us, and a lot of talk and questions make 'em worse."

We all just sat and took it, as Dick says, except for the middle-aged man with the stomach. He'd been swelling up like a poisoned pup. A more unpleasant creature I never saw; and I'm not a snob but I thanked the Lord he was no relation of mine. "I'm a doctor, young man," he said in a much louder voice than he needed to use. He wanted all the rest of us to hear him too. "I'd better examine this woman. She may not be dead. Ever think about that? A layman can't always tell."

The young driver said grimly: "She's dead, all right. Knitting needle in the middle of her heart, and a spot of blood around it"—he put his thumbs and forefingers not too close together, though the spot had really been quite small—"*that* big." And into the dense silence he added after a minute: "Sorry, doc. I guess you mean well. But how would I know you don't want in there to destroy some evidence, see? You got to remember you're a suspect like the rest of us. All of us."

The Red Cross girl repeated it like a sigh. "All of us—"

"That's right," one of the young ensigns said. After that everybody was quiet till the policemen came.

The officer on duty was the first, naturally. But not by much. It seems that the police department is only a few blocks away—everything is, of course, in Annapolis—so the others got there while the first man was still goggling in at the bus window, like a goldfish through a globe. There was quite a group. I thought I could pick out the manager of the bus station by the way he was talking a blue streak and acting as if he'd been insulted personally, and of course the medical examiner by his little black bag. In addition to the three or four young policemen in uniform there was still another man in ordinary clothes. He was in the lead, so I might have figured out that he was the detective in charge even if two of the young naval officers hadn't been whispering behind me. He was quite an important one, it seemed, who'd been borrowed from the Baltimore Department to investigate a case of sabotage at the Experiment Station. According to the respectful whispers he'd just finished solving it rather brilliantly.

I peered at the detective lieutenant with interest—I didn't have my glasses—and got the shock of my life. It was Ben Kramer! I hadn't seen him for twenty years, and certainly I never expected to see him in

Annapolis. Or any place else outside of jail. He was one of the worst boys I ever taught—not mean, but into something every minute. I always feel a little taken aback when my old students don't turn out the way I thought they would; I think I'm a pretty good judge of human nature, and yet it does seem that a lot of my worst prospects have grown up to be preachers. And the boy who was first president of our Student Council is in the penitentiary now. Still, I'm always glad to be favorably surprised, and I was glad to see Ben Kramer. I always had liked him in spite of paper airplanes and trained fleas and never knowing a gerund from a gerundive, though he could have any time he tried.

Ben was glad to see me, too. "Why, Miss Julia!" he said right off, and stopped and shook hands. But he didn't waste much time on me. I was impressed with the way he got down to business. In less time than it takes to tell it he'd marshaled his assistants inside the bus, and flashlight bulbs were going off, and I presumed they were taking pictures of the body, and insufflating for fingerprints, and looking around for clues, and going through the victim's pocketbook for identification. I would have given a good deal to see just exactly what did go on—I've always suspected some discrepancy between murder novels and the real thing—but the windows of the bus were high up off the ground, and anyway two of the young policemen were herding us away from it.

I imagined that the room they took us into was the manager's office. It had a big desk, and a lot of collapsible metal chairs had been set up in a double row in front of it. We sat down, the six or seven of us who'd been waiting for our baggage, and pretty soon the other passengers came straggling in. Some of them were right mad. The young policeman who was going to ask the questions—he had his notebook out—handled them very well, I thought; and I thought the department as a whole showed promptness and efficiency. It's hard to round up a lot of people who are going their separate ways.

As soon as everybody got there he asked us to seat ourselves in the order we'd left the bus, and I took my place, between Mrs. Barnes and the Red Cross girl, with less uneasiness than I reckon I should have felt. Of course I knew with one part of my mind that I was a suspect— in it up to my neck, as Dick says; but the other part, the bigger part, assured me I was still a respectable character in spite of having found a body. I was mighty glad the detective in charge knew I'd been a respectable character all my life. I settled myself to listen comfortably while the young policeman took everybody's name.

The fat woman in overalls was Mrs. Kleinschmidt; she showed her defense plant badge to prove it. "Mrs. Elsie Kleinschmidt, and my husband and I both work at Bendix. His name's Herman. Naw, I don't live in Annapolis—live in Eastport." Eastport, I remembered, was just across the bridge. Between it and Annapolis there was a great gulf fixed, and I don't mean merely Spa Creek. "I come back on this same bus every day, and I ain't murdered anybody yet," Mrs. Kleinschmidt said, looking pointedly at her diamond wristwatch. "You want to know anything else?"

"Were you acquainted with the deceased, Mrs. Kleinschmidt?" asked the policeman, very dignified. Unless I was much mistaken this was the first case of the kind he'd ever worked on, but he was trying to act as if he had them every day and twice on Sunday.

Mrs. Kleinschmidt snorted. "Never saw her before. And you might say I ain't seen her yet. Didn't see her get on the bus, and she sat in front of me and never turned around." If everybody didn't know about the diamond wristwatch by this time it wasn't Mrs. Kleinschmidt's fault. "Anything else?"

"Not for the present, thank you," the officer said. "Lieutenant Kramer wants to speak to all of you after he's finished inside. Name, please?" He turned to the next passenger as Mrs. Kleinschmidt began to splutter. Maybe I was wrong about his being inexperienced; the way he ignored that woman was beautiful.

The next woman said she was Miss Gladys Fulton of Annapolis. That gave everybody a mild shock, because we'd heard her telling about her dear little daughters that she locked up every morning before she went to work. But she went on to explain that she was a divorcée (accent on the first syllable, as in inspector). It seemed that she lived "oh, so quietly" in suburban Annapolis, leaving home only because of the exigencies of daily bread. No, she didn't know the deceased personally, but she'd often seen her on the street and was pretty sure she lived in Annapolis.

After Miss Fulton it was the soldier's turn—Private John Aloysius Tindle, of Coffeyville, Missouri. Like Mrs. Kleinschmidt, he could prove it and seemed to feel it necessary to do so. I certainly hope that nice clean police officer remembered to wash his hands after looking at Private Tindle's furlough papers; they looked as if they'd been carried through the Civil War. On closer inspection I didn't think Private Tindle looked any too clean either, and certainly he was still rather vague—not exactly drunk, but not glowing with health and abstinence either. He'd been making the most of his ten-day furlough from Fort Meade. "I lost my money and couldn't go home, see, so I come down here to take a look at the town. I've seen Baltimore and they can have it. I can't say I think much of this burg either, so far."

I expect we all felt a flash of fellow feeling at that last. I did.

"Did you know the deceased, Private Tindle?"

"That Mrs. Rich-Bitch?" said Private Tindle. "Is it likely?"

The policeman ignored that as became an officer and a gentleman. "Thank you.... Your name, please?" It was the young woman of *True Romances* he was speaking to this time, and I didn't blame him for the subtle change in his voice. He hadn't seen the way she neglected her child on the bus—the child was curled up asleep now, and looked like his mother's little angel—and she certainly was pretty. *True Romances* could have used her for a cover girl. She was twenty-five maybe, with skin as smooth as Anne's and big dark eyes and silky dark hair that I believe would have curled a little if she'd had sense enough to leave it alone. Instead she'd had it tortured into tiers of rolls on top, and the back part dragged up stark and plain, so that it embarrassed you to look at the back of her neck.

Her voice was as affected as her hair. "I'm Mrs. Dorothy Hamilton," she told the policeman. "I'm a war widow; my husband was killed in the Pacific. My little boy and I stay with my mother now, over on Eastern Shore. I guess you'd say we lived there."

"And your mother's name?" the officer said. I hoped he'd be as gentle with me when my turn came.

"She's Mrs. Mamie Bruner, and she lives at Bowiesburg, Route Two."

"Did you know the deceased, Mrs. Hamilton?"

"No, sir."

I was getting tired of people that didn't know the deceased; not that it would have been anything but chance if the two defense workers or the grubby young soldier or Mrs. Dorothy Hamilton had known her. They so obviously lived in different worlds. I could imagine the way she would have looked straight through such people, if she'd seen them alive, and how her lip would have curled at the horrible sound of "Mrs." before a woman's Christian name. Even dead there had been authority and arrogance in her face, and I thought it wasn't just the authority and arrogance that can come from being handsome and having beautiful clothes. But doctors know everybody, even doctors whose own clothes don't fit and who have their offices in West Street, as Dr. James Mosser—questioned next—said he had. I pinned my hopes on him.

But Dr. Mosser wasn't saying anything he didn't have to, and he was downright rude to the nice young policeman who was asking the questions. I couldn't bear the man. He looked smart and capable enough, but he could have lived appropriately back in the days when they called a doctor a leech. I don't see how sick people could have wanted him around. I know if I'd been sick and that man came to see me it would be the last straw.

But the policeman was beautifully patient, and finally he asked the question I'd been waiting to hear. "Did you know the deceased, Dr. Mosser?"

"Yes." I leaned forward in my chair. But the thin mouth had shut with a snap, and opened only with seeming reluctance. "Woman active in civic affairs," Dr. Mosser said, and this time it was a snap you could almost hear. His face reminded me of the turtle that's supposed to hold on till it thunders.

I wished the policeman would thunder at *him*. He was way too polite, I thought; but maybe Dr. Mosser was active in civic affairs too. He thanked the doctor and asked him no more questions. Undoubtedly the police knew who the murder victim was, and didn't need Dr. Mosser to tell them; but they might have had pity on the rest of us. I settled back in my chair with keen disappointment.

The big, greasy young man turned out to be a restaurant owner. "Bill Palougous. I run the Free State on Main Street, best eats in town." He presented his business card with a flourish, grinning from ear to ear as if this were the pleasantest occasion in the world. His teeth were so big and strong-looking that I suspected the two symmetrically placed gold ones had been put in purely for effect. My Euphrosyne has a front tooth like that. "Not on your life I didn't know the lady, or do her in either," Mr. Palougous went on to say. "Sure, I seen her on the street, and I'd know her name if I heard her called. She was a big bug, all right. Husband was some admiral or other."

I wasn't surprised to hear it. The beautiful clothes, the look of authority, the poise that even undignified sudden death can have, if the victim's had enough of it in real life—the dead woman was very much what you'd think an admiral's wife might be. I was grateful to Mr. Bill Palougous for that much information, but it remained for the young man that twitched to identify her fully. But first he said— twitching, and twisting the brim of his hat nearly off between his fingers—that his own name was Ronald Miller and he lived at the Y.M.C.A. He worked at the soda fountain in Tracy's Drugstore on State Circle. "She comes in the store pretty often," he told the policeman. "I mean she did. Sure, I know her. She was Mrs. Roger Barnes. Admiral Barnes's widow."

Another Mrs. Barnes! I thought. I looked over at my Mrs. Barnes to see what she made of that coincidence. But she didn't nod back the way I expected her to, a nice friendly woman like that. She was staring straight in front of her, and her face was as white and cold and hard as stone.

CHAPTER THREE

Goodness knows I ought to know better, after living sixty-seven years and teaching forty of them, than to jump to conclusions. But I was saying to myself, "I don't believe it!" before I thought—denying an idea that I was even ashamed to have. Mrs. Barnes, my Mrs. Barnes, had seemed like the nicest woman I'd met in a long time.

But then lots of murderers seem nice. At least they do in books.

I was so upset I didn't even hear the young sailor answering questions about himself and his wife and baby. The Red Cross girl had to tell me later. He was George Campbell, S1/c, and his wife was named Betty and the baby Betty Jean. They all belonged in Jackson, Mississippi and were going back there. The sailor boy was home for the first time in over two years—he'd never seen his baby, just as I'd guessed—and Betty and Betty Jean had come to New York so they wouldn't miss any of his furlough. They'd come to Annapolis "just to see it," and they'd never laid eyes on the dead woman before. "I don't meet many admirals' wives," young Campbell said, grinning. Everybody sort of smiled back; he was that kind of boy.

The little stenographer-looking woman was, we found out next, a genealogist. Miss Edith Dorsey, Duke of Gloucester Street, Annapolis. "Oh, yes, I knew Mrs. Roger Barnes," Miss Dorsey said. "I did some work for her several months ago—yes, several. The Shaw line, it was. Not direct descent from John Shaw, but interesting. Yes, interesting. Yes." She let her voice trail off; you could see that she had forgotten the murder. She was mentally going over the family ramifications of the Shaws, whoever they were. Acknowledging the officer's thanks with a vague little bow, she vaguely ripped out a couple of rows—for no good reason that I could see—and began to pick up stitches.

I braced myself as the officer with the notebook turned to Mrs. Barnes. For some reason I was taking this pretty hard; stupid of me, for I'd never seen or heard of the woman an hour or so ago, and certainly, after seeing Ben Kramer in a lieutenant's badge instead of a convict's stripes, I ought to know that people don't always turn out the way you expect them to. Apparently I was taking it harder than Mrs. Barnes herself. Her voice was a great deal calmer than mine would have been.

"I'm Mary Barnes, Mr. Green, as you know," she said quietly. The white, stony look was gone from her face, and I hoped irrationally that nobody but me had glimpsed it. "I live on a little farm on Eastern Shore, just outside of Sewall. I didn't know Mrs. Roger Barnes was on the bus. I didn't see her get in, and when I passed her going out her face was turned too far aside for me to recognize. And I—didn't kill her, Mr. Green." The quiet voice went on after an instant's silence. Mary Barnes said (just as if she were saying "I had ham for breakfast"), "But, of course, I hated her very much."

"I know, ma'am," Patrolman Green said quickly and humanly, before he thought. He caught himself up. "I mean, I know you and the lady was—acquainted, at one time. Thank you, Mrs. Barnes. Now, lady, your name, and where do you live?"

I said in a daze that I was Julia Tyler from Rossville, Virginia, and that I was coming to Annapolis to visit my great-niece Mrs. Travers. I pointed out Anne, visible through the plate-glass window that gave on the bus area, and by this time practically hanging over the barrier rail. I wished I could give up and lean on something myself. I felt weak. Mrs. Barnes—my Mrs. Barnes—hadn't said why she hated the dead woman, or what the relationship was. Apparently the officer knew all about it, and maybe that was why she had come out with such an outrageous statement of fact. It was fact, all right; quietly as she'd said it, you could tell that, even if you didn't know what she was talking about.

I had a feeling the Red Cross girl knew. I watched her clear, very specially pretty profile while she told the officer that her name was Ruth Allein, that she commuted to Baltimore, where she did social casework, but lived with her uncle in the commandant's quarters, Naval Academy. She had known Mrs. Roger Barnes for several years, and had spoken to her when she got on the bus. "But I didn't kill her, either," she said with a little smile. I liked her all over again. Ruth Allein. She and Anne didn't know each other, but they were going to.

I didn't pay much attention to the four young naval officers' names, for I couldn't tell the officers themselves apart. Then, and even after I'd been in Annapolis quite a good while, all nice young men in uniform looked alike to me. I could easily see differences when I looked for them, just as you can in identical twins; but similarly I couldn't remember them next time. I could pick out Lieutenant (j.g.) Foster Gibson only by the fact of the extra half-stripe on his cuffs, and which of the three young ensigns was Larimore, and which Dietz and which Smith, I couldn't even begin to tell. Two of them—and I forget which two—knew Mrs. Roger Barnes and had, like the Red Cross girl, spoken when they got on the bus. The others were new to the Navy and didn't know her at all.

Well, there was the lot of us: some likely-looking suspects for murder; some nicer than most people; some obviously upset and nervous, and others calm. There we sat in the manager's office, facing the empty desk like a class of students waiting for the teacher to come in. I never thought I'd sit waiting for Ben Kramer to tell me what was what and why.

But I was more than a little proud of him when he came in and put his hat on the desk and stood behind it. Maybe he still doesn't know who Catiline was, but he's turned out to be a fine-looking man. He must be forty-four or -five; he graduated from high school in Anne's mother's class. I didn't know then what he'd been doing since—college and law school, I found out later, and a few years in the FBI before he married a Baltimore girl who wouldn't live anywhere else—but he'd come a long way. He never could have managed it in Rossville, of course; small Southern towns are like that, and people would always remember that old Tom Kramer ran a barber shop. But here away from home he could have passed for anybody. Just anybody at all.

"I'm sorry to detain you, ladies and gentlemen," Ben began. "I wish the murderer among you would confess. Then the rest of you could go on home." He stopped and let his eyes go over the double row of people. "But I suppose that's too much to expect. We'll have to hunt the murderer down before we hang him—or her. Did you know we hanged murderers in Maryland?" Again his eyes went from one of us to another; but apparently no reaction. I would have given anything to have been sitting so I could see how they took it, too; but of course I couldn't look around, and I wouldn't though I could look over at Mary Barnes, sitting next to me.

"Some people disapprove of hanging," Ben Kramer went on. "And of course it isn't a very nice way of punishing murderers. But murderers aren't very nice people, and this murder was a pretty ugly one. The lady was doped so she'd be drowsy or asleep—morphine, probably. And then somebody stabbed her. Somebody that picked the right place to stab." Dr. Mosser! I thought. And I was ashamed of myself again. Just because he had a loud, arrogant voice; just because he strutted when he walked. "The murdered woman was Mrs. Roger Barnes," Ben said, "as some of you know. She was a prominent woman—clubs and charities and so on—known all over Maryland. Her husband, of course, was known all over the world. The Barnes periscope is pretty famous, and the Barnes System of Submarine Navigation. Famous men often do have enemies; maybe somebody who still had a grudge against the admiral took it out on his widow. Or maybe somebody hated her on her own account. That person is in this room."

I wondered if the murderer's nerves were wearing as thin as mine were.

"I know what you've all been hoping," Ben went on. "You've been remembering the people who got off the bus at the little towns between Baltimore and Annapolis. You've been hoping—the murderer especially has been hoping—that the police would lay the murder on one of those people. Well, we won't. A police surgeon has examined the body, and he tells me that Mrs. Barnes died not more than half an hour ago. He thinks it was less than that. And *we* think that Mrs. Barnes was killed after the bus stopped, when the rest of you passengers were crowding down the aisle to the door. Somebody had a long sharp knitting needle in his hand. Or her hand."

He indicated Patrolman Long, who was standing off at one side of the room, and Long, looking as pleased and modest as if he'd performed some heroic deed, unwrapped a long, thin paper package. The needle was bright silver—steel, I suppose—except for two or three inches at the pointed end. That part was rusted over with Mrs. Barnes's blood.

It was almost too much for me, and when I heard a noise behind me I thought it had been too much for the murderer too. Dr. Mosser, or Mr. Palougous, or the mean-faced, nervous boy was going to stand up and confess. But it was only Miss Edith Dorsey rummaging in her knitting bag.

"Is it a number-three Boye?" she wanted to know, and her voice was little and high and squeaked with excitement. "Because if it is I—I think it's mine. One of mine seems to be gone. A number-three Boye."

There was a rather long interval while Patrolman Long got it through his head that Boye was a manufacturer's name, and that she was talking about the knitting needle. You would have thought he'd spent his life in the tropics where they have number-one boys and, I presume, number-three boys as well. Finally he said yes, it was.

"I must have dropped it on the loading platform in Baltimore, just before I got on the bus," Miss Dorsey said. Her voice still squeaked and her eyes shone. Poor thing, I thought, this is probably the first time in her life so many people have noticed her. "The driver was late opening the bus door, so I pulled my scarf out of my bag and started to knit. My bag hangs on my arm, so my hands were free. I walked up and down the platform knitting. You see I use up all the little scraps of time so many people waste. If they only realized—this horrible war—our poor dear boys shivering in those fox holes—"

I caught Ben Kramer's eye the way he used to catch mine in Cicero class, and his mouth twitched the way mine so often had. I felt better, less like a suspect.

"When did you last see this—weapon, Miss Dorsey?" he asked. "Are you sure it was in your bag when you were walking up and down the platform?"

"That's it," Miss Dorsey said. "I was knitting with it at first, you see, and then I came to my ribbing and changed to a smaller pair of needles. I dropped the number threes down in my bag, or thought I did. I must have dropped one on the platform."

"You couldn't have lost it later, Miss Dorsey? Did you open your bag again?"

"No, officer, I didn't," Miss Dorsey said, looking pleased because she was such a good, positive witness. "That was the only time the—the murderer could have got it. After I was on the bus I held my bag right in my lap."

Yes, I thought, and while you were holding that bag right in your lap you could very easily have got the needle out yourself. Maybe you never dropped it at all. Maybe you're the homicidal maniac. Goodness knows, I thought, genealogy is enough to drive anybody out of her mind.

Ben was going on. "If Miss Dorsey dropped her needle on the platform, before any passengers got on the bus, any one of you had a chance to pick it up. You know what that means. Any one of you might have stabbed Mrs. Barnes."

"I beg your pardon, sir," one of the young ensigns said.

"Yes, Mr. Smith?"

"I believe some of us can furnish alibis, as to that," Ensign Smith said. "I can't; I passed right by Mrs. Barnes going out of the bus, and brushed against her coat. I could have stabbed her just as well as not." He paused and smiled disarmingly around the room; a nice, attractive boy if I ever saw one. "But Ensign Larimore was on my right all the way to the door. He couldn't have stabbed her without reaching across me, and he didn't. And Ensign Dietz, in front of us, had a heavy briefcase in each hand. He didn't set them down."

"Is that correct, gentlemen?" Ben asked. And the two ensigns said, "Yes, sir, it is," together.

Ben said: "Then except for people like Ensign Dietz, who was carrying something that took up room, you came down the aisle two by two. Is that right?" The elephant and the kangaroo, I thought hysterically, as everybody nodded. "If we can get some alibis all the way we'll cut it down considerably. Mr. Dietz, who was in front of you?"

"Lieutenant Gibson, sir, with Miss Allein at the right."

"She couldn't have leaned across me," Lieutenant Gibson said definitely. "You can count her out."

Patrolman Long was making notes, perspiring gently. He wasn't either as smart or as nice as the one named Green. The suspects were being weeded out faster than he could write; he looked as if he didn't altogether like it.

"Now, Miss Allein," Ben said, "did you notice who was ahead of you?"

"Miss Tyler was," Ruth Allein said slowly. "And Mrs. Barnes."

"They walked up the aisle together?"

"Yes."

"And which was on the right?" Ben asked patiently. This was the first uncooperative witness he'd had. He looked a little puzzled at the way Ruth Allein's mouth shut tight after that "Yes." He hadn't heard what the rest of us had heard—Mary Barnes' saying: "I—didn't kill her, Mr. Green. But, of course, I hated her very much."

"Which of the ladies was on the right, Miss Allein?" Ben asked again.

"Miss Tyler was," Ruth Allein said reluctantly.

I could have shaken her. Trying to be nice, she was making a bad matter worse. Where was the presence of mind the Red Cross was supposed to be famous for in emergency? If she'd just come out flat-footed with it, instead of hemming and hawing, Ben wouldn't have thought any more of Mary Barnes' passing next to the dead woman than he'd thought of Ensign Smith's or Lieutenant Gibson's passing her.

But either Ben wasn't too perceptive or he was smooth as owl's grease. I was afraid it was the latter. He went very smoothly on, ignoring any implications he might have got. Establishing alibis, such as they were. Pretty soon we were divided into sheep and goats: those who couldn't have reached the murdered woman and those who could. Unless somebody was lying, of course. And either somebody was lying— or so it seemed to me—or we were sixteen of the most unnoticing, mind-our-own-business passengers that had ever ridden on any bus. Nobody had seen Miss Edith Dorsey drop a knitting needle, to hear us tell it; nobody had seen who picked it up; nobody had seen the quick, sharp, vicious jab that would have been needed to send a weapon not very sharp, as weapons go, into Mrs. Roger Barnes's heart.

I don't suppose these things ever turn out quite to suit you. Of course I know I ought to be ashamed to admit it, and I hereby am, but I certainly hated to think Ronald Miller and Bill Palougous were in the clear, as Dick says. Either one of them was my beau ideal for a murderer. Mrs. Kleinschmidt, too. But they were among the suspects Ben eliminated. The nice young bus driver was eliminated, too, I'm glad to say; Mrs. Kleinschmidt and Miss Fulton had had him in full view all the time. The ones that were left—exactly half the passengers, unless you count the children—were Gordon Smith, Foster Gibson, Mary Barnes, Edith Dorsey, George Campbell, Dr. James Mosser, Dorothy

Hamilton, and Gladys Fulton.

Certainly it wasn't just the list I would have picked, if I'd been picking. But of course I was glad enough to have Julia Tyler out of it.

That was the attitude to take, I told myself. Stay out of it. Don't worry about it. I got up with the rest of the people who'd been given alibis—Ben said we might go—and started for the door. It wouldn't be but a minute until my child would be strangling me with both arms, the way she always does, and I could laugh and straighten my hat and forget all about murder.

But before I left Mary Barnes I couldn't help putting my hand on her sleeve a minute, just casually and accidentally.

CHAPTER FOUR

Anne and Dick had rented a house on Cornhill Street, a little bit of a thing, only two front dormers upstairs and one window and a door below. Circa 1770, I found out later. It had been restored and modernized and painted shiny white, and looked more Williamsburg than Williamsburg itself. Annapolis does, in spots. My crooked little room upstairs had roses on the wallpaper, a fireplace that worked, and a slantwise view of Kentish House from its window. Everything was so nice I decided I'd make my good lengthy visit after all. The bus station murder seemed long ago and far away; I hoped it wasn't true.

From the time Dick got home, though—yelling "Hi, suspect!" as he came pounding up the stairs, and then something less quotable when his head hit a quaint old beam—we had murder and nothing else. He and Anne couldn't let it alone. Useless for me to turn the conversation to some of the things I'd come to Annapolis to hear. "Who lives in that pretty old house across the street?" I'd ask. And Anne would say: "Darling! Your Mr. Palougous, of all people. The neighbors had a fit when he bought it, and now he says he's going to do it over with glass brick, so the Colonial Annapolis members are having fits too. Do you think he did it, Aunt Julia? I do."

"Don't be silly," Dick said. "He had an alibi. Now, that Mary Barnes—"

"She didn't do it either," I snapped back at him. "Do you think I could have walked up that aisle with her, side by side, without seeing her pull out a weapon and stab a woman?"

"I don't," said Anne.

"Yet that's what somebody did do," Dick said seriously. "Mary Barnes or somebody else—without being seen."

"Well, it wasn't Mrs. Barnes," I said firmly. "She isn't a killer."

"Bill Palougous is, Aunt Julia!" Anne said, getting excited. "He shot a man that used to work for him. But he had a big criminal lawyer down from Baltimore and got off."

"He shot a man that was sneaking around his restaurant in the middle of the night," Dick said. "He didn't need a specially big lawyer to get him off. The law was on his side."

"Shooting a man with a wife and three little children!" Anne was indignant. "And he'd just come back to get something that belonged to him. He didn't break in; he still had his key. Professor Gassaway says—"

"Professor Gassaway is president of the Society for the Restoration of Colonial Annapolis. He'd believe anything of a man who'd put glass brick in a pre-Revolutionary house."

"I would too," I said pacifically. I looked with considerable pleasure—smugness, I'm afraid—from Anne in her pale-yellow dress to redheaded Dick in his Navy blues, with a gold stripe and a half on each cuff. They were glaring at each other the way they've glared all their lives. They seem to enjoy it; I stopped worrying long ago.

"Of course," Anne said, capitulating first, "Palougous does have an alibi. But in all the murders *I* read the people with alibis are usually murderers."

I was just starting to express my resentment when the knocker on the front door banged.

Anne has a maid, of all things. She came with the house—which the children took over, furnished, from the officer Dick replaced—and nearly fills it. Now she put a hot dish down on bare mahogany and moved like a covered wagon to the door.

I rescued the dish. Then I sat there with it burning my hand, for the voice at the door was Mary Barnes' voice and she was asking to speak to me. She didn't say it was private, and normally I wouldn't have closed the dining room door behind me. This time it was a good thing I did.

"I have an apology to make, Miss Tyler," Mary Barnes began. She had the air of a person who's determined to say what she came to say and get it over with. I'd asked her to sit down, but she didn't seem to hear me. She just stood there twisting the felt drawstring of her bag. I noticed it because it was a good deal like the bag I'd left upstairs. Her voice was calm but her face wasn't. "I came to ask you for something I put in your bag."

"You what?" Because I was thinking of bags anyway, I thought I hadn't heard that right.

"Something I put in your bag," Mary Barnes said rapidly. "You see I thought they might search our things—the ones of us who didn't have alibis. After you left. They didn't, but— There was a—package in my bag I didn't want anybody to see, so while we were sitting in that office I just slipped it out and into yours. I'm sorry. I took advantage of your kindness. I just didn't know what else to do."

I said automatically: "It was quite all right. I'll get the package for you." But I didn't know what to think. I didn't doubt she was telling the exact truth; certainly she could have slipped something into my bag easily enough. It's a big drawstring affair like so many you see now in wartime, bulky and inconvenient and hard to find things in. Dropping a purse or keys inside is like dropping them down a well, and I for one will be glad when snaps and zippers come back. But I didn't know what was in the package, of course, or why Mary Barnes didn't want the police to see it.

Up in my bedroom I turned it over in my hands. It was about six inches long and four inches wide, flat, and obviously a box of some kind. It didn't exactly rattle when I shook it, but there was a sort of soft thud as whatever it was struck against the inside of the box. It didn't tell me anything. Neither did the wrapping, which was good quality plain white paper and red string; but I did notice that it wasn't the first time the paper had been folded or the string tied. Some inexpert person had unwrapped that package and wrapped it up again—Mary Barnes herself, maybe. Another inexpert person could do the same thing and nobody would know the difference. For a minute I struggled with temptation; but after all there is a long line of ladies back of me, and they were all looking over my shoulder, wearing the expression that as a cake-stealing child I'd seen on my dear mother's face. I took the package downstairs and gave it to Mary Barnes.

She was a different person the minute she got it into her hands. She thanked me with the utmost calm and smiled—really smiled for the first time since I'd met her—when I said impulsively and no doubt wrongly that I wouldn't mention the incident to anyone. She had a lovely smile that lit up her strong, plain face. I felt reassured. She really was a nice woman; it was quite outside possibility that she'd killed the other Mrs. Barnes.

But then I felt worried again when she seemed in such a hurry to get away, and wouldn't even stay to meet Anne and Dick. Probably I'd compounded a felony, or something like that. It was very much on my mind all evening—though the children, fortunately, didn't ask any questions—and when I went upstairs to bed I conducted a little experiment. I emptied a little cardboard box I had and put various things in it, one at a time. The calendar pad didn't make the same kind of noise I'd heard before. Neither did my fountain pen, nor a piece of the dog candy I'd brought Anne's cocker pup. The scissors out of my sewing basket did.

I felt worse instead of better. I turned out the light and went to sleep.

Anne had a party for me next day, three ladies my own age for lunch and bridge. It's always rather interesting to know whom the young consider your suitable companions. I wasn't too flattered by Anne's selection of Mrs. Thomas Beale, who was bright and sharp as a steel trap but hardly visible under layers of powder and rouge, nor by Miss Lucy Dulany, who talked too much about her niece Mrs. Wickliffe. But Miss Sarah Maccubbin I most unreservedly liked. She was a big handsome woman with a voice like a bishop's, an inexhaustible fund of stories about Annapolis people, and the most exclusive boarding house in town. Anne and Dick had stayed there when they first came and were waiting for their house. Professor Gassaway, whose cousin went to college with Anne, had been kind enough to get them in; and kindness it was, for though Sarah Maccubbin did half her own cooking, now that you can't depend on servants, and pinched and scraped to pay the taxes and upkeep on her big two-hundred-year-old house, getting a room there was like being presented at court. She was real society, not the café type that Annapolis and the Navy had before New York ever heard of it.

The ladies were talking about that, in connection with Eleanor Barnes.

"There's just something wrong with the whole system," Mrs. Beale said. "Roger Barnes was perfectly happy with the first wife—personally, that is. They came from the same town out in Kansas, had the same background, really enjoyed the same things. And yet it was a tragedy they married."

"Why?" I said.

"Because Mary Barnes couldn't keep up with the Navy," Sarah Maccubbin said bluntly. "I liked her—"

"Oh, so did I," said Miss Dulany.

"She's a fine woman," Mrs. Beale chimed in.

I heard them all in a daze. "Did you say Mary Barnes?"

Sarah Maccubbin smiled at me. "Yes, Mary Barnes. The Mary Barnes who was on your bus. Quite a coincidence, wasn't it? And"—she stuck her strong chin out belligerently—"that was all it was, too. Mary would never have murdered Eleanor Barnes."

The other ladies agreed.

"But you certainly couldn't blame her," Miss Dulany said. "Divorced after thirty-four years!"

"She was the one who got the divorce, Lucy," Mrs. Beale reminded her.

"Yes, but everybody knew the admiral asked for it. He did want that appointment, and he'd lost it once before. And then when he married again right away—"

"Let me get this straight," I said rather desperately. "Admiral Roger Barnes and his first wife, Mary, were married thirty-four years. They'd come from the same town, had the same background and interests. Then they got a divorce and he married again. Married this woman who was murdered on the bus."

The ladies nodded. "She was a widow with one son," Mrs. Beale said.

"Well, why?" I wanted to know. "I mean, why did the admiral divorce the first wife to remarry? Mrs. Beale said he was perfectly happy with her."

"I said he was perfectly happy with her, *personally*," Mrs. Beale corrected me. "There's more to it than that, Miss Tyler. I was brought up in the Navy, and I know." Her mouth shut grimly.

"You see the Navy's a religion as well as a way of life, Miss Tyler," Sarah Maccubbin said. "They get their officer material from all over the country, from all kinds and classes of people; and then they press them into a mold and they stay there four years.

"Annapolis isn't a liberal education. When they get out of the Academy they're pretty much of a type. The past doesn't matter and the future's mapped out for them, down to the last detail. In almost everything they conform rigidly—very rigidly. They'd better! There's just one time they usually kick against the pricks. They come out of Annapolis trained technically and trained socially and gentlemen by Act of Congress—they *are* gentlemen, I don't care who or what they were before. They could marry anybody. Some of them do—marry well, I mean. But more of them marry the girl back home."

"And that's what Roger Barnes did," I commented.

"If he hadn't been in the Navy everybody would have said *he* married well," Sarah Maccubbin went on. "Mary was a fine, solid, sensible woman. And goodness knows Roger Barnes needed that kind of a wife, promotions or no promotions. Look what happened afterward."

I didn't know what she was talking about, but I let it pass.

"But Mary wasn't the type whose husband makes admiral," Sarah Maccubbin said. "In wartime, I grant you, some men with very unlikely wives get to the top—Army and Navy both. Look at—" And she named an officer who's on the front pages every day. "But this was peacetime, and in peacetime, well, there're lots of brilliant men in the regular services, and other things being equal it's the men whose wives can hold up *their* end that get the top posts. You know how it is in the

Church. Well, Navy wives make or break their husbands the same way. You never see a superintendent whose wife isn't a brilliant hostess. Nor a commandant. It's just up to an ambitious man to marry an ambitious woman. And she has to be talented—really talented—socially. And work hard at it all the time."

"And Mary Barnes wasn't, and didn't?" I asked.

"Miss Tyler, I wish you could have seen her house!" Mrs. Beale said. "They bought the old Governor Tasker place on King George Street, the same one Eleanor has now—had. *Eleanor* had it featured in *House Beautiful* and opened it up for Garden Week. *Mary* had it looking like Platt's Crossing, Kansas. Absolutely. She had lace curtains, and a big picture of her mother in her wedding dress, standing by her father in his fireman's uniform, and actually a bowl of apples on the drawing room table—"

"And once the bank put out a wall calendar she thought was pretty, and she hung it in the dining room—"

"No decorating sense," Sarah Maccubbin agreed with both of them. "No clothes sense. No sense at all, really, in a way. Lots of service wives have backgrounds just about like Mary Barnes', and lots of them would rather have decorated their houses to suit themselves instead of to suit Joe Valiant. Not all the officers' wives you see playing bridge and making calls are crazy about it. Maybe *they'd* rather be home with their slippers on, too. But they realize they're in the Navy just the way their husbands are, and they live the Navy way. If Roger Barnes hadn't been an exceptional officer he'd have been passed over."

"That's true," Miss Dulany said. "And if he'd married a rich senator's daughter first, why, they'd have had to establish five-star rank years ago."

"Is that the right kind of wife for a naval officer? A rich senator's daughter?" I asked. It sounded pretty bad to me, even though Virginia, at least, still sends gentlemen to the Senate.

The ladies laughed. "Oh, that's just a phrase," Mrs. Beale said. "Lucy only means that an officer's wife needs training for her job, every bit as much as the officer does for his. And Eleanor Barnes had it. I've heard she was middle-class Middle West herself, originally; but her first husband was a diplomat, and she learned on him."

"Mary didn't learn at all."

"Mary Barnes didn't even care," Sarah Maccubbin said. "Even if she suspected she wasn't much of a help to her husband, just staying at home and sewing on his buttons and bringing up young Roger, she thought that was the way he liked her. The divorce hit her like—well, like Pearl Harbor."

"She wouldn't take any alimony or settlement," Miss Dulany took up the story. "Young Roger bought her a little chicken farm over on Eastern Shore; it took every cent he could scrape together, but it makes her a living. A bare living, though, and she has to work very hard."

"What about the admiral?" I asked after a minute. "I suppose his second marriage was successful?"

The three ladies just looked at one another.

"You tell her, Sarah," Mrs. Beale said finally. "I'd probably lose my temper and swear. Roger Barnes was my husband's best friend."

Sarah Maccubbin said: "Well, she ruined him, Miss Tyler, that's all. Oh, he got his captaincy, and the tour of service he'd always wanted— superintendent of the Naval Academy here. And later he made admiral. But his first marriage had had everything but front, and his marriage to Eleanor had nothing else. Eleanor was a hard woman. Rule or ruin. Roger Barnes' home life was— Well, I reckon nobody'll ever know the half of it. It wasn't long before he began to drink. He'd never drunk enough to mention before." She paused and looked at me keenly. "I spoke just now of Pearl Harbor. Did you ever hear anything about Roger Barnes in connection with that? Any criticism?"

"Why, no, I don't think so," I said, bewildered. "There was a lot of talk in the papers about court-martialing the officers in charge. But I didn't know Admiral Barnes was on duty there."

"He wasn't," Sarah Maccubbin said. "But his flagship was close by, *and* two cruisers and four destroyers and an aircraft carrier. He got an SOS from Honolulu. He could have been a lot of help, with that much force. Instead— Well, they hushed it up, after he died of his wounds. But people say he needn't have lost those ships. They say he was drunk, Miss Tyler—drunk as he'd been every Sunday since he married again."

CHAPTER FIVE

I had no business at Eleanor Barnes' funeral; but of course I wouldn't have missed it, with Anne and Dick going. I hoped people wouldn't think their aunt was an old curiosity-box, but if they got the impression that was, as Dick says, just too bad.

I also went with some mistaken idea of helping fill up the church. That's done sometimes at home; when the deceased is an unattractive person whose virtues wouldn't have caused the front pew to overflow, some of the pillars of St. Ives' make a point of going. From what I'd heard over the bridge table about the second Mrs. Barnes, mourners at her funeral would be few, too.

But I'd reckoned without the solidity of the Navy, which stands by its own in the face of everything short of court-martial. St. Anne's was full of the flash of gold braid. And certainly I'd reckoned without the power of the press. Anne and Dick take the conservative Annapolis *Capital* and the conservative *Baltimore Sun*; those papers had given the murder its due but no more. I hadn't realized we'd made the tabloids to such a pictorial extent, and it was weeks later when I got hold of a *New York Flash* with "My Interview with the Bus Station Murder Victim," by Mrs. Elsie Kleinschmidt. That one! And I'd heard her say myself she didn't know the dead woman was on the bus.

So what with one thing and another there were actually policemen at the churchyard gates, keeping back the crowd. We went in with the blessing of Patrolman Long, though he gave me rather a supercilious stare—not recalling, evidently, just which of us suspects had turned out to have alibis. If it hadn't been for Dick's uniform I believe I should have been definitely without the gate. As it was, he was barring a good number of indignant women—mostly frank sensation seekers from Baltimore and Washington and even Philadelphia, but a few who claimed to be reporters and at least a dozen who, to hear them tell it, were Eleanor Barnes' close kin. Among others, we saw him arguing with a woman with dyed black hair and yellow clothes—yellow shoes, even, like the woman in *Crimson Friday*. She was taking it very badly indeed, and Anne clutched Dick's arm.

"Mrs. Van Horn!" she whispered. "Hadn't we better go back and tell him? He must be new here—he doesn't know her."

"Leave him to his luck," Dick said out loud. "It's none of our business."

"But she'll have a fit!"

"She's having it," I said grimly. "Don't tell me you know that woman, Anne Meredith! Who is she?"

"She's an admiral's wife and a general's daughter and a senator's daughter-in-law, and she throws all their weights around," Anne said. "She's terrible, Aunt Julia."

I agreed. "She certainly is. I'm like Dick—let her throw her weight around outside."

"But he's treating her as if she were a—a—"

"She is," I said firmly, but I felt bewildered. Navy ideas were too much for me. "Maybe the next time she goes to a funeral she won't wear yellow shoes."

We went inside. St. Anne's, Annapolis, is nothing much to look at. It was built too soon and not soon enough. But some of the windows were nice, and I specially liked the one with the old woman in brown. She reminded me of somebody I knew.

I don't often get out of Rossville; it seemed strange to be in church without knowing all the people in all the pews. I did pick out Sarah Maccubbin, well toward the front, in the blue feather hat she'd played bridge in, and Foster Gibson straight across from us, and one of the young ensigns by the door. Miss Edith Dorsey was down in the Amen corner where I presume she always sat. I didn't see anybody else I knew until Ruth Allein came in with her uncle. At least I thought it must be her uncle. He had a nice face and gold stripes halfway to his elbows.

"Captain Morton," Dick whispered in answer to my nudge and lifted eyebrows. "Yes. Swell. Shh!"

"Don't you hush me, Dick Travers!" I whispered back. "I want to know if you two place that girl?"

"It's his niece, I think," Anne said in my ear. "I've never met her; I don't know her name."

"It's the Red Cross girl that was on the bus," I said. "Ruth Allein. Yes, it is! She just looks different in this hat." And indeed she did. That visored Red Cross cap, pulled down like a Chicago gangster's, makes even a pretty girl look plain. Maybe that's what it's intended to do. Without it, in her black dress and little mink jacket, with a scrap of black felt on her smooth pale hair, Ruth Allein was nothing short of beautiful. I'm not the kind that goes around calling pretty girls beautiful, either.

The service began then, and it went off very well. I kept thinking how convenient Episcopal burial can be in cases like Eleanor Barnes'—everything right in the book, and no leeway given for extemporaneous prayers, and no necessity for making personal remarks. It's all the same for saint or sinner. And it's impressive enough that, no matter which is being buried, some people nearly always get in a funeral mood and cry.

It cast a lot of light on Eleanor Barnes' character, I thought, when I noticed that not a soul in St. Anne's had wiped an eye.

There was no service at the grave; the body was being sent West for burial. We all stood in the churchyard while the uniformed pallbearers lifted the coffin into the hearse that would take it to Baltimore. I didn't think they should have kept their caps on, but they did. It seems they are not supposed to remove any part of a Navy uniform outdoors, and a missing cap is considered as bad as missing trousers would be. I couldn't help thinking of all the boys like Dick, who are only reserve officers; I hoped they wouldn't have too much trouble relearning manners after the war. But I'm afraid a lot of them (not Dick, of course) will go right on letting their wives push the baby carriage and carry the bundles, while they saunter along with both hands free.

We had started around Church Circle to Main Street when we heard someone hurrying up behind us, a good deal faster than most people walk after a funeral. It was young Lieutenant Gibson, and I thought of course he was coming up to speak to me. Not that there was any special reason why he should. I felt like a fool, stopping there on the street all smiles, while Foster Gibson hurried past us and caught up with the man ahead.

"Uncle John!" he said.

The man turned around, and I recognized him as a man I'd noticed in church. He looked like a diplomat out of a novel—cutaway and gray trousers, gray mustache, distinguished profile, and eyeglasses on what Dick calls a leash.

"Good afternoon, Foster," he said, and added nothing to it. The words were like three ice cubes, and the gentleman didn't seem to see his nephew's hand, though the gold stripe and a half above made it rather conspicuous.

Lieutenant Gibson looked like a puppy that had been stepped on. "I didn't know you were coming down, Uncle John," he blundered on, making a bad matter worse for reasons that he apparently understood no better than I. "I'm glad to see you. Did you go by the apartment? I didn't go home at noon."

"I went straight to Carvel Hall from the train," his uncle said. "I'm staying there. This is where I turn." He nodded curtly and stepped off the curb. Foster Gibson stood staring after him as he walked briskly down Main Street. As even I knew, Main Street wasn't the way to Carvel Hall Hotel. You could get there eventually, by going through an alley and zigzagging blocks out of your way, but anybody in his right mind would have gone by way of State Circle. Anybody, that is, who didn't mind walking with Foster Gibson.

"Mr. Gibson!" I said. I didn't think what I was going to say; it just came out.

"How are you, Miss Tyler?" he answered automatically. He looked dazed, but at least he remembered who I was.

"I want you to meet my niece and nephew." I mentioned names, and everybody said how-do-you-do. "We were just wondering," I said, telling an out-and-out lie, "if you couldn't have dinner with us tonight, and play some bridge afterward?"

"Why, that's very kind of you, Miss Tyler," Foster Gibson said, hesitating. He sounded as if he'd like to come but hadn't quite decided to go on living.

Anne said, "Please do!" and Dick said, "We'd like to have you," almost together. Silently I blessed their hearts; they were not only standing by me but being as cordial as if they'd had the idea themselves. But really it was inexcusable for me to invite a stranger to somebody else's house, especially on Fairy's night off, just because his uncle had snubbed him. I apologized to the children as we walked along. Foster Gibson had said he'd come at six-thirty and we left him looking quite a lot happier.

"Why, Aunt Julia, of course you're supposed to invite company!" Dick said. "Anybody you want, any time. Why not?"

"Because it's your house, and I'm company myself, and you're grown up and married and I keep forgetting it," I said. "And just for that I'm getting dinner tonight alone. Anne can set the table and fix the salad, but I do all the rest."

I did, too, and everything was good if I do say it. I spread the ham with mustard and molasses before I broiled it, and stuck in plenty of cloves. I made a chocolate pie, too. I was glad I did. Foster Gibson ate and ate. He turned out to be every bit as nice as he looked, and his bridge was just right, not too good but good enough for anybody. He wasn't one of those who mind talking along with it, either. Well fed, and with everybody obviously liking him, he relaxed and talked a blue streak. I found out a lot about him. One nice thing about getting to what is called a certain age—and at sixty-seven I've been there some time—is the privilege of asking questions without having your motives misunderstood. You have to ask questions, too, when it's a matter of young naval officers. I soon found that out. On the surface they seem pretty much alike. They all look handsome in their uniforms, whether already handsome by the grace of God or not; they all have nice manners, however recently acquired; and either they're all extroverted or they all pretend to be. Even the ones who've been in service only a very short time have learned to be tactful and noncommittal, and to assume ever so politely that civilians don't, for all practical purposes, really exist. Maybe among themselves they break down and admit a political preference, or condescend to hark back to the days before they joined the Navy. They certainly don't outside.

In Foster Gibson's case there hadn't been any pre-Navy days. He'd been born into the service and had had nothing else since, poor child. (Though I understand it's the Navy juniors who feel sorry for everybody else.) His father, a lieutenant then, was killed in the *Macon* disaster. His mother—and *her* mother, of all things, was Eugenia Gresham who went to school with my cousin—died when he was in his plebe year at Annapolis. There weren't any other children. The only close relative he had was an uncle, his mother's much older half-brother, who lived in Philadelphia.

It was at this point that I realized Foster Gibson wasn't telling me everything he knew after all. It would have been the most natural thing in the world to say, "Did you notice the gentleman I was talking with just before you came up today? That was my Uncle John." He didn't.

Then too when we got on the subject of murder—as inevitably we did—he closed up like a clam. I didn't like that. Of course I didn't think he did it; I'm not in the habit of making chocolate pie for people I think do murder. But the fact remained he didn't have the sign of an alibi, and people would naturally draw their own conclusions if he got still and frozen-faced all of a sudden. I liked the boy, and I hated to think how Ben Kramer might interpret his reactions.

Don't tell me there's nothing in mental telepathy. Ben Kramer banged on the front door.

It was purely a social call—at least it started out to be. I enjoyed Ben tremendously, and Anne and Dick were really impressed with him. Shiftless old Tom Kramer and his barber shop were both before their time, and I could see they thought rather more of me since they saw I had such friends. Ben made himself very pleasant indeed. With the exception of Foster Gibson they were all down to first names in no time, the way young people do.

I could have shaken Foster Gibson till his teeth rattled. The charming young man of the dinner and bridge table was quite gone, and instead he was stiff and cold and curt and everything that an innocent person shouldn't be in the presence of the law. Ben, of course, might think he was always like that. I hoped he would. He was certainly very smooth. But with Anne and Dick and me all under a strain, and Foster Gibson just plain scared, though I suppose I shouldn't say it of a naval officer in time of war, it was a relief when the telephone rang. It was extra relief when the call was for Foster Gibson.

The telephone in the little Cornhill Street house is upstairs. The officer who lived in it last was out late a great many nights—why, I don't know—and his wife was nervous, so the telephone was on the table by her bed. Thanks to priorities or something, it has to stay there till the war is over.

So Foster Gibson went upstairs, and I hope Anne's underclothes were picked up better than they used to be at home. We couldn't hear his voice at first, for Dick was pounding back downstairs rather like a troop of horse. The whole house shook. But then the voice came to us as clearly as if Foster Gibson were still in the living room. Anne's eyes went to the ceiling, and ours followed. The register was wide open.

". . . can't get it from Uncle John," he said. "No, I can't. I thought I could, but I can't.... It's very simple." His voice was as bitter as the taste in my own mouth. "He thinks," Foster Gibson said, "that I murdered Mrs. Barnes."

CHAPTER SIX

If I had had the sense God gave geese I would have sneezed, or coughed, or dropped my glasses case. It wasn't my fault that Foster Gibson didn't go on looping a rope around his neck. Instead of doing anything to warn the boy—and he was not a murderer and he hadn't said so, had he?—I sat there like a stone image. So did all of us, while he opened and shut the bedroom door and came downstairs. In the hall he picked up his cap, and with that in his hand he spoke to us from the door.

"I'm sorry," he said, and he smiled the nice white smile we hadn't seen since Ben Kramer came. "It's been a swell evening, and I hate to cut it short. But that was the Experiment Station. I'm subject to call, you know, and something in my department needs my master hand." My charming young friend was back again, but unfortunately and quite too late.

Anne managed to smile back at him. I couldn't. What an actor! I thought. What an accomplished liar! Is he a clever murderer too?

I don't remember what all we said between then and the door's closing behind Foster Gibson. I remember that it was Ben who broke our silence.

"Well," he said, "it looks as if this wasn't my night off after all."

He got busy. First he traced the telephone call; and a lot of good that did him, for it had been made from a booth in Tracy's Drugstore. Patrolman Green, contacted at police headquarters, was sent right over to check. But he got nothing at all. It wasn't late; the store was still full of people, and the soda fountain boy, the only clerk who had the telephone booths in view, had been too busy to notice. There's a dearth of well-located public telephones in Annapolis, and the ones there are used a lot.

Ben came back downstairs. "Well, the spy hole's still open, so you heard what I found out," he said. "Nothing. But maybe you people can give me more."

He pulled out a disreputable pocket notebook that hadn't been much to start out with and looked as old as his career. Before the murder investigation was over it was as familiar to me as my dear mother's face.

"Now, Miss Julia," Ben said, poising over the notebook a pencil that wasn't much better, "what do you know about that young man? Where did you meet him?"

"On the bus," I said a little reluctantly. I didn't like this. "That is, I saw him on the bus, and—afterwards. I didn't actually speak to him till today."

"And then what happened?"

"I asked him to come to dinner."

"Just like that? No build-up? No special reason?"

"I liked his looks," I said.

Anne broke in, backing me up. "We liked his looks, too, Ben. And he really is nice. You can't imagine what fun he was until you came." She stopped a little too late. Certainly she hadn't done Foster Gibson much good by that last frank statement of fact.

"Lots of people are nervous around the police," Dick said. "I remember when I was a kid I wouldn't even walk past the station house. I'd cross the street. Aunt Ticey was always threatening to send for a big blue policeman with a stick."

"But you got over feeling like that," Ben pointed out. "Normal people do. Some psychoneurotics don't—and, of course, the people who have a reason to be afraid."

"Foster Gibson is no psychoneurotic," I began, and stopped.

"Miss Julia, you people make me sick," Ben Kramer said quietly and politely. "This man isn't any kin to you, is he? None of you ever spoke to him until today, did you? Well, then, why the cover-up? It's nothing to you if he's the murderer—and somebody has to be—and maybe he is."

"We like him," I said stubbornly.

"So what?" Ben said. "You like this dog, too, don't you?" He rubbed the toe of his big black shoe over Shenstone Alice-Sit-by-the-Fire, who was being just that, good as gold. Alice nearly purred, which wouldn't have surprised me as I consider cockers half cat anyway. "But if she went mad and bit Miss Anne it would make a difference, wouldn't it? I've got a mighty good hunch you'd tell the doctor the whole tale."

"That's different," Anne said. "The doctor is to cure people. But you want—to hang somebody."

"Not necessarily, Anne, no." Ben's voice was serious. "As a matter of fact I don't approve of hanging. I belong to the new deal in criminology—what some police commissioners sneer at as Bright Young People. I believe most criminals need a doctor instead of a hangman." He smiled across at me. "Miss Julia doesn't like my word 'psychoneurotic.' I admit it's one that's been used—misused—too much. Amateur psychologists are apt to associate it mostly with middle-aged women who have too much money and too little to do, who go in for Pekes and imaginary pains and other people's business. The Helen Hokinson girls." He smiled at me again, and I could smile back because I'm thin. "But now the war," Ben said seriously, "is showing us the real McCoy. In quantity. Thousands—I mean thousands—of men are cracking up in service. Some of them are psychotic—crazy, that is—and have to be shut up. But most of them aren't crazy. They're just psychoneurotic. They weed them out of the services too, of course—they're no good in. Some few of them make a good adjustment back to civilian life. Most of them will be quiet, respectable citizens the rest of their lives—unhappy, but not hurting anybody by it. They look and act like you and me. But some of the others—well, they'll go over the edge. They'll pass from psychoneurosis to psychosis so quietly their friends and relatives may never suspect. Until somebody they hate is—well, stabbed."

Dick broke the following silence. "Foster Gibson hasn't had combat duty."

"That doesn't matter," Ben said. "Not that I'm talking about Foster Gibson, Dick, you understand. I'm just talking generally. As far as I know, Foster Gibson is as normal as you are—or as I think you are." Anne let out an indignant gasp, and he grinned at her. "N.P. cases don't have to be stormed at by shot and shell. Of course a lot of them are what used to be called shell-shock, and the tropic sun has accounted for some. But mostly it's just this: everybody has a breaking point, a point where his nerves just won't take any more. It differs in different people, depending on a lot of factors. It's like the plateau of learning Miss Julia could tell us about. Some boys go through the worst of a war without reaching it. Other boys get there at the induction center, when they have their first taste of discipline."

"Do you think Mrs. Barnes' murderer was a serviceman?" Anne asked doubtfully. "Because it didn't seem to me— Of course there was the Campbell boy, and one of the ensigns, and then the private who'd had too much to drink— Oh, but he had an alibi."

"If I gave you the impression I thought it was a serviceman I'm sorry," said Ben. "I didn't mean to. No, it's just that the war is in the news these days, and the magazines full of half-baked articles about the returning soldier have made us N.P.-conscious. Actually some of the worst N.P. cases have never been near the army. If you want the figures, it's less than half a million that have been weeded out of service, as opposed to three times that many that were too bad to get in. And of course those figures are only on young men subject to induction. It stands to reason there'd be plenty of women and older men. As far as this particular murder is concerned, it's the civilians that seem to have the strongest motives." He grinned at me. "I understand, Miss Julia, you've taken a shine to the admiral's first wife too."

"She didn't do it, Ben," I said earnestly. "Leave the fact that I liked her out of it. Remember I talked to that woman nearly all the way from Baltimore, and we were still talking on our way out of the bus. 'How anybody can sleep with all this going on!' she said. Do you think anybody who'd just stabbed a woman, or was just getting ready to, would have called attention to her like that?"

"It does seem most unlikely, Miss Julia," Ben said handsomely. He wrote in his little book.

"Mrs. Barnes—my Mrs. Barnes—didn't have her mind on anything but her son, anyhow." I was warming to my subject. "She'd just come back from visiting him in the hospital. He lost his right leg and his eyesight at Salerno. Did you know that? But she was so thankful to have him back at all."

"That's interesting, Miss Julia!" Ben's pencil was moving fast. "You're telling me a lot. Now I'll tell you something. Roger Barnes, Jr., will get a pension for total disability."

"Well, I should hope so!" I said.

"Around two hundred dollars a month, I expect it'll be. Two-fifty, maybe. He'll get a fine new leg free, he'll be entitled to vocational rehabilitation if he wants it, and if he'd like a Seeing Eye dog it will cost him just a dollar, special price to disabled veterans. But that's all he will get. It won't be as much as he'll need. Young Roger Barnes," Ben said, "has got a wife and child in an expensive TB sanitarium. He's got two other delicate kids at home with his mother. And he's got his mother."

"Oh, the poor things!" Anne said. "But—"

"I don't see the connection either, honey." Dick turned to Ben. "All that's very too bad, of course, but hardly the second Mrs. Barnes's fault. You think it adds to the motive?"

"In this way," Ben said. "Under Admiral Barnes' will his widow got a life interest. At her death the whole estate went to his only son. Not a fortune, as fortunes go, but the admiral's pay was six thousand a year, plus big extras. He'd lived well under income while he was married to the first wife, and he had a mighty good friend on the Stock Exchange. I understand he bought a lot of Lorillard, for instance, when it first came on the market. It all added up. More than enough to commit murder for, I'd say, even without the motive you knew."

"Oh, Lord!" Dick said.

Anne was anxious. "But Ben, you don't really think she did it?"

"I don't have opinions at this point, Anne," Ben said. "I don't know enough yet. I'm still just collecting facts, and I don't have half enough of them."

"I'll give you one, Ben," I said suddenly. I hadn't been able to say anything for quite a while. I felt a little sick and disgusted, but I'd made up my mind. I wasn't free to tell him about Mary Barnes' mysterious little package, because I'd promised; but I'd made no promises to the attractive young man who'd had dinner with us.

"Yes, Miss Julia?" Ben said.

"It's Foster Gibson." The look on Anne's and Dick's faces nearly made me stop. After all I'd spanked Dick once, at the age of eight, for tattling on Bobby Lanham. And I'd tried to pound it into Anne all her life that a lot of perfectly true things do harm if they're repeated. I felt like an informer but I went on. "His uncle *is* mad at him," I said. "He nearly cut him on the street today. The uncle's still in town. He's staying at Carvel Hall."

"That's fine, Miss Julia. Thanks," Ben said. He wrote in the awful notebook. "Do you know his name?"

"I don't. But he comes from Philadelphia. He's a gray-haired handsome man with a mustache, and glasses on a black ribbon."

"Then we can find him," Ben said. He put the notebook away and stood up. "You two kids wipe off your faces. I don't know about the Navy, but Miss Julia has come out on the side of law and order."

"Where the Navy will join me," I said with confidence. I know my children. "After all, it isn't a question of divulging details about secret weapons. There's nothing Oppenheim about this case that I can see. It's just a matter of accepting—or rejecting—any ordinary person's debt to society. I don't mean to preach, children, but there it is. And, as Ben says, it isn't as if these apparently nice people were anything to us. If you two find my alibi is upset, or I find that Dick was on that bus disguised as Bill Palougous, I expect we have Ben's permission to—er—deviate. Otherwise, I think we ought to help him."

The solemn young faces were smiling at me now.

"Lie ourselves black in the face, you mean," Dick said. "And of course if the secret weapon does come into the picture, later on, I'll have to claim another exemption. Otherwise, Ben, we're with you."

"I expect we'll be pretty good help, too," Anne said seriously. "We all read lots of murders, even Aunt Julia. She can throw Hercule Poirot in your teeth every step of the way,"

Ben agreed. "And Miss Marple. In fact I'm counting on Miss Julia's turning out to be another Miss Marple or Miss Silver. You don't know Miss Maud Silver? She's another of the lady sleuths who solve the crime and give the credit to the police. An expert on human nature."

"Well, you can just get over any such idea," I said definitely. I forbore to tell him that seeing him on the right side of the law had shaken my faith in my ability to judge character. "You'll solve this crime yourself, Ben Kramer. But I can keep my eyes and ears open, and it seems to me Annapolis is pretty talkative."

"You're right, it is," Ben said with some grimness. "Everybody talks all the time, and a lot of the things they say are actionable. And you can pick up stuff I can't, Miss Julia. You'll be getting to some places a policeman can't very well go. For instance, I expect you'll be at the DAR?"

I looked at Anne.

"Why, of course, Ben, if Aunt Julia wants to," Anne said. "But it comes right after a luncheon we're going to, and everybody's going to sew for the Red Cross first—"

"I do want to," I said definitely. "I can rest when I go home to Rossville."

"That's the old detective spirit!" Ben said. He looked around for his hat, and found it. "I expect you'll come back with a tidbit that'll bust this case wide open. You tell me all and I'll tell you—well, nearly all. How would you like to hear a little something now, about Dr. Mosser?"

We all three gazed at him the way Alice gazes before we hand her a bone.

"Dr. Mosser has a lousy practice," Ben said. "But it wasn't always that way. He didn't always have that chip on his shoulder, either. I don't mean he was ever the kind of doctor *I'd* like, but lots of people did swear by him. He had a good growing practice here in Annapolis, four years ago. He was doing swell. He was a smart man, all right. But he got a little *too* smart—got to dispensing drugs on the side. And one day he got caught. Know who caught him?"

"Eleanor Barnes!" we chorused.

"Right, Eleanor Barnes," Ben said. "Dr. Mosser made the mistake of selling morphine to her precious son. It's great stuff to sober up on, you know. Mrs. Barnes was an influential woman and a—determined woman. She saw that he got three years. He deserved it, of course."

"But why did he come back here?" Anne wanted to know. "I should think he'd rather make a fresh start somewhere else."

Ben shook his head. "It just doesn't work, Anne. Somebody always finds you out, and then it's worse than if you hadn't tried to fool people. It's better to go back where it happened and try to live it down. But of course it's hard. Bitterly hard. And of course it was too bad for Dr. Mosser that Eleanor Barnes was still in town. I don't imagine she made it easier for him." Ben slapped on his hat and opened the door. "Dream about that one, Miss Marple."

CHAPTER SEVEN

Anne instructed me carefully in local history before I went to the DAR. She seemed to think it a serious matter that I'd never heard of the Peggy Stewart Tea Party the Annapolis chapter was named after. I'd never even heard of Peggy, and freely said so.

"Oh, she wasn't a *person*, Aunt Julia," Anne said. "Well, maybe she was originally. But the *Peggy Stewart* was a boat—"

"A brig," Dick said.

Anne withered him with a look. "The *Peggy Stewart* was a boat, and nobody cares how many sails it had."

"She had."

"Children!" I said. "I have exactly eleven minutes before Sarah Maccubbin comes by for me."

"Well, I'm *trying* to tell you, Aunt Julia." Anne plunged on. "The *Peggy Stewart* belonged to an Annapolis man who was still trying to import tea. All this was before the Revolution when people got excited about things like that. His neighbors got mad at him, and he thought he'd better burn his old tea up. So he went on board the—*boat*, and set it afire, and it sank right where Farragut Field is now."

"A likely spot," Dick said.

"All that is made land," Anne informed him with dignity. "The Severn used to come right up to where Bancroft Hall is now. Professor Gassaway says so."

"Mark my words, Aunt Julia," Dick said. "When I get my divorce I'm going to name that man as correspondent. Anne quotes him at me all the time. He's made a lifework of ye olde Annapolis, and he's another one that's excited about the pre-Revolutionary tea tax. Nothing since. Able-bodied man, too."

Later in the afternoon I was forced to see Dick's point. Professor Gassaway, who chanced to be the chief speaker at the meeting, certainly lived up to his name. He gave the Daughters quite fifty minutes of a man called John Beale Bordley, his life and works. I knew no more of Mr. Bordley than I had of Peggy Stewart, and was quite willing to be instructed; but after half an hour the young professor's spotted tie and equally spotted face began to blur. I hastily transferred my attention to the ballroom woodwork.

The DAR was meeting that day in the famous Howard House on Prince George Street. I'd never been in it before. Of course I knew it from the outside, as anyone does who's seen Annapolis even once. It's the only five-part house in town with three full stories, and it towers over its neighbors artistically as well as physically. It's *the* house in Annapolis that architects come to see, though of course the smaller Harwood and Brice and Chase houses aren't far behind. But only the Howard House has an upstairs ballroom seven full windows across, with not one Buckland mantel but two, and plaster shells and flowers on the ceiling. It was about the most beautiful room I'd ever seen, and beautifully restored. Some Cincinnati millionaire, trying rather wistfully to make the link with the past he couldn't do via the Sons of the Cincinnati, had paid for the whole thing and given it as a museum. The main part of the house was furnished in the period—1775—and one of the wings housed the millionaire's silver collection and the other his archival library. I wanted to see them both; I wished Professor Gassaway would stop.

He did, of course, eventually, and then we had tea and four kinds of sandwiches and little frosted cakes. Everybody was very cordial to me, and I enjoyed myself after I gave up the struggle to remember names. Sarah Maccubbin could tell me later. But I did identify a nice fat Mrs. Morton as Ruth Allein's aunt, and I was glad to see Mrs. Beale and Miss Dulany again. Then a cowed-looking little woman was introduced as Mrs. Duckett, and I nearly laughed. They can talk all they want to about the tone-deaf Birdsongs and two-hundred-pound Lightfoots we number among the first families of Virginia; here in one afternoon I had met garrulous Professor Gassaway and cringing Mrs. Duckett, and Friday night we were having dinner with the Chews.

Of course I like to think I'm naturally popular, but if so it was strange how soon murder entered into the conversation of the group around me, and how promptly the group increased when it did. I found myself acting the whole thing out, with gestures. The ladies hung on my words. It was pleasant, but suddenly I remembered I was supposed to be finding out things instead of giving out, as Dick calls it.

"I was wondering about the second Mrs. Barnes' son," I said. "Did he come for the funeral?"

"Oh, no, Miss Tyler!" the ladies chorused.

"Eleanor Barnes' only son is dead," Miss Dulany explained. "He was killed in the war—quite early in the war. In the Pacific area, I think."

"He died a very fine death," a thin, beaded lady said approvingly. "Volunteered for some very dangerous mission, when it amounted to suicide to go. Didn't he get a decoration?"

"They sent it to his mother," Mrs. Beale said. "A citation, too. Poor boy, he had to die to get something good said about him."

"Wasn't he popular?" I asked.

"Oh, Shaw Hamilton was popular enough," nice fat Mrs. Morton said. "He had lots of friends. Even my sensible Ruth used to take up for him." I pricked up my ears, Mrs. Morton being Ruth Allein's aunt. "But he was weak all through."

"Oh, worse than weak, Katherine!" somebody said. "I'm perfectly willing to call whisky a weakness, but when it comes to drugs—"

"Oh, did he take drugs?" Nobody—or so I flattered myself—would have suspected I knew already.

"Morphine." Mrs. Duckett lowered her voice. "Everybody was surprised when he was accepted for service."

"Not as an officer, of course," someone added.

"I think that upset his mother more than anything else," said Mrs. Beale frankly. "Of course she should have known before she tried that they *couldn't*; but still—"

"So he went in the army—was it?—as a common private," I said. "How old was he?"

After some conferring back and forth the ladies decided he was twenty-two.

"Was he married?"

Mrs. Morton said, "Yes," and Miss Dulany said, "No," almost together. Everybody laughed a little.

"The truth of the matter, Miss Tyler, is that we don't know," Sarah Maccubbin said. "We wish we did! There was some story about Shaw Hamilton's marrying; but he'd never lived in Annapolis, you know, and nobody knew him well. He and his stepfather didn't get along, and anyway he was off at college when his mother married Admiral Barnes."

"He went to one college after another," Mrs. Beak said, "but it was always the same thing. Thrown out for drinking! I never heard of his taking drugs till later."

The ladies all agreed that they hadn't either.

"Shaw Hamilton was a problem to the admiral," Mrs. Morton took up the story. "His mother too, of course; but though she must have worried she didn't show it. He did."

"She wasn't that kind," the thin, beaded lady said.

"And of course it wasn't just drinking and drugs," went on Mrs. Morton, "though that was the worst. He gambled too, and practically lived out at Pimlico when he was here, and once there was something about a check. But I believe he was married to the girl in New York."

"She said so, certainly," agreed Miss Dulany, though with every appearance of doubt. "My niece Mrs. Wickliffe met them on the street— she was going to see some friends in the part of the Village that's respectable now, and they were coming around the corner from one of the parts that aren't. Shaw had been drinking pretty hard, she said. He didn't want to introduce the girl to Lucy, but Lucy just planted her feet, she said, and kept on talking, and finally he had to. 'This is Miss Wynne, Mrs. Wickliffe,' he said."

"Surely," Mrs. Beale put in, "she wouldn't let him get by with that if they were really married!"

"That's just it!" Miss Dulany came back triumphantly. "She didn't. She asked Lucy to come and see them. 'We've got the sweetest little apartment,' she said, 'and I'm fixing it up too cute! But of course I haven't had time to do much,' she said. 'We've only been married two weeks.' And she sort of gazed up at Shaw and giggled. Lucy said it was sickening. She didn't believe for a minute that they were really married."

"Well, he didn't deny it," Mrs. Morton remarked.

Several of the ladies laughed indulgently. "Oh, Katherine!"

"I don't see how he could have denied it, very well," I said, and they laughed again.

"You didn't know Shaw Hamilton, Miss Tyler," the beaded lady answered. "Married or not, he would have denied it with pleasure if he'd wanted to."

"He was a good deal like his mother," somebody said.

"If I were my grandson, Miriam"—it was meek little Mrs. Duckett, of all people—"I'd call that a dirty crack." Everybody laughed again.

"Oh, possibly Eleanor Barnes wasn't as bad as all that," Mrs. Morton said charitably. "I don't think our Navy life always brings out the best in us. I don't mean it's just what some people say—bridge and needlepoint and other people's husbands—but our time is taken up with trivialities, and we don't get much else done. We dumb ones enjoy ourselves," she smiled cheerfully. "But sometimes it does things to intelligent women. And you'll have to say Eleanor Barnes was an intelligent woman."

"Oh, yes," some of the ladies said unenthusiastically.

Mrs. Duckett spoke up. She wasn't as cowed as she looked. "That's all very well, Katherine. But Edith Dorsey is my own first cousin, and a person can't overlook *everything*."

Edith Dorsey! My mind sat up, and I'm afraid I did too, but nobody noticed. I opened my mouth to ask a question—not the most tactful or ladylike thing under the circumstances, but I *had* to know what Eleanor Barnes had done to the woman who admitted owning the murder weapon. But Mrs. Beale got there first, and changed the subject. I was definitely hacked, as Dick says. Of course I could have turned the conversation back again; but thinking it over, while Mrs. Beale complimented the cakes that the beaded lady's cook had made, and the beaded lady explained that they were really very simple, just raspberry preserves added to plain yellow batter, I decided Ben wouldn't want me to. It was all right for me to show interest in the people who'd been on the bus, the murdered woman and the others who might have done the murder. That would be expected of me. But if I pushed it too hard, if I made anyone suspect that I was curious on behalf of the police, my usefulness in the case would be over.

But my caution was like the lid on a boiling saucepan and I had to hold it firmly while Professor Gassaway and a new Mrs. Kent showed me over the house. I would have enjoyed myself more if Edith Dorsey hadn't been on my mind. And Shaw Hamilton—Hamilton— What was it that name connected with? But the house was breathtaking even so. I'm used to pre-Revolutionary architecture, Rossville being full of it and Williamsburg not too far away, with the James River mansions in between. But there's nothing in all Tidewater to touch the Howard House. That's not just my opinion; the experts say so too. The hall sweeps straight through from front to back, the way it does at Sabine Hall only more so, with the staircase in its own hallway beyond an arch. The arch itself, with its dentils and acanthus leaves, gave me a good feeling in my stomach. That's what Anne used to say when she was little, and I still don't know any better way to express reaction to sheer beauty. I had that feeling all through the house: music room, withdrawing room, state and family dining rooms, nursery with the iron bars still across the windows, and especially the room they call the White Lady's Chamber. Before 1781, Mrs. Kent told me, it had been the best of the six great bedrooms, the one where important guests were put so they could lie in the big tester bed and look out over the town and port of Annapolis. If George Washington hadn't slept there it was only because the Howards of that branch were Tories. And nobody had slept there at all—successfully, that is—since Bladen Howard's patriot wife had been murdered in the great tester bed, with nobody to notice or hear because Annapolis was out celebrating the Battle of Yorktown.

"Do they think Bladen Howard killed her?" I asked doubtfully. "Because I never heard of a man's murdering his wife for political reasons."

Mrs. Kent and Professor Gassaway laughed politely.

"It was rather more fundamental than that, Miss Tyler," the young antiquary said. He was really very nice in spite of his pimples and preciosity. Some people just can't help being tiresome. "Of course the murder was never solved, you understand. But her daughter-in-law was strongly suspected. There'd been bad feeling between them."

"People cut young Mrs. Howard the rest of her life," Mrs. Kent took up the story. She spoke with the enthusiasm Annapolis people do reserve for the past. I like the past myself, but I could see how it rubbed Dick the wrong way, with a world at war. "She never lived it down. She got so she never went anywhere she didn't have to, and always wore a veil—"

I didn't hear the rest. My mind had left the White Lady's murder back in 1781 where it belonged, and was fixed on Eleanor Barnes'. I knew who had killed her. I was marveling at my own stupidity for not having leaped at it before, and at Ben Kramer's stupidity, and at the stupidity of all the good ladies who knew Eleanor Barnes' son's name, and who had read in their *Evening Capitals* the names of the passengers on the bus. Shaw Hamilton—Mrs. Dorothy Hamilton. The war widow whose husband had been killed in the Pacific. The pretty dark-haired girl who'd read *True Romances*, who'd said she didn't know Eleanor Barnes. But she did. She was Mrs. Barnes' daughter-in-law, and she had killed her. I knew it as well as I knew my own name.

CHAPTER EIGHT

Of course it was all I could do to keep from letting out a whoop and rushing out of the house and down the street in search of Ben Kramer. Not that I am in the habit of letting out whoops—in fact I never have; but I'm not in the habit of solving murders, either. I was really proud of myself because I went right on talking to Mrs. Kent and Professor Gassaway. But I didn't even see the rest of the beautiful house they showed me, and I'll have to go back and look at that silver collection some day. I don't remember a thing about it. Silver is my own special hobby, too. As to the Cincinnati millionaire's archival library, I only noticed the Latin deeds and grants the crisp young librarian got out on purpose to show me. Anne had told Professor Gassaway that I'd taught Latin all my life, and they were all very deferential, as if I were from a big university instead of a country high school. I was sorry not to say something brilliant and penetrating, by way of living up to the reputation Anne had given me, but with Eleanor Barnes' murder on my mind I was thankful to be adequate.

I couldn't even wait till I got home to call Ben and tell him. "I have to go in here," I said to Sarah Maccubbin, in front of Tracy's Drugstore on State Circle. We made arrangements to have tea together one day next week. I like Sarah Maccubbin, but I was certainly glad to see her solid handsome back this time. I hurried into the drugstore. Fortunately a booth was free; I believe if it hadn't been I would have kicked the door and screamed.

I had a terrible time finding a nickel and then finding the slot to put it in, and after I got headquarters they didn't want to let me speak to Lieutenant Kramer.

"If you could just tell me, ma'am," the policeman kept saying.

"I can't and I won't," I snapped back finally. "Are you going to let me speak to Ben Kramer, young man, or do I have to come around there?"

Evidently there are some policemen whom politeness is wasted on, just as there are some children who can't be reasoned with, and don't respect you till you give them a spanking. There was a pause, and then Ben's voice came over the wire.

"Lieutenant Kramer speaking."

"This is Julia Tyler, Ben." I was disgusted to hear my own voice tremble and then actually break. "I—I think I know who did it."

"Where are you, Miss Julia?"

"I'm in a booth at Tracy's Drugstore." I laughed shakily. "You needn't worry, Ben. Nobody's following me with a knife; nobody realizes I know. Though why we didn't see it before—"

"Go on, Miss Julia," Ben said crisply. "Who do you think it is?"

"Tell me this first." I was enjoying myself now, basking in his interest the way poor Edith Dorsey had in the bus station, prolonging it like a piece of cake icing held on my tongue to melt. "Was Shaw Hamilton married?"

"Shaw Hamilton? The second Mrs. Barnes's son? Why, yes, Miss Julia. A very dizzy blonde out of a nightclub."

"A blonde?" I said faintly.

"Miss DeLoriese Wynne."

"Was that her real name? Are you sure she was a blonde?"

"Probably not, as to the name," Ben said. "We haven't seen the license. But she was a blonde all right. What did you have in mind, Miss Julia?"

"The girl on the bus, Ben," I told him. "Mrs. Dorothy Hamilton. The last name's the same. *Her* husband was killed in the Pacific—"

"I know, Miss Julia." Ben's voice was kind. Too kind. I knew I'd gone up a blind alley. "Long checked that point. But we did see *her* marriage license. Her husband's name was James."

I sat in the telephone booth a long time after we had said goodbye and hung up.

"What's the matter with you, Aunt Julia?" Dick asked at dinner. "Didn't you have a good time today?"

I told them about Shaw Hamilton and Dorothy who wasn't, after all, his wife.

"Now, Aunt Julia, look," Dick said kindly when I had finished. "You have to cultivate the scientific point of view. Actually you accomplished a lot today."

"I don't see what," I said gloomily.

"Yes, you did. Eat your meat, Aunt Julia; it's good. You made a negative contribution."

"It was negative, all right." But I picked up my knife and fork again.

"Some research chemists and physicists spend their whole lives making a negative contribution," Dick said. "Take the people who've been working on synthetic rubber, or atabrine. That's the new substitute for quinine. You don't think they hit it the first time, do you? You don't think the people that got their names in the paper were the only ones who ever tackled those problems, do you? If things happened that way it would be more luck than sense, like a hole in one. No, sir, Aunt Julia, you have to try and fail, and pick yourself up, and dust yourself off, and start right over again."

"And maybe die of old age while I'm doing it," I said.

"Probably not, darling." Anne patted my arm. "You're always talking about how long-lived the Tylers are."

"No, seriously, Aunt Julia," Dick said, "every time you have a hunch it's up to you to play it, just the way you did this time. You didn't establish a motive for your Mrs. Hamilton, but you're closer to a solution. You can't forget about her because she did have opportunity; but you can count her off your list of people who had opportunity and motive both."

"That's something we've forgotten!" exclaimed Anne, as we got up from the table. "We haven't made a list, and in books they always do."

"But does it ever do them any good?" I questioned. "It seems to me that when they've finished they always sit and look at it for a while, and then sigh, and push the paper away."

The children laughed.

"Oh, but later it comes back!" Anne said. She went to the living room secretary and settled herself to write. Her pen scratched across the paper, drawing lines, while Dick went through his nightly routine of offering me a cigarette before he lit his own. Fresh from the DAR meeting, where the customary percentage had smoked after tea, I refused a little more firmly than usual. Not that I see anything wrong with old ladies smoking. I don't see why a bishop shouldn't wear a rose in his hair, either, if he doesn't think he'd look silly.

"Now!" Anne said at last. She read aloud from her paper. "One. Mary Barnes. Motive, money for her son, also professional jealousy."

"After the admiral has been dead three years?" Dick doubted, and I agreed with him. But Anne shook her head darkly.

"When a woman is scorned, she stays scorned."

Dick conceded the point. "Maybe so."

"Two. George Campbell. Motive, unknown, if any.

"Three. Edith Dorsey. Motive, as above."

I sat up. "But she does have a motive!" I'd forgotten it in my excitement over the Shaw Hamilton angle, when I thought—foolishly enough, now that I thought again—that the Lord had delivered a solution into my hands.

"What?" The children said it together.

I told them, word for word, what Mrs. Duckett had said about Edith Dorsey. They were excited and impressed. We agreed that checking up on Edith Dorsey was my next move, and that it shouldn't be too hard. People in Annapolis, as far as I could see, were quite lacking in the fine art of reticence.

"Four," Anne read. "Gladys Fulton. Motive, unknown, if any."

"Five. Foster Gibson. Motive, unknown, but probably existent.

"Six. Dorothy Hamilton. Motive, unknown, if any.

"Seven. Dr. James Mosser. Motive, conviction on charge brought by the murdered woman."

"You might add to that," I said, "the fact that Ben said she was murdered by somebody that picked the right place to stab."

Anne added it. "Eight. Ensign Gordon Smith. Motive, unknown, if any. And that's all the ones who had opportunity."

"Only two with established motives," Dick said thoughtfully. "Mary Barnes and Dr. Mosser. Edith Dorsey Aunt Julia is going to check up on. I've already been making discreet inquiries about Foster Gibson—nothing from it, though, so far. Which of the others are you planning to run down, my good woman?"

"Gordon Smith," Anne said without hesitation. "I know his wife—not very well, but I could invite her to the luncheon I'm having for Sally's sister."

"You won't be able to get much out of her then," I said practically. "You'll have too much on your mind."

Anne agreed. "Especially since I never know whether Fairy is going to show up. But it will be an opening wedge. Later I can ask her to come to tea or go to the movies, and she will tell me all."

"That reminds me, Anne," I said. "Would you invite a friend of mine to your party? Ruth Allein? I want you two to meet."

Anne and Dick looked at each other and laughed.

"Aunt Julia isn't on to the Navy yet," Dick said. "I hate to tell you, Miss Tyler, but in Annapolis we're very low on the social scale. Oh, we're *on* it—that's something. But Anne's husband is only a lieutenant, junior grade, and Ruth Allein's uncle is a captain."

"That's foolishness."

"Off the record, I think you're right," Dick said. "Oh, it isn't so bad; not half as rigid as they say it used to be. But there's plenty left, and you don't want Miss Allein to think Anne has designs."

"She wouldn't think so; she's got too much sense." I was disgusted. The idea of worrying about things like that in wartime. But I remembered about Mary Barnes, who'd also thought a wife's Navy duties were silly. "Well, would it be all right if I took the blame? I'll ask her myself."

I went upstairs and did. Ruth Allein sounded glad to hear my voice, and sorry when I told her about Anne's party. She couldn't come because it was a working day and she'd be at the Baltimore Red Cross as usual. But she did want to meet Anne and Dick, she said, and asked if she could come over some night soon. We settled on Tuesday, and I hung up the receiver feeling pleased with myself.

Then on an impulse I dialed Sarah Maccubbin's number. "You'll think I'm a gossipy old woman, Miss Maccubbin," I began, "and I don't care if you do. I wish you'd tell me what Mrs. Duckett meant when she said she couldn't overlook something Eleanor Barnes had done to Miss Edith Dorsey."

Sarah Maccubbin laughed her comfortable fat laugh. "I'll be glad to tell you, Miss Tyler. I know just how you feel. And anyway it's common knowledge, though there's nothing much to it."

I thought there was a good deal to it. When I came downstairs again the children swear I skipped. They laughed at me, and so did Ben Kramer, who had knocked and been let in without my hearing it.

"Well, Miss Julia," Ben said, shaking hands, "you got me over here on false pretenses. You sounded so discouraged over the telephone, after I had to slap you down about Mrs. Hamilton, that I thought I'd better come cheer you up. And I find you looking like Christmas morning."

"It's her mercurial psychoneurotic temperament," Dick said. "One minute she's up and the next down. Emotionally unstable."

I gave him a look. "I have something to be emotionally unstable about, Dick Travers," I said. "Edith Dorsey has got as good a motive as you would want to see."

CHAPTER NINE

"This is everything Sarah Maccubbin told me," I began, "with a few gaps filled in.

"You know why Miss Dorsey wasn't at the DAR this afternoon? She never goes when they meet at the Howard House. It makes her feel too bad—and too mad too, I reckon. She was librarian there for twenty years, until this spring.

"It seems there was a small library in the Howard House wing even before the Cincinnati beer man came along. Twenty years ago there wasn't any Hall of Records, of course; so a group of people interested in genealogy formed a little club. They bought a secondhand fireproof safe, so they could put their family papers somewhere, and from time to time they bought lineage books. They didn't have much money or many members. It never was much of a library.

"Miss Agatha Howard let them have the Howard House wing for nothing—nobody else wanted it, the way it was then—and Miss Edith Dorsey worked for nothing as part-time librarian. Then in 1926, when the beer man bought the place and set up the Howard House Association, she began to get a salary. It wasn't much, but they increased it when he sent his own archival library down and she began to take care of that too. Pretty soon she was making enough to live on without doing freelance genealogy, so she stopped. Sarah Maccubbin said she never liked it anyway. She wasn't really interested in anybody's family but her own.

"Then in 1942 Eleanor Barnes came on the board. She wasn't one of those new members that sit back because they think they don't know everything. She pitched right in and told them how they could solve all their problems.

"Mrs. Barnes thought Edith Dorsey was one of the worst problems the Howard House Association had. Here was the place all done up so beautifully, she said, with handmade replacements and concealed furnace heat and period furnishings, and the archival library was one of the best in the country. It wasn't terribly big, but every book was handpicked, and some of them were rare and valuable. Mrs. Barnes said there ought to be a trained archival librarian. And Miss Dorsey didn't even know the Dewey decimal system, and when Mrs. Barnes tried to show her how to set up a card file she couldn't seem to get the hang of it. And she thought it was silly to stamp the books that went out, even the valuable ones. She said all the patrons of the Association

Library were ladies and gentlemen.

"The first year Eleanor Barnes was on the board her motion to replace Miss Dorsey was voted down. For one thing, some of the members were kin to Miss Dorsey, or were old friends of her family, and the rest felt the Association had an obligation to her. After all, she'd served faithfully and done the best she could for twenty years, even if she didn't file alphabetically within the letter.

"But some of the board members felt that Mrs. Barnes was right, even though they didn't vote her way.

"The next year three of the Dorsey cousins and old family friends died, and there were vacancies to be filled on the board. Sarah Maccubbin says Mrs. Barnes went around lobbying as hard as if she was running for President herself. She got her people in, too.

"Then when the new board met and Mrs. Barnes brought up the question of replacing Miss Dorsey she nearly put it over. The motion just failed by one vote.

"This spring when they took the vote again there weren't any new members on the board. But one of the men who had voted for Edith Dorsey last year voted against her. He happened to be a man Mrs. Barnes had—influence with.

"Well, the board hired a young Vassar graduate who'd written her thesis on William Dunbar manuscripts and incunabula. They had to pay her a lot more than Edith Dorsey had been getting, but Mrs. Barnes said she was worth it.

"Edith Dorsey went back to freelance genealogy.

"She hadn't done any for a good many years, and she found the field had changed. There didn't seem to be much room for nice old ladies without training; the new breed of genealogists were rather like the girl with the Dunbar thesis, and clients seemed to prefer them. Then too, Miss Dorsey's eyes had gotten mighty bad. That was one reason she'd had so much trouble with the card file. She found out when she started to do genealogy again that she couldn't see a lot of the old faded writing and had to guess. Some of her mistakes got found out.

"So, what with one thing and another, she hasn't been getting along so well."

I stopped then, and there was quite a long silence. Edith Dorsey's story was the nearest thing to a speech I'd done since I retired; maybe that was why my throat felt funny.

Ben was the one who spoke first.

"Now you see, Miss Julia, why I said you could go places we couldn't very well go and find out things we couldn't. I knew Miss Dorsey had resigned that library job; but I didn't know her resignation was forced, and I didn't know the second Mrs. Barnes was back of it. I didn't know she wasn't doing so well now, either. You've got the story behind the story, and I'm much obliged."

Anne had been looking very unhappy indeed through all this, and now she burst out.

"If Miss Dorsey killed that woman, I think she was exactly right! I hope you can't prove anything on her!"

"You seem to be having a little mutiny among your assistants," Dick said to Ben. "Look, honey, that's not the way to feel. You may sympathize with Miss Dorsey, but you can't think she ought to be allowed to rampage around polishing people off."

"And if it's Miss Dorsey she isn't at herself," I said firmly. Ben had made two strong converts at least—even if I hadn't told him about Mary Barnes' mysterious package. "She ought to be shut up for her own protection, if not for other people's. That's what she'd want herself. Miss Dorsey is a lady if I ever saw one."

Dick and Ben laughed at me, but I didn't give an inch.

"No, ladies *don't* commit murder," I said. "Not if they're in their right minds."

"Well, but how are you ever going to prove it?" Anne changed her tactics. "On her or anybody else? You've got eight people with equal opportunity, and three of them have equally good motives."

"Five of them have," Ben corrected grimly. "At least that's the score to date. I've no doubt we'll find motives for the other three, and if we do—well, this may turn out to be the most impossible case of my brilliant career."

He sounded genuinely discouraged, but none of us wasted any sympathy on him. We were too anxious to hear who the two new suspects were.

"George Campbell and Lieutenant Gibson," Ben said. "Campbell's motive isn't very strong; at least it doesn't seem so to me. But of course you never know how strongly people will feel about things—and he's one that *has* had combat duty, too, a lot of it. Campbell's older brother was on Admiral Barnes' flagship at Pearl Harbor. His legs were blown off, and it took him quite a while to die."

I caught my breath. I'll never get used to the horrors of this war if it lasts a hundred years.

"Campbell enlisted to get back at the Japs who killed his brother. He's hit them plenty hard, I reckon, in the three years he's been in."

"Yes, his service ribbons are all covered with stars," Anne said.

"I'm wondering if Campbell didn't later decide to get back at somebody besides the Japs," continued Ben. "After all, it was pretty common gossip, after Pearl Harbor, that Admiral Barnes was drunk and unfit to command his ships. There's never been a full investigation, as you know, and so the talk goes on. Campbell told me voluntarily that some of his shipmates, since he joined up, were men who had escaped when his brother's—and Admiral Barnes'—ship was torpedoed and burned. The chances are, of course, that they told him a lot: all the gossip about the admiral's being a few seas over at Pearl Harbor, and also what a swell Old Man he used to be, before his second wife drove him to drink."

"But wouldn't George Campbell's brother have been killed anyway?" Anne asked. "Even if Admiral Barnes had been cold sober? After all, the Japanese *were* attacking."

"Maybe so," said Ben. "But Campbell doesn't know that for sure, and maybe he thinks not. Human nature inclines to blame human nature when it can, you know. I think it's entirely sound, if farfetched, that Campbell might hold Admiral Barnes directly responsible for his brother's death, and therefore the admiral's wife for the condition that made him responsible. *Quod erat demonstrandum*, as Miss Julia would say."

I looked at him with my mouth open. He never learned that much Latin from me.

"It's sound, all right," Dick said thoughtfully. "I don't agree with you, Ben; I think it's a pretty good motive."

"Is Foster Gibson's better?" asked Anne anxiously. We'd all been waiting, I think, for Ben to get through with George Campbell so he could start on Foster Gibson.

"I'm sorry to say it is," Ben said. "You three aren't the only ones that like that young man; I like him myself. He's got brains and courage and resourcefulness. He thinks fast, and you know yourselves he's a mighty cool liar. This is his kind of crime; he could have planned it, all right, and put it over without a hitch—I'm not worried about that. I'm just worried about his good chance of getting off scot-free."

"Why do you think it was his kind of crime?" Anne asked with a touch of belligerence. Bless her heart, she still wasn't into the spirit of this thing the way Dick and I were.

"Because it fits him psychologically, Anne," Ben said. "I can't quite see that fluttering little Miss Dorsey stabbing anyone—now, can you?—good motive though she had. Poison would have been her dish, I think, if she'd been planning a crime. Not that I'm saying she didn't commit this one," he hastened to add. "At this point I just wouldn't know. But I can't help doubting that she'd have the strength, for that matter. Remember that Eleanor Barnes was sitting on the left-hand side of the bus. It was practically impossible for her to be stabbed with a weapon held in somebody's right hand; he—or she—would have had to reach too far across and would have been seen. So it looks to me as if the murderer were either a left-handed person, an ambidextrous person, or a person strong enough to use an awkward left hand with enough force nevertheless."

"And that lets out—?" I questioned.

"It *seems* to let out Miss Dorsey and Mrs. Hamilton," Ben said, smiling ruefully at me. "The men were all strong enough, and Gladys Fulton and your friend Mary Barnes are both left-handed."

"Get back to Foster Gibson, Ben," Dick said impatiently.

"Well, Foster Gibson could have stabbed the lady very easily," went on Ben. "And he had, as I've said, everything it takes to plan a crime like that and put it over. As to the motive, he's got one that fits in too. A good plain money motive."

"Money?" we all said. "But—"

"After Miss Julia kindly told me about Gibson's uncle I went to see him," Ben said. "I didn't get much; he wasn't talking. Maybe he suspects his nephew of murder—there's not much doubt that he does—but he's not willing to help us hang him." Anne wasn't the only one who shuddered at that. "But with the help of the Philadelphia police we round out—certain things.

"Mr. Foster—John Biddle Foster; he's Gibson's half-uncle on his mother's side—has been a widower for thirty-odd years. The family never thought he'd marry again, and young Gibson, whose mother didn't have much beyond the allowance Mr. Foster made her, was brought up with the idea he'd inherit everything. After the mother died Mr. Foster settled any doubts by taking Gibson over financially, and making a new will. That will still stands. Under it Gibson inherits around four million dollars, when and if. And he likes money. He's been brought up with plenty of it, and he still throws it around. Have you been in his apartment?"

We shook our heads.

"Go the first chance you get," Ben advised us, apparently overlooking the fact it might be a murderer he was sending us to see. "He likes antiques—not just provincial ones—and he's got a collection of sextants that ought to be in a museum. So ought his brandy." Ben rolled his eyes heavenward. "I don't see how he can bring himself to drink that stuff."

"Go on," I prodded him. I didn't care a thing about Foster Gibson's brandy.

"It's just that he lives beyond his pay," Ben said. "Gets a big allowance from his devoted uncle—which is all right, of course. Only thing is, the devoted uncle has been coming down to visit him quite a lot lately. Maybe Gibson was beginning to suspect why; anyway, last week he found out for sure. He got a letter saying his uncle was engaged to marry Mrs. Barnes."

"Eleanor Barnes?" I said incredulously.

"Eleanor Barnes. She was an attractive woman, Miss Julia. And Foster Gibson took the first train for Philadelphia.

"Mr. Foster's servants couldn't tell the Philadelphia police what he and his nephew said to each other. It's one of those well-built old brick houses; the walls and doors are pretty thick. But they all agree that there was a violent quarrel. Foster Gibson slammed out of the house. He took the next train back to Baltimore; and from Baltimore he took the bus on which Mrs. Barnes was killed."

We all sat in silence for quite some time.

Dick said at last: "It's a strong case against him. But it's all circumstantial, Ben. You'll have to have something else."

"We've got something else," said Ben quietly. "We've got the letter from his uncle, that Gibson went home and burned the night I saw him here. Too bad he didn't scatter the ashes better. And we've got a small Damascene dagger that disappeared from his uncle's house the day Gibson quarreled with him. You see, he couldn't know ahead of time that Miss Dorsey would drop a nice sharp knitting needle. We found that dagger in the secret drawer of Gibson's desk. He'd sharpened it, for use."

CHAPTER TEN

After that it was hard for me to be natural when I saw Foster Gibson. I saw him once at a football game, once at Anne's friend Sally Lewis's house, and again at a dance at the North Severn Officers' Club. He came over to speak to Sarah Maccubbin and me and stayed quite a time talking. Murderer or not, I couldn't help liking him all over again when he spoke so nicely of Anne and Dick. Anne did look pretty in her long white dress. But all of the girls looked pretty, and I fairly caught my breath at Ruth Allein in a pale gray that matched her eyes, and long-dark-red velvet gloves that matched her sandals. She had on an exquisite garnet clip and earrings, and her smooth blond hair was parted the Madonna way that only real beauties can stand. I pointed her out to Foster Gibson, and he agreed with me with some enthusiasm. I didn't think much of it at the time because I was busy planning to have my dear mother's garnets reset for Anne's Christmas present.

But it came back to me later, for Tuesday night when Ruth Allein came to see us—preceded and obscured in the doorway by her nice fat aunt—Foster Gibson was behind her. There was quite a difference in the way he helped the two of them off with their coats, and throughout the evening he kept looking over at Ruth as if he'd invented her. It worried me a little, even though she wasn't paying much attention to *him*.

We had the nicest kind of evening. Mrs. Morton was an awful gossip, but of course that made her entertaining—at least to an old woman who isn't above gossip herself. And Ruth Allein was entertaining from anybody's point of view. Some of the stories she told about her work at the Baltimore Red Cross—without names, of course—were the funniest things I ever heard, and she told them well. She could have been an actress, not just a model as I'd thought before. She was smart, too. I think we all had to revise our concept of social workers a little that evening. I know I always think of them as terribly earnest and dedicated and unattractive people, or else like Myrtle Mason at home. Myrtle is about Edith Dorsey's age and general type, with just about Edith Dorsey's ability to face the world. She hides her feelings, whatever they are—insecurity, I suppose—under an arrogant manner that's always encouraged me, for one, in habits of thrift. I've never wanted to get old and poor and have to tell Myrtle Mason about it. Oh, doubtless she means well. But that isn't enough anymore.

There are a lot of such people in the new professions, people left over from the days when training wasn't thought necessary for taking care of books or following the doctor's directions or interviewing people in trouble. The new order is hard on them, and some of them are pretty bitter about it. (Bitter enough to murder, as in Edith Dorsey's case?) I can understand that bitterness because it was only luck I missed tasting it myself. We Tylers were as poor as any other good Virginia family, in the years after the War Between the States; and if my dear father hadn't got the clerical cut-rate, as Dick calls it, I wouldn't have gone to college either.

Nevertheless I think it's a good thing, and high time too, that people like Ruth Allein are replacing people like Myrtle Mason. And from the purely personal point of view, watching Ruth as she sat in the big blue chair, and watching Foster Gibson watching *her*, I was mighty glad she had casework training. Good caseworkers, or so I'm told, are hard to fool when it comes to people. They can even tell by looking at a person's hands whether or not he's lying.

Foster Gibson said something just then, and I looked at his hands myself. As far as I could tell, he was just lighting his pipe.

I had been thinking and stewing so hard I missed a lot of the conversation. When I came back to it Ruth was telling Anne how sorry she'd been not to come to her party.

"Who else was there?"

Anne rattled off a list of names, ending with Elizabeth Smith's.

"Elizabeth? Oh, Gordon Smith's wife," Mrs. Morton said. "Do you know her well?"

Anne said no, just a little, and I said I doubted that anyone did. Maybe I said it a little tartly, for I hadn't liked Elizabeth Smith. She was a tall, dark, handsome girl who came, I found out, from a good Atlanta family; I knew her husband was attractive; her clothes looked like plenty of money; and one of the other guests, having asked her how Betsy was, told me in an aside that she had the most adorable child in Annapolis. I couldn't see why Elizabeth Smith should have a chip on her shoulder; but have it she certainly did. She kept making little snippy remarks all through the luncheon, and afterward when everybody was saying goodbye, and she told Anne how kind she'd been to invite her, her voice was definitely sarcastic.

Mrs. Morton laughed when I made my own not-too-nice remark.

"Oh, she's a very sweet girl really, Miss Tyler. She dislikes the Navy—got off on the wrong foot, as it's really very easy to do—and of course that makes her unhappy. Such a mistake to show it, I think, since her husband is in the service to stay."

"Oh, is he?" I said. "I somehow got the idea he was a reserve officer."

Foster Gibson smiled at me and shook his head. "Third generation Navy."

"Then you and he are old friends?" Anne asked casually. Gordon Smith was the suspect she'd promised to check up on.

"Old but not close. We used to see each other, off and on, when we were kids, but it so happens we've never been shipmates. And, of course, Gordon was two years ahead of me at the Academy."

"Two years *ahead* of you?" I could see that Anne was starting to say something else; her mouth took the shape it takes for "But." Instead she shut it firmly.

Nice fat Mrs. Morton reached over, laughing, and patted Anne on the knee. "*You'll* not get off on the wrong foot in the Navy, my dear! You've got a smart wife, Mr. Travers. She thinks before she speaks, and sometimes she thinks better of it and doesn't speak at all." She laughed again. "What you wanted to say, my dear, was, 'But he's only an ensign, and you, graduating two years behind him, are a lieutenant junior grade. Why is that?' Wasn't that it, my dear? Well, I'll tell you anyway."

"Oh, Aunt Katherine!" Ruth said in mild protest, and apparently just for form's sake. Even I who had met Mrs. Morton only twice could see there was no stopping her when she got started.

"But, Ruth, why not?" asked Mrs. Morton innocently. "There's nothing to it. Everybody knows it. Gordon Smith just didn't get his promotion when he should."

"But if you leave it at that it will be the shock of my life," Ruth said, smiling. "You know perfectly well you're going to tell them why, and when, and how it could have been avoided."

"Of course I am!" exclaimed Mrs. Morton, unrebuffed. "They want to hear!"

We all laughed, and she did too.

"Well, it didn't start right after Gordon and Elizabeth were married," Mrs. Morton said. "They were somewhere on the west coast; I forget the post but it was a small one and not a bit formal. Elizabeth got along very well.... I make her sound as if she drank out of finger bowls," Mrs. Morton broke off to say, "and of course it wasn't that way at all. Elizabeth's social background is *very* good, and she has some money, too. It's just that the Navy is different.

"Well, anyway, right after Betsy was born they were sent to Newport. I don't know whether you know Newport or not?"

She looked from Anne to me, and we shook our heads.

"Well, it's one of the places where society means a lot; and the Navy usually takes a good deal of character from whatever town it's in. Here in Annapolis, for instance, society means a lot too—but there's not much money in town and never has been. That's a difference right there. Then the people you meet are nice and well-bred and well established, for the most part; they've got background, so they can afford to be casual. Newport society, now, is full of people with nothing but money."

"How Uncle Bob ever got to be a captain!" Ruth murmured. But she and her aunt exchanged a very nice smile.

"Well, it is," Mrs. Morton maintained. "And when you're only a generation or two or three removed from fur trading or ferrying or meat packing you *have* to go in to dinner in gloves. Once you took them off, why, there you'd be."

She finished rather helplessly, but of course we got her point. We reason the same way in Virginia.

"Hams instead of hands, no doubt," Dick said gravely.

"No doubt." Mrs. Morton beamed on him. "Well, anyway, they were in Newport, and they went out to dinner. Elizabeth hadn't wanted to, because the baby was sick and the nurse they had was young and not a bit reliable. But it was an important dinner, and she went. She kept worrying, though, and finally about ten o'clock she couldn't stand it any longer, and she thought she'd done her duty anyhow. She explained as nicely as she could to her hostess, and went home."

"I think she behaved very properly," I said.

Mrs. Morton spread out her hands in a curious, helpless little gesture. "Of course. But, strictly speaking, in the Navy the ranking lady always leaves the party first. We don't feel half so bound by that old foolishness nowadays, and even in Newport, if the ranking lady had been a nice, reasonable person—"

I happened to look over at Foster Gibson. He was looking into the fire—not at Ruth Allein, for a change—and for some reason his face was a hard brown mask. He didn't look either nice or reasonable, himself.

"But this ranking lady made an issue of it?" asked Anne.

Mrs. Morton nodded vigorously. "Then and later. When poor Gordon came up for his promotion—and he's a very able young officer—well, everybody knew why he didn't get it. Gordon took it better than Elizabeth did. He's Navy. But it *was* a shame. There are lots of people glad that woman's dead."

"What woman?" Anne asked, startled out of her commended habit of thinking first.

"Why, Eleanor Barnes," Mrs. Morton said. She seemed surprised to find we hadn't known who it was right along. "That's why I thought you'd be interested. You didn't think we had a lot of them like that, did you? No, really, my dear, you'll find Navy people very nice."

We began to talk about some of the nice ones.

After the company had gone Anne and Dick and I had a spirited argument over whether to call up Ben. Dick and I were for it; Anne insisted Ben would have gone to bed. It *was* half-past eleven. But we strongly suspected that Anne's real reason was less concern for Ben than concern for Gordon Smith. Well, we'd been over all that before. Anne really agreed with us, but in the same way she used to agree with me when I'd say that either the mice had to get out of our house or we'd have to. She never could bear to set the traps, and it was always up to me.

I called Ben finally.

"We were afraid you'd gone to bed," I began, "but we found out something to tell you. Another motive."

Ben groaned. He sounded wide awake and said he hadn't even thought about bed. "Matter of fact I was just sitting here wondering whether to call *you*. I've got a new development myself—one you'll like. But tell me yours first."

"Well, I don't like *it*," I said. I told him about Gordon and Elizabeth Smith. "Not that I think he did it. Now if it had been his wife who had a good chance like that—she looks half Borgia at least."

Ben laughed for politeness' sake, but he answered seriously.

"Not a bad motive, even so, Miss Julia. After all, Smith was the injured party, not his wife. She might have felt hacked socially, but his career was really hurt. Third generation Navy, you said? That kind would take it hard."

"I can't think murder would fail to hurt a career, either," I said snappishly. "If he cared so much for the Navy he surely would have considered that."

"Maybe he didn't count on getting caught," said Ben dryly. "You know, Miss Julia, up till tonight I've had an almighty fear that the murderer—whoever he is—*wasn't* going to get caught. It's looked like a perfect crime. Apparently there weren't any witnesses, and thanks to your invaluable researches we find that most all the people with opportunity had motive too. Good strong motive. We've been widening the field instead of narrowing it down. But now things are beginning to break our way."

"How?" I said. "What's happened?"

"I want to read you a letter I got today." Ben rattled some papers with a loud crackling sound. "I don't know whether he's going to confess he did it himself or going to prove it on somebody else—"

"*Who* is going to confess?" I nearly shrieked.

"Keep calm, Miss Julia," Ben drawled back. I could have killed him. "You're not the only one with a sense of the dramatic. I'm going to read you the letter first."

"Oh, all right," I said resignedly. "But wait till I get a pencil. I've got to get this straight for Anne and Dick."

"No, Miss Julia!" This time Ben's voice was not just serious but intensely so. "Don't write anything down. Just pay close attention, and tell Anne and Dick the best you can. I've got no business telling you all this—as you know. No matter how much you've helped *me*. But the main reason is that there's a murderer loose—going in and out of your house, very likely—and you can't be too careful."

Normally I would have protested, for that *was* ridiculous. But I was too anxious to hear the letter. "All right," I said. "Go ahead."

"DEAR LIEUTENANT KRAMER [read Ben]:
"As a passenger on the bus when Mrs. Roger Barnes was killed, I feel that in justice to everyone concerned I should provide you

with certain documents in connection with the case. I shall have these, I think, by Monday afternoon, and will bring them to your office at five o'clock. I should prefer you not to come here. "Yours very truly.

"Now, Miss Julia," Ben said deliberately and maddeningly, "do you think he's leading up to a confession, or do you think the 'documents' will incriminate somebody else?"

"Ben Kramer!" This time I did shriek at him. "Who is it?"

"The signature on the letter," Ben said, "is 'James Mosser, M.D.'"

CHAPTER ELEVEN

I cannot pretend to a continuous passion for football. I had gone twice with the children, and had committed myself to the rather special Army-Navy game coming up, as Dick says, in December. The War Bond that had to be bought before the ticket could be was in my stocking box upstairs. But I cannot and will not drag out every Saturday or so to sit on a cold hard bench in a cold hard rain and yell for a Navy team when I feel more like yelling to go home. So this time Anne and Dick had gone to Baltimore without me, and Fairy had fixed me a nice lunch on a tray. I ate it before the living room fire, and Alice had her own bowl down beside me. The big blue chair had a feather cushion, the chrysanthemums on the desk smelled nice and spicy, and I was perfectly happy because I had Leslie Ford's new book propped up in front of me. She is my favorite right after Agatha Christie, though Dick says that by the time the heroine has looked in the carved and gilded Queen Anne mirror that's reflecting also the pair of sunburst tables with pale creamy tea-rose petals spilling onto them from the pair of fluted Sheffield urns that have stood there nearly as long as the Corinthian columns have stood on the wide porch overlooking the river George Washington used to travel by barge, rowed by his liveried slaves, he's forgotten who she is and why.

I was tired. I am, after all, sixty-seven years old—I wouldn't like this if anyone else said it—and Annapolis is a strenuous place. It's go, go, go all the time. Even this one free afternoon would end early, at half-past four, when I was meeting Sarah Maccubbin for tea. I like Sarah better than anyone I've met in Annapolis (I call her Sarah to myself, though in public my generation here say "Miss" and "Mrs." for the first fifty years); but I wished she was coming to me instead of my having to pull myself out and up the hill to State Circle. It was just a little way, but my old bones fairly ached.

We had tea in a nice little place with flowers on every table, and real napkins instead of paper ones. War or no war, that's still a good way to judge. The room was half full when we got there and still filling up, but we got a splendid table in the front window, where everybody had to pass us going in or out. Sarah knows all Annapolis, I think. She says you're bound to when you've run a boarding house as long as she has. I knew a reasonable number myself, and of course I was specially interested to see Miss Gladys Fulton in a chair up front, obviously waiting for somebody, and Miss Edith Dorsey with a handsomely furred fat woman I hoped was a client. Those two were at a table for four right next to ours. Over in the corner Foster Gibson was talking earnestly to my friend Mary Barnes, of all people. I thought she looked rather old and worn. Watching her as she sat against the light, I realized suddenly that it was Mary Barnes I'd been reminded of in St. Anne's Church, the day of Eleanor Barnes's funeral. The old-woman saint in the brown stained-glass robe had the same kind of fine, strongly marked, patient face Mary Barnes had.

I pointed her out to Sarah. "She and Lieutenant Gibson look like old friends."

"Well, of course they are," Sarah Maccubbin said comfortably, taking some more toast. "He's a Navy junior, you know, and Mary Barnes was in the Navy herself for thirty-odd years. They'd known each other from Pensacola to the China Station, I expect, before Foster's father died."

"I like Mary Barnes."

"Everybody does. But," said Sarah, lapsing into the vernacular, "a lot of good that did her."

I was watching a little scene near the front door. "Well, will you look at that!"

Miss Gladys Fulton was getting up to greet a man who had just come in—obviously the person she'd been waiting for. Teetering on her high heels, and with her blond pompadour built up even more incredibly than it had been on the bus, she towered inches above the insignificant-looking, fat-stomached little man. But he didn't seem to mind. I never thought I'd see Dr. James Mosser with such a happy, silly smile on his face.

"Disgusting!" Sarah Maccubbin said. "Even if he doesn't have any reputation to lose, he ought to think about his wife. She may not have long red fingernails, but not every woman would have stuck by him the way she has."

"Shh!" I said. "They're coming this way." They were, and Dr. Mosser looked more natural because he was scowling now instead of smiling.

Evidently he was mad because they'd come too late to get a table to themselves, and the hostess was getting ready to put them with somebody else. I didn't know why Dr. Mosser should specially object to Miss Edith Dorsey or her companion, but his scowl certainly did deepen when the hostess pulled out the two empty chairs at that table and asked the ladies if they'd mind.

Of course they said they wouldn't, but I thought Miss Dorsey, at least, looked far from pleased.

There was a great flurry of getting settled. We couldn't hear a word anybody said, for though their table was right next to ours and we could *see* everything, the whole roomful of people was talking and laughing and tinkling spoons against teacups, and back by the pantry door some girl was playing the piano.

They couldn't hear us either, of course, so we had quite a nice time talking about Dr. Mosser. Sarah didn't like him at all—never had. We were still at it when Mary Barnes and Foster Gibson got up to leave. Somewhat to my surprise, they stopped when they came to that queerly assorted group at the next table and talked for quite a while. As far as we could tell, Mrs. Barnes knew the fat woman in the fur coat, and hadn't seen her for a long time. She and Foster spoke cordially to Miss Dorsey, too, and pleasantly to Miss Fulton and Dr. Mosser.

Miss Fulton was pouring the doctor's tea. She put lemon in it—no sugar. No wonder the man had the disposition he did. Sarah Maccubbin and I agreed on that, and then immediately felt like fools when Dr. Mosser took a box of saccharine tablets out of his pocket.

We could see the little box perfectly and it was lovely. I shouldn't have suspected Dr. Mosser of liking things like that. It was old, for the chased-silver edges were worn almost smooth, and the top was set with a flowerlike design of opals. I suppose it had been a snuffbox originally; but it was smaller than any snuffbox I'd ever seen.

Foster Gibson's face lighted right up. I remembered Ben's saying he was interested in antiques. Evidently he admired it aloud, for Dr. Mosser handed the box over to him. He was so prompt about it I gathered he was used to showing it off. I would have liked a chance to see it up close myself, for evidently it was something rather special. Foster Gibson was like a child with a new toy. He held the little box up so he could read whatever it said on the bottom; he ran his fingers over the opal flower; he opened it, holding it carefully so as not to spill the three little pellets inside, and felt the inside cover very delicately with his thumbnail. When he finally passed it over so Mrs. Barnes could look at it, too, you could see he hated to give it up.

I don't think Mary Barnes cared much about antique snuffboxes; but after Foster had made such a fuss over this one she couldn't very well just glance at it and pass it on. So she and Miss Dorsey and the fat lady all examined it carefully too, looking inside and holding it up to read the mark on the bottom. Miss Fulton watched them with an expression of utter boredom, but Foster Gibson watched very much the way he'd watched Ruth Allein.

By the time the box got into her hands Miss Fulton had an idea that saved her from having to gush over it too. With a pretty little shriek—or maybe it wasn't so little, because Sarah and I heard it distinctly over the teatime noises—and much fluttering of hands she pointed out that Dr. Mosser's tea was getting cold. The little box stayed in her lap while she poured him a fresh cup and added a slice of lemon. Then with considerable manner she dropped one pellet in.

Mary Barnes and Foster said goodbye then, and moved on to our table. But they didn't stay but a minute, for Mrs. Barnes was looking at her watch and saying she mustn't miss the ferry. I remembered she lived on Eastern Shore. But she was mighty nice and said she hoped she'd see me again. I hoped so too.

Sarah Maccubbin took her party smile off as soon as they'd left our table, and turned to me so seriously I was surprised. "Miss Tyler, I'd like to ask your advice. You know Lieutenant Kramer pretty well, don't you?"

"Ben Kramer? Why, yes. I taught him in high school," I said. I was a little bewildered at the turn the conversation had taken.

"Is he reliable?" Sarah Maccubbin asked. "I mean, if you told him anything would he keep it to himself?"

"Why, yes, I think so." Then I thought I'd better qualify that. "Of course, if it were information he needed to complete a case, he'd have to use it as he thought best. After all he's a police officer, sworn to do his duty."

"I understand that." Sarah picked up a clean teaspoon and began to draw intricate patterns on the tablecloth. "I shouldn't mind his using it—later, if he found out it fitted in. But it's something I really ought not to tell, and I wouldn't want it to get out unnecessarily. It could cause a lot of trouble if it did. I don't know what to do."

"If you're asking my advice, I'd tell him," I said bluntly. "It's something to do with the murder, isn't it?"

Sarah nodded.

"Then he ought to know." I made her the same little speech I'd made the children, the night I told Ben about Foster Gibson's uncle. As then, the mysterious package I hadn't told about myself weighed heavily on my conscience. "Just tell him you don't want it known unnecessarily, and why. He won't tell anybody."

Except me, I said to myself. He'd better tell me, after all this.

"Well," Sarah said uncertainly. But she looked relieved.

What I wanted to tell her, of course, was that I was Lieutenant Kramer's first assistant, and that she'd better just tell me all about it. I hated to think of her having a chance to change her mind, and maybe not tell anybody anything. But of course that wouldn't have done.

"You just tell Ben all about it," I told her again, and Sarah said, "All right, I will," quite decisively. I felt better and so, apparently, did she. She was quite cheerful and commonplace when she picked up her check and headed for the door.

It was only half-past five, and we decided to go to the picture show. I knew the children wouldn't be home yet, and I was perfectly free till seven, when we were going to a spaghetti supper at the commandant's house. Sarah was going too; she and Mrs. Morton were close friends. Fortunately all her boarders but two were either away for the week end or going out to dinner, and the cook was fixing those two trays. Poor Sarah, I don't think she often had both an afternoon and an evening off. I've had people pity me almost to my face because I've spent my life with iambics and Latin verbs, but at least they don't whine or ask for hot-water bottles or claim they're allergic to perfectly good things to eat, the way Sarah's boarders do. She has to wait on them hand and foot. Of course her boarding house is a very exclusive one; but I've never noticed that sixteen quarterings make people pleasanter to get along with.

The picture was pretty good. Oh, it was impossible, of course. It was all about an actor named Sylvester the Great (Bob Hope, really) who for some reason was touring around in the Caribbean when it was full of pirates. All this was supposed to be back in the seventeenth century. The pirates attacked the ship Sylvester was on, and he had an awful time getting away from them. For instance, he started to jump overboard and hung his coat and hat on a hook first, and then he found out the hook was part of one of the pirates he was trying to get away from. I couldn't follow the plot very well; maybe it was my fault, but Sarah couldn't either, so I don't think so. Anyway in the end he got the beautiful princess, though why she wanted him I do not see. It was really very funny, especially the scene in which he takes a bath with the governor who is aiding and abetting the pirates, and has to keep lathering his chest so the governor won't see the treasure map somebody tattooed on him while he was unconscious. But it was so ridiculous and improbable that I was ashamed of Sarah Maccubbin and myself, two grown-up, presumably sensible women, for sitting up there laughing.

But then I got to thinking that improbable and ridiculous things really do happen, and sometimes there is nothing funny about it. What could be more improbable and ridiculous, for that matter, than my being mixed up in a murder case? I, Julia Tyler, who everybody in Rossville (including me) had thought was neatly catalogued and filed away, had actually found a body. I'd turned a strange dead woman over and screamed when I saw a knitting needle sticking out of her heart. And since then I'd been batting around, as Dick says, with all sorts of suspicious characters, my favorite among them being the young man who was, in all probability, the murderer himself.

It was quite dark when we got out of the picture show. I was glad I was only half a block from home, and didn't have to go all the way around to Duke of Gloucester Street, the way Sarah Maccubbin did. Annapolis sidewalks may be quaint, but they certainly are treacherous; and Sarah and I are both nearing the age at which, whether you fall on your head or your hands, you always break a hip.

Anne and Dick were home from Baltimore. Every window in the house was lighted, as far as I could see, and light was streaming from the doorway too. In spite of the cold Anne was standing there in her thin dress.

"Aunt Julia, where have you *been?*" she demanded, pulling me in, and calling for Dick as if a St. Bernard had just dragged me home, unconscious, from the topmost alp. I didn't see anything to be so excited about. I looked at the clock, and it was only twenty minutes to seven.

"Sarah Maccubbin and I have been at the picture show," I said with dignity, removing my hat.

"We've been so *worried*," Anne said. "Ben came here twice, and Dick went by the tearoom for you, and you'd gone, and you weren't at Miss Maccubbin's house—"

My patience was at an end. "Dick," I said, "can you collect yourself sufficiently to tell me what this is all about? Why was Ben Kramer here, and what has happened?"

"It's Dr. Mosser," Dick said. "He's dead, Aunt Julia. He died about an hour ago."

I just looked from one of them to the other.

"Ben thinks he was murdered," said Anne.

CHAPTER TWELVE

It seems that Dr. Mosser had left the tearoom shortly after Sarah and I did. He and Miss Fulton parted at the door. She went on home to her dear little daughters whom she locked up while she worked and also, presumably, while she cavorted around with married men. Dr. Mosser started on an emergency call—some accident west of town. But he never got there. He never even got to his car, parked over on North Street. He collapsed on the sidewalk, and in less than half an hour he was dead.

Maybe he shouldn't have been moved; but not everybody has taken First Aid, and anyway it was a cold, damp night—already dark, as I've said. The people who saw him fall helped carry him into the nearest place with lights. North Street is only a little short street without many houses, now that the big new bus station takes up half of one side, and most of them were dark. So they carried Dr. Mosser into the bus station to die.

When I heard that, I couldn't help thinking what a break, as they call it, that circumstance was for the reporters. They'd all been writing up Eleanor Barnes' death as "The Bus Station Murder," and now they could go right on, just adding an s.

Of course I didn't know Ben's plans then.

But none of it mattered to Dr. Mosser, poor thing. I can pity him now that he's dead and not strutting around sticking out his pompous fat stomach, showing off in his arrogant loud voice. From the time they brought him in he just lay there as if he were already dead. He didn't recover consciousness at all.

At first they thought he'd died a natural death. Certainly his wife had no doubts about it. "I've been expecting it," she said, when they told her over the telephone, and began to sob. She got there almost at once, her neat black coat flung on crookedly over the print house dress and fancy apron she'd been wearing to cook supper. There was a little flour still on her hands, and her broad plain face was shiny and splotched with tears and her hair stringing down every which way. All that was the least of her troubles. She wasn't thinking about anybody but the man who'd pulled her down with him when he sold out his professional integrity, who'd left her to earn her own living the best she could, and who'd never stopped running around with other women. All his sins of omission and commission were forgiven him—or forgotten, more likely. They let Emma Mosser go in the restroom where the doctor was lying on a couch, and shut the door behind her; but even out in the waiting room—quiet for once—they could hear the poor soul crying and carrying on.

Maybe there was some good quality in Dr. Mosser, after all, that accounted for such heartfelt devotion. I don't know. Maybe I'm just getting soft and sentimental in my old age.

Dr. Lucius Kent was hard to find, as all doctors are nowadays, and he didn't get there till right before Dr. Mosser died. Like poor Emma Mosser, it didn't occur to *him* at first that death wasn't from natural causes.

"Worst heart I nearly ever saw," he said briefly. "Angina. High blood pressure, too—I could give you a list of things. The wonder's only that he didn't die years ago." Then he lifted one of the dead man's eyelids and drew a sharp little breath. Poor Mrs. Mosser didn't notice, but the policeman did.

Well, I won't go into the details Ben told me. I wasn't there, and I'm mighty glad of it. But the upshot was that though Dr. Mosser had died of a heart attack the attack was caused by his taking a morphine tablet. It was 0.15 grams, they later found out—heavy dosage, but not enough to kill an ordinary well person.

It was the same dosage that Eleanor Barnes had had, the same thing that had made her sleep so she could be neatly stabbed.

Even then it didn't look like murder. Quite a lot of people in Annapolis, and certainly the police, knew that Dr. Mosser had got in trouble selling morphine, and they weren't surprised to gather that he took it himself.

Dr. Kent settled that.

"Not unless he wanted to commit suicide," he told Ben bluntly. (All this was later, of course, after the autopsy.) "James Mosser was an intelligent man and a first-rate doctor. He had a big future, once. And even a layman would know better than to dope with a heart like that."

"Did Dr. Mosser realize his condition?" Ben asked.

"Of course he did!" said Dr. Kent vigorously. "You can't lie to a professional man about that, lieutenant, even if you want to. I told James Mosser four years ago the state he was in. I told him he was done for if he didn't take the utmost care—and maybe if he did. And he didn't want to die. Never has since. God knows why not."

"Please go on, doctor," Ben said.

"Nothing much more to say," said Dr. Kent. "He did take care of himself—bent over backward doing it. Stopped all smoking, for instance—he wouldn't have needed to do that—and cut things out of his diet that wouldn't have had bearing one way or the other. I told his wife the shape he was in, too, and she kept him wrapped in cotton wool. Cooked all his food specially and brought it to the jail, when he was waiting trial." Dr. Kent cleared his throat as if he were embarrassed personally. "Then when he went to prison he asked me to send along a statement to the authorities: what he couldn't eat and do, and so on. They gave him light work in the penitentiary office. Probably would have anyhow—educated man like that. He had two foreign degrees, you know, on top of Harvard Medical. Point was about it all, though, Mosser made sure he wouldn't be told to do something his heart wouldn't stand."

"Possibly he changed his outlook later? Grew more lax, maybe?" Ben asked.

Dr. Kent was positive. "Not at all! I saw Mosser not a week ago. He was as finicky about his heart as ever."

"But about this morphine?" Ben said.

"Well, what about it? James Mosser knew exactly what morphine could do to a heart like his, if that's what you're getting at. Now look, lieutenant." Dr. Kent's big booming voice became soft and gentle, for him. He snapped his bag shut and put on his hat. "You needn't ask me whether Mosser committed suicide or not. I don't know. I've told you what he died of. I've told you what kind of a man he was, and that's all I can do. But if I were in your business—instead of having to go over to Eastport and deliver a half-Filipino illegitimate baby—I'd consider a certain possibility."

"Yes, doctor?" Ben said.

"Well, murder," said Dr. Kent, and left.

Ben is a kindly, tactful soul—witness the way he's kept telling me what wonders I've uncovered in this case, when of course I know better. So he didn't tell Dr. Kent what he told Anne and Dick and me.

"Actually, I knew it was murder the minute I heard Mosser was dying," he said. "I believe in coincidence, all right, but this was just too much. Leading suspects don't die natural deaths just before they turn evidence over to the police. I could feel it in my bones."

"Well, you're no credit to that scientific police school you went to, then," I said, sniffing. "Feel it in your bones!"

Ben laughed. "You can't beat the old-time methods, Miss Julia. Sometimes they work when nothing else does."

"And sometimes they don't," I said. "Look at the feeling I had in my bones about young Mrs. Hamilton. I had woman's instinct back of *me*, too. And look what that came to. Nothing."

"Now, Aunt Julia, think about your successes instead," Dick urged. "You can't expect to hang a motive on everybody. It's plenty good enough to get six out of eight."

"Bad enough, you mean," Ben corrected him grimly. "It's awful."

Anne made a literary contribution. "In *And Then There Were None* there were *ten* suspects, and every one of them had a motive."

"Well, any time that happens to Lieutenant Kramer, you'll find him floating in Spa Creek," Ben said. "Mosser's death at least cuts down the list. He was beginning to be my choice for the murderer himself."

Dick said thoughtfully: "I believe Dorsey's my choice. Look, Ben, she's bound to be the one. Look at that motive, and she only says she dropped the knitting needle. I bet she had it in her bag all the time. And she's neurotic as hell. Repressed. You've only got to hear that flat, monotonous little voice trailing off into space— That's the kind that finally goes berserk with a butcher knife."

"Not necessarily," I said tartly. "Your Grandmother Nelson had that same tiresome little voice, and she died at eighty-seven of double pneumonia."

"Who do you think, Anne?"

Anne smiled ruefully. "I'm afraid I'm in favor of Aunt Julia's Mary Barnes. But maybe it's just wishful thinking. I like Foster so much, and I feel so sorry for poor Miss Dorsey—"

"Don't you feel sorry for Mary Barnes?" I demanded. "A blind son with his leg shot off, and money troubles, and worrying about that tuberculosis, and having another woman take her husband away?"

"Not about that—the husband, I mean," Anne said firmly. "If she'd hung on to him—yes, she could have, Aunt Julia, because the wife always has a *great* advantage—maybe none of the rest would have happened."

They say youth is such a difficult time; but it seems to me things are quite a lot easier at the age when you think black is black and white is white, with nothing in between.

"Well, I wish it would turn out to be that Gladys Fulton. I certainly don't like *her*," I said. "Or the fat woman Miss Dorsey was with. What did you say her name was, Ben? Stark?"

"Park. Mrs. Mervin Park." Ben stopped at Anne's command and waited while she rummaged through the secretary for her suspect list. "Her first name's Euphemia, I'm sorry to say. E-u-p-h-e-m-i-a. Nice easy names we have in this case: Euphemia, Palougous—"

"Smith—"

"Did you find out where Mary Barnes knew her?" Dick asked, ignoring Anne.

Ben nodded. "With the greatest of ease. And checked it. Mrs. Morton and Mrs. Beale were there too. It seems that Mrs. Park's husband was a major in the last war, and she knew these other ladies when they were all stationed together in Washington. They were about the same age and pretty good friends. But they lost touch when Mrs. Park went back to Des Moines. The only reason she turns up now is that her husband was called—he'd kept a reserve commission. He's a brigadier general this time, and stationed in Washington again."

"What's her connection with Miss Dorsey?" Dick seemed determined to pin the rap, as he calls it, on that poor woman.

"Just professional," Ben said. "Mrs. Morton introduced them, after Mrs. Park told her she wanted to trace some of her Maryland ancestors while she's here. She and Miss Dorsey had been out at Herring Creek the whole day of Dr. Mosser's murder, clambering over tombstones at a great rate."

"Symbolic," Anne said.

"Something, anyway," agreed Ben. "I can't think the Park angle is going to get us anywhere. The FBI investigated her when the general came to Washington—he's got one of the very important hush-hush jobs—and apparently her life is an open book. She said she'd read about Eleanor Barnes in the paper, but she'd never even heard the doctor's name."

"Then you're eliminating Mrs. Park?" I asked.

"Not at all, Miss Julia. I'm not eliminating anybody, in this murder or the last. And that reminds me. You noticed that the news story in the paper didn't call the Mosser death a murder?"

We nodded.

"Well, don't you call it that either," Ben said. "We think maybe we'll get along better if people just think he died of an ordinary heart attack. If the murderer thinks *we* think that. Or the murderers, of course."

"Well, maybe I read too many whodunits—" Dick began.

"It isn't that you read too *many*, Dick, it's just that your *taste* is so low," Anne said. "He likes those old gangster murders, Ben. And—can you imagine?—he likes Philo Vance."

Dick got on the defensive the way Anne and I do when he criticizes Lord Peter Wimsey. "Philo Vance is all right."

"Philo Vance needs a kick in the pance," I contributed—appositely, I thought.

"Why, Miss Julia!"

"That is a quotation," I said with dignity.

"Maybe you'll meet Ogden Nash while you're here, Aunt Julia. He lives in Baltimore," said Anne. "That ought to make up to you for Leslie Ford's moving away."

"I think we're all moving away from the subject," Dick said. "As I was saying when my wife interrupted me, Ben—and incidentally maybe that was how the second Mrs. Barnes got the admiral away from the first Mrs. Barnes, since even ex-officio advantages fade beside the art of listening—I think these murders are dead sure to be connected. Don't you, really? You said you felt Dr. Mosser was killed because he was about to spill the beans."

"Well, frankly," Ben said, "I do. The only thing that bothers me is how the murderer knew he was going to spill the beans."

"The telephone," suggested Anne. "The operator is always kin to somebody."

"I thought afterward, Ben," I said, "that maybe I should have waited to tell you about Elizabeth Smith, and you shouldn't have read me that Mosser letter, either. People do listen in on telephones."

"But not on dial telephones," said Ben. "It's a mechanical operation, you see; that's why there don't have to be so many girls on duty. The calls go through automatically, and the operator doesn't even know about it. She doesn't get a signal unless you dial 'Operator.'"

"So unless she just listened in every minute," Anne said, "there wouldn't be a chance in a hundred."

"Not in a thousand," answered Ben. "We feel just about perfectly safe since the dial phones came in. And is our leg work cut down! In the good old days the police were afraid to say, 'It's a nice day,' over the Annapolis telephone."

"Well, that's that," I said. "We're right back where we started."

"Not quite, Miss Julia," said Ben. "We know that somebody broke in Dr. Mosser's house the night he was killed. We think that person was hunting for the 'documents' the doctor mentioned in his letter. Maybe they were there and he got them. We don't know. Maybe they hadn't arrived—they weren't expected till Monday, remember. Maybe they never existed at all. Anyway, we hadn't gone through the house ourselves, before that—didn't know what all was supposed to be there. But we *had* been through Eleanor Barnes' house on King George Street, and that house was entered the same night. The same tool was used to open both windows."

Ben paused for effect. He certainly got it.

"There wasn't but one person who would have been interested in the piece of paper that disappeared out of Eleanor Barnes' desk that night. There wasn't anything else taken. Of course, there weren't any fingerprints; we can't prove a thing."

"But the one person?" Anne asked breathlessly.

"It was Bill Palougous," Ben said.

CHAPTER THIRTEEN

After that I spent quite a lot of time in the front window, watching for the Palougous' goings out and comings in. I kept my hat and bag conveniently on a chair, so I could step right out and happen to meet him the first chance I got. There were things I wanted to know.

"You'll need your coat too, Aunt Julia," Dick said, surveying my preparations. "He'll think you're crazy if you come dashing out without it in this weather."

"I can't help that," I answered firmly. "It's bad enough to get my wits collected and my hat on. You can laugh, Dick Travers, but it's harder than it looks."

It really was. I don't see how naval officers keep the watch, as they call it, as well as they do, and it seems to me surprising that sentries who drop off are the exception rather than the rule. I'd get to reading, or even just thinking about something else, and the first thing I knew the door of the house across the street would slam and Bill Palougous would be halfway to the corner. I did almost make it one time, though, and would have if Alice hadn't got under my feet. Alice has the impression that every time I put my hat on I am going to take her walking.

"I'm surprised you can't *hear* him coming, Aunt Julia," Anne said, as we watched—too late—the great tweed-coated figure going down the street. "That plaid!"

"I'll get him yet," I said determinedly.

I did, too. The Thursday after Dr. Mosser died I stepped neatly out of our house—with my coat on, even—just as Bill Palougous stepped out of his.

"Good afternoon, Mr. Palougous," I said.

He looked at me as if he'd never seen me before. At the same time I got the strangest feeling that he did know me perfectly well, and was just pretending not to. But I couldn't see why he would.

"I don't suppose you remember me," I went on, a little taken aback. "I'm Julia Tyler, and you and I were both on that bus—"

"Oh, sure, Miss Tyler!" Bill Palougous' memory appeared to come back then, and his smile was wide and golden. "I seen you at the window lots of times, too. Nice to look out, ain't it, when you get so you can't bat around so well?"

I had the grace to blush. At least grace was what it started out to be, but it changed to indignation. I can bat around as well as anybody.

"I seen your niece and nephew, too," Mr. Palougous went on. "That's what it is, ain't it? Nice young folks. Mrs. Palougous was saying to me just the other day, 'Bill,' she said—my first name's Bill—I sure do like that girl's looks.'"

"She is a nice girl. I wish all the Navy things didn't keep her so busy," I said hastily. I hated to pass over this golden opportunity—Heaven only knows what Anne could have got out of Mrs. Bill Palougous if they'd become bosom friends—but from what I'd heard of the Navy, Dick would probably lose all his gold braid in consequence and be put to scrubbing decks.

"Oh, that's all right," Mr. Palougous said expansively. "They keep 'em jumping, sure. Look, how'd you like to go in here for a coke?"

We had reached the drugstore at the top of the hill. Maybe it was the most natural thing in the world for him to ask me, but the sudden question startled me considerably. It's always startling to get an answer to subconscious prayer, and I'd just been thinking how unsatisfactory it was to launch a murder discussion while you were walking along the street. I wanted to watch Bill Palougous' face, for one thing, and then there was always the danger he'd stop in front of one of the little tailor or souvenir shops and say, "I go in here."

So of course I said I'd love to have a Coca-Cola. I only hoped the Senate, or superintendent, or whoever it was wouldn't hold his great-aunt-in-law's erratic social conduct against young Lieutenant Travers.

I'd certainly advise anybody who plans to lead a double life not to try it in Annapolis. When Bill Palougous and I walked into Tracy's Drugstore practically everybody I knew was there.

"Anything you want," my escort told me with a fine gesture, as we sat down. "How about a beer?"

I repressed a shudder and explained how fond I was of Coca-Cola. I'm not at all; it tastes too much like the Castoria I used to give Anne, taking a dose first myself to show her how good it was.

"Probably couldn't get it anyhow," Mr. Palougous said. "Now over at my place, the Free State— Say, Miss Tyler, why don't you and the young folks come eat at the Free State some night? Just been done all over fresh, everything the best. Next time your girl goes off for the evening just come around and get some real good eats." This idea seemed to please him mightily. "You do that, now, Miss Tyler, and the beer'll be on the house."

I thanked him as nicely as I could. He seemed like a good-natured, kind young man. All of a sudden he couldn't do enough for me—first the Coca-Cola and now the offer of free beer—and it couldn't be designs on Anne and Dick because I'd nipped that in the bud. Evidently I'd been mistaken in thinking he recognized me. He really hadn't, and thought he'd hurt my feelings and was trying to make up for it.

But then I got a good look at his little black eyes, buried in rolls of greasy fat, and I wasn't so sure. They were hard and unmoving as a snake's.

The fountain boy set our glasses down then, slopping them over because his hand shook. I recognized those hands before I even looked up. It was Ronald Miller, of course, the mean-faced, nervous clerk who'd been on the bus. He hadn't improved in looks since then. Sipping my Coca-Cola as slowly as I could, I was glad he'd had an alibi for the first murder and hadn't been on hand for the second. Being drug clerk part of the time as well as soda fountain boy he certainly could have put lots of morphine tablets in lots of people's drinks. It seemed like a really ideal job for a homicidal maniac.

Mr. Palougous said, beginning to interview me before I'd decided how to start on *him*: "Remember that guy? He's one that was on the bus, too. Miller, his name is. Say, Miss Tyler, who do you think done it?"

"I must say I thought it was Dr. Mosser," I said. I felt mean to say it about a dead man I knew was innocent, but I wasn't going to confide my suspicion of ladies like Miss Dorsey and Mary Barnes, or a nice boy like Foster Gibson, to this Palougous person. But with all my caution I saw I'd made a mistake. I'd forgotten that the public in general didn't know Dr. Mosser was murdered, and the murderer didn't know the police knew it. I felt ashamed of my stupidity in using the past tense; Bill Palougous was sharp, all right.

"You mean you don't think so now?"

"Oh, no, I didn't mean that," I said, looking him in the eye the way liars should, I understand, if they want to be convincing. "I just meant that he is dead, and since he didn't leave a confession or anything, I thought it was kind of mean to—pin the rap on him."

I brought that last out after only momentary hesitation and (I thought) quite triumphantly. If I expected to get anywhere with Bill Palougous it might help to speak his language.

Mr. Palougous nodded benevolent approval. "I think that's a real nice kind way to look at it, Miss Tyler. Tell me though, what's the dick think?"

"I couldn't tell you what my nephew thinks, Mr. Palougous," I said promptly and more than a little pointedly. If I'd thought first I would have realized that, presumption or not, it was no time for what Dick calls pulling the FFV stuff.

Mr. Palougous, however, appeared more puzzled than hurt. "Your nephew? I don't— Say!" An idea seemed to strike him, and his broad gold grin curved up. "Is that your nephew's name, Miss Tyler? Dick?" He began to laugh, and if there is anything in the theory that a really bad man can't really laugh then Bill Palougous was a snow-white dove. Mrs. Duckett turned all the way around to look at us, and the thin, beaded lady I'd met at the DAR—she didn't have on the beaded dress this time, but I never did find out her name—nearly fell out of her chair.

"I got to ask your pardon, Miss Tyler," Mr. Palougous said finally, wiping his eyes with his paper napkin. He then polished his whole face and neck while he was at it. "I never meant what did your nephew think; I said, 'What did *the* dick'—the detective? The guy I see going into your house all the time. Lieutenant Kramer, ain't that his name?"

"I'm afraid I don't know what Lieutenant Kramer thinks either, Mr. Palougous," I said with as much dignity as I could muster. I may add that I had given up all idea of speaking his language, rapport or no rapport.

"He don't talk, huh?" Mr. Palougous said. "I thought he was an old pal of yours."

I thought I'd better explain fully and get it over with. "He is. Lieutenant Kramer used to go to school to me when I taught down in Virginia. I haven't seen him for a good many years, and naturally I'm interested to hear all the things he's been doing since then. And of course we can tell him a lot, too, about people he used to know. My niece's mother, for instance—she's my great-niece really—graduated from high school the same year he did."

I thought Bill Palougous' sharp black eyes had relaxed a little. "Oh, you talk about the old times, huh?"

"That's it," I said, a shade too eagerly. "Like the time I put him out of class for bringing trained fleas—and who married whom and how many children they have. I expect he feels a little homesick sometimes, you see, and so do my two."

"I see. Well, Miss Tyler, it looks like I got to apologize to you again." Bill Palougous laughed, but his little black eyes were watchful. "I thought you were one of these lady dicks."

I just gasped.

"Well, you know you did come into town at a funny time," Mr. Palougous said defensively. "And then seeing the lieutenant go in and out of your house—well, I just said to Mrs. Palougous, 'I bet those two work together,' I said."

I had recovered enough to smile and shake my head. "No, I've never been around a murder before. I live in a little country town where nothing happens, and I've just taught Latin all my life."

"Taught Latin?" Mr. Palougous was interested and diverted. "How about Greek? You know that too? I got my papers and all, I'm American now; but I come over from Greece myself, thirteen years ago this May."

"I used to." Laboriously, for though I can read it, of course, I haven't ever had occasion to speak the language, I asked him from what part of Greece he came. I gathered very little from his answer except the fact that it wasn't a part where Homeric Greek survived. However, by going slowly we did finally get a few questions and answers back and forth. Bill Palougous' face shone with such real happiness that I almost liked him. And speaking of faces, Mrs. Duckett's and the beaded lady's were certainly something to see when they passed our table and heard us muttering away in some foreign language. I'm sure they went right out and reported me to the FBI.

"Mr. Palougous, let's go back to this murder," I said at last. "Tell me what you think. Did you know Mrs. Roger Barnes?"

I'd thought rapport had finally been established by my talking Bill Palougous' language, even though it wasn't the one I'd first tried. I was wrong.

"Seen her on the street, just like I said." The little black eyes were like a snake's again, unwavering. "I did know her name, too, but when that guy asked me right quick I couldn't think. But I never did know *her*. We never did have no dealings."

Well, of course, there were two stories right there. The paper stolen out of Eleanor Barnes' desk—whatever it was—was proof that they'd had dealings of some kind. And the policeman hadn't asked him right quick at all. Bill Palougous was the sixth person to be asked that question; he'd had plenty of time to anticipate it and think.

"She never came to your restaurant?" I persisted, though I knew perfectly well she hadn't. I'd seen the Free State from the outside.

"Never did," Mr. Palougous said amiably. And no more.

"You never went to her house, either?" This was even more unlikely, so I added lamely, "I hear she had some beautiful things, and liked to show them."

"Never did," said Mr. Palougous again, and not so amiably this time.

"Then I don't suppose you have any ideas on the murder," I went on, rather desperately. I wasn't a bit fond of the way those steady little black eyes were looking at me. "You wouldn't know who disliked Mrs. Roger Barnes, and might have wanted to kill her?"

Bill Palougous didn't answer directly. He folded his arms and leaned across the table. "Miss Tyler, you and I are friends, ain't we?"

"Why, I—suppose so," I said, flabbergasted.

"What I mean is, why, we're neighbors and all," Mr. Palougous said.

He went on hurriedly; all of a sudden he seemed less happy and less at ease. "I mean we live right across the street from each other, and if it wasn't for all them Navy things Mrs. Travers goes to—and I been in Annapolis long enough to know Navy people got to toe the line, like you said—she and Mrs. Palougous would visit back and forth. And you and me— Why, here we are drinking together." His expansive gesture took in our messy Coca-Cola glasses. "What I mean is, anybody would say, 'Why, Miss Tyler and Mr. Palougous are real good friends.'"

He actually mopped his brow.

"All right, Mr. Palougous." I came to the point for him. "We're neighbors, and neighbors ought to be friends. Is there something I can do for you?"

"You can talk to that dick for me, ma'am," Mr. Palougous said. Unquestionably his relief was nothing short of exquisite. I still didn't know what it was all about. "Tell him how you know I'm all right, and all. He'll listen to you. Tell him I knew when I done it I ought not to have lied to him. I ought to have spoke right out. But, jeez, Miss Tyler, I was scared. I know it don't sound very good to say I was scared of that little— But I just happened to look over, see, when he was taking his hand away. We was going down the aisle of the bus together. He knew I seen him. And he give me a look as if to say, 'You keep your trap shut, you, or you'll be next.' And, jeez, he didn't have nothing on me, but the whole thing wasn't nothing to me, either. So I kept still. I was in the clear, see."

I was proud of myself for being so calm. "So you saw the murder, Mr. Palougous?"

"I saw him take his hand away," Mr. Palougous corrected. "He done it, all right. I'll tell the dick myself. I got to, I know—get this thing cleared up." He used his napkin on his forehead again. "But you tell him first, Miss Tyler—tell him you know me, I'm okay, all that—" He pushed his chair back and rose. Now that he had got it off his mind he seemed in a tearing hurry to go.

I wasn't. There was one pretty important point he hadn't mentioned, and that I certainly had to know. He hadn't said who it was he'd seen taking his hand away, and who it was he'd been afraid of.

"Why, it was the dead guy," Bill Palougous said, when I asked him. Stupidly, he seemed to think. "It was the doc that done it. Mosser."

I got up then, and around to the police station like the Water Witch coming out of the engine house.

CHAPTER FOURTEEN

Not that I thought Bill Palougous had been telling me the truth. I didn't. And Ben agreed with me, especially after he'd talked to Palougous himself. We didn't believe the doctor had killed Eleanor Barnes at all. In the first place, we knew Dr. Mosser had been murdered himself; Palougous didn't know we knew that, and it blew his story sky-high. Ben says that some such story is a feature of any self-respecting murder case. Either some crank confesses to the crime, when he didn't do it at all, or there's an attempt made to fasten it on somebody who can't defend himself. The first is purely pathological, Ben said. The second *may* be psychopathic personality, which involves among other things a taste for slandering innocent people, or it may be the much more simple instinct for self-preservation. Ben thought it was self-preservation this time. He believed that Bill Palougous wanted the Barnes case closed for reasons of his own, and thought this was the quickest, safest way.

"And he really wanted it closed, Miss Julia," Ben said. "He was scared to come to me, even after asking you to pave the way. He knew how the police feel about the testimony of a murderer, when it comes to another murder case."

I was shocked. "A murderer? Dick said he shot a man who was prowling around his restaurant at night—"

Ben said: "He did. But he turned on the light first. He could see then the man wasn't armed. He could have ordered him off the place, or called the police to take him on a storehouse-breaking charge. He shot because he wanted to. I call that murder, Miss Julia."

I told the children what Ben had said, next morning at breakfast. We'd gone out to dinner the night before and hadn't had a chance to talk.

"I wish I thought he killed them himself," I said, meaning respectively Bill Palougous, Eleanor Barnes, and Dr. Mosser.

"He's the one I wanted to do it from the first," agreed Anne. "I never could bear those little snake-eyes, and it will be *awful* if he puts in glass brick, and now pretending that poor woman's husband did it, with all she's got to stand—"

An outsider might have found that hard to follow, but we are used to Anne.

"Not very sound reasons, honey, but you may be right," Dick said. "I'm beginning to think myself Palougous is it."

"But he had an alibi!"

"Established by Dr. Mosser." Dick ticked off his points impressively. "One. Palougous tells Aunt Julia Mosser didn't have anything on him. That shows the way his mind is running. Maybe he was unconsciously telling her *he* had something on Mosser. Maybe on account of that something Mosser let him reach across to stab Eleanor Barnes, and then alibied him.

"Two. He *could* have reached across. Have you noticed those arms? I believe they're six inches longer than an ordinary man's.

"Three. The 'documents' Mosser was going to show Ben are not in his house. That house was entered, presumably by the same person who burgled Eleanor Barnes'. And the Barnes burglar, Ben feels pretty sure, was Bill Palougous himself.

"Four. Somebody murdered Dr. Mosser by putting a morphine tablet in his saccharine box—"

"And right there your theory breaks down," I said, "unless you can show a connection between Palougous and one of the people who handled that box. I don't think it was Foster or Mary Barnes, or Miss Dorsey or Mrs. Park. It could have been that Fulton woman. But something would have to be proved."

"My dear Aunt Julia," Dick said with maddeningly kind patronage, "don't you remember *The Simple Way of Poison?*"

I did, of course, after he'd told me about it. I was ashamed not to have thought of it myself.

"If you're going to poison anybody—and this Mosser murder amounts to that," went on Dick, "—the best way isn't to handle the vehicle in full view of a tearoom full of people. Somebody might see you. Or somebody who was morally sure you did it might feel justified in saying he saw you. Ben says that's been known to happen; and if the witness against you were a reputable person, and the circumstantial evidence were strong, and you had as good a motive as Edith Dorsey and Foster Gibson and Mary Barnes all have, you'd hang just as high."

"Then you think the morphine was put in before, and that he just happened to take it when he did?" Anne was still uncertain. "But how could the murderer know he'd get to it before he gave the 'documents' to Ben?"

"Because there were only three tablets left on Saturday, honey, and he'd naturally finish them before Monday afternoon."

"Not if he filled the box up first," Anne persisted. "You often put in more of a thing like that before you're quite out of it."

"That's right, you do," conceded Dick thoughtfully. "Well, if that had happened, the murderer would have had to kill by other means at the last minute."

"That's a side issue anyway," I said impatiently. "Dr. Mosser did take the morphine. The point is that not just the people at the table Saturday, but anybody who'd handled that box even a month ago—"

"Say two weeks ago, Aunt Julia," suggested Anne. "You said it was quite a little box."

"You said he seemed used to showing it off, too," Dick contributed. "Lord knows who all have handled the thing."

"I still think whoever did this murder did the first one, too," I said firmly.

"Oh, so do I." It was a duet.

"But even so," Dick said, "it means the case is pretty wide open again. We have to worry about not just Dorsey and Gibson and Barnes and Fulton and Mrs. Park, but Aunt Julia's Mrs. Hamilton milking the cows on Eastern Shore, and George Campbell on furlough down in Jackson, Mississippi—"

"And Gordon Smith that we saw ourselves at the Navy–Notre Dame game—"

"And now even Bill Palougous who may not have an alibi for the first murder," I finished gloomily. "I won't be surprised if some of the other alibis explode on us, too."

"Well, I've always been a little suspicious of Miss Julia Tyler," mused Dick.

"This is no time to be funny, Dick Travers," I said with dignity.

Anne patted my arm. "Especially when Aunt Julia is hand in glove with the police."

"So was Dr. Sheppard."

I gave him a look. This was no time for Agatha Christie either.

"Poor Ben!" Anne said. "Somebody besides me has got to tell him."

"How do you mean, tell him?" Dick wanted to know. "Why, honey, he knows it. He just doesn't tell *us* everything—including the things we ought to have figured out long ago, like this. Did you think he did?"

"He certainly didn't tell us about Eleanor Barnes' house being broken into," Anne admitted. "At least not till a long time after it happened."

"And he never has told us what was on the paper they took," I said.

"Well, when you come right down to it, he's got no business telling us everything he knows," Dick said reasonably. "Maybe it's all right to give us enough to keep us on the scent. It helps Ben to talk things over with somebody outside, even if he figures out the answers himself— and we *have* found out some stuff he said he couldn't. No Navy person would have told him that tale about Gordon Smith, for instance, and no Howard House board member the one about Edith Dorsey."

"If we gave him something really good, now," Anne said dreamily, "do you suppose he'd tell us what happened when he interviewed Bill Palougous?"

"I can tell you that—third degree." Dick was prompt. "Good bright lights and maybe rubber hose."

"You know Ben Kramer wouldn't use rubber hose!" I exclaimed, outraged.

"Well, it took something pretty drastic to bring about that drastic change," Dick said reasonably. "He's what the novelists call a broken man."

He really was. Every time I saw Bill Palougous—and now that I'd had the interview I wanted it seemed as if we met twice a day at least—I marveled at the difference. It wasn't just that the cheerful, common voice wasn't cheerful anymore and only about half as loud. He actually seemed to have shrunk in his clothes. As to the little black eyes that I'd disliked because they never wavered, they never met mine now at all. Altogether Bill Palougous reminded me of one of those cowed-looking dogs you see hanging around garbage cans.

"I think I'll get the *Baltimore Sun* file out of the library and read about his shooting that man in the restaurant," I said thoughtfully. "There may be a connection or a clue somewhere, and I think it's about time we started out and *did* something, instead of just working on people to tell us things."

"You're absolutely right, Aunt Julia!" Anne pounded on the breakfast table so hard that Fairy pushed open the kitchen door and peered around it. Satisfied that Dick wasn't beating his wife—she adores Anne and can't look at her without beaming, but that doesn't keep her from staying home from work about two days out of six—she giggled and withdrew. Fairy is so dull that we really could talk about the murder in front of her and she'd never know it; but of course we always wait.

"I don't know what you two call action," Dick said then, mildly. "Aunt Julia has been in at the kill both times. First she discovered a body, and then next time she actually saw the victim drink the morphine. What more do you want?"

"I want to *go* someplace and *do* something," Anne said. "The way we've just been *sitting* and *talking* about these murders is enough to drive anybody *wild*."

"But the best murders are solved that way, or so you tell me," Dick countered.

I hope those children get over their pleasure in baiting each other before they get my age. It may be all right now—Anne is certainly extra pretty when she's upset, and Dick's eyes get as bright as his red head—but it isn't going to look nice for an old lady and her husband to glare at each other over the breakfast table.

Dick went on. "They just sit and talk, and then they have tea, and then they go up and dress, and then they eat their dinner—"

"That's all right in a *book*."

"—and you say my taste is low because in my kind of murder bodies get snatched and amateur detectives go helling around in taxicabs chasing suspects."

"I have no desire to go helling around in taxicabs," Anne said with dignity. "You can't even take a taxi to the place I want to go." She turned her back as well as she could, considering that she was sitting across the table from him. "Aunt Julia, how would you like to go over to Eastern Shore and call on your friends Mrs. Hamilton and Mrs. Barnes?"

"I think it would be wonderful," I said.

"Gas."

"Oh, we have *hogsheads* of gas!" cried Anne, turning on him. "I haven't used the car for *weeks*, and the tank is practically running over."

"Yes, and we have to get to the Army-Navy game."

"We can go with somebody. Sally and Jim will take us— Oh, they're having company. Well, Foster Gibson, then."

"He doesn't want us."

"Of course he wants us! He thinks we're wonderful. He says so."

"He doesn't want us around the day of the Army-Navy game," Dick said patiently, "because he's got a date. D-a-t-e. With Ruth Allein. And you know how fast things are moving in that sector."

"Oh. Yes, they are." Anne was thoughtful. "Jane and I saw them at Miller's the other day. Did I tell you? And they just mostly sat and looked at each other, and didn't eat enough to keep two little birds alive."

If people don't eat the seafood they have at Miller's in Baltimore it really is serious. I put in what Dick calls my two cents' worth. "In that case I think we *ought* to go with them," I said firmly. "We certainly don't want that nice girl getting involved with a murderer. Well, I don't think so either; but it could be, and you know it."

It took the children a little while to admit that, but of course they knew I was right.

"That's settled, then," Anne said briskly. "Dick, you just tell Foster Aunt Julia and I are definitely bound and obliged to go over on Eastern Shore, and we won't get to the game unless he takes us. You might as well tell him you know it won't be convenient but it's just up to him."

Dick still wasn't pleased.

"Go on, I do lots of things I don't like to do too. Suppose you had to go to a baby shower for Mrs. Van Horn's daughter-in-law."

"Or make a speech at a library tea," I said.

But the tea turned out to be extremely nice and I was glad I'd felt I couldn't refuse Professor Gassaway. He might be tiresome, but it was largely thanks to Anne's being at Sweet Briar with his cousin that my two were in both the college and the old-family cliques, instead of having to stay in just the Navy one. The Navy is all right and some of the people are just as nice as anybody, but the Tylers have always gone everywhere.

Sarah Maccubbin and I ran right into Ben when we were coming home. He walked down College Avenue with us, and Sarah proceeded to review my speech. Ben was much impressed, or pretended to be, that I'd been asked to perform at St. John's College. It seems they're considered very highbrow now that they've gone back to the classics. I thought they were just nice. Everybody sat around the library informally, not in rows, and I got to sit down too while I talked about Lucretius the best I could. As I explained to them first, I'm just a teacher from a little country town; but my dear father made quite a study of *De Rerum Natura* and I remembered some of his points. The talk went off very well, and everybody was kind as could be.

Sarah turned one way and we another when we got to State Circle, and then Ben and I could talk. I told him about our projected trip to the Eastern Shore, and he agreed it was well worth taking.

"I only hope it turns out better than my trip to Baltimore," he said gloomily. "I've been trying to see this man for a week, Miss Julia, and when I get to him he won't talk. 'Privileged communication,' he said. Of course he's inside his legal rights, but—"

"What man? What did you want to see him about?" If Ben didn't want to tell me he shouldn't have told me as much as he had.

"It was the lawyer who defended Palougous when he shot John Evans," Ben said. "I don't blame him for not wanting to talk about *that*. But all I wanted to know was why Palougous himself didn't pay the fee, instead of Eleanor Barnes."

I was considerably startled. "Mrs. Barnes paid Bill Palougous' lawyer's fee?"

Ben nodded. "And the lawyer wouldn't say why. It was a thousand dollars, even. Now, Miss Julia, what do you make of that?"

"Maybe Palougous didn't have a thousand dollars," I said promptly, seizing on the consideration which would have applied in my case.

"Maybe not. But why would Eleanor Barnes fork it over?"

I didn't know the answer to that.

"And why was the receipt so important," Ben said, "that Palougous risked breaking into her house to get it?"

I didn't know the answer to that one either.

CHAPTER FIFTEEN

Well, we went to the Eastern Shore. In spite of certain aspects—I did like Mary Barnes, and didn't like the idea of snooping around her house—I must say I enjoyed the trip. This whole murder problem was rather like the fox hunts we used to have in Virginia when I was a girl. There are still fox hunts, of course, but now that the rich Yankees have taken hunting over, lock, stock, and barrel, practically, it isn't what it was. I learned when I was very young how to squeeze the last bit of enjoyment out of the dog music and the fine crisp mornings and the good horse under me, and how to drop a little behind at the last, so I wouldn't have to shut my eyes.

One of my aunts used to live across the bay in Virginia, so the Maryland Eastern Shore didn't look the least bit strange. It's a lovely country. The scenery isn't spectacular, in spite of the glimpses you keep getting of Chesapeake Bay, and the old houses scattered around are for the most part pleasant rather than splendid. But all the same it's easy to see why Eastern Shore people feel that Eastern Shore is the Garden of Eden. Some of them make the ferry trip from the mainland twice a day and don't complain; and that's love, as Dick says. Not that the ferry isn't a fine big one, because it is; but there was an awful lot of rough gray water between one bank and the other, the day Anne and I went across, and it looked very cold. I had expected to be only mildly interested in seeing the little village of Claiborne, where the ferry landed—William Claiborne is one of my collateral ancestors, though I understand I shouldn't brag about him in Maryland—but the longer we stayed on that bay the more interested I got.

We took the road to Easton and Anne pointed out the sights. Rich Neck Manor, right after we left the ferry, was back from the road, but we could see it plainly because the leaves were off the trees. I understand the people are nice about showing it, and I would have liked to see it inside; but of course we couldn't start that. But we went past slowly, and slowed up again when we passed Elberton and West Martingham, which were little white-clapboard houses, very attractive, and one at least very old. When we got to St. Michael's Anne went down Mulberry Street so I could see what they call the Cannonball

House. It seems that during the War of 1812 a cannonball came through the roof and bounced right down past the lady of the house, who happened to be standing on the stairs. Poor woman, I knew just how she felt. I'd felt the same way when I turned Eleanor Barnes' body over and saw that knitting needle sticking out of her heart.

We turned just beyond St. Michael's into the little side road that led to Sewall, and all the while we were bumping along it I kept thinking about Eleanor Barnes, and about Mary Barnes whom we were going to see, and wondering what kind of split personality man could have wanted to marry two such different women. Everybody in Annapolis had told me how different they were; but even if I'd never heard that I'd have known from the house we finally came to. Eleanor Barnes wouldn't have lived in that house five minutes, even done over, the way she'd done over the old Tasker place on King George Street. This place was just plain common and hopeless. Inside—well, everything the ladies had said over the bridge table was true.

We had plenty of time to look at Mary Barnes' living room, for the pale little girl who let us in had to go way out to the chicken houses to get her grandmother. It was rather an interesting room, I thought. First of all, it was clean and comfortable, and nothing in it was very new. The furniture might have been bought secondhand at some country auction; I expect it was. There was a round table in the middle, with magazines like *Good Housekeeping* and *Woman's Home Companion*. Over on the leather-and-golden-oak couch—the kind that opens up into a bed—was a row of dolls, and in one corner there was a child's table with a tea set on it. The bay window was full of big healthy-looking ferns. I hadn't seen a windowful of ferns in years. I hadn't seen a parlor stove, either, and I'm afraid I shuddered a little at this one: ugly potbellied thing, sticking out into the room and hiding a mantel that wasn't half bad. But I lived in a furnaceless house long enough to know that stoves give a lot more heat than even the most beautifully carved fireplaces do; and I'm not so decorator-conscious (though I am a little, after watching the Restoration all these years) as to begrudge Mary Barnes the family photographs she had around. I didn't see the fireman and his bride; but young Roger Barnes in his army captain's uniform was certainly more ornamental than any of the Kuhns and Hesseliuses I'd seen in Annapolis, and I'd like to know why it isn't better to look at a picture of your own son, whom you love to distraction, than a dingy old painting of somebody dead a hundred or so years when you were born.

Mary Barnes came in while we were looking at the picture of her daughter-in-law in her wedding dress and the later, frailer picture that showed young Mrs. Barnes with her three children, the baby boy in her lap and the little girls one on each side. Anne and I both jumped as if we'd been caught going through the desk. There wasn't any reason why we shouldn't have looked at the pictures, of course—Mary Barnes had presumably put them out for people to see; but I think we were both disliking the detective business just then, and hoping perversely that we wouldn't find out a thing.

Mary Barnes was so glad to see us that I was ashamed all over again. We had the nicest kind of visit. The little girls came in: Suzanne who was six and having lessons at home this year, because she was underweight and run-down, and Mrs. Barnes' four-year-old namesake Molly. They moved the dolls so they could sit on the couch with Anne, and pretty soon she was telling them a story about some little pig who was plump and therefore socially self-conscious, while their grandmother and I talked. She raises dahlias, too, and she says that soot put around the roots of delphinium makes them quite a lot bluer.

We turned down an invitation to lunch. I think Anne and I both had the same idea, that it was bad enough to come spying on Mary Barnes without eating her bread and salt. But we'd got our wish; we hadn't found out a thing. Two or three times I'd been on the verge of mentioning the murders, but somehow I never did. I couldn't even casually ask the way to Dorothy Hamilton's, as I'd meant to do, for Ben said that according to the address it would be way off the highway and probably hard to get to. The nearest we got to the murders at all—and nobody came out with it then—was in saying goodbye.

"I appreciate your coming, Miss Tyler," Mary Barnes said at the door, and she sort of held on to my hand. "It was—very good of you to think of me."

I realized with a shock that she took our visit for a vote of confidence, and that she needed it. It hadn't occurred to me that people might be avoiding Mary Barnes and Edith Dorsey and Foster Gibson—I'm afraid I didn't care about the others—on account of the murders.

"Goodbye, Mrs. Travers," Mary Barnes was saying to Anne. "And thank you, too, for coming to see me."

"You must come and see me, soon, the very first chance you get, and please don't call me 'Mrs. Travers,'" Anne said very fast. Her eyes were big and bright, the way they always get when she's tuning up to cry. She got down the path in a hurry and was holding the car door open before I could reach in my bag for Kleenex. Really I felt I needed some myself. It wasn't just seeing the delicate little girls, or the pictures of their gay pretty young mother who hadn't even suspected she had tuberculosis until the little boy turned up with it, and the doctors started checking back. It wasn't even the blinded, crippled son. It was the fact that Mary Barnes, with all she had to stand, was *feeling* suspected of murder. I made up my mind that, gas or no gas, Anne and I were coming back, and that furthermore I was going to invite Miss Edith Dorsey to lunch or tea, tiresome though she was, and be extra nice to Foster Gibson.

We had lunch ourselves in a trashy little place at Easton, where the food was cold and the waitress so friendly I wanted to slap her. But of course that's the kind you get information out of, as we found when we asked the way to Mrs. Bruner's. Mamie Bruner was the name of Dorothy Hamilton's mother.

"Oh, yes, the lady that hooks rugs," our friend the waitress said. We hadn't heard about that, but we said yes, Mrs. Mamie Bruner, and got elaborately directed.

"I hear Mrs. Bruner's daughter is with her now," I ventured. "Does she help her with that work?"

The waitress laughed merrily. "That one? No, *ma'am*. I know her, see. I'm from Bowiesburg myself. Dotty never did what I'd call an honest day's work in her life. She wouldn't be caught dead carrying a tray like me, f'rinstance."

"What does she like to do?" asked Anne.

The girl looked Anne up and down, and not so much at Anne as at the raspberry-tweed suit that had cost, I knew, more than a j.g.'s wife should pay. Her voice wasn't as cordial as it was when she'd answered me. "Nothing, if you ask me," she said. "Oh, Dotty always said she wanted to be an actress. To hear her tell it, she was all the time just a jump ahead of getting her name in lights. But she never *worked* at it. She just set back and waited to be discovered."

"Sometimes *that* works, I understand," I said.

"Yes, but sometimes you set a long time. Look at America."

The girl seemed to like Anne better because she laughed, so Anne tried again. "But doesn't she have a little boy? I should think she'd want to stay home with him."

Our friend laughed raucously. "Stay home, nuts! Why, Dotty Bruner ain't stayed home since she was sixteen! Ran away from high school and got her a job in the chorus, when the rest of us didn't know where babies come from."

I didn't see the connection, but I thought I'd better not go into that. I said instead: "You haven't noticed a change in her since her husband was killed? Maybe she's settled down now, even though she's been rather slow doing it."

"Maybe so." But the girl was doubtful. "I ain't seen her since then. I wouldn't know. All I know is, she lights down here just long enough to drop the kid, same as old times, and off she goes. You talk about her wanting to stay home with her little boy—she don't care no more about that kid than I do about this tin tray."

"He's such a sweet child, too," I said. He wasn't at all—spoiled, sticky little wretch.

"Well, he must have had a sugar daddy, then." Our friend laughed uproariously, slapping an area ladies don't. "Say, that was pretty good! I guess maybe he did at that!" She sobered. "No, what I mean is, Dotty was a hateful little snip all her life. And still is, I guess, from what Bernice told me."

"What was that?" asked Anne.

"Well, it was like this." She shifted the tray, and the people at the next table brightened up. They'd been trying to attract her attention for five minutes. She gave them what's called a dirty look and went right on. "Bernice met Dotty in front of the five-and-ten in Bowiesburg, see, and of course she stopped and said Hello. She knew Dotty wouldn't have cared whether she spoke or not, because she never knew anybody but boys was on earth. But, as Bernice says, just because somebody else is no lady is no reason why *she* shouldn't act nice. So she said: 'Say, I sure was sorry to hear about your husband, Dotty. That was tough.' And what do you think Dotty did?"

"What?" We spoke together, and with flattering eagerness.

"Why, she just stood there and glared at Bernice—like this—and her face kept getting redder and redder, and finally she just simply screamed at the poor kid! She said, 'Don't you call me Dotty, you— you—' Bernice said she was afraid there was going to be a fit thrown, actually."

The restaurant patrons who'd been watching this spirited impersonation seemed to fear so too.

"And then what happened?" Anne wanted to know.

"Why, nothing did. You don't think Bernice was going to just stand there after that, do you? She just went off and tended to her own business, same as I got to do."

It was a good exit line, but she lingered. "Say, if you buy a rug of Dotty's mom, don't you pay her first price she asks you. Her rugs are high class, all right, and I guess there's a million dollars' worth of work on each and every, like she says. But she counts on being beat down some. I'll get your change."

"No, you keep all that," Anne said.

"Oh, gee, thanks!" The girl's eyes were big.

She didn't know, of course, anything of what we'd had in mind, but now she looked at us with frank speculation. I could just see her telling everybody she knew about the two ladies who'd given her a big tip for talking about Dorothy Hamilton. Maybe the raspberry tweed had fooled her at first, but the tip had given Anne away. Rich people give a dime in a case like that, or nothing at all. And they don't end up in the poorhouse the way Anne is going to do.

Anne saw her mistake too, and covered it up pretty well. She said sweetly, "You saved us more than that, telling us about the rug," and we swept out the best we could, I marshaling the points of an article I'd read about inflation.

"But she did, Aunt Julia."

"She would have if we'd been going to buy a rug. But," I pointed out, "we're not."

"Well, maybe we'll have to, Aunt Julia. To make her talk. I know if I were selling rugs I wouldn't say a word till somebody bought one. Anyway, we *need* a rug: one with a lot of blue in it, to go in front of the living room fire."

"You need no such thing," I said. I remembered a few more points brought out in the article. "Now get your mind off hooked rugs, Anne Meredith, and think about this murder."

We thought in a rather stiff silence. Anne is sensitive about her extravagance and I am sensitive about her penniless old age. Meantime we drove and drove. We must have passed a county line, maybe more than one. I got distinctly worried about our gas, especially when we got on the wrong road and had to go back. After that we stopped about everybody we saw and asked the way.

"Why, lady, you're there," the last little boy said. "There's Bruners' right in front of you, down that lane."

Anne turned into the lane with expressions of deep thankfulness. She'd been worried about the gas too. We had no idea the place would be so far—or so lonely. There hadn't been a house in miles: just the Bruner house, standing lank and gray on the bank of a sorry little creek, with bare sycamores behind. The place was clean and respectable—all of that; but I didn't blame young Dorothy Bruner for leaving home, not if she had any normal young girl's love for fun and excitement. This was the stillest place I ever saw.

I said as much to Anne. And just then came the scream. It rose and fell, and wavered and rose again. It didn't sound human, and yet I knew it was. It didn't sound like anything I ever heard in this world, or hope to in the next.

CHAPTER SIXTEEN

Anne wobbled the car nearly off the lane.

"Anne!" I said, making at least three syllables of it. "Go back. Stop this car. That noise came from inside the house."

"I know it." Anne's voice wasn't a great deal better than mine. "But I can't back, Aunt Julia. I'd land in that ditch, and then whatever—screamed—could come right out and get us."

"Do we have to go up to the house and save it the trouble?" I was beginning to get hold of myself.

"I have to go up there and turn around, Aunt Julia. Then I'll step on the gas, and we'll leave so fast we'll meet ourselves coming back. Oh, damn!"

I don't understand a car, but whatever Anne stepped on it wasn't the gas. The engine spluttered and died.

"Damn, damn, damn, damn, damn, damn, damn—"

I felt like chiming in. The motor, for its part, was making the kind of noise motors make when they're being repeatedly flooded.

I don't know what we expected to see come out of the kitchen door when it opened. Something with horns and a tail, at least. I mean that quite seriously and literally, as nobody would doubt who'd heard that scream. As Dick says in another connection, it was just out of this world.

Actually it was only a middle-aged woman who came out. She had a crocheted shawl thrown over her head, and her round face was even pinker than it was. She was smiling and composed. Either she was stone-deaf or she was stone where her nerve ends ought to be. Anne and I looked at each other wildly. We couldn't both be going crazy, but the woman couldn't be going to ignore that scream.

But she was. She said Howdy-do and Ain't-it-cold and Come-right-in just as if nothing had happened. And maybe we were fools, but we went in. We didn't know what else to do.

The kitchen was reassuring. It was even more ordinary than Mary Barnes' living room had been, part old-fashioned-tenant farmer and part too-much-money-for-the-first-time. There was a big beautiful white stove with steaming, shaking pans on it and gingerbread in the oven. We could smell it baking. There was a baby tied in an armchair. Back of the stove six or eight diapers were drying on an improvised line, and they smelled too, the way diapers do when they dry. A big expensive radio-victrola, the kind that plays a dozen records, stood at one end of the room—which must have been twenty-five feet long, two rooms thrown together. At the other end were the frames Mrs. Bruner worked on, and some of her finished rugs.

The rugs were the loveliest things I ever saw. She'd used old-fashioned patterns, and her sense of color harmony was incredibly fine. I say "incredibly" because I'd seen her daughter wearing three different shades of red at the same time. Mrs. Bruner was a real artist. No two of her rugs were alike, and there wasn't a one I didn't instantly want. And there was a little oval one hanging in the corner, just the right size to go in front of a fireplace, and with quite a lot of blue in it, that I hoped Anne wouldn't see.

Just because I comment on the hooked rugs is no sign I wasn't still scared to death. I was. And it was something that only time could cure: not the lovely rugs, and not nice hospitable Mrs. Bruner—just time and place. Some other place. I was so scared I even forgot I was scared of getting undulant fever from farm milk, and accepted a glass to drink with some of the gingerbread Mrs. Bruner was taking out of the oven. I couldn't relax; I was expecting momentarily to hear that scream break out again.

But the house was silent as a tomb.

Anne wasn't at her best either, visiting with Mrs. Bruner. But we drank our milk and ate our gingerbread, and we bought a rug. At least I did—the oval fireplace one, for Anne's Christmas present. I'd been worrying over what to give her ever since the Baltimore jeweler said he couldn't fix the garnets in time. Sure enough, just as our friend the waitress had told us, Mrs. Bruner came down quite a bit on her price. I believe she would have come down more if I hadn't been in such a hurry, trying to buy the thing while Anne's back was turned. Fortunately Anne can't keep away from babies; dirty or clean, black or white, it's all the same to her. So I hadn't had to wait long before she went down on her knees in front of the armchair. I maneuvered Mrs. Bruner behind a pile of hooked rugs, thinking Anne disposed of for quite a while.

But it wasn't but a few minutes till she called me. "Look, Aunt Julia, come here and watch this baby."

There wasn't a thing to watch, as far as I could see. I don't profess to know much about children. The baby was just sitting there in the pillowed armchair, tied in with two diapers knotted together. Anne was down on the floor in her good suit, swinging her little round lapel watch back and forth in front of his eyes. No wonder it gains time if she makes a practice of taking it off and playing with it. The baby was doing just absolutely nothing. His eyes didn't even follow the little gold and crystal ball as it swung.

"See, Aunt Julia, he doesn't pay any attention at all."

"He's good like that all the time," Mrs. Bruner said complacently. "Don't pay no mind to nothing. Never cries, never gets into no mischief. And it's natural, too, don't think it ain't."

"How do you mean, natural?" I asked.

"Well, some people dope their kids," explained Mrs. Bruner. We hadn't known that, and Anne visibly shuddered. "Lily Ingalls, up the creek, gives all three of them paregoric every time they get too wild. Not just when she has to go to town, the way some folks do. Now me, I don't believe in it at all."

We agreed.

"I don't hold with dope or liquor either," Mrs. Bruner went on virtuously. "I seen too many homes broke up, and fine young fellers ruint, all by the sin of self-indulgence. I always said to Fred, 'Fred,' I said, 'let's not cast no temptation in the path of our young ones. Home ain't the place for liquor,' I said. 'I couldn't face my Maker if I'd been the one to set my kids' feet on the wrong path.'"

We endorsed these laudable sentiments, too, though I had to choke back hysteria when she said, "Home ain't the place for liquor." I couldn't help thinking about the woman in Rossville who bought a best-seller and then donated it to the public library because, she said, she'd be ashamed to keep such a book in her house.

"How many children have you, Mrs. Bruner?"

"Five living and four dead," Mrs. Bruner said cheerfully. "Course I don't have but the two little ones at home, and then my daughter's kid."

"You surely don't have a grandchild?" Anne's flattering disbelief was overdone, I thought; but Mrs. Bruner swallowed it hook, line, and sinker.

"I sure do. Getting to be a big boy, too." She produced a picture from a top shelf. "He ain't here today; his mother taken him into town to the doctor. But this is him."

We admired the picture of the handsome dark-eyed child in his mother's arms.

"And his mother is a beautiful girl, Mrs. Bruner," I said. "You must be very proud of her."

Mrs. Bruner sighed loudly. "I'm having a time with her, I know that. Would you believe it, her pension ain't never come through *yet*, and her husband's been dead over two years?"

"Oh, is her husband dead?" Anne asked with sympathy.

"Killed in the war." Mrs. Bruner left it at that. "Now, why would they want to make her so much trouble? Course they was separated when he was drafted, but so was lots of others we've heard tell of. I think one of them guys up in Washington has just went off with the money, that's what I think. Fred says it's more likely a mistake, but I just say, 'Well, Fred, maybe you wasn't old enough to remember Teapot Dome, but I was.'" She laughed heartily.

"What does the Red Cross think?" Anne asked.

Mrs. Bruner spread out her hands. "She won't go to the Red Cross, Dorothy won't. She don't like telling women her business."

She wasn't much like her mother, then. Mrs. Bruner was having the time of her life.

"But if they could help her get the pension—"

"Sure, I know," Mrs. Bruner said. "That's what I tell her. 'The Red Cross ladies are nice, too,' I say, time and again. 'Mrs. Mitchell is a fine, nice woman, and the *young* lady is just as sweet as peaches and cream.' But she won't go, and that's that. *She* don't care how long I wait for board money for the kid. *She* don't care if I work my fingers to the bone—"

"But didn't her husband leave insurance?" Anne asked hastily. "I thought they made them take it out."

"He took it out, all right." Mrs. Bruner laughed bitterly. "Made it over to his mother."

This wasn't getting us anywhere.

"Well, I don't think that was right," I said with as much indignation as I could muster. It was the right approach—Mrs. Bruner beamed on me. "I think his wife should have got it," I went on vigorously, "and then she could pay you, and you wouldn't have to work so hard—"

I had succeeded only too well. Mrs. Bruner wept.

I've seen people cry in my time, but I've never seen anything even approximating that flood of tears. Her voice came from behind it muffled like the voice of somebody standing behind a waterfall. It was actually funny, or so it seemed to us, keyed up and nervous as we still were. And talk! I had to fight back a laugh when I remembered how Anne had said she mightn't talk unless we bought a rug; I wondered what would have happened if, instead of the little fireplace oval, I'd bought the big room-size rug on the wall.

"It's all my fault," the poor woman was saying. "Never a mite of trouble with any of the others, and this one trouble from the day she's born. Trouble, trouble, trouble— I can stand it about Fred, and I don't care if I do have Uncle Willie— I oughtn't to signed the papers. I oughtn't to let her come back. I knew there'd be trouble. God forgive me, I wanted the money. Well, he punished me, all right. He's punishing me now. Trouble, trouble— Show me the way, Lord. Show me the light. I don't mind Uncle Willie—"

How long it might have gone on I don't know. A bell rang sharply, and Anne and I nearly jumped out of our skins. It was just an alarm clock going off—an ordinary metal alarm clock going off at twenty minutes past three in a nice warm commonplace country kitchen. But I couldn't have moved to save my life. We all just sat there while the alarm rang itself out and ran down. Then Mrs. Bruner spoke. The tears had stopped as if somebody had turned off a spigot, and her voice was calm and cheerful again. It was the strangest thing I ever saw. It was like the time I went with Bertha Harrison to the séance where she talked with her mother—or thought she did, poor thing—for five dollars a conversation. That medium, when she "came out of it," acted quite a lot the way poor Mamie Bruner did. The only difference was that Bertha's woman was a fake. I could tell that the minute I saw her. And this—whatever it was—was real.

"It's almost half-past three," Mrs. Bruner said. "Would you ladies like to see some nice hooked rugs?"

I was still perfectly paralyzed. I was proud of Anne when she said, "Yes, we would, please. How much is the gray and blue one in the corner?"

"Well, now, I'm sorry you've took a fancy to that one," Mrs. Bruner answered benevolently. "That little rug up there is sold, and that's a fact. How about this nice little Rose of Sharon? That's been a good seller, now. I done a set of three for Mrs. Byington Spence, up in the Green Spring Valley."

I never heard anything calmer or more normal in my life.

"No, that one wouldn't go with my other things." Anne was magnificently calm too. "Just the gray and blue. You're sure that one's sold?"

Mrs. Bruner winked at me out of the eye more remote from Anne. "Dearie, I'm just as sorry as you are. But it's sold, it sure is, sold to a young lady that come down here in a big red car with a Jersey license. Just last week, it was—"

"Then we'd better be going." I'd found my voice. We said goodbye and thanked Mrs. Bruner for the gingerbread. Somehow we got out of the car, though my knees, at least, felt definitely weak. I felt panicky, too, the way you can get at the last minute, when really everything is all over; it was all I could do not to run the last few steps.

Thank the good Lord, the car started without any trouble. We drove down the lane, leaving our hostess waving cordially from the kitchen doorway. I knew I ought to look back and wave in return, but until we got to the main road I couldn't. I just couldn't. And when I did finally turn around I forgot all about waving to Mrs. Bruner. Her flapping apron was in my line of vision, and I was vaguely conscious of it; but mostly I was looking at the little window in the gable. Unless I was very much mistaken the girl behind the curtain was Dorothy Bruner Hamilton.

"Anne!" I clutched her skirt and told her what I saw.

Anne didn't turn her head. "Aunt Julia, I don't even care. I don't care if Fred's up there too, and even Uncle Willie. Especially Uncle Willie. Let 'em all stay up there and count the money. The Lord will show them the light." She drew a deep breath and relaxed. I think the main reason was the fact that we'd just run into quite a stream of traffic—civilization again. I felt the same way she did. "I've had all the action I want in this murder case," Anne said. "Just let me get out of here."

CHAPTER SEVENTEEN

I got to worrying afterwards about the twenty dollars I'd paid for that rug, and wondering if I'd thrown my money away. It's quite all right to falsify before Christmas, of course, but after that wild harangue about Uncle Willie I wouldn't have been surprised if Mrs. Bruner had shipped the rug to the mythical young lady in the red car. But it duly came to me, fortunately while Anne was out rolling bandages. I took it over to Sarah Maccubbin's. You couldn't have hidden a postage stamp in that little Cornhill Street house, but Sarah's attic was huge.

I stayed for tea and had a nice time. At first Mrs. Marsden, the whiniest of the boarders, was underfoot and we couldn't talk about anything more exciting than the Book Review Group of the Navy Women's Club. There'd been a regular fight the day before over *Forever Amber*.

But finally Mrs. Marsden wandered off upstairs, and I could tell Sarah about our trip to Eastern Shore. Anne and I were still just popping with it. Dick said all he'd heard for three days was speculations about Fred's faults and Uncle Willie's identity, and whether it was Uncle Willie or Dorothy Hamilton who had screamed. Anne held to the former theory and I to the latter, feeling absolutely that if that girl were a homicidal maniac it would explain everything.

Of course I didn't tell Sarah the whole story, the way I'd told it to Ben. I let her think, for instance, that we'd just taken a little trip so I could see the Eastern Shore, and that we'd stopped in Mrs. Bruner's because we'd heard how beautiful her hooked rugs were. Stopped in! I didn't tell Sarah it was miles and miles off the highway. I didn't tell her Mrs. Bruner's daughter was Dorothy Hamilton, either, or that she'd lied about her being away from home. But I told her about the scream and the hysteria and the mysterious allusions to Fred and Uncle Willie, and the alarm clock set to go off at twenty minutes past three in the afternoon.

Sarah was disgustingly calm about it. She said she thought it was quite possible the Bruners had a lunatic shut up upstairs, and if so it was enough to make poor Mrs. Bruner nervous and hysterical. She said she'd known of a number of families who had afflicted children and wouldn't hear of putting them in institutions. She said there was a case right in Annapolis, a dressmaker whose daughter, a woman thirty-four or -five years old now, had never developed mentally beyond the age of six. She'd just spent most of her life in her own room upstairs, playing quite contentedly with her dolls. Of course, Sarah said, that woman was perfectly harmless, but she knew of another case, outside Chestertown, that was far from it. The man was an epileptic, perfectly normal most of the time, but when the attacks came on him he turned on the nearest person like a maniac. Once he beat his poor old mother over the head with a piece of kindling, so the doctor had to take several stitches; but even then she wouldn't give in and have him committed. She said she could take better care of him, because she loved him, than anyone else could or would.

Well, after Sarah got started on all the privately maintained crazy people she knew of, I thought of a few myself: Mr. Bolton down in Rossville, and the aunt of a girl my dear mother visited once. By half-past five we had turned up so many half-remembered cases that we'd about concluded a feeble-minded relative in the attic was indispensable to the well-run household.

"I expect Ruth could tell us quite a few, too, if she would," Sarah Maccubbin said. "You know that's what she specialized in after she graduated: psychiatric casework. Can you imagine why a nice young girl would pick *that* out?"

"No, I can't. But she certainly is nice," I said warmly. We'd seen quite a lot of Ruth Allein in the last few weeks, and I liked her more every time I saw her. It was amazing that anybody so lovely-looking was so much else as well.

"That child has surprised me lately," Sarah went on musingly. "It just shows you never can count on people till they're dead, doesn't it? Well, I wasn't the only one; everybody in Annapolis thought Ruth would marry Peter McClean."

"I never heard of him."

"Well, he hasn't been much in evidence since you came," Sarah said dryly. "But for the last year, ever since they put him out of the Army, he's been down here most weekends Ruth hasn't been in Baltimore. He's a doctor, doing research at Hopkins. Nicest kind of boy, plenty of money from his father's side of the house, and his mother was a Tilghman from Queen Anne's. He and Ruth had so much in common, too. Everybody thought they'd marry. Oh, well!" She sighed heavily. "He never loved who loved not at first sight, I reckon. Lieutenant Gibson seems mighty pleasant, too."

"Oh, I hope she won't marry *him!*" I said involuntarily.

Sarah showed her surprise. "Why, I thought you liked him."

"I do." I could have bitten my tongue out. Sarah is my best friend in Annapolis, but she does repeat things. That's what makes her such good company, of course. But I didn't want her to know I suspected Foster Gibson of murder. "It's just that she's known him such a little while."

"Well, time will take care of that. I didn't mean they'd marry right away." Sarah was looking at me rather hard, and I realized I hadn't fooled her for a minute. "Miss Tyler, I'm surprised at you! You surely don't think Lieutenant Gibson had anything to do with Eleanor Barnes' murder?"

"Well," I said defensively, "he could have."

"So could lots of other people. There's no reason to think he was the one." Sarah was vigorous. She didn't know about the good strong money motive, which Ben says is behind more murders than all the other motives put together. And she had no idea there was a Damascene dagger, freshly sharpened and carefully hidden, in Foster Gibson's desk. "Don't you worry about *that*, Miss Tyler."

"Do you mean you know who did it?" I asked bluntly.

Sarah looked slightly annoyed. "Well, no. But Lieutenant Kramer—you know you advised me to tell him anything I knew—Lieutenant Kramer agrees with me. He thinks it's very likely, indeed." She looked smug. "He's an exceptionally nice man, Miss Tyler. It's too bad he's a policeman, isn't it? But I understand some very brilliant young men go into the FBI. now."

"It's becoming quite a profession," I said. I got up to go.

I'd meant to ask Ben before this what Sarah had told him. It was a good thing he was having dinner with us that night. Otherwise I would have had to pound over to the police station, as Dick says. He further says that if I go any more than the two times I've already been, Annapolis will conclude I am an old lag—a chronic ex-convict—who is on probation and has to keep reporting back.

I don't think any of us especially enjoyed our dinner, for Ben had nodded yes when Anne took his hat and asked if he'd found out about Uncle Willie, and of course he couldn't tell us in front of Fairy. With Uncle Willie and Sarah's evidence both on my mind, I thought she'd never get through lumbering around the table; and Ben and Dick annoyed me by taking second helpings of everything. But finally she was gone, after stopping in the door to make Anne another long thank-you speech about Marnell's present. Marnell is Fairy's son, who had just been inducted. She'd been doleful for weeks because his eighteenth birthday was approaching and "Uncle Sam was breathin' down his neck"; but the extravagant going-away present helped to reconcile her, and now that induction has actually happened she seems quite cheerful.

"Well, Miss Julia, first of all," Ben said, "I'll have to tell you that Anne was right and you were wrong. The screamer was Uncle Willie."

Anne was insufferably triumphant.

"But, much as I hate to disappoint you, my dear child," Ben told her, "I have to say that Uncle Willie is no homicidal maniac. He's not even a lunatic. He just merely doesn't have all his buttons. He's what they used to call a natural, and describe nowadays as a happy little moron who doesn't give a damn."

"Well, he didn't sound like any happy little moron to me," Anne said stubbornly. "If he's harmless, why do they shut him up?"

"They don't, usually. That was just in honor of your arrival," Ben said. "As a general thing Uncle Willie shambles around the farm quite as he pleases, and sometimes even goes into town on simple errands. He's got a beautiful disposition, and it's never occurred to anybody in Bowiesburg to be afraid of him. He's always been that way, you see, and they just don't pay any attention. It's the strangers who come to buy the hooked rugs that don't care for Uncle Willie."

"They certainly don't," I shuddered.

"It seems that Mrs. Bruner lost two or three sales because Uncle Willie was too much in evidence, breathing down the ladies' necks the way you say Uncle Sam's been breathing down Marnell's. He's just like a child, you see. When he catches sight of something glittering, like a pin on somebody's dress, or a pair of big bright earrings, he just naturally reaches out his hands to touch it. And the ladies just as naturally scream. Maybe that's what gave Uncle Willie the idea."

"Well, thank the Lord for small mercies," I said solemnly. "At least he was shut up when *we* got there."

"But I thought you and Anne wanted action," said Dick.

I gave him a look.

"So Mrs. Bruner started locking Uncle Willie up whenever she saw a strange car turn into the lane," Ben went on. "Usually, as I understand it, she maneuvers him into a little shed some distance from the house, where he can scream his head off. And does. He isn't angry, you understand; he's just disappointed. Uncle Willie likes company, and naturally he's hacked when he doesn't get to come out and see them."

"Oh, naturally!" Dick said.

"The day you came, though, Mrs. Bruner was busy and didn't see the car as soon as usual. She and her daughter just barely had time to hustle Uncle Willie into the attic. The daughter and the little boy stayed with him to keep him company, and that's why he was quiet while you were in the house. But Uncle Willie doesn't like being pushed around, and when they were getting him upstairs he did balk and let out that one howl you heard."

Anne and I shuddered, just remembering it.

"But you see it's very simple," Ben finished. "There's one like Uncle Willie in every community. As long as he isn't dangerous—and especially if it's out in the country, where there aren't neighbors to be bothered—there's no reason to put him in an institution. People of that class"—I don't mean to be ugly, but the way Ben said that you'd have thought old Tom Kramer was an FFV—"have a horror of what they call being put away. But of course it doesn't make the home happier to have a half-wit underfoot and needing care. No wonder Mrs. Bruner gets nervous and upset and cries easily. I'd think it would be specially hard on her, because Uncle Willie isn't her blood kin. He's Mr. Bruner's uncle."

"Yes, and what about Mr. Bruner?" Anne wanted to know. "'I can stand it about Fred,' she said."

"Well, Fred is another of Mrs. Bruner's crosses, poor woman," said Ben. "It seems he isn't saved. He won't be baptized and join the church. He doesn't mind her going every time the doors are opened, and once in a while he'll even go with her; but when the preacher calls for sinners to come up to the mourning bench Fred Bruner just sits still."

"Is he all right except for that?" asked Dick.

"Highly respectable. Good worker, good father and husband. He's been on Judge Rousby's farm thirty years, and the judge says he's a fine man in every way. No, it just upsets Mrs. Bruner to think she's going to heaven and Fred isn't."

"Another thing, Ben," I said. "You promised to find out about the alarm clock, if you could. It may not have meant a thing, but when she said in that strange voice, 'It's almost half-past three,' Anne and I both got the impression half-past three was some special time."

Ben nodded. "It is. It is the time the Reverend Leander Dawson,

Christ's personal representative evangelizing the Eastern Shore, starts on his daily broadcast. Mrs. Bruner wouldn't miss it any more than you'd miss brushing your teeth every day. She sets the alarm so she won't forget the time, and she puts it a little ahead so she can finish up whatever she's doing. She's like a cat on a hot griddle after that bell goes off. It rang while I was there, too, and she was scared to death I wouldn't get out before the Reverend Leander Dawson began to pray."

"Ben," I said impressively, "that woman's a natural-born liar. The way she said her daughter had taken the little boy to the doctor, and then when she mentioned the big red car—" I stopped abruptly. I'd almost let the cat out of the bag about Anne's Christmas present. "What I mean is, did Mrs. Bruner just tell you all this, or did you actually *see* Uncle Willie?"

"Oh, I saw him all right," Ben said. "Sorry to disappoint you, Miss Julia, but Uncle Willie and I had quite a nice little talk. I talked to the police in Bowiesburg, too, and to Judge Rousby whose farm he's lived on thirty years. Uncle Willie is just as represented—a harmless, ordinarily contented half-wit."

"Like that poor, pitiful little baby," Anne said. "Did you get down and play with it the way I told you to?"

Ben nodded yes. "I'm afraid you're right. Another mental defective."

"Now, listen to me, Ben Kramer," I said forcefully. "That makes a clear case of the kind of mental trouble that runs in families. Do you deny that Dorothy Hamilton could be affected too? She obviously isn't feeble-minded, but she could have mania instead, couldn't she?"

"Oh, yes, she could, Miss Julia," Ben said. "I don't think she does; I talked to her too, and she seemed perfectly all right. Of course I'm no psychiatrist. I do know and admit, though, that it's possible to have several types of mental trouble in the same family. Dorothy Hamilton knew it too, poor kid."

"What do you mean?"

"Well, you know what the girl in Easton told you about her blowing up when 'Bernice' said, 'I sure was sorry to hear about your husband, Dotty'? Now Dotty's a very common nickname for Dorothy, and under ordinary circumstances nothing to take offense at. But little Dorothy Bruner's uncle was the village idiot. Can't you just see the dear little schoolmates standing on the street when she passed and chanting, 'Dotty's dot-ty! Dotty's dot-ty!' Children are mean, Miss Julia."

After teaching school for forty years I didn't need anybody to tell me that.

"'Poor kid' is right," Dick said gruffly.

"Oh, I *don't* think she did it, Aunt Julia!" exclaimed Anne. "It's true, with two crazy people in the family there certainly could be another; but then again lots of children in families like that are perfectly normal. Aren't they, Ben?"

"Oh, yes. It works both ways," Ben said. "You've got a good case there, Miss Julia, but it's all theory like—some of the others we've made out. It's evidence we need. And we're beginning to get it—all at once. I can't tell you who it is, or anything about it; but we're going to make an arrest."

CHAPTER EIGHTEEN

The next three afternoons I fairly snatched the *Evening Capital* out of the paper boy's hand. But there wasn't anything new in it about the murder, and we didn't see Ben. I did know this much (though I didn't find out from Sarah Maccubbin, who for once was being close-mouthed and impervious to hints): her information was part of the case against this person, whoever it was. I figured that out from Patrolman Long's sudden fondness for Duke of Gloucester Street. There wasn't going to be another murder if Ben could help it.

The days passed slowly. I couldn't seem to get my mind on anything but murder, which is an awful confession for a respectable woman to have to make. I went to the UDC, I went to the Army-Navy game, I played in the bridge tournament at Carvel Hall and got as far as the semifinals. But the stream of talk about promotions and servants and who'd been seen having lunch in Baltimore with whose husband passed for the most part right over my head.

I had no more idea than a rabbit who it was Ben was intending to arrest—or had intended to. Maybe that was all off. He'd certainly talked as if they meant to make the arrest without delay. From the way Ben had looked that night—sort of stern and sorry at the same time—I was mightily afraid that it was either Mary Barnes or Foster Gibson. But I still couldn't and wouldn't believe either of them was guilty, and remembering my good resolutions I made a point of sending Mary Barnes some recipes I'd told her about, and I was extra nice to Foster when I saw him.

I didn't see him often, though, except at a distance. His affair with Ruth was in what Dick calls the second stage. They wanted to go off by themselves now, and the afternoon of the Army-Navy game was the last nice time we all had together. I watched Ruth closely that day, worried because the children seemed to think she was getting serious too, and for a while her offhandedness relieved me. But when we got home from Baltimore, and Foster Gibson slipped on the ice outside our house and took what was from Anne's and Dick's and my point of view a perfectly ludicrous fall—well, right there and then I had to give up. I gave up, too, the idea that trained caseworkers aren't easily fooled. Maybe Ruth was foolproof on the people she wasn't in love with, but she was no more competent to judge Foster Gibson than a doctor is to operate on his own dying child.

Of course Ruth didn't know any of the evidence against him. It was one thing for her to act happy and oblivious—being in love *is* nice— and quite another for Foster. You can't just ignore everything, after all. But he seemed to be doing it. I watched him that Sunday with Ruth in the Naval Academy Chapel, kneeling together with their heads bent down. Mine was irreverently up, I'm sorry to say, and my eyes wide open. I haven't got used to the Navy custom of singing part of "Eternal Father, strong to save," all kneeling, after the final prayer. I always start to get up. Foster's eyes were open too; he was watching the stained-glass light on Ruth Allein's serious beautiful face, and if he was thinking about the love of God, or even about little things like being arrested for murder and losing out on four million dollars, I'm very much mistaken.

No use worrying about that young man, I thought. He doesn't have gumption enough to know he needs it. But I went right home and called Miss Edith Dorsey.

Judging from the eagerness with which she accepted my invitation to lunch, I'd been right in that case anyway. Miss Dorsey did need and welcome a vote of confidence. We arranged to meet next day at Carvel Hall. Lunch at home might have been pleasanter, but I was determined to do my good deed out in public, so people could see for themselves that Julia Tyler, at least, didn't think Miss Edith Dorsey was a murderer.

Miss Dorsey was late. I felt my righteous Christian glow evaporating fast as I sat in the lobby with nothing to do. I wandered up into the old part of the hotel (originally it was a house belonging to William Paca, one of the Maryland Signers, and though it isn't architecturally great it's very nice indeed) and sat there looking at the mantel till I could have gone home and drawn a picture of it from memory. Finally in desperation I went back to the little gift shop cubbyhole and bought a book. There was a very poor selection—not a single murder, and nothing much at all but *Richard Carvel*, which I read forty-five years ago, and several different books about colonial Annapolis, which Professor Gassaway says are none of them worth reading. Finally I bought a biography of Charles Carroll of Carrollton, whose townhouse Anne took me to see last week. It cost three dollars and seventy-five cents, so

I read it with the tips of my fingers, thinking I could give it away for Christmas.

I'd read quite far along when Miss Dorsey arrived. She came huffing and puffing up the steps as if she'd been to a fire, and her eyes were shining with excitement the way they had that day in the bus station.

"Oh, Miss Tyler, I'm so sorry to be late!" Miss Dorsey said rapidly. She wasn't at all. "But wait till you hear. I was just passing the police station—and of course I wouldn't have stopped and stared usually—but I think when people make a commotion like that it's because they really want to be looked at, don't you? And naturally I was interested on account of having been on that bus—and I said to myself, 'Oh, this is going to make me late for lunch, but Miss Tyler would want to hear about it too—'"

"You mean somebody was being arrested? For Eleanor Barnes' murder?" I demanded.

"Oh, yes!" Miss Dorsey looked at me gratefully, as if she weren't used to being interpreted so fast. Of course I couldn't have done it if I hadn't talked to Ben before. "Yes. They were just bringing her in."

Her? My mind flashed to poor Mary Barnes.

"I was never so surprised. I hadn't thought—"

"Miss Dorsey!" I said in desperation. "Who was it?"

"Why, it was that Miss Fulton," Miss Dorsey said. "Did you think—Why, it never had occurred to me—but she must have been guilty. She acted *extremely* guilty. Why, Miss Tyler, you'd never believe the way she was crying and sobbing right out loud, and her hair was all untidy and her—complexion streaked, and when the young policeman attempted to help her out of the car she struggled quite violently and actually tried to bite his hand! Of course quite a crowd had gathered. Very undesirable people for the most part. I didn't see a soul I knew except Tom Beale, but of course I couldn't see well at all, for naturally I kept at the outside edge of the crowd. I shouldn't want anyone to think I wasn't just passing by."

"Naturally not," I said dryly. I felt dazed and inexpressibly relieved. "Did you hear what people were saying, Miss Dorsey? Do you know why she did it?"

"Nobody seemed to know," Miss Dorsey said with regret. "I wish your friend Lieutenant Kramer were here. He could tell us all about it." We were at the dining room door by this time, and her eyes and mine went around the room in what I at least knew was ridiculous search. Of course with an important arrest just made Ben Kramer wouldn't have been lunching at Carvel Hall. But then I saw Sarah Maccubbin waving to me across the room, and I knew the Lord had answered prayer the way He so often does, giving you not what you asked for but something just as good.

"Come on," I said to Edith Dorsey. "Let's join Miss Maccubbin." And to the great annoyance of the waiter, who was pulling out chairs at a table by the window, I started over to the larger table where Sarah was sitting with a vaguely familiar-looking woman. I thought it was a DAR I'd met somewhere before; but instead it was a Mrs. Smith, Ensign Gordon Smith's mother and his identical image. Well, that couldn't have been more fortunate, because naturally she was interested in the murder too, and we could start talking about it right away.

Miss Dorsey gave her account again, making a worse muddle of it than before, but remembering a few extra points.

"And the last thing before the door shut," she finished, "Miss Fulton said: 'Oh, my babies! My poor little babies! Whatever will become of them now?' I declare I felt right sorry for her, murderess or not."

Sarah Maccubbin's mouth was grim. "She ought to have thought about her poor little babies before."

"Oh, maybe she killed Mrs. Barnes for *them*," Miss Dorsey said sentimentally.

Mrs. Smith snorted, and I felt like it.

"Well, as a matter of fact she did," said Sarah Maccubbin slowly. "I might as well tell you all this, Miss Tyler. I wanted to the other day, but I'd promised Lieutenant Kramer not to say a word. He said he had to get more proof before he could make an arrest, and meanwhile talk would be dangerous."

I must admit my feelings were a little hurt. Ben might have trusted me.

"The reason I'd waited so long to tell him what I knew," Sarah went on, "was that I wasn't sure I had any business telling anybody. You see I got the information because I was a member of the Children's Home board, and of course it was supposed to be confidential.

"This is a story with a beginning way back last spring," Sarah said. "That was when this Gladys Fulton started work at the defense plant in Baltimore. Up till then—ever since she'd got her divorce, that is—she'd been a waitress in one of those Greek restaurants on Main Street. The Free State, I believe it was."

Miss Edith Dorsey and I both made small noises under our breath. I looked over at her quickly, wondering what *she* knew about Bill Palougous, before I realized she was just protesting Miss Maccubbin's use of the new upstart name for Church Street.

"Well, that job had worked out very well," Sarah was saying. "She didn't go to the restaurant till four in the afternoon, and by that time the oldest girl was home from school. She's fourteen and old for her age, and I understand she took very good care of the little ones. It was an imposition on *her*, of course. But when the mother went to work in this Baltimore plant she left home early in the morning, and there wasn't anybody to stay with the children till the oldest girl got home from school."

"You don't mean she left them in the house by themselves?" Mrs. Smith asked incredulously. "How old were they?"

"Five and four, the ones at home. There was a nine-year-old, but of course she was in school too. All girls. Somehow," Sarah Maccubbin said, "that seemed to make it a little worse. You read of so many cases in the paper—"

"But didn't they cry?"

"Yes, they did. At first they cried so much the neighbors complained about it to their mother. She was unconcerned as you please. I believe something would have been done then; but the school term ended about that time, and the eldest girl could be at home.

"Well, things were all right during the summer; but this fall it started over again. The little girls had got used to doing without their mother and didn't cry so much when she went off and locked them up. But they still cried enough to disturb the neighbors, and Mrs. Feldhaus, next door, had a sick old mother the doctor said needed absolute quiet. Besides, the neighbors worried about the children themselves. One day the baby—Sheila Fay, I think its name was—burned her arm on the steam radiator and screamed till they thought she was dying. Mr. Feldhaus finally broke a window and got in. Miss Fulton was awfully mad at him, I understand, but Mr. Feldhaus just told her a few things right back. And Dr. Kent told her he'd known cats and dogs that took better care of their children."

"Well, I should think so!" Mrs. Smith said.

"But you know how it is. Everybody in the neighborhood said she ought to be reported to the child welfare authorities, but nobody wanted to bell the cat."

"I declare, I don't see why there's such a prejudice against anonymous letters," I said. "It seems to me they'd fill a real need."

Sarah smiled at me and went on. "Of course, something was bound to happen sooner or later. One day the children got hold of some matches, and while they were playing they managed to set the living room curtains on fire. It spread fast, and by the time the fire department got there not much of that room was left. But the little girls were all right. They'd had sense enough to run back in the bathroom and shut the door, and were screaming their heads off out the window. It was the only one in the house their mother hadn't nailed shut, because it was too little and high for them to fall out of."

I think we all shuddered.

"Well, naturally, the whole thing got in the papers, and there was a lot of criticism; and at least one person who didn't mind belling cats—who really liked belling cats, if you ask me—heard about it."

"Eleanor Barnes, of course," I said. It was like all roads leading to Rome.

"Yes, Miss Tyler. Eleanor Barnes went to see the Fulton woman and told her that, unless she turned over a new leaf, she'd report the case to the Children's Home board."

There was a short silence broken by Miss Dorsey's precise, monotonous little voice. "Well, I'm sure somebody needed to speak to Miss Fulton. I think Mrs. Barnes always did what she thought was her duty."

Hadn't I said Miss Edith Dorsey was a lady?

"Well, it seems this Gladys Fulton tried every way and anyhow to get a woman to stay with the little girls; but she couldn't do it for love nor money." The other ladies nodded vigorously. They could well believe it. "And she couldn't see herself giving up the big money she was making in Baltimore to be a waitress again in the Free State Restaurant. And she didn't hear any more from Eleanor Barnes, and she did hear a lot *about* her: how hard she was working for Bundles, for instance, and how absorbed she'd got in the new Society for the Preservation of Maryland Antiquities. She very naturally thought there was a good chance Eleanor Barnes would forget all about it. She didn't know her as we did."

"Eleanor wasn't that breed of cat," Mrs. Smith said succinctly.

"So Miss Fulton learned when she happened to meet her in Baltimore, the day Mrs. Barnes was murdered," answered Sarah dryly. "Eleanor told her she'd had her chance and thrown it away, and so she'd have to be reported to the Children's Home board, and her little girls would certainly be put somewhere they'd get better care. The Fulton woman cried and carried on, I understand; but it didn't do any good. She said she offered Eleanor Barnes anything she had—"

"She said? Sarah, where did you hear all this?" Mrs. Smith wanted to know.

It was Sarah's turn to stare. "Why, Gladys Fulton told me herself," she said. "She came to see me the day after she killed Eleanor Barnes."

CHAPTER NINETEEN

At first I was definitely hacked, as Dick says, at Sarah for not having told what she knew quite a lot sooner. I didn't mind her not telling me, of course, but she should have gone straight to Ben. This was a murder case, after all. Maybe if she'd spoken up in time Dr. Mosser wouldn't have been killed too.

But Ben set me straight on that. "Actually what Miss Fulton told Miss Maccubbin was nothing but good strong motive," he said. "She didn't confess to the murder. She just felt she had to talk to Miss Maccubbin, for two reasons. In the first place, she knew Eleanor Barnes had already talked privately with Miss Maccubbin herself, about the children. Mrs. Barnes told her that. She was afraid the case would get brought up at the board meeting anyway, in spite of Mrs. Barnes' death—"

"Well, why didn't she kill Sarah Maccubbin too, then?" I broke in.

"That's what Miss Maccubbin wondered, after she got to thinking about it. She was scared to death." Ben grinned reminiscently. "But then she figured out—and I think she was right—that Miss Fulton wasn't really a killer. She killed Eleanor Barnes because there wasn't any chance of getting mercy from her. Eleanor Barnes wasn't that kind of woman. But Miss Maccubbin, who has about the softest heart in Annapolis, underneath, was a very different proposition. Miss Fulton thought she could talk her out of another chance."

"Anyway," Anne said, "Gladys Fulton couldn't have gone around killing all the people who knew she locked her children up. Why, it had been in the paper."

"And then she talked about it herself," I added. "Bragged about it, almost. She was telling Mrs. Kleinschmidt, that day on the bus, what a nice arrangement it was, and how happy the little girls were at home with their beautiful toys."

"Rationalizing," Dick said, wisely. "Go on, Ben."

"Well, in the second place Miss Fulton wanted Miss Maccubbin to promise not to tell that Eleanor Barnes was interested in the case and had threatened her. *That* part hadn't been in the papers. And Miss Maccubbin promised."

I sniffed. Then I remembered a promise I'd made, too, the one to Mary Barnes, and didn't feel so smug.

"But didn't she know she might be shielding a murderess?" Anne demanded. "Even if Miss Fulton denied doing it—"

"She did deny it, of course. For that matter she still does. But Miss Maccubbin believed she was telling the truth. At first, that is. Later she wasn't so sure." Ben smiled and shook his head. "You can't afford to be guided by your beliefs and disbeliefs in a case like this. Evidence is what counts, on top of motive and opportunity."

"You haven't told us what the evidence is," I reminded him.

Ben smiled at me. "I probably shouldn't tell you now. But you've been such a help to me—yes, you have, Miss Julia, all of you— Well, the evidence is pretty damning."

He ticked off the points on his fingers.

"One. Gladys Fulton had what amounted to a quarrel with Eleanor Barnes, in Hutzler's store in Baltimore, and Mrs. Barnes threatened her again. She admits that much. Undoubtedly she wanted to kill Mrs. Barnes then and there; but didn't have either the opportunity or the means.

"Two. Later in the day— This was the day of the murder," Ben said, interrupting himself. "I should have told you that Miss Fulton was unexpectedly off from work; a boiler had burst in her department, and they had to close down. Well, later in the day she had lunch in Baltimore with Dr. Mosser. We don't know that she got morphine tablets from him at that time, but we do know the one given Eleanor Barnes was the exact size and type he used to peddle. He must have cached a supply the police didn't find when he was arrested. We've found part of it since. And remember that Mosser hated Eleanor Barnes too, on his own. I expect he was glad to cooperate.

"Incidentally, we think it was at this luncheon—rather than the day he died, when she had tea with him—that Miss Fulton slipped one of the morphine tablets into the doctor's pillbox."

"It seems to me that was a pretty good day's work, for a woman you say wasn't a real killer," commented Dick.

Ben laughed and admitted it. "But Miss Fulton was a student of human nature. Waitresses get to be, just like policemen and schoolteachers. She felt pretty sure Dr. Mosser was a dangerous ally, just as she'd felt sure Miss Maccubbin was a nice, kind-hearted woman.

"Three. When Eleanor Barnes had a Coca-Cola at the bus station soda fountain, half an hour before the bus was called, Gladys Fulton served her."

"This is beginning to sound like one of the murders I read," Dick said. "How'd she put that over?"

"Well, that was a piece of luck," Ben said. "The regular girl was an old friend of Miss Fulton's; they'd worked together right here at the Free State Restaurant. They got into a conversation, of course, and it came out that the regular girl had a boyfriend leaving on an earlier bus. Gladys Fulton offered to take her place for a while, so she could be with him."

"And you mean to tell me Eleanor Barnes didn't even recognize her?" I asked incredulously.

"I doubt that she even looked at her, Miss Julia. People don't really look at waitresses, you know. And if she did, well, Gladys Fulton in a pink cap and wrap-around wouldn't look much like Gladys Fulton in a dizzy hat and a fur coat.

"Four. Miss Fulton talked on the bus about locking up her children. Do you think she'd have dared that defiance if she hadn't known Eleanor Barnes was passed out and couldn't hear her?

"Five. In that alligator bag of Miss Fulton's there was a nice sharp new paring knife. She bought it in a Baltimore dime store after her quarrel with Eleanor Barnes. As I said before in another connection"—Ben smiled apologetically at Foster Gibson's friends—"nobody could know Miss Dorsey was going to drop a knitting needle.

"Six. When she got it home Miss Fulton buried that knife under a rosebush. Maybe Gibson's secret drawer was just a good safe place for a valuable antique, but nobody could say being buried helped a paring knife.

"Seven. Last week Miss Fulton sent Mrs. Elsie Kleinschmidt, over at Eastport, a check for a hundred and twenty dollars. Mrs. Kleinschmidt says it was for a piece of costume jewelry—jade bracelet, I believe—Miss Fulton commissioned her to buy in New York. War workers *are* throwing their money around like that, and Miss Fulton does have a jade bracelet. But remember Mrs. Kleinschmidt walked up the aisle of the bus with her."

"You mean she might have seen her stab Eleanor Barnes? Well, why doesn't she say so, then? Miss Fulton is in jail; she's got nothing to lose."

"Oh, yes, Anne, she has," Ben said. "Now that we know about the hundred-and-twenty-dollar check. Blackmail isn't murder, but it's a pretty serious offense."

"Oh!"

"And, finally, point number eight. I thought I'd left something out," Ben finished, "but this is what I've told you before. Gladys Fulton is left-handed. Otherwise, I don't think she could have delivered that strong a blow. But she uses her left hand the way you and I use our right."

"Well, Ben, you've certainly got a case," Dick said after a minute. "I should think you'd easily get a conviction. Congratulations."

"Thanks." But Ben didn't look very happy, so I said, "Aren't you pleased?"

"Oh, in a way, Miss Julia," answered Ben. "But this is the part I don't like, the part ahead. I guess I'm just a sissy."

"No, you're not," I said warmly. I knew just how he felt. As I think I've said before, I always used to enjoy a run across fields as much as anybody, but the first time I was in at the kill was my last as well. I always managed after that to drop behind.

"Well, it's just that I always hope it will be somebody we can send to a nice modern nut house," Ben said. "Gladys Fulton will hang."

He got up and found his hat and went home.

The day after that, Gladys Fulton's preliminary trial, or whatever they call it, was held, and she was sent back to the county jail, to wait trial for murder in May. I think that's the refinement of cruelty. Why don't they do a thing like that and get it over? They had all the evidence, the state's case was complete, and Miss Fulton's lawyer had turned up all he could in her defense. It wasn't much. She still wouldn't confess; but, as Ben says, lots of them never do break even right at the end. He says a murderer with the nerve and resourcefulness and poise to put over a crime like this one can stick it out all the way. And Gladys Fulton, after that first hysterical outburst when she was arrested, had been like a woman turning to stone.

Nobody seemed to worry or even think much about her, after the nine days' wonder had run its course. But every once in a while, especially in the middle of the night when you wake up and never by any chance think of cheerful things, I'd think about that poor woman down in the jail, lying awake too, I had no doubt. I'd think besides of the four little girls up the creek in the Anne Arundel Children's Home. Sarah Maccubbin had reported them as good as gold, apparently happy enough but more than a bit bewildered. Poor little things, I wondered what was ahead for them. There didn't seem much future for a murderess's children; and somehow I couldn't get out of my mind the picture Ben had called up of a slim, dark-eyed, white-faced child running past a group of jeering little devils—well, that's what children can be when they like—who pointed their fingers and chanted, "Dotty's dot-ty! Dotty's dot-ty!" Things would be even worse for Gladys Fulton's little girls, after she was hanged.

I met Dorothy Hamilton on the street a few days after the preliminary trial. Strangely enough, I saw all of the former suspects—with the exception of George Campbell—within the space of that next week; but Dorothy was the first. We met on Maryland Avenue and stopped and talked. Dorothy had had to come over, she said, to try to find some decent stockings. She'd painted her legs all summer and had meant to go on all winter, but now it was getting too cold for her. Oh, yes, ma'am, she'd be glad when nylons came back. Putting on leg make-up was a nuisance, summer or winter, but so was pulling up rayon stockings all the time. Embarrassing, too, especially on dates. She giggled. Oh, yes, ma'am, she had dates. Jimmy'd been dead for over two years now, and anyhow he'd want her to have a good time. She wasn't thinking about marrying again, oh, no, ma'am; but she did love to go dancing, and some of the Coast Guards at Curtis Bay really knew how to show a girl a time. Oh, yes, ma'am; she was glad she'd seen me, too, and a merry Christmas to everybody at *our* house.

I walked on feeling rather ashamed of myself. The girl really was a sweet little thing, in her way. She was common as pig tracks, of course, and her clothes and hair and make-up made me think of another Hamilton by marriage, Sir William's poor dear Emma, who had so much taste, and all of it bad. If she'd only let her pretty dark hair alone! I believe she'd actually had a henna rinse. But she did have beautiful manners—you don't often hear a young girl these days say Yes, ma'am, and No, ma'am, as meticulously as naval officers say No, sir, and Yes, sir, to their seniors—and under that frivolous exterior there was plenty of good hard intelligence. Dorothy Hamilton was a girl who knew what she wanted and would get what she started out for. I don't like to see that in a young girl, but I expect it's inevitable when she's made her own way since sixteen. And, remembering Uncle Willie, I'd be the last person to blame Dorothy for running away from home. I hoped her pension would come through soon so she could get away from him again—and from that overreligious, overemotional mother, who couldn't have been easy to live with. I don't mean I couldn't see the mother's side too; I didn't doubt that Dorothy'd been nothing but trouble from the day she was born, as Mrs. Bruner said. Probably just about everything she liked to do was on the Reverend Leander Dawson's black list, poor child. It was no wonder to me there was a shadow in her big dark eyes.

I met Miss Edith Dorsey and Gordon Smith that same day, walking down the street with nice Mrs. Smith between them. We didn't stop to talk, but Sarah told me afterward why Miss Dorsey had looked so happy. Mrs. Park, the woman who'd been having tea with her that day when Dr. Mosser was murdered, had decided to take up genealogy in a big way, as Dick says. She'd got so interested in looking up some ancestor or other who'd fought in the Revolution and left a diary that she'd decided to write a book about him. It seemed quite a lot of her friends thought she was very talented. But even she didn't believe she could do the research without help, so Miss Dorsey was going to help her—at a rate, Sarah said, to make you believe there really was a tide in the affairs of men.

But Sarah said there wasn't any reason, so far as she knew, for Gordon Smith's looking happy too. She said it was probably just because he was young and felt good.

The Sunday after that, Anne and Dick and I went over to spend the day with Mary Barnes. Thanks to our educational but otherwise barren little jaunt to Dorothy Hamilton's house, we didn't have a drop of gas, and coupons still not due; but Mrs. Barnes met us at the Claiborne ferry and took us back to it. We had the nicest kind of day and a beautiful big turkey for dinner. It was their Christmas dinner, Mary Barnes said, fixed ahead of time because when the real day came they'd be down with the little girls' father at White Sulphur Springs. The old mean sanitarium, as four-year-old Molly told Anne, wouldn't let them come to see their mother and little brother; but Daddy's hospital was nicer about things like that, and anyway Daddy needed them the most because—did Anne know?—Daddy couldn't see anymore. Grandmother said they were going to be the biggest kind of help to Daddy, so he wouldn't even miss his eyes.

Sitting across the room from Anne and the children, Mary Barnes had tears in her own eyes. But at least some of the trouble was gone out of her fine plain, patient face—the money worry, I guessed it was. Things were still just about as bad as they could be for her, but almost anything is easier to stand if you don't have to worry about money too. Money gives you a chance to catch your breath and think about other people. For the first time since I'd known her, Mary Barnes seemed really interested in outside things, not just polite. She was just as concerned as I was, she said, about Gladys Fulton's poor little girls, and just as happy about Foster Gibson and Ruth Allein.

Those two were actually engaged. Mrs. Morton called to tell us about the big announcement party she and the commandant were giving: first a dinner for the intimate friends, and then a reception and dancing for "practically everybody in town." I believed her, too, when she went on to say they'd love to send Lieutenant Kramer a card, if I thought he'd come. Not that Ben isn't nice; he is. He's one of the nicest men I know. But strict and snobbish as Annapolis usually is I never thought I'd live to see a policeman dancing gayly in the commandant's house. Mrs. Morton knew exactly what I was thinking, of course, because she laughed a little before she went on.

"You see Ruth and Foster feel they owe Lieutenant Kramer a special debt of gratitude, and of course it *was* sweet of him never to think

Foster had anything to do with killing Eleanor Barnes, when he did have every bit as much chance to as that Miss Fulton did."

I didn't correct her.

"And if he hadn't been so clever about finding her out people would have said Ruth and Foster were marrying so Ruth wouldn't have to testify against him," Mrs. Morton burbled on. "Yes, they would, Miss Tyler—oh, indeed they would! You don't know Annapolis as I do. And they do want to marry without delay, because Foster is waiting for orders, and he hopes he'll be sent to the South Pacific—"

That's the trouble with young naval officers, all of them. They don't have any sense. Here's Dick, for instance, who admits himself that teaching physics to midshipmen is highly essential, but who talks about combat duty with a light in his eyes that makes me want to spank him.

Well, it was a beautiful party, and speaking of light in people's eyes I've never seen a happier young couple. Ruth had on a white and silver dress and needed nothing extra but a pair of wings, and Foster was so bemused it was a wonder he got to the party at all. He got there late as it was; he couldn't make the bus he'd meant to take from Baltimore, and had to catch the very last one, the one that gets in at twenty minutes to eight. And dress afterwards, of course. But Mrs. Morton said nothing would be spoiled by waiting, and didn't seem to mind. I like to see a woman relax and enjoy herself at her own party, the way Mrs. Morton can. Maybe that's one reason it was so successful. Everybody was having a wonderful time. I kept seeing Ben Kramer dancing past with, as Sarah said, the most unlikely people, and he was having the night of his life.

Sarah Maccubbin and I were sitting together about twelve o'clock when Ben came over to us, looking annoyed. "Miss Julia, I may not be the ranking lady at this party, but I've got to leave. Call just came from the bus station. Probably it's nothing important, but they said nobody but me would do, and hung up. They got kind of used to me while I was working on the murders, I reckon."

"Oh, that's too bad," Sarah and I said.

"I can't find Mrs. Morton," Ben went on. "Would one of you tell her I was called away, and thank her—in case I don't get back?"

But just then Mrs. Morton herself sort of came to the surface of the crowd, the way people do when they've been dancing and the music stops. She looked mighty nice, almost thin, in a handsome black dress with sequins. I got up and put my hand on Ben's arm.

"There she is, Ben, and if you don't think your call's important I'd like to say good night too and go with you," I said. "I'm not the ranking lady either; but I'm old and tired and staying up too late, I know that."

But before that night was over I thought there was something to be said for Navy etiquette, after all. I wished I'd stayed where I was.

CHAPTER TWENTY

It was just beginning to sleet a little when Ben parked his car around the corner from the bus station—the closest he could get. I decided to wait for him right there. I couldn't afford to get my new black velvet wet. But I was already shivering—the car didn't have a heater, and it was getting bitterly cold—so when my eye lit on an inconspicuous little back or side door to the bus station, so close that I wouldn't get wet enough to mention, I decided I'd go inside.

It was the bus station's main waiting room the door opened into, but a remote corner of it. The ticket agent's enclosed cage stuck out so that you couldn't see the newsstand at all, and only a corner of the soda fountain, way on the other side of the big room. The front door, opening onto North Street, that Ben Kramer hadn't come through yet because my door had been a short cut, was in plain sight, and so were the big entrances to the two big loading platforms, as they call them, where the Baltimore and Washington buses come and go.

But I didn't notice all those things till later. Much later. I couldn't take my eyes off the thing I saw the minute I came through that little door.

It was Bill Palougous. Bill Palougous of all people, sitting upright on the high-backed bench facing me, with his gay yellow necktie spotted and stained with blood, and his fat, greasy face hurt and surprised-looking above it, and his little black snake-eyes staring unwaveringly for the last time.

There wasn't any weapon in the wound—no knife, or dagger, or knitting needle like the one that had killed Eleanor Barnes. Just the blood. It was all over the left side of his coat, too, as well as on the tie; it just didn't show because the cloth was dark. You couldn't see it at all unless you came closer.

"Don't touch him, Miss Julia!" Ben Kramer said.

I saw his face and the station agent's, a thin mediocre middle-aged face with pale blue eyes and a scraggly mustache and a receding chin. Then suddenly I had to put out both hands to catch hold of the bench back, and I reckon I made it because when I came to there were no bones broken.

I was all by myself when I opened my eyes—not that first person, as

Dick says, bending over me to ask if I was all right. For all Ben Kramer knew I had a weak heart and might have waked up in the next world, after a shock like that.

I was ashamed of myself too, though, in the midst of my indignation. Never again will I criticize poor Mrs. Latham for being upset when she finds a body. Theoretically she should, as I'd thought, have got used to it by this time. But so should I.

I kept on lying there and listened to Ben Kramer's voice, four or five feet away on the other side of the high-backed bench. I was perfectly able to get up and walk around there; but when a person has just dumped you down unconscious and gone off and left you it seems unnecessary to rush him reports on your condition. He too obviously isn't interested. Besides, I was afraid Ben would tell me to go on home; and, while I certainly wished I'd never come with him, now that I had I wanted to hear what the station agent had to tell.

Ben was saying: "Enough of that, now. Answer questions. What was Palougous doing in here, Mr. Jenkins? Was he waiting for a bus, or what?"

"He was waiting for a bus," Mr. Jenkins said unsteadily. "The nine-thirty bus. He just missed the seven-thirty by a minute or two, so he had to wait. It was such a bad night he said he'd rather wait here than go away and come back. That way he'd be sure not to miss the nine-thirty bus, he said. But he missed it after all."

The thin, scraggly voice rose hysterically.

"Now, Mr. Jenkins, no more of that." Ben was firm and not too kind, I thought. I knew just how Mr. Jenkins felt. "Did Palougous sit right here, or did he move around? What did he do? Did he talk to anybody?"

"Why, yes, he moved around," Mr. Jenkins said. "He moved around quite a bit. He went over to the soda fountain and had some coffee, I remember, and to the drinking fountain for water, and to the gents' lavatory once or twice. And then when anybody'd come into the station that he knew, why, he'd get up and come over and pass the time of day. He was just kind of bored waiting so long, I guess, and he just acted about the way anybody would."

"I'll take the names of the people he talked to," Ben said. Without seeing him I knew he had that disreputable notebook and pencil poised.

A lot of the people that Mr. Jenkins named I didn't know. But among the several ladies from out of town who stopped by "because we've got such a nice new powder room, decorator from Baltimore and all," there was one that I'd been unconsciously hoping was safe on Eastern Shore. I knew perfectly well that Mary Barnes was not a murderess three times over, but I couldn't blame Ben's voice for quickening as he repeated her name.

"Then there were two or three people I didn't know at all," Mr. Jenkins went on. "There was a fat man with one of those hand-painted neckties on, and a colored lady, and then the young lady Mr. Palougous drank his coffee with. A real pretty young lady with dark reddish hair. Ronald can tell you who she was, though."

"Ronald?"

"Ronald's our fountain clerk. Ronald Miller," Mr. Jenkins said. "This young lady came in to have a cup of coffee at our fountain, and Ronald had fixed it for her, of course, and she was standing there drinking it and talking to him, and Mr. Palougous heard them talking and came over. He bought the young lady another cup of coffee, and they took it over here and sat down, where Mr. Palougous had left his overcoat and things."

"That the Ronald Miller that's been working at Tracy's Drugstore?"

"Yes, sir," Mr. Jenkins said, wrenching his mind with obvious effort from the topic of the real pretty young lady with dark reddish hair. "Ronald just started here with us this week. He's a good fountain clerk, and I hope he's going to like it here and stay. Not that I see why he would," Mr. Jenkins added hopelessly. "Not with all this going on. Why, as far as I can remember Ronald was the last person to see Mr. Palougous alive, and so of course you'll want to question him too. I'm an old employee, I was at the other bus station before they built this one, and I don't mind. But for a new boy here—well, it *isn't* pleasant, lieutenant."

Ben said grimly: "It isn't meant to be. Tell me when Ronald Miller last saw Palougous. Can you fix the time?"

"It was just about nine-five or nine-ten," Mr. Jenkins answered promptly. "I know because it was just exactly eight fifty-six when the young lady went out the front door. I don't know why I looked at the clock right after I watched to see if she'd shut it, but I remember I did. And it wasn't ten minutes after that that I had occasion to pass in front of Mr. Palougous, sitting right here where he is now"—Mr. Jenkins gulped audibly but went on—"and noticed the dirty coffee cups on the floor. I went back and told Ronald to come and get them, and he did it right away."

"How about bus passengers? Nobody that left on the nine-thirty bus see him after Miller did? And isn't there an eleven-thirty outgoing bus too?"

"Yes, sir. They both go to Washington. But there weren't but a few people—people don't like to travel by bus at night after it starts to sleet and snow. And the loading platform for Washington is way over on the other side of the station from where Mr. Palougous was. No, sir, the only bus passengers that saw Mr. Palougous were the ones that came in on the Baltimore bus, and of course that was way before he was killed."

"When was that?" Ben asked. "You understand, Mr. Jenkins, I'm interested in anybody and everybody that saw Palougous waiting here, and had reason to know he'd be here for a while. Because maybe somebody came back. Came through this little door right here, while you were looking the other way."

Mr. Jenkins said, gulping: "Yes, sir. Well, sir, the Baltimore bus gets in at seven-forty, and I guess everybody on it saw him. And heard him, too. You see, that bus—it's the last one of the day that comes from Baltimore—got in just a minute or two after Mr. Palougous came tearing into the station and found out he'd missed *his* bus: the seven-thirty bus to Washington. He was plenty mad, I can tell you that. He said our clock was fast. I tried to tell him how we get our time from Western Union, and so on, but he didn't like it a bit. He made quite a commotion settling his things down over here, and saying he'd be damned if he was going out in the storm. He'd just sit right here till the next bus came, he said, and make damn sure *it* didn't go off without him."

"I want all the names of the passengers on that bus," Ben said then, of course.

But poor Mr. Jenkins had come to the end of his rope. He couldn't remember even one of the passengers who'd come on the seven-forty Baltimore bus.

Next day's *Evening Sun* had a partial list, though, compiled mostly from responses to the *Morning Sun's* appeal. Of course a citizen who had nothing on his conscience had nothing to lose by sending his name in. Neither had the citizen (the paper didn't say this, but it was the first thing I thought of) who knew somebody else would report him if he didn't do it himself.

I ran my finger down the list, looking for names I knew. Lieutenant (j.g.) John Foster Gibson, USN. Well, I was prepared for that. I knew that Foster had been in Baltimore that day, and got back late. Then— I thought my heart couldn't sink any lower, but it did. Miss Edith Dorsey. Ensign Gordon Smith, USN.

Foster and Ruth had lunch at our house the next day. It was a weekday, but Ruth's leave of absence had started when her engagement was announced. She'd stay in Annapolis till she married, and as long after that as Foster was there too. If he was ordered to his ship—and everybody seemed to think that was pretty sure—she'd go back to her job with the Baltimore Red Cross. She was crazy about it, in the first place, and used to having something to do. Besides, trained caseworkers are so scarce, these days, that it would be a crime for one to quit for a little thing like getting married.

Foster smiled back across the table at her, of course, when she said that, but *his* smile was definitely forced. Apparently it hadn't occurred to Ruth, bless her heart, that the groom might be spending the honeymoon in jail. The groom knew it all too well. He'd come considerably out of his pre-engagement daze, I thought, watching him; I was reminded of the night he'd mentioned his uncle's murder suspicions over our telephone, with the living room register wide open. Maybe he didn't realize, as we did, that he was Lieutenant Kramer's pet suspect, now restored to favor; but he had something else on his mind we didn't know about till later. He didn't have an alibi for the time of the murder. (Between nine-ten and eleven o'clock, the medical examiner said.) He hadn't been continuously at the Mortons' all evening. I could have sworn he had—it seemed to me every time I looked up he and Ruth were dancing past. Actually, as he later said himself, he'd slipped out right after dinner and made a quick trip to his apartment. In the hurry of getting dressed that night, knowing that he was already late for dinner, he'd forgotten to empty one set of pockets into the other. Among the things he'd left in the uniform he wore from Baltimore was the main thing he'd gone to Baltimore to get. There couldn't very well be an engagement party without an engagement ring.

It was a perfectly reasonable story, but nobody could verify it. Plenty of people had seen him leave the party and come back to it, but there was only his word for it that he'd gone to the apartment. He might have gone back to the bus station and murdered Bill Palougous. Quite a lot of people were going to think he had, that his conspicuous dash off the bus and through the station had been conspicuous on purpose, and that later he'd come back through that unobtrusive little back or side door, not six feet from the bench on which I'd found Palougous dead.

So might anyone else, of course. Gordon Smith might have come back. Or Edith Dorsey. Or Mary Barnes. And of course Ronald Miller, who'd been the last person to see Bill Palougous alive, might not have needed to come back. For all the police and Mr. Jenkins knew, he might have sat down beside his victim on the bench, and reached over and stabbed him without fuss, and then calmly got up and carried the coffee cups away.

And of course any of the other people, the ones I didn't know, could have come back and stabbed Palougous too. That was a possibility the police had to bear in mind, but they didn't really think so. Nor did I. Nor did the newspapers. They all thought Bill Palougous' connection with Eleanor Barnes' murder was too obvious to be overlooked. Even the conservative *Baltimore Sun* ran a big headline this time, and the *Post* really went to town, as Dick says. There was even what they call a sob story about poor Gladys Fulton, locked up for killing Eleanor Barnes when actually the murderer was still at large.

I never could get used to the way the papers mentioned Mrs. Barnes' murder but not Dr. Mosser's. That was so sharply in the front of my consciousness, too, that it was always surprising to remember that the Mosser murder had been hushed up, and the papers and almost everybody else thought he'd died of ordinary heart attack.

But Bill Palougous' death was, as the *Evening Capital* said the day after, a palpable murder in the most horrible tradition.

Poor Ben! I thought to myself. But it wasn't Ben I mostly felt sorry for.

Dick had to go back to the Academy right after lunch, as usual, and not long after that Foster said he must be going, too. We were all surprised, because Wednesday is one of the afternoons which, according to the Experiment Station's rather complicated schedule, he usually has off. Finally it developed that Lieutenant Kramer—Foster didn't look at Ruth as he said it—had asked him to drop in about two o'clock.

It was another one of the nasty bad days we'd been having, all sleet and snow, and Foster had a cold. Anyway it always goes to Anne's head when her coupons come due and she gets the gas tank filled. So what with one thing and another she insisted on driving Foster to the police station, and of course Ruth and I went along.

We didn't drive right on after Foster left us. We just sat there and watched the people going in—all the people, apparently, who had any connection with the Palougous murder. It was quite a procession. The seven-forty bus from Baltimore had been full, and quite a lot of people had, as Mr. Jenkins told Ben, stopped in the station to buy magazines or cigarettes, or drink a Coca-Cola at the soda fountain, or use the beautiful new powder room. Most of them were people we didn't know. It didn't seem tactful to call out greetings to the ones we did, so we let them all go past in equal silence. Miss Edith Dorsey, first, and Gordon Smith just behind. Then Dorothy Hamilton and her mother. Mrs. Bruner saw us and waved; you would have thought we were old friends, and of course we all waved back. Dorothy smiled and bowed too, after her mother pointed us out. She had on a quite amazing hat with a tall blue feather, and her hair underneath it had had still another henna rinse. Of course! Dorothy Hamilton had been the girl of Mr. Jenkins' testimony, the one who'd had the cup of coffee with Bill Palougous. "Dark reddish hair"—well, it certainly was. Awful. Then came Mr. Jenkins himself, and Ronald Miller close behind. I looked at that poor boy's twitching, skin-and-bones hands and an idea struck me. It was worth developing, I thought; but just then Mary Barnes passed by, and I forgot all about it. She was the last of the line, following a group of people I didn't know. She walked slowly by herself, and her face was the saddest thing I ever saw.

"Please let me out at the corner of College Avenue and Bladen, Anne," Ruth said abruptly.

I looked at her in surprise; Anne hadn't even started the car. She did then, of course, and we drove the few blocks in silence. I didn't know what to say to the poor child—Ruth, I mean. Naturally she was upset. But she'd got hold of herself by the time we turned into College Avenue, and thanked us for lunch and said goodbye as nicely as usual.

"Come back and see us, my dear. Oftener, now," I said.

"Oh, much oftener!" Ruth answered, smiling. "I'll see you again soon."

It was much sooner than we thought.

I'd just gone to bed, and the clock had just struck eleven, that night when our telephone rang. I could hear Dick answering, though I couldn't hear what he said, and then he banged on my door.

"Aunt Julia! Can you get dressed and be on your way to Baltimore in fifteen minutes?"

"Is anything— Is it Anne?" I managed to get out. I was scared to death, the way you naturally would be.

"Anne's all right. She's right here. It's Ruth, Aunt Julia. Hurry, can't you? Ruth's in the hospital in Baltimore, and Ben can't locate the Mortons, and we were the only friends he knew to call. I'll have the car out in front right away."

Ben? Well, it certainly wasn't any time to talk or ask questions. I put my clothes on with shaking fingers—hind part before, as likely as not. But then I did think of something I had to know, and I opened my door and called across the stair landing to Dick.

"Have they got hold of Foster Gibson?"

Dick came to his door with his clothes half on, pulling desperately at a coat sleeve.

"They've got hold of him all right," he said grimly. "They've got him in jail. Now, Aunt Julia, scram."

That trip to Baltimore was the wildest ride I ever hope to take. Dick is a good driver, and normally I never think of worrying; but this night the road was slick, and we were going faster than we should have on those old tires. We didn't talk much. At first we said a few things like

"Thank goodness we could get gas this morning!" and "I wonder where the Mortons are." But the last three-fourths of the trip we made in silence.

I'd never been in the Johns Hopkins Hospital before, and I hope I never have to go again. If that's the finest hospital in the world I'd rather be sick at home. It was a gloomy, ugly old red-brick building—the main building, that is—and a big statue of Jesus loomed up frighteningly at us as we went in the lobby. It was more the size for Bedloe's Island than indoors, and judging from the effect it had on me, a lifelong Christian in perfectly good health, I could imagine how some of the incoming patients might react. Dick told our life history to a girl at a desk, and then we went up in the elevator, and down one corridor and up another, till I was completely lost. Finally the nurse who'd come with us stopped at a door with a "No Visitors" sign.

Ruth was lying in the high white hospital bed looking more dead than alive. There was a bandage covering part of her head, and her eyes were half open and rolled up till she looked perfectly ghastly. Her breath was coming in short jerky sobs that were alarming enough, but the way she looked it was a relief to hear her breathe at all. There was a nurse at the head of the bed, holding Ruth's wrist and looking at a chart the way they do, and there were two doctors who spoke to us very nicely. The gray-haired one had a big, booming voice that shocked me; it seemed to roll from one side of the sickroom to the other and bounce back off the wall. I must have showed what I felt because the doctor laughed. That was awful, like an earthquake.

"She can't hear me, you know," he said cheerfully. I didn't see anything very funny about it. "Miss Tyler, isn't it? I'm Dr. West. This is Dr. McClean, Miss Tyler. Mrs. Travers. Mr. Travers. Miss Allein's going to do nicely now, I'm glad to say. She had us scared for a little, but now she's coming right along."

Anne and Dick shook hands with no special reaction; Dr. Peter McClean's name meant nothing to them. But I looked with considerable interest at the young man Sarah Maccubbin had thought Ruth would marry. He really was attractive, big and blond and dependable-looking, and apparently as nice as I'd thought Foster Gibson was. I felt completely dazed. Foster Gibson might have murdered Eleanor Barnes and Dr. Mosser and Bill Palougous, but I couldn't imagine him hurting a hair of Ruth's head, and that was what Dr. West was booming out.

"Understand the police have got the young man who did it in jail. Good work. All sorts of young men in uniform these days; can't tell a thing by the way officers look and act. Guess you've found that out, Mr. Travers. But then, maybe it'll be an ill wind. Miss Haynes here tells me Miss Allein's engagement to him was in the paper."

Dr. Peter McClean looked acutely uncomfortable. I expect we all did.

"These social workers! Get so they don't think there *are* any bad characters, you know," Dr. West went on chattily. "And never think anything's going to happen to *them*. That's a bad district her Red Cross building's in—dark as your hat. These women ought to know better than to go in and out late at night. Feel sorry for this one, though. Not a nice thing to wake up to—come out after a hard day's work and find your fiancé waiting to tap you on the head."

White-capped Miss Haynes had been waiting patiently to say something. Medical etiquette is at least as strict as the Navy's, and this Dr. West was, as we found out later, a very famous doctor. Nurses and younger doctors didn't interrupt him even when the patient was dying, much less just coming to.

I didn't think a thing of him, myself. However much Ruth had heard of what he said, it was too much. She was white as a sheet and looked as if she'd lost ten pounds since afternoon—maybe that part was the effect of her injury. But it was the doctor's fault that her eyes were desperate and her voice sounded as if she were choking. "He did not! Don't you dare say things like that! I—I fell. The pavement was icy, and I fell."

"There, there, Miss Allein," Dr. West said. "Go easy, there. Don't you worry about anything. Just take it easy, and you're going to be all right."

His insultingly soothing tone had even worse effect on Ruth than it did on me, and I'm sure it didn't help to hear Miss Haynes saying under her breath, "Poor girl! Poor girl!" I could have slapped her too.

"Where's Foster? Why isn't he here?" Ruth flung off the doctor's hand and tried to sit up in bed. She almost made it, but her head must have been pretty badly hurt. She fell back before Miss Haynes could catch her, and for a minute she looked like death itself. But as soon as Dr. West bent over her with some more of that take-it-easy-just-don't-worry kind of talk her eyes popped open again and she was wide awake and fighting mad.

"Dr. West, you're doing more harm than good," I said finally. I'd stood all I could. I motioned him and Miss Haynes out of my way, and they were both so flabbergasted they actually stood aside. Miss Haynes' mouth was really all the way open. "Ruth, my dear, it's Julia Tyler," I said. "You've had a bad knock on the head. I don't think Foster did it either. I don't see how he could. But you know policemen aren't any too smart"—I was thankful Ben Kramer wasn't there to hear me, because I didn't really think so—"and they put him in jail. But he's all right;

he'll get out again. And you want to be all well by then, don't you?"

"I want him out now!" Ruth said, and began to cry. "Miss Julia, you know that police lieutenant. Please go talk to him. Tell him I slipped and fell. It wasn't Foster's fault. He was just waiting for me. He didn't hit me, Miss Julia. You know that."

I said firmly: "Maybe not, Ruth. But I'm not going down to police headquarters and tell Ben Kramer you slipped and fell. People don't fall on ice and hit the top of their heads. I'll go down and see him, though, and I'll see Foster and bring you a message. I'll go right now. Will that make you feel better?"

"Get him out," Ruth said feverishly. "Tell Lieutenant Kramer a client hit me. Don't tell him I slipped. Tell him a client did it. It happens every once in a while. Sometimes they hate you and think you're working against them. Tell him it was a client that wanted to kill me—"

Dr. West gave me a dirty look, as Dick calls it, as if to say I wasn't doing too well myself. He nodded to the other young doctor, and Dr. McClean came up to the bed with a hypodermic needle in his hand. The needle went in so smoothly and casually that Ruth hardly noticed it, but anyway he was the kind of doctor who didn't need to sedate his patients to calm them down. They calmed themselves. Ruth smiled and spoke to him in quite a different voice, and put out her hand as if she wanted to touch something solid, poor child. Maybe this solid young doctor, who was supposed to be so brilliant and so rich and whose mother was a Tilghman from Eastern Shore, and who liked and disliked the same things Ruth did, could make her forget the charming young naval officer who'd turned out to be a murderer. It didn't seem too likely. But then I remembered *Death in the Air*, where exactly the same thing happened, the man everybody'd thought was the hero turning out to be the murderer instead, but the other nice young man being right there in reserve. I take some pride in being able to adjust to circumstances suddenly changed, and before young Dr. McClean had finished bending over the bed I'd worked out a nice new little romance with a happy ending.

It was funny that I felt so low in my mind as I went down the hall.

CHAPTER TWENTY-ONE

I took a taxi to the Baltimore Police Headquarters, which had both Ben Kramer's office and the holdover in it. It wasn't too far away, a five-story brick and stone building on the Fallsway. I'd seen it before, I remembered, the day Anne and Dick took me down in that part of town to see the Flag House and the old Shot Tower and so on. It looked grimmer now, in the middle of the night; or maybe it was just because somebody I liked was shut up in it.

I didn't have a bit of trouble getting in to see Ben Kramer. Evidently they didn't take him so hard, as Dick says, in his own department as they did in Annapolis. Detective lieutenants on the Baltimore police force were probably a dime a dozen.

Ben and I shook hands—neither of us felt like smiling much while we did it—and I asked if I could see Foster Gibson. "Ruth seems to think you've got him in leg irons anyway, and not even bread and water to eat."

"On the contrary, Miss Julia, he doesn't have a care in the world," Ben said. "He fought arrest, but now he's settled down and relaxed—says he doesn't mind a bit staying in jail while we find the real murderer. He told the guard he didn't expect it would take me long—I didn't really think he'd hurt Miss Allein."

"Well, what *do* you think, Ben?" I asked.

Ben spread out his hands. "Well, I keep thinking about the way he looked at her when they were dancing, Miss Julia. I never saw it done better in the movies. But of course the movies aren't the real thing, either. He was caught right in the act, you know. You can't get away from that."

"No, you can't. Well, I'd like to see him anyway, Ben. I promised Ruth," I said. "Can I see him by myself?"

Ben shook his head. "This is a man in jail for attempted murder, Miss Julia; and probably for the three bus station murders too. You'd better let me stay around. We'll have him in here, and I hope you'll get a better story than I've been able to."

But I didn't get a better story. Foster told me just exactly what he'd told Ben. He'd been waiting in his car across the street, he said, when Ruth came out of the Red Cross building. She'd called him late in the afternoon and told him where she was, which was a surprise because she hadn't intended, so far as he knew, going into Baltimore that day. She asked him to pick her up at the door at nine o'clock, but said she might be a little late.

Actually it was after ten when she turned out her office light and came downstairs. Foster'd been watching that light, but when the time came he didn't see it go off after all. He was tired and bored and hadn't had but four hours' sleep the night before. He wasn't exactly asleep this time, he said, but he was too far gone either to see or hear Ruth the first minute she came out. He looked up just in time to see her collapse on the wet pavement, and to see a dark figure cast something dark from its hand—the police had found a bloody half-brick, Ben said, sans fingerprints—and streak around the corner of Calvert Street.

"I can't describe him any better than that, Miss Julia," Foster Gibson said. "I don't even know whether he had on a topcoat, or what he had on his head. I just couldn't see. But he was young, I'd swear to that much. I could tell by the way he ran. I'm not sure I could have caught him even if those two policemen hadn't caught *me*. But I was hacked at the time, you understand. I hope I didn't mess up your men too much, lieutenant."

"You damn near broke one of 'em's back," Ben said. "Been practicing up to fight the Japanese, haven't you?"

"So you started after him, Foster," I prodded. "You mean you didn't even stop to see about Ruth?"

Foster Gibson laughed shortly. "Miss Julia, you're as *Romantische Schule* as the lieutenant here. He thinks that's the weak spot in my story too. He thinks I should have stayed there and held her, or carried her over to the car, or something. He thinks the fact I left her lying in a puddle is proof positive I was the one that hit her on her head."

Well, I didn't say anything, but leaving that poor child on the cold pavement, much less actually in a puddle— Well, I could see Ben's point of view.

"But, Miss Julia, I thought she was dead. She looked dead, and the blood was coming out of that place on her head, and I couldn't find her pulse. I tried. And of course I'd have stayed there with her if I hadn't had a job to do. But it seemed to me my job was to catch the man that killed her. That's what Lieutenant Kramer here can't see."

Ben said wearily: "I see it all right, Gibson. It could have happened, of course. But it also happens that every last murderer we've ever caught running away from the scene of the crime has told exactly the same story you have."

It made me feel strictly awful, as Dick says, to watch Foster Gibson going back to the lockup between two policemen. Maybe Ruth was going to marry the other young man after all, but this one had never looked nicer to me than he did in his torn, disheveled Navy blues that I'd never even seen mussed before, nor his hair either.

I was just gathering up my bag and gloves to go when the young policeman who seems to be Ben's personal maid knocked on the door and brought in Anne and Dick. I wasn't surprised to see them, of course. I rather thought they'd be along as soon as Ruth dropped off to sleep and everything seemed all right. Dick feels strongly about my taking taxicabs at night by myself, and had told me so within the last hour.

But I was surprised to see him handing a big plain Manila envelope to Ben, and telling him Ruth had sent it and it was all right for him to read it. She'd got permission.

"She had it in her bag all the time," added Anne. "But she just didn't think to give it to Aunt Julia, because she was so fit to be tied at the time. And when she thought about it she got all upset again, and the doctor had to give her another hypodermic."

"Is she all right now?" I asked anxiously, and they nodded.

"Dropped right off as soon as we promised to sit here and watch Ben read it. Otherwise she'd be awake yet, hypodermics or no hypodermics. That girl is plenty stubborn," Dick said.

"That girl gets too many things promised her." Ben included me in the official glance of rebuke. "But all right. I love to read at half-past one in the morning."

There was complete silence in the little office for quite a long time then, broken only by the crackle when Ben turned a page. There were twelve or fifteen of them: stapled, closely typed, rather blurry carbons, with what looked like topic headings at intervals on the page. But I couldn't read even those upside down. Several times I made out a word or so, but just then Ben would turn a page.

He read it fast, and then he turned back to the first and read it straight through again. Finally, without saying "Boo pussy cat" to any of us, much less please excuse me, he got up and bolted out of the room and was gone a good hour anyway.

After the first fifteen minutes Anne said something about going home and getting to bed. "He's probably gone to Annapolis chasing a clue. I bet he won't be back at all."

But Dick and I glared her down. "Things are popping. I'm staying here," Dick said, and I agreed.

Even we were pretty tired, though, by the time that Ben got back. It was way after half-past two. But Ben was fresh as a daisy—excited about something, and not trying too hard to hide it. "Still with me? Well, I'm glad you like it here so much," he said. I sniffed. "Because I have to stick around awhile myself—just a little while, maybe—and I'm glad to have company. What do you want to talk about?"

"There's only one thing in this world we're interested in, Ben Kramer," I told him solemnly. "And that's murder."

"Well, that's a nice thing for a Virginia lady to say, Miss Julia!" Ben certainly was feeling plenty high, as Dick says.

"You could sum up the case, the way Hercule Poirot does," offered Anne. "And take the suspects one at a time, and say why you thought they did it and then how you found out they didn't—"

"Afraid I wouldn't get very far," Ben said blithely. "Not that I don't know plenty now. But any minute—any minute, my dear child—that little black telephone in front of you may ring, and *whoo-oo-osh!*"

You would have thought I'd taught him in high school two years ago instead of twenty-odd. I said dryly, "Well, you could make a start," and finally Ben calmed down and did.

"Not that I was any Hercule Poirot in this case," he began ruefully. "I was nearly the world's biggest fool. But we had eight suspects without alibis, and a couple more whose alibis were pretty shaky; and as for the assortment of first-rate, watertight motives—well, if *all* the suspects had taken a poke at Eleanor Barnes, on their way out of that bus, I wouldn't have been surprised."

"Like *Murder in the Calais Coach*—"

"But since there wasn't but the one stab wound," Ben went on, smiling at Anne, "we were up against the problem of finding, not necessarily the best motive, but the motive that had prompted action. That made it into a psychological problem. We had to look for a person who would react to a solution like murder.

"At first glance it didn't look like Mary Barnes, in spite of her good strong motive and the evidence against her. She'd already taken so much—and taken it so well. Even the people who criticized her admired her, too, for letting the admiral go as she did, so his career wouldn't be hurt, and refusing to take any alimony. Don't think she didn't want to hang onto him, either. There aren't any pictures of him downstairs, naturally, but up in her bedroom she's got just exactly eight, counting snapshots. And by the way, Miss Julia!"

I recognized the tone I've often used when students didn't bring in their homework.

"I expect you'd like to know what that package had in it, the one Mary Barnes put in your handbag."

Anne and Dick looked at me in wonder; it was the first they'd heard of it. I had the grace to blush, but I said defiantly, "Yes, I would."

"It was still another picture of the admiral," Ben said. "A miniature he gave her on their tenth wedding anniversary. She'd taken it to Baltimore to have the ring on it fixed—it's the kind that hangs round your neck—and when Kirk said he couldn't do it till after Christmas she wrapped it up again and brought it back with her. I reckon she couldn't do without it that long. Talk about a man's being a hero to his valet—Mary Barnes was married to him thirty-four years, but she still thought Roger Barnes was Lord God Almighty."

"He must have had something, definitely," Dick said.

I said: "I've felt bad about not telling you about the package, Ben. But I promised Mary Barnes—it was before you even came to see us—and a promise is a promise."

"Of course it is, Miss Julia. That's all right," Ben said, very nicely, I thought. He went on with his story. "Well, I never did think it was psychologically sound for a woman like Mary Barnes to wait three years after his death and then kill a successful rival, no matter how much she resented it and hated *her*. But when her son needed money—Well, that was something else again. She was nearly out of her mind worrying about him. And she was just about as worried about her grandson, of course, and about that sick daughter-in-law of hers. Lots of women don't care much for their relatives by marriage, but Mary Barnes was the kind that loved hers like real."

I reached over and patted Dick's Navy-blue knee.

It still didn't sound like Mary Barnes, as I've said. But people can be pushed just so far.

"Then there was Foster Gibson—take him next because his was a money motive too. He stood to lose quite a bit of cash if old Mr. Foster married Eleanor Barnes. Add to that the fact that Gibson knew the lady personally and by reputation, knew what a wreck she'd made of the admiral after she married him, and naturally didn't want his uncle messed up too. He's crazy about his uncle, over and above the money part. It just about killed him when Mr. Foster decided he murdered Eleanor Barnes."

"What about the dagger in the secret drawer?" Dick wanted to know.

Ben laughed. "Fine touch of melodrama, wasn't it? And perfectly simple, once you know the answer. Mr. Foster just gave it to him. They didn't start quarreling the minute Gibson got to Philadelphia, naturally; they talked about other things for a while and it was all very nice till they got on the subject of Eleanor Barnes, and Gibson started giving out good advice. Old people just can't take it."

"Neither can young people," I said snappishly, and Ben grinned.

"Nor middle-aged people, like me. Nobody can. Well, anyway, they started out nice as pie, and Mr. Foster showed Gibson a lot of stuff he'd just had sent to him from a friend's estate—personal property, everything from junk to good antiques. Gibson took a fancy to the dagger and two or three little medallions, and his uncle insisted he take them. He put the stuff in his pocket, with appropriate speeches, and then forgot about it in the heat of the quarrel."

"When did he sharpen the dagger?" asked Anne.

"Not till several days later, he says. And he didn't actually sharpen it then. It just looked as if he had. The blade was rusty—good steel, but

Mr. Foster's friend had lived up on Cape Cod and the salt air had attacked it—so Gibson just polished it off with emery cloth. He likes antiques, but he likes them all nicely cleaned and refinished."

"One more thing," Dick said. "That telephone conversation we heard, when he said his uncle suspected him of killing Eleanor Barnes. What'd he mean when he said he couldn't get it from Uncle John?"

"What do you think? Money again," Ben said. "Friend of his wanted to borrow and couldn't put up enough security. Gibson promised to ask his uncle; but then they quarreled, and he couldn't very well. At least not successfully."

"Well, that's that. I always knew Foster Gibson was no killer," I said smugly.

"But he is, Miss Julia. That's why the Navy's sending him to the South Pacific." Ben took the wind out of my sails. "Gibson's a trained, cool-headed killer, and so is Gordon Smith, and so is George Campbell. Gibson and Smith haven't had their chance yet, but Campbell's got Germans and Italians and Japs, all three, and one of those ribbons is for the prettiest piece of wholesale killing I've heard of in this war."

"How about your other killer? Palougous?" Dick wanted to know.

"Well, Palougous. He looked like a good chance until he got it himself, in spite of having an alibi for Eleanor Barnes' murder," Ben said. "He *might* have reached across Mosser. Matter of fact, though, he didn't have any reason to kill her at all. They were on good terms. They'd had one little deal a few years back that came out fine; she paid his lawyer when he was in a tight place, and he did a job for her. Of course after she was murdered he thought he'd better remove the evidence of the deal."

"What was the job he did for her?"

"Let me save that for a while, will you, Miss Julia?" Ben said. "Let's just say for the present that he didn't have any reason to kill Eleanor Barnes or Dr. Mosser, either one.

"Miss Edith Dorsey, now, had an excellent reason to want to kill them both. You know the part about Mrs. Barnes. But did you know that Dr. Mosser was the man who voted *for* her, the first time Eleanor Barnes tried to get her out of her job, and *against* her this year? He was back in Annapolis, trying to make a fresh start, and Eleanor Barnes said she was willing to help if he'd do that little thing for her."

"But what was a man like Dr. Mosser doing on the Howard House Association board?" I couldn't help asking. "A jailbird?"

"He wasn't a jailbird when he was elected, though, Miss Julia," Ben said reasonably. "Election is for a five-year term, and he stayed right on the board the whole time he was in the penitentiary. He even got to proxy his vote while he was in there. The by-laws hadn't foreseen a situation of that kind, and didn't provide for disqualifying a board member that fell from grace in the middle of his term."

I sniffed.

"Oh, that's common enough, Aunt Julia," Dick said. "I doubt they'd have put Palougous on the Annapolis draft board after he shot John Evans. But he was already on, he was technically clear, and so he got to stay."

Anne broke in. "Before you get off Dr. Mosser, aren't you going to tell us about the 'documents'? Didn't you ever find out what they were?"

"Oh, yes, we did," Ben said. "And they were so unimportant that I forgot to mention them. One of those blind alleys you go up in every murder case. I got all worked up about those 'documents,' thinking they were going to be either Dr. Mosser's own confession or his implication of somebody else. Actually they were just statements from two of his friends, saying they'd been with him continuously all afternoon and had put him on the bus. Meaning, of course, that he'd had no chance to give Mrs. Barnes morphine. The two friends had their statements all nicely typed out and notarized, the way Dr. Mosser had asked them to do, but then when they heard he was dead they didn't see any use sending them."

"Did Bill Palougous know about the papers? Is that what he went to Dr. Mosser's house to steal, the night after he died?"

Ben shook his head. "No, he didn't, Anne. And he didn't go to Mosser's house to steal anything. He went there to plant some evidence, so the police would think the doctor had murdered Eleanor Barnes and would close the case. He must have thought the police were pretty dumb. The evidence was kid stuff."

"But why was he so anxious to get the case closed?" I asked. "If he wasn't the murderer—"

"Because he was like a lot of other people who've been in trouble before," answered Ben. "He believed the police had it in for him. Matter of fact, we did. We knew as well as he did that John Evans' death was cold-blooded murder. But the law is pretty law-abiding; you'd be surprised. We wouldn't have hung a murder on him that he didn't do.

"Well, then there was Ronald Miller," Ben went on. "He had an alibi for the Barnes murder, just as Palougous did. But none of those alibis was too hard and fast, and anyway I thought he was more likely to be an accomplice than the actual murderer. I couldn't scare up any motive for his killing those people, though I've certainly tried since I found out why they fired him from Tracy's Drugstore. He'd been making way with morphine."

"I'm not surprised to hear it," I said. "The way he jerks!" I felt rather pleased with myself. Ronald Miller's possible addiction to drugs—and they say people like that will do anything in the world to get it—had been the idea that struck me while I watched the witnesses going into police headquarters.

Ben nodded. "I found out finally he just stole it for himself. He didn't have anything to do with the murders. I'm just telling you so you'll know how much work I did."

"You certainly worked up a good case against that poor Fulton woman," Dick said with an impolite grin.

"Well, it *was* a good case," said Ben defensively. "She did have that sharp knife in her bag—but all the rest of the ladies would have had paring knives, too, if they'd known that dime store had just got in a shipment. Cutlery's been hard to find, since the war. That's why it looked so extra bad when she buried it. But she was no fool by any means, and she got the wind up about her potential weapon just the way Gibson did.

"The other points against Miss Fulton evaporate the same way. She did ask Mrs. Kleinschmidt to buy her a bracelet in New York, and she did serve Eleanor Barnes a perfectly innocent Coca-Cola. Just as she said. But I still say she had a swell setup for the first murder. All the alibiless ones did—including Dr. Mosser, who looked about the blackest of the lot till he got his. And some of them were naturals for Dr. Mosser's murder, too. But only one had the shadow of a reason for killing Bill Palougous.... Well, I did get through. I wish that telephone would ring."

It didn't, but there was a knock on the door instead.

"Okay, lieutenant," the personal maid said.

"Okay?" Ben was around the corner of the desk before you could say "Jack Robinson," but this time he did stop at the door and speak to us. "Well, Miss Julia, Anne, Dick, I'm going down to make an arrest. Not the kind they can sue me for this time. The real thing. Wait for me if you want to, or get to bed and read it in the papers."

"We won't do either," I said firmly, getting up. "Do you seriously think, Ben Kramer, that after all this we don't intend to see it through? We're going with you."

"You certainly are not, Miss Julia." Ben was madder than I was, mad at being delayed. "Who do you think I am—Lieutenant Weigand, taking my friends along for the ride? I'm going on police business in a police car."

The door banged.

"Well, it's a good thing we've got our own transportation," Dick said. He jerked open the door Ben had slammed, and pushed Anne and me out in front of him. Ben was already out of sight around a corner, but we were right behind the sound of his footsteps. In just a minute we were out in the cold clammy fresh air, and the police car was lurching away from the curb with the siren already going, and Dick had slid into ours and started the engine while Anne and I got in the best way we could.

It was another wild ride we took, I suppose, but this time I didn't notice. I was too excited to feel anything else, and when our car drew up in front of the Baltimore bus station, right behind the car that Ben was in, I just tumbled out with Anne and Dick and followed at his heels.

He didn't even notice us. A young policeman met him at the door and pointed across the waiting room, and Ben nodded his head and started walking that way, fast, with the young policeman behind him. And Anne and Dick and I weren't the only ones behind *him*. There was quite a crowd to see when the slim young figure in dark slacks jumped up from a bench and whirled around and tossed a mop of dark-red hair back from a frightening face. But they only heard the first few words of the charge that I for one had read in so many murder books: "Dorothy Hamilton, I arrest—"

The slim dark-sleeved arm shot up then, and somebody in the crowd screamed. Ben wasn't touched; one policeman had made a flying tackle, and another had grabbed the knife arm at the wrist. Held up in the air like that, the knife was there for everybody in the crowd to see, as if it had been a trophy. It was a trophy, too. Though she hadn't been able to reach Ben Kramer with it, the knife was brown two inches up the blade with dried dark blood.

CHAPTER TWENTY-TWO

"I'm sorry I was impolite, Miss Julia," Ben Kramer said. He was standing on the sidewalk outside the police headquarters, and Anne and Dick and I were sitting in our car at the curb. I'd wanted to go on home, now that it was really over—the sight of that poor girl's face had been enough for me, much less the knife with Bill Palougous' blood. I think Anne would have liked to go home too. But Dick had started the car after Ben's with so much enthusiasm that I hated to say a word.

Ben had gone back alone in his car. They'd had to call a police wagon for Dorothy Hamilton. Even with Ben and the two strong young policemen who'd located her—calmly waiting for the next bus back to

Annapolis—there wasn't any chance of getting her to the lockup in an ordinary car. She was really violent. They often are when they realize the game is up, Ben says.

I felt a little ashamed of myself, sitting there waiting to see the humiliation and fear of another human being. It didn't alter the fact that she was a murderess three times over, or that as a citizen and taxpayer—well, of course I don't pay taxes in Maryland, but Anne and Dick do—I had a perfect right to be there if I liked. It just wasn't a very nice thing for a person to do.

I had plenty of company, though. Two cars besides ours had followed Ben's back from the bus station, and now at least half a dozen more were stopping in the wake of the Black Maria, which drew up and parked in the space reserved for police vehicles. I don't see how they do it in these days of gas rationing, but Ben says there are always cars that follow after when they've made an arrest, no matter how bad the weather or what time of night it is.

I'd hoped Dorothy Hamilton wouldn't see us, but she did. Naturally she glanced in the direction Ben had come from, when he left Anne and Dick and me and joined her as she got out of the wagon. She was perfectly calm and composed now, poor thing. Of course they couldn't tell when or how she'd break out again, though, so a handcuff linked her wrist to a big fat policeman's, and the two young policemen who would get credit for the arrest—one of them bleeding like a stuck pig from the lines those long red fingernails had dug in his face—stood behind her with their espantoons fairly twitching.

Dorothy Hamilton and Ben stood there and talked for what seemed to us a long time. We couldn't hear a word they said; but she seemed to be telling him off, as Dick says, still quietly but in no uncertain terms, and he was trying to reason with her. Finally Ben shook his head as if to say, "I give up," and to our surprise made his way back to our car.

Anne rolled the side window glass down so we could talk.

Ben said, halfway between apology and irritation: "Miss Julia, will you do the Department a favor? The prisoner wants to talk to you. Not to me. She says she's perfectly willing to tell all about the murders, how she did them, why she did them—everything. But if she can't tell it to you, she says, she won't tell it at all. She says as far as she's concerned we can wonder about it till hell freezes over."

"Well, but you can get your information other ways. You've got plenty to convict her already," Dick said. "I haven't got that first idea of letting Aunt Julia within talking distance of that hyena."

"Oh, I'm not afraid of her, Dick. She'd still be handcuffed, wouldn't she, Ben, and you'd be right there?" I asked, and Ben nodded. "But I don't understand why she wants to tell me about it. It's not any of my business, as she knows."

Ben said: "Well, she just seems to think you'd get her point of view better than I would, Miss Julia. They want to justify themselves sometimes, and apparently it matters to her what you think about her. She just likes you—says you were always nice, and stopped and talked on the street, and so on. I'd appreciate it a lot if you'd humor her, Miss Julia. She's not normal, you know. We have to make allowances. And we can't push a case like that. Of course, as Dick says, we can convict without a full confession; but I'm mighty anxious to hear it all and I bet you are too."

Well, after considerable argument back and forth we agreed that I'd do it—interview her the best I could, that is; and we settled ourselves in Ben's office, and Dorothy Hamilton was brought in. We were all there, even Anne, who wouldn't leave me but who was frankly scared. I wasn't exactly scared, but I was nervous; and I nearly laughed hysterically when I saw Anne take a paperweight off Ben's desk, a heavy bronze thing shaped like a horse, and sit down with it in her lap.

"I'll begin anywhere you want me to," Dorothy Hamilton said. "Do you want me to tell how I killed them first, or why I had to do it?"

I said: "Suppose you tell it in your own way, any way you want to. And maybe I'll ask you some questions as you go along. Will that be all right?"

"Yes, ma'am." Dorothy looked at me with the trusting dark eyes of a nice little dog. It was hard to believe she was the same girl I'd seen half an hour before with her face contorted and her body twisting and that horrible brown-stained knife in her hand. "I'd like to begin at the beginning. I want to tell you everything. I just didn't want to tell *him*."

She said it as if Ben Kramer weren't sitting right there in plain sight, all ears.

She began: "Well, you know what it was like at home, Miss Tyler. Mamma thought it was awful when I left, but time I was sixteen I just couldn't stand it any longer. They let you stop school then and go to work. I got me a job entertaining at the Mirage."

"That's right here in Baltimore, isn't it?" I asked. Sarah Maccubbin had told me about that place, a regular dive down in the burlesque district. She was on the board of something or other that was trying to clean it up.

"Yes, ma'am. I danced in the chorus, and after the show I'd sit with the customers. It's not a regular joint, Miss Tyler, but it's not the Mount Vernon Club either. People like Jimmy don't come there unless they've had a few first. Jimmy was a regular souse. Maybe I oughtn't to talk about him now that he's dead, but he was."

"If you knew that before you married him, why did you do it?" I added, trying to soften the impertinent question: "A pretty girl like you—"

"Well, I guess it was because I *was* a pretty girl, Miss Tyler," Dorothy Hamilton said, unsmiling. "And I'd been through sophomore in high school, and I knew I could do as good in society as anybody, if I just had the chance. Jimmy was society, all right. But I thought he had money, and he didn't. I wouldn't have married him if I'd known that. I wouldn't have married him if I'd known about that old—about his mother, either. She treated me like dirt. What that woman got was a lot too good for her."

She spoke with a calm detachment, but it wasn't that that made me gasp.

"Yes, ma'am, that was why I killed her," Dorothy Hamilton said earnestly. "She was awful. She was a devil. She wouldn't even let me in when I went to see her. And when I'd write to her she'd send the letters back. I tried, Miss Tyler. I tried awful hard to get acquainted. But she never even got close enough to know what I looked like. I guess she was sorry for that in the end." She laughed suddenly. "I knew what *she* looked like, see—her picture was always getting in the paper. But she didn't know me. That's why I could follow her around the way I did when I was planning it out, and sit by her on the stool at the fountain in Baltimore. That's when I put the morphine in her coke."

"But I don't understand," I said, dazed. "Your husband, Jimmy Hamilton, was Shaw Hamilton after all? Eleanor Barnes' son?"

"I don't know what you mean by 'after all,' Miss Tyler," Dorothy Hamilton said. "But, yes, ma'am, sure he was her son. Her only son. James Shaw Hamilton, his full name was. I was surprised when the detective didn't figure that one out right away. It looked pretty easy to me."

I was too polite to glance in Ben Kramer's direction.

"Well, first she lost me my job, and made it so I couldn't get another, and we had to go to New York. And Jimmy couldn't get a job there. Not that he tried any too hard." She said it without bitterness. "Poor kid, he didn't know which way to turn when she cut off his allowance. I got a job, all right, but after we got married Jimmy didn't like me sitting with the customers anymore, and of course they do make passes. But it was either that or not eat. You understand that, Miss Tyler. And I didn't know any other kind of work to do that would pay good enough to keep two people and a baby coming."

"I understand," I said. I was beginning to, too.

"I just started that baby because I thought it would make the old—make Jimmy's mother come around," Dorothy went on. She spoke in the matter-of-fact way that even nice people speak of such things now. "What would I want with a kid? I was the oldest of nine, Miss Tyler, and before I got away from home I'd taken care of kids till just the sight of one made me sick to my stomach. But I'd read a lot about baby hands bringing people together, and stuff." She laughed bleakly. "I guess old Mrs. Barnes never had heard about that. I wrote her a note and sent it up by the girl, after she'd told her to tell me she wasn't at home. And there 'wasn't any answer.' I got it through my thick head then that she wasn't ever going to come around, not ever. I went on back to New York and tried to get rid of the baby."

I covered up a gasp by saying, "Go on."

"But it didn't work," Dorothy Hamilton said drearily. "All it did was make me good and sick, so I couldn't work except sometimes. And Jimmy couldn't, or wouldn't, or something. And whenever he did get hold of some money he'd likely as not spend it on whisky, when I was going without things I'd need. And then he took to morphine again."

She laughed again, bitterly, shockingly. "That was how I got so good dropping things in people's drinks without them knowing it. I tried every way in God's world to make that kid lay off the drink and dope, Miss Tyler. I'd argue with him, and I'd cry, and once I took him down in Chinatown and showed him the hopheads laying around. You wouldn't think anybody'd want to get the way they looked. But I never did any good fast. And then I saw an ad for this stuff in *True Confessions* and I got some."

"What stuff?"

"White Rose Anti-Alcoholic Pills," Dorothy Hamilton said seriously. "The ad said that if you'd put one pill in a person's coffee, every time he had a cup, he'd soon lose all taste for liquor. And it was liquor that made Jimmy take the dope, to sober up on. So I thought I'd kill two birds with one stone. I put a White Rose tablet in every time I poured Jimmy's coffee, and at first I thought it was working. He'd stayed on the wagon a whole week. And I was so glad I couldn't keep my big mouth shut. I told him about it, and he just hit the ceiling. After that he watched me like a hawk, and I had to get pretty good, I can tell you. If vaudeville hadn't washed up I could have got in one of those sleight-of-hands, all right."

She laughed again, but this time it was the happy, carefree laugh of a child. "The old woman was looking the other way when I put the morphine in her coke, that day. But when I put it in Dr. Mosser's box he was looking right at me."

"Well, I think you were mighty smart," I said. I'd read that it was a good thing to flatter cases of this kind. "Why did you want to kill Dr. Mosser? And how did you know one morphine tablet would do it? Did you know he had a bad heart?"

Dorothy nodded. "Yes, ma'am. He told me so, one day when I went to his office to ask him about my sick headaches. I've had sick headaches all my life, Miss Tyler, and I didn't really think he could help them, and he didn't. But I thought it was a good way to get in with him. He said something about the dirty deal he'd got, getting sent to the pen for selling dope. He said lots of doctors sold it for years and got by. And I asked him if he ever took it himself. I was just kind of making conversation. And he said: 'My God, no! I've got too bad a heart. One morphine tablet—just one—would finish me off.' And so one morphine tablet did."

I wished she wouldn't laugh like that. I could stand the poor girl's recital of facts, horrible as it was, but when she laughed it made me shudder in all my nerves.

"Of course he was way up on my list," Dorothy went on matter-of-factly. "If he hadn't given Jimmy dope, way back years before I knew him, a lot of the troubles I had never would have happened. Yes, ma'am, that was why I killed him."

I said feebly, "You say you had a list—"

"Yes, ma'am. I've got a little list," Dorothy answered, nodding, smiling.

The words sang themselves horribly through my mind, over and over, to the Gilbert and Sullivan tune:

> I've got a little list—I've got a little list
> Of society offenders who might well be underground,
> And who never would be missed—who never would be missed!
>
> But it really doesn't matter whom you put upon the list,
> For they'd none of 'em be missed—they'd none of 'em be missed!

No, Eleanor Barnes would not be missed. Nor Dr. Mosser. Nor Bill Palougous—

"What about Bill Palougous?" I asked suddenly. "Why was he on your list?"

"Because he got Jimmy drafted into the army. Because he sold her his vote." Dorothy went on swiftly before I could say, "How do you mean?" "He was on the Annapolis draft board, see, and Jimmy was registered there, and his number came up. His old—Mrs. Barnes—had been trying every way and anyhow to break it up between Jimmy and me, and she went to the board and told them Jimmy had married me when he was drunk, and he wasn't supporting me and the baby anyway, and there wasn't any reason why he shouldn't go into service."

"You mean she just deliberately sent her only son off to be killed?" Anne asked incredulously. She couldn't keep still any longer.

"Yes, ma'am."

I said determinedly: "Now, look, my dear. Give the devil his due. Maybe she didn't see it that way. She didn't know he was going to be killed. All this was before Pearl Harbor, wasn't it?" I went on in spite of Ben's shaking his head at me, as if to say you should never contradict or argue with a crazy person. I'd heard that too, but I didn't think Dorothy Hamilton was as crazy as all that, even if she had killed three people. "I expect she'd heard the admiral talk about Navy discipline and how much good it did—and it's the truth, too. There isn't any finer training for a young man than service in the Army and Navy. I think Mrs. Barnes very sincerely hoped and believed the Army might succeed where she, and you, and all the colleges had failed."

Dick spoke from behind me, backing me up the way he always does. "I'd say it did succeed. Shaw Hamilton was cited for gallant and meritorious service, wasn't he? And he certainly stopped the dope habit, or he wouldn't have stayed in."

James Shaw Hamilton's wife said stonily, as if she hadn't heard: "And two weeks after he went overseas he was dead. I was awful sick then. Daddy was good to me. He came up and got me and the baby and took us back to the farm. They wanted him to send me to Bellevue, but he wouldn't. And then Mamma was real good too. After I got better she kept the kid when I went to New York to work, and then when I joined she signed the papers to say she'd go on keeping him. I was dancing in a burlesque show when I joined. I was just walking down the street and saw the poster."

"What poster? Joined what?" I asked, thoroughly puzzled.

"Why, the WAC," Dorothy Hamilton said, while all of us gasped but Ben. "WAAC, it was then. I went right in, and the recruiting sergeant said sure, it was the best way in the world to get back at the Japs for killing my husband, and I'd get over being nervous as soon as I was in uniform being useful. But I didn't. I was worse."

I could well imagine it. The fine lessons the WAC has to teach would mostly bounce right off a girl with that background plus that emotional instability. She'd learned her lesson on yes-ma'am and no-ma'am, though; I remembered how surprised I'd been, the day we stood and talked on Maryland Avenue, at her having such old-fashioned meticulous good manners. And of course she'd profited by the WAC physical program, that makes girls hard as nails even if they aren't dancers to start out with. Otherwise she might not have had the strength for that hard backhand stab that had killed Eleanor Barnes, that Ben had thought only a man or a naturally left-handed woman could do. But by and large Dorothy Hamilton would make the kind of soldier Ben had told us about that first night, the kind that can't adjust themselves to discipline and routine, and that get to their breaking point in a mighty short time. She got to hers in just a matter of months.

"At first they kept putting me in the guardhouse," Dorothy went on. "But then they sent me over to the hospital, and I was awful nervous there. You could hear folks screaming and groaning all the time." Just like home, I thought. Poor child, poor child! I felt rather like screaming and groaning myself. "And somebody was always watching me through a little hole in the door. I know that for a fact. Maybe I did imagine it about people talking about me and trying to poison me. I was sick, see. But I could really see the eyes."

"I expect it was the doctor or the nurse, checking up to see how you got along," I said pacifically.

She nodded. "Yes, ma'am. And then they wrote to the Red Cross at Bowiesburg, and they sent a girl out to snoop around the farm." She laughed bitterly. "Sweet as peaches and cream, Mamma said she was. You know how Mamma is, Miss Tyler. She couldn't tell anything much about Jimmy, who his folks were or where he was from, because he and Mamma never met, either, any more than I and Mrs. Barnes." Again that nerve-shattering laugh. "But Mamma said she said it was mostly me she was interested in, anyhow, and what about my early life, and did I sleepwalk or have temper tantrums or bite my fingernails or wet the bed, and was I a social or discipline problem when I got to be adolescent. And Mamma just opened her big mouth and went to town. And Uncle Willie howled for her, too, the way he did for you that day." She smiled and nodded. "It was nice of you not to go out and talk about that, Miss Tyler. And lucky for me, too. She'd have put two and two together, if you'd mentioned it to her. And then I'd have been sitting here in handcuffs that much sooner, without getting to kill that Palougous rat. She's the reason I'm here now, but it wasn't your fault. Her head was just too hard."

"You mean Ruth Allein." I said it without surprise. Nothing surprised me anymore. The pieces were all falling together, fairly jumping together the way they do toward the end of a jigsaw puzzle. It was a psychiatric social history that Ruth had gone to Baltimore to get, and that she'd sent to Ben Kramer to read, after its subject had hit her on the head. I've heard her say that when she's loaned out to one of the little country Red Cross chapters that don't have trained caseworkers, or whose caseworkers are sick, or something, she always brings a copy of the history back to the Baltimore office. She's saving a copy of every one she does in a private file there, and she'll base her dissertation on them some day. I knew she did a lot of those histories, too, and that most of them were pretty dramatic. And this case must have been quite two years old.

Still and all, though, I think she should have remembered about it sooner, and I said so.

"Well, but she never laid eyes on me before that day on the bus, Miss Tyler," Dorothy Hamilton said. "I was in the army hospital when she went out and talked to Mamma. And she was the reason I stayed there till I was discharged—all that stuff she got out of Mamma and wrote up and sent back to the hospital. I'd have gotten a pension except for her, too. And if it hadn't been for Mamma and Daddy signing the papers to take me out I'd be in that veterans hospital yet. The doctors didn't want me to leave. But Daddy said he wouldn't let any of his blood kin stay in an asylum as long as he had a home to give them. Much less his own kid. And Mamma wanted the money. She thought everybody that got a disability discharge got a disability pension too."

"Were they nice to you at the veterans' hospital? Will you mind going back?" I asked. It was all too apparent, had been apparent ever since the poor child started to talk, that Ben was going to get his wish. This murderer was the kind they send to a nice modern nuthouse. She wasn't the kind they hang.

"Oh, but I'm not going back," Dorothy said eagerly. "That's why I wanted to talk to you instead of to that policeman." Again she spoke exactly as if Ben weren't in the room. "I knew you'd understand why I had to kill those people. They asked for it, didn't they, all of them?"

"Except Miss Allein." Again I saw Ben's head shaking to warn me, and again I paid no attention. "She didn't mean to hurt you. She was just doing her job."

"But she did hurt me. She kept me from getting my pension. She'd have kept me from getting out if she could. Of course she was on my list," Dorothy said, surprised. "And that's why I can't go back to the hospital. It was nice enough, sure. But you explain to him I have to get finished with it."

"You mean you have some more people on your list?" I inquired carefully.

"Five."

I said, controlling myself: "Five. Well, Dorothy, it will take me quite a while to explain that many people to Lieutenant Kramer. He might not mind just one or two, but five— Why don't you go lie down, while I see what I can do? I see they've sent a nice nurse to help you get undressed."

The nurse had been standing in the doorway, back of Dorothy, ever since she started to talk. She did look nice, though why a nice girl would ever pick out a job taking care of lunatics— It was worse than Ruth Allein's. She smiled at Dorothy and held out her hand, and to my intense surprise—I hadn't known I was a psychiatric expert myself— Dorothy got right up and went to her, without a word. The policeman who was handcuffed to her left wrist stumbled to his feet and went along too, of course. She didn't seem to know he was there.

Ben sat back in his chair and wiped perspiration. "Well, Miss Julia, any time you want a job as a policewoman— And I haven't apologized to you yet. I do. I take off my hat to your woman's instinct. As the prisoner strongly inferred, I ought to be pounding a beat. You were on the right track right there at the first, and I threw you off. If I hadn't maybe nobody besides Eleanor Barnes would have been— Well, anyway, it was all my fault."

"Skip the humble pie, Ben," Dick said. "It's not your fault you don't have woman's instinct."

"And anyway that was enough to fool *anybody*," Anne put in loyally. "How could you possibly connect a brunette named Dorothy with a blonde named DeLoriese, especially when their husbands' first names were different? Didn't you say you saw Dorothy Hamilton's marriage license?"

"We did, and the husband's name was James. Not even a middle initial. But the service papers all had James S. Oh, I ought to have figured it out," Ben said. "I knew as well as anybody that the services make them go by their first names, no matter how much they hate them, or whether they've used their middle names all their lives, the way Shaw Hamilton had. Nobody but his wife ever called him Jimmy."

"Well, we should have figured it out too," I said firmly. "We knew Foster Gibson's first name was John." We did, too; it had been right there in the paper, for one thing, the day after Bill Palougous was murdered.

Ben shook his head. "I still think I'm not much of a detective without you, Miss Julia. The next time I can't break a murder case I'll call on you."

"Don't you dare," I said, getting up to go.

I certainly feel that way now, as if I never even wanted to read another murder. I change the subject every time it comes up at home; I didn't come to Annapolis just to talk about suspicious characters. I'm going to stay on till the last of February as I'd planned, and Anne and I will go shopping in Baltimore, and I'll look up William Claiborne in the Hall of Records, and take Alice walking out to the end of Duke of Gloucester Street, and play bridge and drink tea and gossip the way everybody in Annapolis does. And some day I'm going to climb up in the State House cupola and see the view from there. Sarah Maccubbin says I'll find it really exciting.

"After the bus station murders?" I doubted.

But maybe so.

THE END

No Pockets in Shrouds
LOUISA REVELL

CHAPTER ONE

My great-niece Anne is quite a business woman when she wants to be. She rented my house in Rossville at a price I'd have been ashamed to charge any young army wife, I don't care how rich she was; and the OPA let her because my house had atmosphere, whatever that is, and some of the original furniture, and was mighty close and convenient both to Fort Eustis and the tourist attractions at Williamsburg. Of course, all that's true, but I'm afraid Anne didn't tell my tenant and the OPA that it had the original plumbing too, and mice whose ancestors had lived there about as long as mine had.

Anyway, it was mighty nice to have that extra two hundred dollars piling up every month, the four months I'd spent visiting Anne and Dick in Annapolis, and I was hard put to it for arguments when they insisted that I prolonged my visit. But I still thought four months was the extreme limit of visitation, even to your nearest and dearest.

"Well, then, Aunt Julia, you can just take a trip," Anne said finally, giving up. "You just *can't* go home."

"Mexico City," Dick said. "San Antonio. Sea Island. Sun Valley. Well, New York, if it comes to that. What's the matter with New York?"

We'd all just spent a weekend in New York, and I never had such a good time.

Anne told him kindly, "You're letting Aunt Julia's money go to your head. All those cost too much. But there really are lots of nice places, Aunt Julia, where you could go and have fun and still make money on the deal. *Mexico's* cheap, all except Mexico City, and lots of towns in California— You could sit in the sun—"

I let her go on talking, but as a matter of fact I'd already made up my mind. Sit in the sun, my cat's foot. Sixty-eight years old isn't a hundred and fifty, after all; and if I was going to take a trip I'd do what I wanted most of all to do, though I ought to be ashamed to admit it.

So I went where murder was.

I'd read murder books since the first of the Mary Roberts Rineharts, and after I actually got mixed up in those murders in Annapolis I took a personal interest, naturally. It's right much fun to collect the newspaper clippings—and nothing short of awful how many there are, every day. I just hadn't realized. Even in Rossville, which is as sleepy a little Virginia town as you would want to see, there were three homicides in 1944. I admit that none of them was very interesting, but, as Dick says, the people involved were just as dead as the New Jersey golf pro they found face down in the water hazard, or the Hollywood starlet who wasn't the one that turned the gas on after all.

Dick says, too, that he doubts those murders were any more glamorous than Rossville's, really. I've noticed myself that the newspapers have a tendency to—well, I reckon "dramatize" is the nicest word for it. Their thumbnail sketches may not be actually untrue, but they certainly aren't recognizable. What I mean is you form a certain concept when they say "blond debutante heiress," and it isn't much like effaced little Emily Craig. And nobody but a reporter would have called Mrs. Thompson a "prominent clubwoman," when all she belonged to was the Methodist Missionary Society and the Order of the Eastern Star.

I never would have known Mrs. Thompson or Emily Craig or any of the others if Charlotte Buckner hadn't lived in Louisville. And I hadn't thought of Charlotte herself in years. It was a long, long time since the summer we both visited Jennie Mason—even before Charlotte married and I started teaching Latin in the Rossville High School. There'd been occasional Christmas cards since, but nothing more; when I got a letter I couldn't imagine what awful thing had happened. But Charlotte, bless her heart, had merely read in the papers about my finding a body, and wrote to sympathize with me about the terrible experience I'd passed through. She went on to say she hoped that I was quite all right now, but shocks like these made us all realize we weren't getting any younger, and someday while we were both still well and active she did want me to come to Louisville and make her a visit. We could talk over old times.

I wrote a nice letter back, of course, thanking Charlotte for her sympathy and not mentioning the fact that I'd enjoyed myself. I told her I'd love to make her a visit, someday. But I certainly never meant to do anything of the kind.

It must have been two or three months after that that I read in the papers about the Helm butler's murder. I made a new page for it in my scrapbook, and pretty soon I had to add another. The murder got a lot of publicity right from the first. There were a lot of pictures, too, and among them was one that said underneath, to my complete shock, "Miss Emily Craig, blond debutante heiress to the Helm tobacco millions, after being questioned by the Louisville police. With her are her lawyer, W. Blodgett Fownes, and Mrs. Thomas Crittenden Buckner." *Charlotte.*

Well, I don't know much about the Buckner genealogy, or the Murray genealogy either. Charlotte was a Murray. But I gathered that she must be some close kin to these Helms or Craigs. I couldn't imagine why else she'd let a newspaper take her picture with them. As far as I could make out, this Emily Craig, whoever she was, was actually suspected of the butler's murder. The papers didn't come right out and say so, but all the Helm tobacco money didn't keep them from inferring it.

I'm sorry to say that it was right then, in a flash, that I remembered Charlotte's invitation and began to think seriously about going to visit her.

Margaret Ware had invited me too, if I wanted to visit, and of course I can always stay with my Tyler cousins in Richmond, and Lucy Wingfield is an invalid and always anxious to have company in her big old house. They were all much closer and more recent friends of mine than Charlotte was. The only thing, as I told Anne and Dick, was that nobody but Charlotte could provide a murder to entertain me with.

Dick said doubtfully, "Well, Aunt Julia, I see your point. Of course, looking at Mrs. Ware's tulips or pushing an old lady around in a wheelchair isn't as exciting as a murder case would be. But—"

"But murder isn't a very nice ladylike hobby, I know," I finished for him. "And why can't I get interested in my ancestry or polishing the brass in church, like other people's great-aunts? Or maybe I should just make me a few lace caps."

Dick didn't laugh. "It isn't that, Aunt Julia. Bless your heart, I think it's cute of you to have that scrapbook. But *mixing* in murder is a kind of dangerous hobby, don't you think? We don't want you to get yourself hurt—or even scared."

"My dear boy, they wouldn't be interested in hurting an innocent bystander," I said, and Anne agreed.

"They won't even know she's interested in murders, Dick. They'll think she just came for an ordinary visit, just because she wanted to come. Oh, Aunt Julia, I think it sounds wonderful! I don't see how you can hesitate a minute. This is just exactly the kind of murder you read about in books—all those rich people and butlers and all. And you and this Charlotte Buckner can just walk right in."

"Well, that's the only thing, right there," I admitted. "I don't care about walking right in with Charlotte Buckner. You don't know Charlotte Buckner."

"What's the matter with her?"

I said reluctantly, "Well, she's just tiresome, that's all. She means well—she's a good, kind Christian woman, and a lady too, of course. But she never was what Dick calls a Brain, and now Jennie says she doesn't know there's a thing in life except Kentucky families and the Altar Guild and other people's business."

"But, Aunt Julia, that's *wonderful!*" Anne said. "Other people's business is the sum and substance of solving a murder."

Well, of course it is, and finally, after writing to Charlotte and getting an enthusiastic answer, I went to Louisville. I not only went, I flew. I think the children are as surprised at my newly acquired taste for flying as they are at my newly acquired taste for murder—at my age. But I've come to the conclusion that air is the only way to go. It isn't that I'm not scared to death; I am. The trip we took to New York scared me so I didn't think I'd live to get there. But I did, in exactly one hour and seventeen minutes, and it taught me a lesson. You can stand almost anything for an hour and seventeen minutes.

It took nearly four hours from Washington to Louisville, but I had my air legs my second trip. I read my magazines and had a nice time, and I was fresh as a daisy when I stepped out of the big silver plane and let Charlotte Buckner fall on my neck.

Charlotte wasn't as bad as I remembered her. She'd improved with age. She still looked a good deal like a sheep, but old sheep who've spent their days gazing mildly at the world do acquire a certain dignity. Charlotte was dignified. So were her clothes—a good black dress and coat, and a black hat that came down pretty well in front but still managed to look like one of Queen Mary's. And, yes, she had on toe-rubbers. Charlotte was always mortally afraid of getting her feet wet.

We took a taxi from Bowman Field to Charlotte's apartment.

"It always seems strange to say 'The Puritan' instead of 'South Sixth Street,'" Charlotte told me sentimentally, as we started. "Of course, I've lived there six years now. But it was mighty hard to leave the old rooftree." Charlotte says things like that, which may be all right in books but would embarrass most people to pop out with. "Papa and Mama both passed away there, you know, and all my brothers and sisters except Ella."

"I expect it was way too big for you, though," I said. I'd never seen the old rooftree, but it must have been big if all those people had passed away under it. Charlotte was one of six or eight children.

"Oh, it was," Charlotte said. "Seven bedrooms—imagine! And then the neighborhood wasn't what it was when Papa's father bought there. I was about the last of the old families to go."

"It's hard to make up your mind to move," I said, politeness covering my utter boredom—I hope. I didn't see how I was going to stand Charlotte Buckner very long, murder or no murder.

Charlotte said eagerly, "Oh, it is! I don't think I ever would have if it hadn't been for Mary Preston. 'You've just got to, Aunt Charlotte,' she said. 'There's that nice little apartment vacant right across the street from us, and Emily and I'll help you move your things.' You know I had a lot of things I couldn't have trusted to the transfer men. Mama's Tanagra figures, and the Lowestoft and all."

"Are Mary Preston and Emily your sister's daughters?" I asked idly. I didn't really care, but if I got Charlotte started on the Murray family I could look out the taxi window for the rest of the trip.

"Oh, *no*, Julia!" Charlotte was honestly shocked, though I don't see how she could expect me to remember. "Lucy was the only one of us that left any children, and all three of hers were boys."

"Tom's nieces, then? Or courtesy kin?" I asked. There was something stirring in the back of my mind, but—I needn't talk about Charlotte's being slow on the uptake, as Dick calls it—I couldn't get it out.

Charlotte said, "Oh, courtesy. Well, of course they are *some* kin. Way back. The Murrays and the Breckinridges have intermarried two or three times, and of course the Allens— But Mary Preston and Emily just call me aunt because their grandmother was such a friend of mine. Emily Powell, she was."

"It's nice to have them right across the street from you," I said. "Nice for me, too. They'll keep me from missing Anne so much. What's their last name?"

I'd gathered, of course, that Mary Preston was a double given name, the kind that's so often heard among us. It's the rarest thing, in Virginia as well as Kentucky, for parents to name a girl just plain Mary.

"Well, Mary Preston's last name is Helm," Charlotte said. "They aren't sisters, you know, though they've been brought up together. Just cousins. Emily is Emily Craig."

Well, it dawned on me at last. Emily Craig. Mary Preston Helm. And they lived right across the street from Charlotte. It was almost too good to believe.

The taxi pulled up in front of the Puritan right then, before I could ask any more questions. Charlotte and I got out. It was a nice-looking red-brick and white-tile apartment house, quite big, and inside the lobby everything was bright and fresh and modern. The only antiques were the liberal sprinkling of ladies Charlotte's and my age. I found out later that the Puritan is considered just about the nicest place in Louisville for ladies alone in the world. If they can afford it, that is. It's pretty high. But the address is good, the service stays excellent even in wartime, and they let you keep a dog or cat in your apartment if you want to.

When we got upstairs—Charlotte is on the third floor—I found out they'd let you use your apartment for storage too. I never saw so much furniture in my life. Charlotte had evidently been unable to part with much of anything from the old rooftree, and my room had, I think, knickknacks from all seven of its bedrooms. As for the living room, it was so full of tables and sofas and rocking chairs that only a laboratory rat, accustomed to mazes, could have got around without practice. I thought I could master it in time; I only hoped I wouldn't knock over some of Mama's Tanagra figurines first. Mama had been quite a collector.

"Which way do your windows face, Charlotte?" I asked, over the hot cocoa Charlotte thought I'd better have before I went to bed. "I'm all turned around."

"Ormsby. West Ormsby," Charlotte said. "The Puritan is on the corner of Fourth and Ormsby." She went over to the window and pulled the curtains aside. "See, it's still a nice-looking block. Most of the houses are apartments now, and there's a doctor up at that end, but I think they keep them up mighty well."

"Do Emily and Mary Preston live on Ormsby? Or are they over on Fourth?" I asked. It was blunt, but Charlotte is far from sharp herself. She answered quickly and unsuspectingly.

"Oh, they live on Ormsby. See the red stone house, the biggest one with the balcony and towers? That's where they live. And, Julia, this will interest you—" Charlotte lowered her voice. "Do you see that dormer in the fourth story, the one at the far left? The only one that's dark? Well, that was Gus's room."

"Gus?" I said. I knew perfectly well who Gus was, and my heart was beginning to pound. Gus was the Negro butler who'd worked for some people named Helm—Mary Preston Helm's family, of course. And Emily Craig's. The butler who'd been found dead in bed one morning, but without previous despondency or reason for it, so far as anyone knew, and without a suicide note. The murder that wasn't a suicide after all, though it had happened in one of Louisville's very best families.

And Emily Craig. The "blonde debutante heiress to the Helm tobacco millions." The nice little girl whose grandmother had been such a friend of Charlotte Buckner's, who'd helped her move all those shelves of china pigs and shepherdesses into the Puritan. Emily Craig whom the police had questioned about Gus's murder. Whom the police suspected—if I had any ability to read between the lines of a newspaper story—of doing the murder herself.

I was writing a letter in my mind to Anne and Dick.

"... killing himself," Charlotte said with an air of finality. I came to with a start. Not realizing, apparently, that I could read—the Helm butler's murder had been spread all over the front pages of papers from coast to coast—Charlotte was undertaking to tell me about it from beginning to end. I hadn't heard a thing but those last two words.

However, naturally I knew the facts as the newspapers had given them, and though I'd missed Charlotte's interpretations as she went along, I doubted that I'd missed much. Certainly I hadn't if they resembled her peroration.

"At first I just couldn't believe it wasn't suicide," Charlotte said. "But the detective said there weren't any fingerprints on the glass. Not any at all. He said that proved it." She drew a deep, triumphant breath. "So it just must have been a tramp."

A tramp on the fourth floor of a Louisville town house, especially anno Domini 1945 when—whatever the other ills of our country—tramps are as extinct as the American buffalo!

But Charlotte seemed completely pleased with her solution, and on that optimistic note we went to bed.

It always takes me a good while to get to sleep in a strange place, even when the mattress is as supremely comfortable as Charlotte's guest room Beautyrest. It was after midnight when I finally dropped off. The lights in the houses across the street had all gone out one by one, until only one was left, a dimly lighted window on the second floor of the red stone Helm house. Once, about half-past eleven, a girl's figure was silhouetted for a minute against the shade and I wondered which of them it was, Emily Craig or the other one, Mary Preston Helm. Then that light went out too.

It was daylight when I woke up again, pale but unmistakable. I reckon it was the birds that woke me; they were making an awful racket in the trees. It's an early spring. I could see one or two people walking along on the other side of the street, and a newsboy on a bicycle was throwing papers with beautiful accuracy. He threw one into the vestibule of the red stone Helm house. I looked at the Helm house, and then I looked again. No, I wasn't mistaken. There was a light in one of the fourth-floor windows—the one at the extreme left. It was the window of the room where Gus had died.

CHAPTER TWO

It wasn't till two days later that I met the family across the street. I had to meet all Charlotte's friends first—friends her own age, that is. We went out to dinner and tea at different people's houses, and one lady took us driving, and we were invited to have lunch at the Pendennis Club. It wasn't much quieter that way than Annapolis had been.

The ladies I met were like the ones in Annapolis, too—and like the ones in Rossville or Richmond or Baltimore or any other Southern town. The Southern gentlewoman of my generation certainly is a type, whether we like it or not, and I felt right at home in the midst of the Louisville ladies and their talk about people and food.

But the people they talked about weren't people I knew—knew of, that is. I mean they didn't talk about the Helm-Craig connection. It was all too apparent to me that the Helms and the Craigs were considered almost like Charlotte's family, and that was why everybody tactfully avoided mentioning their troubles. I was scared to death that, in getting up close to this particular murder, I'd got too close to see.

Charlotte talked, though. Everything I asked her later about the Helm household she answered freely and fully, as if it never occurred to her I'd come to Louisville to sit in, as Dick calls it, on their murder case. She seemed perfectly sure I'd just come to visit her. Really, as my visit went on I felt right bad about it—as if I were taking hospitality under false pretenses. Charlotte was like the husbands who never dream their wives have married them for money.

It's nice to have people straight in your mind before you meet them, the way I was able to do with the Helms. Being distant kin, as she'd said, they were duly charted up on the big family tree that covered half of one wall in Charlotte's living room. Climbing over and around three chairs, two little tables, and a sofa, I could see where Lucy Breckinridge, Charlotte's mother, had been a second cousin once removed of a certain Susan Breckinridge. Susan had married a Judge Henry Clay Helm, according to the chart, and their only son was named Breckinridge Helm.

This was the same Breckinridge Helm, Charlotte said, who was head of the family and lived in the red stone monstrosity across the street. He was an old man and an invalid now. He'd had trouble with his heart for years, it seemed, and high blood pressure, and just within the last few weeks he'd had a stroke of paralysis.

Breckinridge Helm was married twice. His first wife was named Emily Powell—that was Charlotte's friend—and by her he had two children, a boy and a girl. The boy married and had two children too. One of them was the Mary Preston Helm that called Charlotte aunt. The other—I presume he called her aunt too—was Breckinridge Helm the third, and according to Charlotte he was a captain in the AAF and the most beautiful thing in or out of uniform. I was pretty sure he wouldn't compare with my handsome redheaded Dick in his Navy blues, but of course I didn't say anything.

Well, the other child of Breckinridge Helm I and Emily Powell Helm married a Craig, and Emily Craig was their daughter. Two other Craig children had died in infancy.

Breckinridge Helm I didn't have any children by his late-in-life second marriage. His wife, though—she was Elizabeth Rowan in the first place, and a widowed Mrs. Todd when he married her—had one daughter by the first husband. The daughter made an unfortunate marriage, Charlotte said, and came back to live at the Helm house with *her* two children. It seems old Mr. Helm always treated his wife's grandchildren just like his own. They hardly knew the difference themselves, and people in general had almost forgotten that John Todd Brown and Martina Brown—Martina Greer, she was after her marriage—weren't really his blood kin

Charlotte said, "Actually, I think Johnny is his favorite—and not a drop of kin except way back where a Todd married a Crittenden woman. Aren't people odd? You'd think his own namesake—"

"Or his own granddaughters," I said. "It's a wonder Emily or Mary Preston doesn't have him wrapped around her little finger. Specially if they're pretty as their pictures." Charlotte had pictures of the girls in a big double standing frame, and they really were lovely, Emily very fair and Mary Preston with dark hair and eyelashes a yard long.

Charlotte said doubtfully, "Well, he's fond of Emily, of course. Everybody is. But Breckinridge and Mary Preston are too much alike."

"They don't get along?" I asked neutrally.

Charlotte sighed. "They just rub each other the wrong way. Mary Preston is just as sweet as she can be, sometimes—I don't want you to think I don't love the child, Julia, because I do. But she just has to have her own way. It's funny, because she wasn't spoiled. Of course, Breckinridge is that way too. And she lost her mother when she was just a little thing—and her father was just plain wild—"

Well, I didn't pay too much attention to Charlotte, because I like to form my own opinions of people, and when I saw Mary Preston I was glad I hadn't. She was as nice a child as you would want to see. And pretty! The black and white picture had done justice to her hair and skin, but it didn't show how blue her eyes were or how her face lit up all over when she laughed. A good many times in the next few weeks I was glad I'd seen Mary Preston Helm that way, and I made myself remember how she'd looked standing in Charlotte's living room doorway, laughing and clutching that ridiculous Kerry pup. She was as young and happy that day as the birds that kept waking me up every morning, or the dogwood in bloom a whole month early, or the first act of *Oklahoma!* that Anne and Dick and I saw in New York.

Charlotte was introduced to the Kerry pup before Mary Preston was introduced to me.

"Aunt Charlotte, isn't he beautiful? His name's Merridale Blockbuster and his father is Champion Tyrone of Derwentwater and his mother is Champion Merridale Dark Rosaleen. And I'm going to bring him right up by this book." She rescued the book from Blockbuster's mouth and Charlotte seized the opportunity to introduce me.

"How do you do?" Mary Preston said. "Do you like dogs, Miss Tyler? Would you like to hold Blockbuster a minute? He seems to want to lick you."

Blockbuster was handed over. His mistress watched with the purest maternal pride, and I felt sure all over again that Charlotte's estimate of her character was wrong. It takes a really lovely nature to watch your dog make over a stranger the way Blockbuster was making over me.

"Where did you get him, Mary Preston?" Charlotte asked when things had quieted down. Blockbuster had played with a rubber plate-scraper which was the nearest thing to a toy Charlotte had, made a puddle on the rug, and finally gone to sleep. "And what kind of a dog is he, for goodness' sake? I never saw one like that."

"He's a Kerry Blue, Aunt Charlotte," Mary Preston said eagerly. "Bill gave him to me. We passed by a kennel out on the Bardstown Road, and the puppies were all looking through the fence, and so of course we had to stop. And the rest of them were cute and sweet, but Blockbuster climbed right up on his brothers' backs and licked me through the wire. The kennel man said he was by far the best dog in the litter. He said if I'd bring him right up by this book and groom him every day and not feed him trash, I'd have about the finest Kerry Blue in this country."

"But a Kerry *Blue*," Charlotte said again. "Mary Preston, he's black as a blind man's pocket."

"That's because he's a pup. He'll get bluer and bluer every day, Aunt Charlotte. You just wait and see."

Charlotte was still doubtful. "I never heard of a black dog's turning blue."

"Well, I don't see why it couldn't," I said, though I didn't know a thing about Kerrys myself. "We've all seen red babies turn white, and cream-colored babies turn dark brown."

Mary Preston turned to me eagerly and gratefully. "We absolutely have, Miss Tyler. You just wait, Aunt Charlotte. Bill used to have a Kerry—he says they're the nicest dogs in the world, that's why he wanted me to have this one—and he says Blockbuster will be the most beautiful slate-blue you ever saw."

Mary Preston was sitting on the floor looking up at us between the extravagant lashes, and I thought, slate-blue to match those eyes, the way that Bill, whoever he was, undoubtedly had too.

"Which one is Bill?" Charlotte asked. I was glad she did.

"Captain Howard. He's out at Fort Knox. You've met him, Aunt Charlotte—don't you remember that time in the Bluegrass Room?"

Charlotte said vaguely, "Oh, yes, of course." But I could see that she was like me, and all nice young men in uniform looked pretty much the same to her.

Mary Preston was scooping up the sleeping Blockbuster, preparatory to departure. "I have to go. I have to take him around to show a lot of other people. I'm glad I met you, Miss Tyler. Emily and I came to see you yesterday, but you were in the bathtub."

"You and Emily must come again," I said. "Bring Blockbuster."

Maybe I shouldn't have added that last, when they weren't my rugs.

"Oh, we will. We come every day," Mary Preston said. She went out struggling with the puppy, who had wakened in full possession of his faculties. We could hear her laughing and talking to him as they went down the hall, both of them tangled up in his leash.

Charlotte closed the door and, as I've said, it was like the curtain going down on the first act of *Oklahoma!*

I said, "Well, Charlotte, I don't believe I'm going to like your neighbor Mr. Helm. If that child rubs him the wrong way there's something the matter with *him*."

"Well, there is, of course," Charlotte said. "I mean, Breckinridge always has been pretty dictatorial. And as Tom used to say, you can't make that much money sitting around worrying about other people's rights and feelings."

"Does he have a lot of money?" I asked innocently. I don't know where Charlotte thought I'd been living the last few weeks, when the phrase "Helm tobacco millions" had been on the front page of every paper every day. The papers had had to play up the Helm family's money and social position to justify devoting so much space to a Negro servant's death.

Charlotte said, "Oh, *yes*, Julia. I reckon Breckinridge Helm has more money than anybody in Louisville—any *nice* family, that is." She went on to tell me how he'd made it manufacturing pipe tobacco and cigarettes—which of course I knew. "Of course I don't have any idea how much there is now; I reckon it's a lot more. But Breckinridge told me himself, when he made his will—oh, that was twelve or fifteen years ago, when the children were little—that he'd leave three or four million dollars to be divided among them."

"My!" I said, impressed. "Mary Preston and Emily will be really rich, won't they? And young Breckinridge Helm III."

"Breck, we call him. Yes. Oh, but so will the others," Charlotte said. "The second wife's grandchildren get equal shares too, just as if they were blood kin. I told you Breckinridge had always treated them alike."

I said comfortably, "Well, I think that's nice. Especially when there's plenty of money to go around."

Charlotte shook her head. "There never is enough to go around, Julia. Not when it's money you're talking about," she said with surprising wisdom. And, of course, I've seen it happen again and again myself. Good people who'll share their last crust of bread won't share bounty when it's translated into dollars and cents, and any time you want to see your nearest and dearest at each other's throat just look down from heaven after you've died without leaving a will.

We went out to dinner the evening of Mary Preston's visit. Charlotte's friends were a Dr. and Mrs. Speed, very attractive people and good bridge players. It was past eleven o'clock when Charlotte and I were back in the Puritan, drinking the cups of cocoa that Charlotte thinks as necessary as prayers and cold cream at bedtime. I remember I had on my expensive immoral black negligee that Dick picked out for my Christmas present, and Charlotte admired it extravagantly. She would have liked somebody to give her one like it, I think. Handsome her so-called nephew Breck may be and undoubtedly is, judging from his picture, but not many people go to the trouble Dick does for me.

We heard the steps running along the hall only a second or two before the knock sounded on the door. It was a harsh, imperative knock, and the person didn't give Charlotte a chance to get there before he knocked again. Before *she* did, rather, because it was a girl's voice that began to call.

"Aunt Charlotte! Aunt Charlotte!"

"I'm coming, Mary Preston," Charlotte said calmly. She'd put her cup down without haste and walked across the living room adjusting her sash. I was never so surprised. I never would have recognized Mary Preston Helm's voice; it just didn't sound like her.

It was Mary Preston, all right. She almost fell into the living room. Bat she didn't look much more like herself than she sounded. She had a smoky-blue net evening dress on and should have been lovely in it, with her blue eyes and silky black hair. Instead, the blue eyes were so wide open you could see the whites all the way around, and her face was a dull dark crimson. At first I thought the child was hurt or scared, or both; but then I realized that she was just plain mad, madder than I'd ever seen anybody get in my life.

"Oh, Aunt Charlotte! Aunt Charlotte! Aunt Charlotte!" Mary Preston said, and burst into tears in Charlotte's arms.

At first I was impressed with Charlotte's almost professional calm, but then I realized this was a scene she'd played many times before. No wonder Mary Preston had wanted her to move conveniently across the street if she did this sort of thing often. And, if she did, Charlotte must love her a lot to put up with it. Mary Preston's tears were absolutely ruining the front of Charlotte's robe, which though not like mine was a perfectly nice, good one.

"Aunt Charlotte," Mary Preston said between sobs, "someday I'm just going to kill Grandfather!"

Charlotte said soothingly, "Now, Mary Preston, now, honey. It's all right. Aunt Charlotte loves you."

"It is not all right!" Mary Preston cried. "Oh, Aunt Charlotte! Aunt Charlotte!" And the tears broke out again.

I'd tactfully retreated to my room by this time, but I'm sorry to say I didn't shut the door very completely. So I could hear every word, and see too, when Mary Preston finally dried her eyes and raised her head and looked Charlotte straight in the face. "Aunt Charlotte, you know how sweet Blockbuster is, and how he wouldn't hurt a thing."

"Yes, honey." Charlotte didn't even glance at the spot on her grandmother's sheaf-of-wheat rug.

"Well, Grandfather told me I couldn't keep him, Aunt Charlotte. He said he was too sick to have a dog around, and he said Blockbuster was too expensive a present for me to take from Bill. And I said Blockbuster was my dog and I wouldn't give him up. And we both got mad and yelled at each other. And then while I was out this evening he called the transfer company and they took Blockbuster back to Bill at Fort Knox."

She was lucky they hadn't taken him to the pound, I thought indignantly. A nice character, old Breckinridge Helm.

Charlotte said softly, "Honey, I'm so sorry. I'm just as sorry as I can be."

"I hate Grandfather! I wish he were dead!"

"Now, honey," Charlotte said. "You mustn't say you hate your grandfather. He loves *you*; he'd do anything for you. But he *is* sick, and he's old—"

"And he's a devil," Mary Preston said. I could see her straighten up and shake off Charlotte's arms. "No, Aunt Charlotte, you can't get around facts. I hate Grandfather. I wish he'd go on and die." There wasn't the slightest doubt that she meant it. "If he doesn't, some of these days—"

CHAPTER THREE

The first upshot of all that was that I telephoned Captain William S. Howard at Fort Knox and arranged to buy a dog. I need a dog anyway. The second was that old Breckinridge Helm had a heart attack next day, and the doctor told Mary Preston that if he died she'd be responsible.

I didn't think the doctor should have said that, for several reasons. In the first place, Mr. Helm wasn't in any real danger of dying. It was a light attack. In the second place, he didn't even have it till the next morning, and probably it wasn't over Mary Preston at all. Charlotte admitted he was always getting mad about something. And finally, I couldn't much blame the child for telling him off, as Dick calls it. Of course, she shouldn't have talked that way to a sick old man, but then a sick old man shouldn't have acted the way he did, either. The more I thought about his sending that child's dog away the less I thought of *him*.

"Where does he expect to go when he dies, anyway?" I asked Charlotte indignantly.

Charlotte said mildly, "Why, I reckon he thinks he's going to heaven, Julia. He couldn't very well go anyplace else—he's senior warden at Grace and St. Peter's." I looked at Charlotte sharply, thinking maybe I'd underestimated her, but she was perfectly serious.

I said dryly, "Well, Charlotte, I was brought up in a rectory and educated in a church boarding school, but you're more orthodox than I am. I reckon I'd better just concentrate on what to do with Blockbuster. I wonder if that same kennel won't board him."

"Why, Julia, of course we can have him here."

I protested, of course. It really was asking too much, a little puppy like that, not even housebroken. But Charlotte had said just what I'd hoped, for Mary Preston's sake, that she would—and finally we agreed that Blockbuster was to come. I engaged to buy his food, whatever the book said he was supposed to have, and Mary Preston would come twice a day to take him walking, and Charlotte said it was nearly time to take the rugs up for the summer anyway.

After the dog episode I wasn't in much of a mood to make a friendly sick call on old Breckinridge Helm. But he was Charlotte's neighbor and distant kinsman, and I was Charlotte's guest, so of course I had to go with her when she asked me to. I even carried the bowl of eggnog, though actually she'd made it strong enough to walk across the street by itself.

I've been in ugly houses, but I believe the Helm house was the ugliest I ever saw. Red stone and gingerbread outside, gingerbread and black walnut inside, it was a regular monstrosity. I always think ugliness that cost a lot is worse than the equal ugliness of poverty. It was depressing to think that house was so well and solidly built that it never would fall down, or even crumble and mellow around the edges.

Mr. Helm's bedroom was elaborately ugly too; it was no wonder they couldn't keep a nurse, even if Mr. Helm had been a pleasure to take care of. I could imagine he'd be no nice patient. But the old man was looking deceptively mild when we saw him. He was lying propped up against pillows in his big carved walnut bed, apparently a long way from dying. He was even smiling grimly at something that had just been read to him out loud.

The girl who'd been doing the reading shut her book when we came in and hurried over to meet us. I knew who she was, of course, before Charlotte introduced her. It was Emily Craig.

Well, if the Louisville police suspected Emily Craig of having murdered the butler Gus, it was because they'd swallowed the detective-story maxim that the murderer is always the most unlikely person. Emily certainly did look unlikely to me. She was a scared little white rabbit of a girl, apparently about sixteen, though Charlotte had told me she was well past eighteen, three years younger than Mary Preston. The studio picture on Charlotte's table had glamourized her considerably, but it was recognizable, and just went to show how thin the line really is between beauty and the lack of it. All Emily Craig lacked was the long dark eyelashes the photographer had painted on, instead of the stubby blond ones the Lord had given her, and clearer skin and a light behind her head and mysterious shadows behind her shoulders; but, lacking them, she was just plain insignificant. She looked sweet and good—the kind that's born to be a doormat and dies a maiden aunt—but she obviously wouldn't say boo to a goose, much less do murder.

It was Breckinridge Helm who would have been my choice for a cool, cruel murderer, if I hadn't known he was out of the question as Gus's. He hadn't been out of bed, Charlotte said, since he'd had a stroke a month ago. It was all up and down his left side at first, but now it was just his leg. He could have been up in a chair, but since he had heart trouble too and was always having light attacks of *that*, the doctor had kept him in bed. They tried to spare him excitement, of course, and Charlotte said they hadn't ever told him that Gus met a violent death. Mr. Helm thought that Gus had just died.

Maybe I haven't said enough about that first murder in the Helm house, and ought to do it now.

Gus Johnson had been a Helm darky originally, as I understood it; but after he married Charlotte's family's cook he went to Charlotte's house to work. He'd been there untold years. Charlotte had given him back again only when she gave up the old rooftree and the car and moved to the Puritan—six years ago—and of course she still kept in close touch with him and with Martha, his wife. Martha cooked for the Helms the way she'd done for Charlotte, and Gus had the same duties he'd performed on South Sixth Street. He waited on the table and drove old Mr. Helm and worked in the yard—not that Louisville yards are big enough to mention—and generally supervised the other servants. He was a good servant himself and some of the new families in Louisville, Charlotte said, would have given their eyeteeth to get him. But Gus was a dyed-in-the-wool snob like all old colored people, and would rather work for the Helms in spite of old Breckinridge's yelling at him when things didn't go just so, and some of the things the young people did. It seems Gus was inclined to be critical of the younger generation. Charlotte said he never did help young Johnny to bed without lecturing him throughout on the evils of drink and riotous living, and once when Mary Preston was starting out for the evening he told her her grandmammy would turn over in her grave to see her and she'd better go back upstairs and put a shawl around her shoulders.

"And how did Mary Preston take that?" I asked.

"How do you think?" Charlotte said resignedly.

I had to admit that Mary Preston did have an awful temper. But she was just a child and as far as I could tell she'd had a right hard life. An opinionated, high-tempered old man like Breckinridge Helm has no business trying to bring up a little girl. Charlotte said he'd never spoiled her and I believe it. It was about time somebody did; I was glad I'd bought her dog back for her.

Well, getting back to Gus, Gus was annoying sometimes, as old colored servants can be when they think they own the family; but still the family seemed devoted to him. It sounded fantastic to say that one of them had murdered him, but Lieutenant Bates said that was how it was. It couldn't have happened any other way.

Gus was found dead in bed the morning of March the thirty-first, which was a Saturday. He'd had a cold the night before and Emily had fixed him some medicine the doctor left. She went up early the next morning to see how he'd passed the night, and there he was dead, with his body convulsed as if he'd died in agony, and the sheets and covers halfway off the bed every which way, and the medicine glass knocked off the bedside table.

The medicine glass didn't have any fingerprints on it at all, not even Gus's or Emily's. Emily freely admitted giving him his medicine the night before, but she said she'd washed the glass afterward and put it on the bureau, not on the little table by the bed. Gus could have got up later and got it, of course. He wasn't that sick. And he could have got hold of the poison, too, that the police found in the bottom of the glass. But he couldn't and wouldn't have wiped the glass off afterwards.

The police were tactful about it, of course, because the Helms were a prominent family and Breckinridge Helm wasn't a man to anger unless you were absolutely sure of your ground. But they said they didn't see how anybody outside the family could have done it. Unless some member of the family had admitted the murderer in the middle of the night, of course, and that didn't seem much more likely than Charlotte's tramp. Leaving that out, the fact remained that there were chains as well as locks on all three of the house's outside doors, and no windows below the third-floor level had been open.

"And there was only the family at home?" I inquired. "Don't the rest of the servants sleep on the fourth floor? Where was Gus's wife?"

"Martha? Oh, Martha'd gone off on a visit," Charlotte said. "Her daughter was in the worst of the March flood, down below town, and she went down to help her clean out the house. She's staying with her still."

"But I saw a light on the fourth floor the other night," I persisted. I didn't add that the light had been in Gus's room.

"Well, the new servants sleep up there now," Charlotte said. "They had to get a whole new set after Gus died."

I said tentatively, "I'm surprised they're willing to stay there, right after a murder."

"Oh, Mary Preston talked them into it," Charlotte said. "She can talk the birds out of the trees when she wants to. I don't know anybody else who could have gone out and hired four new people right in the middle of this servant shortage—and they seem right good ones, too. But she couldn't get any of them to sleep in Gus's room, if that's what you mean. They said they'd rather double up in the two other fourth-floor bedrooms."

That was just what I wanted to know. But then who could have made the light?

"The pre-murder servants slept out, did they, except Gus and Martha?" I asked instead, and Charlotte nodded. "And with Martha away, and Gus the murdered person so he couldn't be the murderer too, that just left the family for the police to suspect. Old Mr. Helm, Mary Preston, and Emily Craig."

Charlotte said, "Oh, but Julia—all of them were there."

"All of them?"

"Why, all the grandchildren," Charlotte said. "The doctor sent for them when Breckinridge had his stroke. You see, he couldn't tell at first how bad it was. Breck got an emergency leave and flew from the West Coast, and Johnny came from New York, and Martina and her husband from Cincinnati."

"Oh." It took me a minute to digest that. "What day did old Mr. Helm have his stroke?" I asked finally.

Charlotte said promptly, "On the twenty-third of March. His whole left side just seemed to crumple up, and he couldn't talk at all. And then even before the children got here he got just a lot better, all of a sudden. Dr. Jordan said he never saw anything like it. He didn't talk very plainly when he first began, but you could understand him if you tried. And in a few days even that had cleared up."

"H'm. So he was a lot better by the time Gus was murdered," I said.

"Oh, but he couldn't get out of bed, Julia. He can't yet. His left leg is just as bad as it ever was, and of course these little heart attacks he keeps on having— And anyway, Julia," Charlotte said, earnestly, "you ought not to get such a prejudice against Breckinridge Helm, just on account of Mary Preston's dog. He's a very fine man, really. I don't say he isn't difficult sometimes, but he's very generous and public-spirited— gives a lot to the Community Chest and the settlements and Woodcock Hall, and sits on all kinds of charity boards, and takes up the collection in church."

Sitting by old Breckinridge Helm's bed, looking down at the handsome, arrogant, high-nosed face on the pillows, I conscientiously went over that list of virtues in my mind. But list or no list, I wasn't impressed. I couldn't help thinking about Mary Preston's dog. You old hypocrite, I thought. You old whited sepulcher, you. I didn't like him at all.

But Breckinridge Helm himself was impressive, even in his helplessness—I had to admit that—and he certainly did have beautiful manners. He'd entertained ladies in bedrooms before. I could see a good deal of his grandchildren in him—not only Mary Preston, with her temper and her high-handedness and her ability to talk the birds out of the trees when she wanted to, but the favorite wild-oat-sowing grandson Gus had had to help to bed. But there I went forgetting too, along with everybody else in Louisville, that John Todd Brown was only a step-grandson. I still say there was more resemblance, though, than I saw to Emily Craig. She wasn't a thing in the world like her grandfather, or any of the other handsome, self-possessed people in that family. She sat off at one side all the time we were there, speaking when she was spoken to and smiling at all the right times. She was just as nice and sweet as she could be. But I couldn't much blame Mr. Helm for the tolerant, smiling contempt he didn't bother to hide when he looked at her. She'd bore me to death in fifteen minutes if she were any kin to me. I'd take Mary Preston any day, temper and tears and all.

We didn't see Mary Preston and it didn't seem tactful to ask about her in front of Mr. Helm. But Martina Brown and her husband, whose name was Dr. Robert Greer, came in while we were there, and later downstairs we met the two grandsons; so before I got out of the house I'd seen the whole family.

Old Mr. Helm was crazy about Martina Greer; I could tell that. I think she was pretty much the kind of woman he admired—handsome and beautifully dressed and intelligent without being intellectual, and perfectly poised and at ease. There was something about her I didn't quite like, myself, though she was charming to me and of course I admired her too. Maybe it was because she was the kind of woman who rather obviously doesn't care whether other women are on earth, and my instincts resented it if my mind didn't. I'm sixty-eight now, as I've said.

I couldn't imagine why Martina had picked out Dr. Robert Greer to marry. Of course, you very seldom do see why people marry the ones they do, and six or eight years ago, when Martina married him—they were both thirtyish now—Robert Greer might have been very good-looking. By this time he was pretty bald. But dentistry isn't a society profession at best, and anyway it struck me that Dr. Greer, though pleasant and smart enough, was the kind of person not likely to go very far in any profession or business. He just didn't have push.

I said so to Charlotte going down the stairs.

"Oh, I don't know," Charlotte answered, when I said I didn't think Robert Greer would ever amount to much and Martina wouldn't like *that*. "Remind me to tell you about him, Julia. Right now I want you to meet the boys."

We could hear the boys talking in a room near the foot of the stairs, but when Charlotte and I paused in the door they stopped talking and set their glasses down and got up fast. They acted interrupted. The blue-eyed one put his glass down so hard he spilled a good deal of his highball on the mahogany table, but he didn't seem to care.

They were both nice, attractive boys. Charlotte's precious Breck looked a lot like Mary Preston, except that his eyes were brown; and he was handsome, but he was thin and tired-looking, and seemed older than his twenty-four years. Maybe his two rows of campaign ribbons explained that. Maybe that was the difference between Breck Helm and John Todd Brown, who hadn't gone to war; for they were as different as day and night.

Charlotte had told me the Brown boy was rejected for something the matter with his heart, and if that was so he certainly shouldn't have been drinking highballs at half-past eleven in the morning. He'd had several more than one, if I'm any judge—and, coming straight from Annapolis, I think I am. But he was carrying them beautifully, and his manners were as beautiful as his grandfather's—step-grandfather's—and his blue eyes made you like and trust him right away. They looked at you straighter than any blue eyes I ever saw. Maybe that boy was weak, as Charlotte thought and as the half-empty bottle on the table seemed to show, but I agreed with old Mr. Helm. I liked him better than any of them.

We talked for probably fifteen minutes, very pleasantly, before Charlotte and I said goodbye and started home. We were halfway down the outside steps when I discovered I'd dropped one of my gloves.

"No, you won't, Charlotte. I'll go back myself," I said, disgusted. "I think I see it, right there by the urn."

There were big ugly stone urns flanking the door we'd come out. Sure enough, the little spot of white beside one turned out to be my glove. I'd picked it up and brushed the dirt off the best I could, and was turning to go again when I heard young Captain Breckinridge Helm's voice. The window wasn't open much but I could hear him perfectly well.

"You knew Gus better than that," Breck Helm was saying softly. "You goddammed bloody fool."

John Todd Brown just laughed.

CHAPTER FOUR

Blockbuster was waiting for us when we got back to the Puritan, Blockbuster and a young man who had him under such perfect control, exuberant puppy though he was, that I wondered if I couldn't rent the young man by the week. I certainly wasn't looking forward to coping with Blockbuster in a three-room-kitchenette-and-bath apartment, especially one that didn't belong to me.

But then I thought of a career for young Captain Howard that was just as useful and that he'd probably like better. I hoped Mary Preston liked *him*, because to my mind he was just what she needed around the house the rest of her life—an example of perfect self-control, among other things, and the ability to make other people behave.

Charlotte and Captain Howard and I had lunch together—the Puritan has a nice restaurant downstairs, as well as kitchenettes—and he and Charlotte had a good time. I didn't. I kept thinking about what I'd just overheard, and turning it over and over in my mind without getting anywhere. And then I got to thinking about the smiling, sneering way that nasty old grandfather had looked at Emily Craig, who'd stayed indoors all that nice bright morning to read to him, and how he'd practically purred when Martina merely stopped in to say hello. Martina knew how to handle men, all right. If the rest of them weren't careful, old Breckinridge Helm would leave her all of his money, instead of just the share Charlotte had said she'd get.

But Charlotte had said it was the blue-eyed step-grandson who was the favorite.

It wasn't poor little Mary Preston, anyway. Listening to Charlotte and Captain Howard talk about her, I felt sorrier and sorrier for the child. Of course, I could see her faults, just as I freely admitted that John Todd Brown shouldn't have been a few sheets to the wind, as Dick calls it, at half past eleven in the morning. But I believe in making allowance for circumstances, and Mary Preston had had a harder time than a lot of people would have been willing to admit, since in a way she did have everything. But there'd been just a succession of incidents like the one about Blockbuster, all her life; and not only that, there'd been big things too.

Charlotte was telling Captain Howard about the one that seemed the biggest thing to Mary Preston. It certainly was a surprise to me.

"... always, from the time she was a little girl," Charlotte was saying. "The other children would change around every change of the wind; Emily wanted one day to be a missionary nun, I remember, and the mother of six children the next. And Johnny never could decide whether to be a cowboy or a pilot or somebody in the French Foreign Legion. But with Mary Preston it was always the same. She always said she was going to be a doctor."

"A doctor?" Captain Howard was as surprised as I was.

"A surgeon," Charlotte said firmly. "She always did like to cut things up. She used to operate on worms and June bugs when she was just a little thing, and later, when she got to biology, she had the time of her life. She used to stay way late after school in the afternoons, working on her frogs. She's still crazy about cutting up anything she can lay her hands on. I think that's the main reason they have so much fried chicken at that house, just so Mary Preston can cut it up."

Well, really, I thought, and looking over at Captain Howard I could see he felt the same way.

"Mary Preston certainly did get poor little Emily through biology, all right," Charlotte went on reminiscently. "Emily said she just *could not* do that laboratory work. She said it made her feel sick even to look at a grasshopper stuck on a pin, much less take his legs off. So Mary Preston did all her experiments for her."

"That was nice," I said feebly.

"Oh, but she wanted to do it," Charlotte said. "I remember Emily offered to give Mary Preston her new blue dress that she liked, after the teacher graded Emily's notebook A. But Mary Preston wouldn't take it."

"Well, why didn't she go to college, if she wanted to be a doctor?" I asked. "I thought you told me she went to that French finishing school in Washington, where they won't let them speak a word of English for two years."

"Miss Manet's. Yes, she did," Charlotte said. "She graduated last June. And of course she didn't know any more about anatomy and medicine than she did when she started out. It just wasn't that kind of a school."

"Has she been studying here since she got back?" I'd heard that Louisville had a right good municipal university.

Charlotte shook her head vigorously. "Oh, no. Her grandfather wouldn't hear of it. He said it was all foolishness, her wanting to be a doctor. He said she'd get over it."

"Well, most girls do," Captain Howard said. It was the first time he'd spoken since Charlotte started to tell how the beautiful young maiden he was romantic about just loved to cut up frying chickens and frogs.

I agreed with him that they did. But Charlotte shook her head at both of us.

"You don't know Mary Preston," she told Captain Howard. Really, I thought in exasperation, Charlotte has no sense at all. First the frogs, and now telling him he doesn't know her, when he undoubtedly thinks he knows her better than anybody else in the world.

"Once she gets the bit between her teeth you can't do a thing with that child," Charlotte went on complacently. "If she says she wants to be a doctor, she'll be a doctor yet."

Captain Howard didn't have anything to say to that, and I felt ready to change the subject too. I didn't see what Mary Preston's frustrated career had to do with Gus's murder, which I was mainly interested in. It wasn't as if Gus had been cut up and sent some place in a trunk.

"What did *you* do before you went in the Army, Captain Howard?" I asked politely. "Or have you always been in?"

"I was a metallurgical engineer," Captain Howard said. "When I enlisted, I was doing research at the Colorado School of Mines."

Charlotte was impressed. "My! My! You must be pretty smart, Captain Howard. I don't even know what all that kind of an engineer does."

"Well, Mrs. Buckner, you wouldn't want me to tell you, either." The Howard boy had the nicest kind of smile and Charlotte fairly beamed back at him. I could see she was beginning to get the idea I'd had since I first laid eyes on Captain Howard—about him and Mary Preston, I mean.

"Did you like Colorado?" she asked brightly. "Or is it too different from where you live?"

Captain Howard said, "Oh, I live *there!* Mrs. Buckner. I've lived in Denver all my life."

"Well, I hear some very good people do live in Colorado," Charlotte said broad-mindedly, with an effort. "They go there for their health, and then they just like it so well they stay. Was anybody in your family delicate, Captain Howard?"

Not so good, Charlotte, I said to myself. Naturally you don't want your courtesy great-niece's hypothetical children turning up with tuberculosis, but that wasn't very subtle. Next thing you'll be asking him his mother's maiden name, and what his prospects are.

Which Charlotte actually proceeded to do.

"Well, I've got to be starting back," Captain Howard said finally, to my relief. He got up and untethered Blockbuster, who, believe it or not, had been lying by his feet all through lunch, licking the polish off his shoes occasionally but for the most part good as gold.

"Wait a minute, Captain Howard," I said, rummaging in my bag. "I want to write you a check. How much do I owe you for Blockbuster?"

"Not a thing, Miss Tyler."

I just gave him a look and unscrewed my fountain pen.

"But, you see, he isn't my dog," Captain Howard said. "I got him for Mary Preston, and the papers are made out in her name. Grandfather or no grandfather, he belongs to her." Even Charlotte smiled back in spite of herself. But though she talks about old Breckinridge Helm herself, she certainly does not like it when other people seem to criticize. "If you want to take him with you when you go home, Miss Tyler, you can settle with Mary Preston. He's her dog."

"Now that's what I call a nice young man," Charlotte said when we were going up in the elevator.

"Even if he comes from Colorado and his mother was a Jones?" I asked meanly.

"Why, a lot of nice people are named Jones, Julia!" Charlotte was indignant. "They're a little hard to tell apart, I admit. But there are

Joneses and Joneses."

I said frankly, seeing that Charlotte was thoroughly converted to Captain Howard, "I'd like to see Mary Preston marry that boy."

"So would I." But Charlotte shook her head, and a frown developed between her eyebrows. "But something will happen, Julia. You just wait and see. Mary Preston was born to go through the woods and pick up a crooked stick."

"Well, I hope not!"

"You wait and see," Charlotte said again darkly. "Mary Preston has young men coming and going, always has ever since she was sixteen years old. And poor little Emily mostly just has the dates that Mary Preston gets her—and in her first season, too. And it isn't the war, either, because there are plenty of nice young men out at Fort Knox and Bowman Field. But you just wait. If there's a good marriage made in that family, Emily'll be the one to make it."

Charlotte and I planned to go shopping that afternoon. There are two good department stores in Louisville, she says, and quite a lot of nice smaller shops, and I'd probably see something I'd want to get for Anne. It really was high time to be thinking about summer dresses.

"And then we'll have dinner downtown," Charlotte said, planning happily. "We can go to the Canary Cottage, or anywhere you like. I like the Blue Boar, myself. Do you mind cafeterias, Julia?"

"I definitely like them best," I assured her, and I do.

Charlotte went on happily, "Then we'll go to the Blue Boar. It's really very nice, Julia, and some of the best people in Louisville go there for Sunday dinner. Even the ones that still have cooks. Well, I reckon I'd better get me a clean handkerchief and some fresh gloves, and then we'll start."

But the telephone rang instead.

"Why, yes, of course, Thelma," I could hear her saying. "Why, yes, tell him I'll be delighted." But I could tell she wouldn't be delighted at all. "Are they all there now? Well, then, you ask them for me when they come in. Tell them I want them all at half-past four and not to fail, because I'm making a chocolate cake."

I couldn't say "Well?" because I was company, but I'm afraid I looked it.

Charlotte said, "Well, there goes our nice trip downtown. I'm sorry, Julia; maybe we can get there tomorrow. But I never turn Breckinridge down when he asks me to do something for the children, and specially now that he's sick in bed— That was Thelma, the new upstairs maid across the street. She says Breckinridge wants me to ask the children over for tea. All six of them. At half-past four."

That was a funny thing to ask, I thought. Charlotte thought it was perfectly all right because it was Breckinridge Helm's idea, but it seems to me it takes a lot of nerve, as Dick says, to call up and tell somebody when to have a party and whom to ask. I don't care how close the friendship is.

We had little enough time to make the chocolate cake. I helped Charlotte, who I will say is a good cook, and then after she got her cake out of the oven and it was cooling, waiting to be iced, I turned the oven way down low and made some little egg kisses. They're nice with tea.

"Not that many of them will take tea," Charlotte said, sighing. "Emily will, and maybe Mary Preston—she knows I don't like to see her drink. And Martina's husband. But the boys will want cocktails, and Martina— I'm sorry to say it, Julia, but it's so. She never shows it"—Charlotte sounded outraged, as if that were the worst part—"but Martina drinks like a fish."

"Do you want me to make the cocktails?" I asked. "I've seen so many made lately, in Annapolis, that I think I know how."

"No, Johnny will make them. He likes to," Charlotte said. "You put the potato chips in the pan ready to heat, Julia, and cut up some cheese and open this bottle of olives. And you can get the whisky out of the sideboard if you like."

I got it out and I never saw such a collection of bottles. Besides the plentiful supply of rye and Scotch and bourbon, and brandy and rum and things like that, Charlotte had stuff I'd never even heard of.

"I hope you haven't turned out to be a secret drinker, Charlotte," I said severely, and Charlotte said, with a vague smile, "Oh, well, there is a lot, isn't there? But I always like for the boys to feel at home."

Out to old Aunt Mary's, I said to myself, seizing Blockbuster and trying to hush his barking while Charlotte went to answer the door.

It was a right nice little party. The children all loved Charlotte—you could see that. Except maybe Martina Greer. I don't mean she wasn't nice as pie; it was "Cousin Charlotte, wouldn't you rather have this chair?" and "Cousin Charlotte, you make the best chocolate cake in the world," all the way. It was just that I didn't think Martina loved anybody much, except the lady that she saw in the mirror.

Everybody was nice to me, too. Mary Preston sat on one side of me on the sofa—she and I were bosom friends now on account of Blockbuster— and young Johnny Brown on the other side. He certainly was the most attractive young man I'd met for a long time, and I couldn't understand why Charlotte didn't like him best. I did. I liked him best of all.

I'll have to quit calling him "young Johnny," though. I could see when

I sat close to him that there were lines around his nice clear blue eyes, and when I asked Charlotte afterward she said yes, he was the oldest of the lot except Martina and her husband. He was nearly twenty-nine, she said, and had been in advertising for seven years, first for the Helm Tobacco Company and then, the last three, for an agency in New York.

Johnny was on his feet a good part of the time, getting up and down to help Charlotte, but mostly making trips to the cocktail shaker for his own benefit. That's how he happened to see the old man with the moustache and the big black briefcase going up the steps of the Helm house across the street.

Johnny went over to the window and pulled the curtains aside. "Well, boys and girls," he said, and his voice didn't sound a bit the way it did when he'd talked to me, "there goes the reason why we were invited to this very nice little party of Cousin Charlotte's. Mr. W. Blodgett Fownes, come by request to change Grandfather's will."

I looked around from one young face to another, during the silence that followed. They weren't any of them very nice to see. And then Emily Craig, of all people, burst into tears.

CHAPTER FIVE

Charlotte says I read too many murder books. Maybe I do. But even without that, even without the fact of Gus's death in the background, I believe the same thoughts would have gone through my mind. Mr. Helm ought to have died, I thought. Died before this had a chance to happen. Maybe he would have died, if the grandchildren had known ahead of time he was going to change his will. There are so many ways to kill helpless old people. You can push them downstairs, or feed them things they're not supposed to have, or even just forget to give them their medicine. And nobody ever suspects, except maybe the doctor sometimes, and he doesn't say anything because he realizes nothing could be proved and all that would come of stirring it up would be a lot of trouble and unpleasantness, and maybe professional oblivion for *him*.

Of course, there wouldn't have been much chance, in the Helm grandchildren's case, for old Mr. Helm's sudden death to go uninvestigated. Not when the police suspected them of Gus's murder already. Killing another old man would be a dangerous thing for them to try. And yet there wasn't any doubt in my mind that one of them *would* have tried it if he—or she—had known ahead of time about the change of will. It's the kind of thing that really does happen. That's why for every fantastically reasoned murder book there are a dozen about rich people killed before they can change their wills. Fantasia makes interesting reading sometimes, but the old moth-eaten plots are real.

Old Mr. Helm was lucky, I thought, going to sleep at last. He changed his will without talking too much beforehand.

It must have been half-past twelve that night when the telephone rang. I answered it. The telephone is in Charlotte's room, right on the little table by her bed, but she was sleeping the sleep of the just.

"Aunt Charlotte?" Breck Helm's voice came over the wire, hurried and hushed. He went on before I had a chance to say it wasn't his Aunt Charlotte he was talking to. "Can you come over here right away? Grandfather—"

If he paused at all it was only for a second. And yet in that second things went through my mind that would have taken minutes to say. All that I'd thought before, and then, in bewilderment: But he's already *changed* his will. Killing him now would be like locking the stable door after the horse was stolen. No, old Mr. Helm can't be murdered. It wouldn't make sense.

Breck Helm was going on, answering as if I'd spoken out loud, "It's all right, Aunt Charlotte. I mean it isn't—Grandfather's just had another stroke. He looks—bad. The doctor's on his way, but would you come too, please?"

"This is Julia Tyler, Breck," I said, a little sharply. Somehow I was afraid of what he might tell me if he went on thinking I was Charlotte. Yet I couldn't have spoken before. I said, feeling the reaction of anticlimax, "I'll wake your Aunt Charlotte. She'll be right over, I know. Is there anything I can do?"

Breck said there wasn't, and thanked me and hung up; and then I waked Charlotte, who is the kind that can sleep through the most earsplitting noise but wakens at a light touch. She was amazingly calm, I must say, and she certainly did make record time getting into her clothes and getting the curlers out of her hair.

I didn't go with her, of course—after all, I'd known the people only three days—but next morning, after Blockbuster and I had met Thelma out sweeping the walk, and she said old Mr. Helm was still alive and everything was at sixes and sevens in the house, I thought I'd better go over and at least offer to help. So I shut Blockbuster in the kitchenette where he couldn't hurt much of anything, and gave him Charlotte's plate-scraper to play with, and went back across the street.

Charlotte met me in the hall, looking, from lack of sleep, as if she'd been drunk last night, drunk the night before. I said, "Charlotte, why don't you go on home and get some rest? There's nothing here that I can't do, and I'll be glad to, and they'll probably need you worse later on."

From what Thelma had told me there wasn't much doubt old Mr. Helm was going to die. "Well—" Charlotte said uncertainly. She knew she needed the sleep, but she liked to feel indispensable, too. After a while she did go, though, and then I made a list of the flowers that were already beginning to come, and answered the telephone for Mary Preston and Emily while they got a little sleep too, and established friendly relations with the servants. All four of them seemed very good, as Charlotte had said. I agreed with her it was nothing short of miraculous that Mary Preston could round them up in the middle of a servant shortage; and not only that, she had them firmly under her thumb. They quoted Miss Mary Preston to me as if she were fifty years old instead of twenty-one, and knew all the ins and outs of keeping house. That child had a lot more good points than bad ones, it seemed to me.

I'd been prepared to dislike the doctor on Mary Preston's account, and maybe that was why I did. Dr. Jordan, his name was. He came downstairs while I was standing in the hall looking at the war headlines in the *Courier-Journal*, and I nearly jumped out of my skin when he pussyfooted up behind me and stopped and cleared his throat.

"I find Mr. Helm more than holding his own this time, Mrs. Buckner. Oh," he said then. "I beg your pardon, madam. I thought you were Mrs. Buckner."

"Miss Tyler," I told him stiffly. I wear my skirts a good three inches shorter than Charlotte Buckner does, and though my hair is just as grey I don't fix it like Charlotte's, or Queen Mary's either. I resented being mistaken for her even with my back turned.

"Miss Tyler. I suppose you're a friend of the family, Miss Tyler?"

I admitted it, and added, "Idiot," under my breath. Who did he think I was, the paper boy?

"Mr. Helm is doing very nicely by this time," Dr. Jordan told me condescendingly. "Very nicely. I feel very much encouraged about him. You understand I would hardly care to be quoted, Miss Tyler. Especially to the press. But I hope very much that I can pull Mr. Helm through."

"That's good," I said automatically and insincerely.

"Mr. Helm is a very valuable citizen, a very fine man. I assure you I feel my responsibility keenly, Miss Tyler," Dr. Jordan went on pompously, and I murmured the way you have to at such points. "I have the best nurse in the city with Mr. Helm. Specialist in paralytic cases. She was relieved from a paralytic case only yesterday." He cleared his throat. "And by the way, Miss Tyler—"

I was beginning to get tired of my name. I said, "Yes?" It wouldn't have hurt me to say, "Yes, doctor?" but I didn't.

Dr. Jordan took his nose glasses off and put them on again, for no good reason that I could see. I never met a man with so many irritating habits—this, and the throat-clearing, and presently he put the tips of his fingers together and looked at me over them, wise as an owl.

"I've instructed Miss Kittinger to allow no visitors to Mr. Helm's room. Nobody at all, that is." He cleared his throat again. "Normally, such orders don't cover members of the immediate family. But in this case I felt it was—ah, members of the family who might have the worst possible effect on Mr. Helm. Miss Mary Preston—" Something in the way he said it made me look at him sharply. I was right. He didn't mean just that Mary Preston tended to upset her grandfather's temper. Dr. Jordan, with all his irritating faults, was sincerely worried about his patient. I ached to tell him that he needn't be, that old Mr. Helm had already changed his will, that the danger he was afraid of—that I'd been afraid of too, subconsciously—was past. But of course I couldn't say it, any more than he could say what was on *his* mind. Dr. Jordan and I merely looked at each other for a minute, with Gus's shade between us.

"You realize I can't actually prevent Mr. Helm's family from visiting his room, Miss Tyler. But perhaps if you would use your influence—"

I had a regular reception after the doctor left. Ten o'clock had come, the hour after which, in Louisville as well as in Charleston and a lot of other Southern towns, it's all right to pay calls. Suddenly the telephone stopped ringing and people came instead. The horrible gilt and red velvet parlor was full of them—all kinds and conditions. It seemed to me I met that morning all the Louisville people I hadn't met before. All the *nice* families, as Charlotte would say. And then there were a lot of business men, and executives from the Helm Tobacco Company, and workers from the various welfare organizations Mr. Helm was interested in. The rector of Grace and St. Peter's was there too, hovering over one decayed gentlewoman after another like a fat black buzzard.

I got along very well, with the new butler's help. He announced the names as if it had been a ball in an English novel. But Mary Preston felt awful about dumping so much social burden on a stranger in Louisville, and couldn't apologize enough when she finally came downstairs. She'd had no idea, she said, that she would sleep so long.

I told her, "It didn't matter a bit. I was glad to do it. Are you sure you slept long enough?" She still looked mighty tired and pale.

Mary Preston said she had. She didn't seem to want sympathy or what Dick calls the soft stuff.

I said in a businesslike way, "These are the people that called you up while you were asleep. This one and this one want you to call them back, but the others just asked if there was anything they could do, and said to let them know if there was. And some Sergeant Morgan," I went on, reading from another piece of paper, "called Emily four different times. He seemed to think I ought to wake her up, and maybe she would have wanted me to herself. But I thought: she needed her sleep. I told him I'd have her call the minute she did wake up."

"Oh, he can wait," Mary Preston said. She got the same worried little frown between her eyebrows that Charlotte had had when she talked about *her* going through the woods and picking up a crooked stick. Obviously that was what Sergeant Morgan was, in Mary Preston's opinion at least.

I said tentatively, "I hope Emily's sergeant is as nice as your Captain Howard, Mary Preston. Your Aunt Charlotte and I had lunch with him yesterday, you know, and we liked him *very* much."

"I like him too," Mary Preston said, too readily. "He was an angel pie to get Blockbuster for me, and you're an angel pie to keep him, Miss Julia. I hope—that is, I hope it isn't too much trouble."

I felt pretty sure she'd started out to say, "I hope you won't have to keep him long." When old Breckinridge Helm died, of course, Blockbuster could come home.

I turned down Mary Preston's invitation to stay for lunch, and was just gathering up my things to leave when the telephone rang. I was right beside it in the hall. "I'll do just this one more call for you, Mary Preston," I said, and put my things down again.

The voice over the wire, a crisp, efficient woman's voice, answered me with, "Who is speaking, please?" the way I was taught was impolite when you haven't given your own name first.

I said a little stiffly that it was Miss Tyler.

The voice hesitated then a minute, sounding more human. "Oh—Mr. Helm's nurse? We didn't know he was getting a new one."

"I'm not the nurse," I said briefly. I saw no reason to go into the matter of Mr. Helm's nurse, or Mr. Helm's second stroke, before I even knew whom I was talking to. "I'm taking all the messages this morning. Who is this speaking, please, and what can I do for you?"

Evidently I can still sound like a Latin teacher of forty years' experience. The voice over the wire said meekly, "This is Mr. Fownes's office, Miss Tyler. Mr. Fownes wants to send a message to Mr. Helm, please. Will you tell him that Mr. Fownes has had his will typed and wants to know when Mr. Helm would like to sign it?"

I just stood there. So did Mary Preston, who, at my elbow, had heard every word. Finally I said, "Will you repeat that, please?"

"Mr. Fownes drafted a new will for Mr. Helm yesterday afternoon," Mr. Fownes's office girl told me obligingly. "And Mr. Fownes brought the draft back to the office to have a fair copy typed. It's ready, and Mr. Fownes will bring it out himself for Mr. Helm's signature any time that it's convenient."

I said, after a shorter pause this time, "I'm afraid it won't be convenient any time soon, Miss—? Evidently you haven't heard. Mr. Helm had another stroke last night, in the night. He's holding his own, but he certainly won't be able to sign anything for a while."

I heard a sound like a sigh behind me. Mary Preston said rapidly under her breath, as if she were talking to herself, "He won't be able to sign it— You mean he *hasn't* signed it—it isn't any *good*—"

And then with the last word there was another sound, and, looking out of the corner of my eye, I could see that Mary Preston, whose manners if not her self-control were usually such a credit to Charlotte's teaching, had left me to finish coping with Mr. Fownes's office and to let myself out of the house the best way I could. I was alone in the hall.

CHAPTER SIX

"Suppose Mr. Helm had signed that new will, Charlotte? Suppose he still gets well enough to sign it?" I said at lunch. I'd gone back across the street for a little while, and Charlotte and I had a good mushroom omelet she'd made. "Do you have any idea what was in it? Who would get the money then?"

Charlotte hesitated and I said quickly, "I'm sorry, Charlotte. It's none of my business, and I'm being too inquisitive. I know better, really."

"Why, Julia, of course you're not being inquisitive," Charlotte said, very nicely. "I like to see you interested in those children across the street. Their grandmother and I were nearly as much like sisters as you and Anne's grandmother were; and aren't you pleased when your friends notice Anne and take to her the way you took to Mary Preston?"

I said, feeling ashamed—for though I do like Mary Preston and the others, too, it was mainly because of Gus's murder I was interested— "Well, yes. And of course anything you tell me I keep to myself." Which I did, especially since I hadn't been in Louisville long enough to know anybody to tell it to.

"About the will," Charlotte said. "The reason I hesitated was because

I don't know what *was* in it, really. I only know what Gus said."

Gus!

"Servants don't always get things straight, and anyway, Gus was getting mighty old," Charlotte resumed. "And then I was so busy trying to calm him down, while he was telling me about it, that I didn't halfway get what he said."

"What was he upset about?" I asked bluntly.

"Well, he didn't think Breckinridge ought to change his will at all," Charlotte said. "That is, he thought it was fine for him to leave the money to the church and the university library and the charities he was interested in. 'There ain't no pockets in shrouds,' he said, 'and the best pocket to leave your earthly substance in is the pocket of the Lord.' And he thought it was all right for Breckinridge to cut down on the one grandchild that had made him mad. Gus thought that one grandchild ought to be punished. But he didn't agree with Breckinridge's idea of cutting them *all* down, just because of that one. They had quite a fuss about it."

I said, "I expect it would sound funny up North, the way people in our part of the country discuss important things like their wills with old colored servants. And get into fusses with them. But we all do it—if we're lucky enough to have any servants left."

Charlotte agreed. "Breckinridge knew that Gus was the most loyal friend he had, I don't care what color his skin was. He talked a lot of things over with him, and of course whenever Gus had anything on *his* mind he went to Breckinridge with it. That was right. The only thing was," Charlotte said, frowning, "maybe I shouldn't have let Gus come over and talk to *me* the way he did. He'd come over and tell me just everything that happened in that house across the street, and of course it wasn't any of my business."

"Well, I don't see how you could have kept him from it," I said. "Gus knew you were really interested, almost like close blood kin. And then he'd worked for *you* so long, before he ever came to the Helms, that it was hard to break old habits."

Charlotte said doubtfully, "Yes, I reckon that part was all right. But he oughtn't to have talked to anybody else, Julia. And I'm afraid he did."

"Johnny knew." I nodded. "Or suspected, anyway. And the rest of them were shocked and upset and all. But I'm not sure they were surprised to see Mr. Fownes going up those steps, are you?"

"No, I'm not," Charlotte said.

We sat for a minute or so in silence.

"So Mr. Helm told Gus that one of his grandchildren had made him mad about something and so he was going to change his will and cut down on all of them," I prompted. "Did he give any reason for that last? What did Gus say?"

"Well, Gus said that Breckinridge had decided too much money wasn't good for young people," answered Charlotte. "The grandchild that made him mad wouldn't have acted that way, he thought, if there hadn't been so much money around and so much in prospect. He said too much money to spend could very easily ruin a young person."

I nodded. Much as I hated to agree with old Mr. Helm, I thought so too.

"Breckinridge's idea was to leave them all a reasonable income," Charlotte went on. "Two hundred a month apiece, Gus said. That way they'd never be in want, and yet they wouldn't just have money to throw around."

"Two hundred a month is plenty, really," I said thoughtfully. "I've lived on half of that most of my life. Small-town teachers are lucky if they get that much. And I've had a good life, and no complaints to make. But maybe if I'd been brought up to expect a million dollars—"

"That's just it," Charlotte said. "Martina, for instance, goes to Hattie Carnegie for her clothes, and that means she and Dr. Greer can't be saving anything. And it's silly, too—there are plenty of good dressmakers in Louisville and Cincinnati both."

"I expect Mary Preston spends a lot on her clothes too."

"Yes, she does. Mary Preston likes good things," Charlotte said. "Now Emily doesn't care about dresses. She spends a good deal on them too, because her grandfather gives it to her *to* spend, and then Mary Preston goes with her and picks everything out. But Emily could get along fine on two hundred dollars a month, even if she didn't marry."

"How about the boys?"

Charlotte said, frowning, "Well, Johnny's the kind that never does have enough, no matter how much it is. Two thousand a month would slip through his fingers just the way two hundred would. And nothing to show for it. Now when *Breck* spends money," Charlotte said proudly, "he puts it right into Holliday Hall."

"Holliday Hall?" I'd never heard of it.

"That's his father's place in Bourbon County. Breck's father bought it from one of the Hollidays—well, maybe he did win it playing cards," Charlotte said in a burst of honesty. "People said he did, and the deed *was* for one dollar and other valuable considerations. Anyway, Breck inherited from his father, of course, and he loves it better than any place in the world. It really is a nice old house. But of course it takes a lot to keep it up, and Breck doesn't have anything except just what he makes and the little his grandfather gives him. A lot of people think he's silly to try to hold on to it, especially when it isn't a family place. Breckinridge, I know, thought he ought to let it go."

I'll bet he did, I said to myself grimly.

"But Breck wants to live out there and have a stock farm, after the war," Charlotte went on. "Of course he'd have to start in a small way—"

"But after his grandfather dies he'll have plenty," I finished for her. "Or would have under the old will. But suppose old Mr. Helm gets well and signs this new will, Charlotte—could Breck run a stock farm on two hundred dollars a month and what he makes?"

"Well, no," Charlotte admitted, frowning. "You see, it's all outgo and no income the first few years, Breck says. And then he'd have to compete with all those rich Northern people who've come into Fayette and Bourbon Counties. Most all the people with stock farms have money to burn."

No wonder Breck Helm's face had been so ugly yesterday in Charlotte's living room. No wonder they all had looked that way. Breck seeing his cherished Holliday Hall plans going glimmering; and Johnny who always needed money on general principles; and Mary Preston who wanted to go to college and medical school; and Martina who probably didn't agree with Charlotte that the dressmakers in Cincinnati and Louisville were as good as Hattie Carnegie. Only Emily Craig, according to Charlotte, would be able to get along nicely on two hundred dollars a month.

Yet it was Emily Craig, out of all the rest, who had burst into tears.

I said abruptly, "Charlotte, which was the grandchild that made him mad?"

"I don't know."

"Didn't Gus know?"

"Oh, yes, Gus knew. But he wouldn't tell me that. I asked him, right square out," Charlotte admitted. "All he'd say was it was 'a bad, bad thing that child done'—it made him feel ashamed for the whole family. He said it was bad enough for Mr. Johnny to carouse around and Miss Emily to slip out at night and Miss Mary Preston to sass her grandpappy, but this—whatever it was—was 'the last straw and the worstest one.'"

"Don't tell me Emily slips out at night!" I said.

"She probably went out to mail a letter. It didn't take much for Gus to disapprove of," Charlotte said. "He didn't even like for Emily and Mary Preston to come see me after dark unless he walked across the street with them. And Mary Preston just drew the line at that. She and Gus used to fuss something awful, about everything under the sun."

"Charlotte, who do you really think killed Gus?" I was shocked to hear it coming out at last. But I had to say it. I thought it was about time I took the bull by the horns and Charlotte faced facts. I thought she could, too. Charlotte had gone up in my estimation since I came. That first night when she told me it must have been a tramp that killed Gus I thought she really believed it, though a more ridiculous idea I never heard in my life. But I remembered Charlotte as a mighty silly young girl. She was silly, too. I won't give an inch on that. But it seems to me that by now she's got right much sense. Underneath, of course.

"You don't really think it was a tramp, do you?" I asked again, when Charlotte didn't answer. I put my dessert fork down and looked her straight in the eye.

Charlotte was crying.

I felt awful, of course. I'd been wrong to try to bring things out in the open; keeping up that pretense, I saw now, was all that had been keeping Charlotte up herself. I picked up my fork and began eating my pie again fast, praying for a diversion.

Sometimes I think I'll just quit praying like that. Not that I always get results, of course. But sometimes when I do they're entirely too effective. I certainly didn't want Charlotte's living room ceiling to fall, scaring us both to death and scarring her great-grandmother's mahogany table, where we'd been eating lunch. Charlotte got all the good china off, though, before the plaster came down. I had to laugh afterwards, remembering how long the drops had been plopping down before it dawned on me that it was unlikely, really, that their loud juicy noise was Charlotte crying into her plate. And Charlotte and I must have been a funny sight, too, rushing around getting things out from under the place where, obviously, somebody had let a bathtub overflow upstairs. We were both too excited to feel scared for ourselves. Of course, plaster is heavy when it does fall. I believe this would have stayed up quite a while longer, though, if Breck Helm hadn't knocked on Charlotte's door and come right on in, shutting the door behind him not specially hard but, apparently, hard enough.

An hour later I was unpacking my things in the big corner bedroom on the third floor of the Helm house, across the hall from Mr. Helm's room.

It was just about the last place in the world I wanted to be. Goodness knows I'd tried every way I knew how to keep from coming. It would be much too much of an imposition, I said. I'd come back and visit Charlotte another time, some time when it was more convenient. I couldn't think of adding to the burdens of even an old friend whose plaster had fallen, and certainly not of comparative strangers with serious illness in their house. But Breck and Charlotte beat me down on every point I raised, and of course I couldn't mention my one unanswerable reason for not wanting to move across the street into the Helm house. I didn't really think, as I'd told Anne and Dick, that the murderer would hurt an innocent bystander. All the same I didn't want to stand too close.

I did gain one point, though. I just insisted that Charlotte and I could share a room instead of making Breck move in with Johnny, to give one of us his. Charlotte wasn't my idea of much protection, but she was better than nothing, since I couldn't take Blockbuster. For once I would have been glad to have him. He barks almost as well as he chews the furniture. But on account of old Mr. Helm, of course, we had to leave him with the janitor at the Puritan.

Our room at the Helm house was nice and we had our own bathroom, a marble-topped old-fashioned place that a modern architect would have considered big enough for a bedroom, not just a bath. It was all ready for company, with beautiful thick pink towels and pink soap and a whole row of bath salts jars on the shelf over the tub, every kind you could think of.

Charlotte said, coming out, "Julia, I've finished, and I've started your bath for you. But let me warn you. Don't waste your time using those Pink Clover bath salts. They don't smell a bit. Somebody must have left the top off the jar or something, and they've lost all their strength."

They really had. It was too bad, too, because while the other bath salts were all nice by themselves, they smelled sort of hybrid when you put their flower odors with the soap. It was Harriet Hubbard Ayer Pink Clover. But the Pink Clover salts were obviously, as Charlotte had said, not worth bothering to use. Only the faintest smell came up from the jar of fine white crystals, though I put my nose practically inside.

I had a nice bath, though, and plenty of time left to get dressed for dinner. Charlotte had dressed in a hurry so she could sit for a while beforehand with old Mr. Helm, so I had the big ugly, comfortable bedroom to myself.

I heard the footsteps over my head for quite a while before I paid much attention. After all, there was nothing very remarkable about somebody's walking around in the room above. But then all of a sudden I stopped with my hairbrush mid-air.

The room above us was the corner room that Charlotte had pointed out to me that first night, the one with the window on the extreme left. Gus's room.

And Gus was dead and gone.

CHAPTER SEVEN

I looked around the Helm dinner table pretty thoughtfully that night. Mary Preston was at the head, looking lovely the way she always does. She seemed ten years older, though, than the girl who'd run down the hall to Charlotte's apartment that first day I met her, laughing and hugging that little varmint Blockbuster in both arms. I was beginning to doubt I'd ever see her looking that happy again. But she laughed in all the right places and kept the conversation going with a skill that was amazing at twenty-one. I remembered, though, that she'd been her grandfather's hostess ever since Martina married and left home.

Martina looked beautiful too, that night. "Lovely" is never a word to use on her, though it's just right for Mary Preston. Martina is too sophisticated. But Hattie Carnegie would have swelled with pride to see the way she looked in that plain black long-sleeved dinner dress with the silver lobster, or whatever it was, across her stomach; and her hair and her make-up and fingernails were all just right. And the most amazing thing about her, or so it seemed to me, was that she looked exactly that perfect at the end of the evening.

I didn't agree with Charlotte, though, that drinking had no effect on Martina. I thought all those little glasses were the reason she got quieter and quieter as time went along, until finally she just sat as if she were posing for her portrait, smiling but never saying a word.

There were nine of us at the table, besides Breckinridge Helm's empty chair. I sat between Emily, sweet and meek as usual in a pretty pale blue dress, and my favorite, John Todd Brown. I can see right through that young man—I mean I know he's probably weak on the solid virtues and doesn't mean half the nice things he says—but he really is attractive. Miss Kittinger certainly thought so. She sat on the other side of him, giggling so hard at everything Johnny said that her starched white uniform fairly rattled. It annoyed me, rather. Maybe she was the best paralytic nurse in Louisville, but I like to see a nurse take a little more personal interest in her cases. Miss Kittinger was as little distressed over her patient upstairs as the family was, and that was saying a lot.

I don't believe there was one out of all those children who really cared a thing for their grandfather. Oh, maybe Emily did, or thought she did. And of course maybe when he did die some of the rest of them would look back and be sorry, and remember his good points and forget his bad ones, and decide they really had loved him after all. But there weren't any signs of it now.

They talked a little about the new president and about the war, at least the men did, and I found out that Breck Helm had been flying the Hump, which is what they call the mountains between China and India. Undoubtedly that was why he looked so strained and worn out and old for his age, and why he'd been given so much latitude in the matter of leave. He'd come home on an emergency, after his grandfather had his stroke, but he was due a regular leave anyhow, and so they were letting him stay on. He had sixty days. Poor boy, he needed every one of them to rest up in, judging from the way he looked; and yet he couldn't be getting much rest, with sickness in the house and the police suspecting his family in a murder case. I felt sorry for him, after all he'd been through.

"I wish poor Breck didn't have to go back at all," Emily said to me softly, under cover of the talk about war. "I wish he could just go out to Holliday Hall and stay."

"Well, maybe he can soon. The war looks pretty nearly over," I said. Of course I wasn't letting on that I knew Breck's life at Holliday Hall depended on their grandfather's will.

Emily said doubtfully, "Well, but if Grandfather should need him at the factory— He was saying just the other day he wished the war were over so Breck could come back and handle the labor union people. That's what he did before he enlisted."

No wonder he enlisted, I thought. From all I hear, I'd rather fly the Hump myself.

"I imagine Johnny would be good at that sort of thing, too," I said aloud. "He gets along with everybody so well and everybody seems to like him. And he's not nervous like Breck. If anybody could make the lion and the lamb lie down together—and that's what it amounts to, isn't it?—I should think he'd be the one."

"But Johnny's so good at advertising," Emily said quickly—and a little uneasily, I thought. "I don't believe Grandfather would want to take him away from that."

It didn't sound much like Grandfather until I remembered that Johnny was supposed to be old Breckinridge Helm's favorite, just as he was mine and Miss Kittinger's. But even Miss Kittinger was certainly having the happiest evening of her life. Her giggles pealed out almost continuously. She was so pleased to have Johnny bending over her, acting as if she were the only woman in the world, that she didn't seem to mind the fact that he was more than a little drunk, or that Mary Preston, at the head of the table, kept giving them what Dick calls dirty looks.

Charlotte was sitting across the table from me, and I caught her eye and saw that she noticed it too.

"Mary Preston certainly didn't like the way her cousin was drinking tonight," I commented to Charlotte after we'd gone to our room. "She just fairly glared at him."

"Him?"

"At Johnny, of course." She doesn't have but one *him* cousin, I felt like adding. Of course, Dr. Greer was a sort of cousin too, but nobody ever seemed to think about him. He was just one of those people.

"Why, Mary Preston doesn't mind Johnny's drinking, Julia," Charlotte said, puzzled. "She drinks herself, more than I wish she would."

"Well, she certainly did glare at him tonight," I maintained. "You've just forgotten, Charlotte. You noticed it yourself at the time."

Charlotte remembered then and laughed, a little condescendingly, I thought. "Oh, yes, but that wasn't why she was mad at him, Julia. It was that nurse, Miss Kitty—whatever her name is. It just makes Mary Preston wild and crazy to see Johnny notice another girl."

"*Johnny?*"

"Why, yes," Charlotte said complacently. "Mary Preston's always thought Johnny was the sun, moon, and stars. She'd do anything for him. Anything in this world." Charlotte. paused for effect. "And three years ago—it was the year Mary Preston came out—they got engaged."

"Engaged?" I repeated feebly. "Are they still engaged?" Charlotte certainly hadn't talked as if they were, the time she and I were discussing Captain Howard.

"Oh, no, they aren't engaged anymore," Charlotte said. "Mary Preston got to thinking it over. Two weeks before the wedding—with the presents already coming in, Julia, and the dresses all fitted. She said—you know how Mary Preston talks—she said the whole thing was giving her grandfather too much pleasure. She said she'd be damned—excuse me, Julia—if she played into his hand."

Well, really, I thought, the way I so often did when it was something about Mary Preston. But I couldn't help liking the child, and I was glad that Charlotte and I, since we had to be there, could be of some help to her and Emily. Somehow you never thought of Martina Greer in connection with things to be done, and neither did she. There were a good many things, of course, that couldn't be left to servants. Fortunately the nurse had stayed—the first one they'd had any such luck with. I attributed it about half to Johnny and half to old Breckinridge Helm's condition. He *couldn't* hurt Miss Kittinger's feelings, because he still wasn't able to say a word.

"But he'll get well, all right," I heard Martina telling Emily one day.

"There's not a doubt in my mind Grandfather will get well."

I was shocked by the way she said it. The words were perfectly conventional and proper, but her light, usually attractive voice was as bitter as gall.

And Emily. Emily didn't sound bitter, but *her* voice, when she said, "Oh, Martina, I think he will too," had a definitely hopeless tone. In spite of myself, I felt a flash of pity for old Breckinridge Helm. Of course, it was all his own fault that his grandchildren disliked him, and valued the money he'd leave more than they did his continued presence on earth. But it seems to me pretty sad, anyway, to come to such a pass. Except for Charlotte Buckner, there wasn't a soul I knew of that really wanted him to get well.

Charlotte apologized to me for being so gloomy, as she called it. "You're not having a very nice visit, Julia. You haven't even got downtown."

"Oh, I'll get downtown soon enough," I said politely, and I did. Too soon. I broke a piece off a tooth and had to go downtown to the dentist. My tooth didn't hurt, but the edge was sharp against my tongue and, anyway, it was on the side that's my favorite for chewing. What made me the maddest was that I hadn't been eating anything hard when it happened. I was just eating an ordinary hot biscuit, of all things.

"Well, Charlotte, I hope Louisville dentists aren't booked as far ahead as they are in most places," I said. "Do you think yours could take me right away?"

"Well, Julia, to tell the truth, I don't have a dentist here," Charlotte answered hesitantly. "That is, he's *here*— I mean I've changed, and I'm Dr. Greer's patient now. Martina's husband. But of course his office is in Cincinnati, and all his instruments and things—he couldn't do you any good. And Dr. Leidner was sort of mad when I left him for Dr. Greer, I think. I don't believe I'd have any influence with *him*."

"And influence is what I need somebody to have, these days, when I'm a stranger in a strange land." I nodded. "Well, what about these children here? Maybe Mary Preston could get me an appointment. You say she can talk the birds out of the trees."

Mary Preston could and did. She not only got me an appointment that very same morning, she drove me to the Heyburn Building herself, and afterwards took me to lunch at the Brown.

"It's mighty nice of you to spend so much time, Mary Preston," I said when we were eating our ice cream. "But are you sure there isn't something you'd planned to do this afternoon, instead of taking me to see the stores?"

"I haven't been able to plan anything at all on account of Grandfather,"

Mary Preston said, shaking her head. "Aunt Charlotte would have had a duck with lavender feathers if I'd stuck my nose out of the family vault. But now that we had to come, and we're already *here*—"

"We'll make an afternoon of it," I said. I didn't see why not, either. I called Charlotte up and explained, and then Mary Preston and I went through the big nice Stewart Dry Goods Company, with middle-aged and elderly clerks that reminded me of the ones in Richmond and Baltimore, and Kaufman-Strauss's, and a lot of smaller shops. Mary Preston bought a pink wool suit I would have liked to have for Anne. It was very pale pink, not much more than flesh color, and soft and warm as a kitten's ear. The only thing in this world the matter with it was the price tag. I don't believe in paying as much for a suit as you would for a house and lot.

Well, we had the nicest kind of an afternoon, and on top of it we walked along Fourth Street right into Mary Preston's Captain Howard and a friend of his from Fort Knox, a Major Barry. They asked us to tea and I accepted against my better judgment. I really thought we ought to be getting back. But Mary Preston had been mighty nice to me, and she had been shut up in the family vault a long time, and she was looking at me the way Blockbuster does when he wants his plate-scraper thrown.

Captain Howard and I talked about Blockbuster, I'm sorry to say. I mean I was sorry it turned out like that—Mary Preston walking with Major Barry, who was very nice but not what I had in mind for her, and then the two of us. Mary Preston seemed perfectly satisfied, though. Captain Howard did too, talking to me, but I hope and believe that was nothing but nice manners.

"I certainly do like Captain Howard, Mary Preston," I couldn't help telling her again, when we were driving home through the five-thirty traffic. "Is everybody you know as nice?"

"Well, just about," Mary Preston said, to my annoyance. "But I'll tell you, Miss Julia"—I'd not been "Miss Tyler" since the Blockbuster incident—"when you get to my age, of course you realize that men aren't really anything but men, after all."

When you got to her age. Twenty-one. I don't often think of the right quotation at the right moment, but this time it went through my mind. *But I was one and twenty. No use to talk to me.* It just suited Mary Preston.

"Other things are more important," Mary Preston said. "Like brain operations, for instance. Of course it's all right for Emily to talk about wanting to get married. She's only eighteen. I was that way myself my first season. But it's just a phase; she'll get over it."

I sincerely hoped she would. I'd known more than one sweet, nice girl like Emily Craig—every quality to make a good wife, and some man would be lucky to get her. The only trouble was, she'd be lucky to get the man.

"Charlotte was telling me you wanted to be a doctor, Mary Preston," I said carefully, instead.

Mary Preston told me about it all the way home.

Some years back, when my Anne was starting off to college, I'd rather worried because she didn't want a career. All her friends seemed all worked up about what they were going to do and be—which is perfectly normal and a nice idea, even though it doesn't often work out for girls. I talked to Anne very seriously about careers, I remember. But the best I could do was get her to take kindergarten training, which she said she could use on her own children. It worried me, as I've said. Anne had always been such a nice, uncomplicated, well-adjusted child. But listening to Mary Preston now, I decided I'd worried for nothing. I'd rather have had a child lacking the drive for recognition than this intense young thing with the blazing blue eyes.

"Nothing can stop me," Mary Preston said in conclusion. She'd parked the car outside the house, and as she talked she drove the fist of her right hand into the palm of her left, over and over again. "And I mean *nothing!* Miss Julia. I'm going to medical school, and I won't wait till I have to go in a wheelchair, either." She said again, "Nothing can stop me," and opened the car door.

"Well, maybe she's a genius," I commented, telling Charlotte about it later. "She certainly knows what she wants, and they say geniuses do."

Charlotte shook her head decidedly. "No, she's not, Julia. Mary Preston's smart enough, but— She's just Breckinridge all over again, that's all. But of course she's a girl, and that makes a lot of difference. I'm afraid Mary Preston will have a hard time."

We sighed together.

Charlotte said then, brightly, "Well, let's talk about something else. What did the dentist think about your tooth?"

"That's not what I'd call a very nice cheerful change of subject, Charlotte!" I said, but I told her.

"There's nothing worse than having trouble with your teeth," Charlotte agreed with me. She ran her tongue over her own the way nobody can seem to help doing when teeth are the topic of conversation. "That awful grinding and polishing, and the time I had my bridge put in I actually thought Dr. Leidner was going to beat off the top of my head."

"And then knowing it probably isn't any use after all," I said gloomily. "I always thought they ought to speak of the three terrors of old age, instead of two—Loneliness, Poverty, and False Teeth."

Charlotte said doubtfully, "Well, of course they've improved a lot nowadays. Dr. Leidner showed me a set that was downright pretty. You could look right through the pink part. But still I'm glad I won't have to have any myself."

"How do you know you won't?" I asked bluntly.

Charlotte got up and swished dramatically into the bathroom. "This is why," she said, coming out.

I looked doubtfully at the little bottle of capsules she'd put in my lap. They were ordinary white things and didn't look miraculous. As for the label on the bottle, which said only, *One capsule three times daily, as directed*, it was depressingly like what I'd read many times before, on many bottles of medicine that never did enough good to mention.

"That's bonemeal," Charlotte said, as if she'd invented it.

I was scandalized. "Fertilizer?"

"Well, on that order, yes. But I expect this is extra clean," Charlotte answered conscientiously. "I take it for my teeth. It's the newest thing, Julia, and it really works. I've taken it for five months now, and not the sign of a cavity. I used to develop cavities thick and fast. But this stuff that comes in bonemeal makes your teeth as hard as rocks."

"What stuff?"

"Well, I can't always think of the name of it," Charlotte said, looking flustered. "It'll come to me. Or I'll ask Dr. Greer, if you're really interested, Julia. It's one of those long chemical names."

"Then I wouldn't understand it anyway. Never mind," I said. "Just tell me how it works."

Charlotte did. I never thought I'd sit and listen to Charlotte Buckner lecture on scientific subjects. This time, though, my tooth was as sore as a boil and I listened hard.

It seems there's a part of Texas called Deaf Smith County, which probably isn't as bad as it sounds. But it's a bad place for struggling young dentists to live in, because they really do have to struggle. People in Deaf Smith County may have pyorrhea and trench mouth and things like that—Charlotte didn't know—but they don't get cavities in their teeth.

She went on to tell me about the experiments that dentists had made, there and other places, after they realized it couldn't be just luck. To make a long story short—and Charlotte couldn't have been longer-winded about it if she'd had two or three medical degrees—they'd found out that people who took bonemeal capsules stopped having trouble with tooth decay. No new cavities at all, and the ones they already had didn't get any worse, even left unfilled to see what would happen. Apparently it wasn't a balanced diet, and it wasn't fighting off acid condition, and it wasn't brushing your teeth that kept them healthy and strong. It was this stuff they had in the water down in Deaf Smith County, Texas, and also in the bonemeal capsules.

"Well, what are they waiting for?" I wanted to know. "Why don't they hurry up and get these things on the market, so everybody can take them? I'm tired of getting cavities in my teeth, too."

Charlotte said reasonably, "Because the whole thing is in an experimental stage, Julia. A lot of dentists don't even approve of it."

"I can imagine they don't," I said, sniffing. "A thing like that could ruin their business. But are we going to appease the dentists, the way we did the Japanese about silk stockings?"

"Now, Julia," Charlotte said. "It isn't that. You oughtn't compare dentists with the Japanese." Which was all very well for *her* to say, I thought, feeling the edge of my sore tooth with my tongue. It may have been broken off before, but at least it hadn't hurt. "It's just that a lot of dentists are like a lot of doctors—they're slow to change to the new ways," Charlotte went on. "And even the ones in favor of it say it isn't ready yet for the general public. They just haven't experimented for a long enough period of time. For instance, in some places the dentists don't give it in capsules; they put it in the water supply instead, so the whole town can get it. Those towns won't know the full results for ten years, I understand."

"And by that time I'll either be dead or have false teeth. I wonder," I said, musing, "if I'll wear them or keep them in the bottom part of the clock, the way my dear father did."

Charlotte was diverted. "Oh, remind me to show you Mrs. Thompson, across the street, Julia. She won't wear her teeth around the house either; she just keeps them down inside the front of her dress, where she can grab them in a hurry when company comes. Isn't that awful? And Mary Preston always did think they'd bite her someday. She was simply fascinated with Mrs. Thompson when she was a little girl. It was sort of embarrassing, because the families didn't call, but every time they'd miss Mary Preston they knew right where to look. She'd be hanging around Mrs. Thompson's, hoping to see her whip those teeth in or out."

"It's all right for Mary Preston to laugh," I said grimly. "She's young. And it's all right for you, if those capsules of yours are as good as you think they are. Personally, after what that dentist told me this morning, I wouldn't think it was very funny."

Charlotte said, hesitating, "Well, Julia, you could take some of my capsules, of course. But maybe you ought to talk to Dr. Greer first. I had a very serious talk with him before I started taking them myself. He was very particular about making me understand that they *were* still experimental, and that he couldn't guarantee good results or even guarantee against bad ones. I thought it was mighty nice of him."

"I think so too. It was the right thing to do," I said, unscrewing the top of Charlotte's bottle. "And if I were Anne's age, with perfectly good teeth, I wouldn't try it till they were sure. As it is, I've got everything to gain and not much to lose.... What, Charlotte?"

I was in the bathroom by that time, and with the water running I couldn't understand a word Charlotte said.

"I said I'd remembered the name of that chemical," repeated Charlotte. "It was sodium fluoride."

"Sodium fluoride. I never heard of it," I said, washing my capsule down.

"I never had either. But I don't see why I can't remember it now, especially after all that trouble they had about Gus," Charlotte complained.

"Gus?"

"Why, it was sodium fluoride he died of," Charlotte said innocently. "Too much sodium fluoride, of course. Not like this. They found it in his glass."

CHAPTER EIGHT

After that I thought I'd better have a talk with Dr. Robert Greer, sure enough. I certainly wasn't going to take any more of Charlotte's wonderful capsules until I did.

But as things turned out I didn't see him alone for several days. There was too much going on. As rapidly as he'd recovered before, after he had the first stroke, old Breckinridge Helm came back to life. He could move his body—all except that left leg, which seemed to be permanently paralyzed—and suck through a tube and swear at poor Miss Kittinger. She couldn't understand the words at first but she could hardly mistake the meaning. And every day the goddamns got clearer and clearer, and fuller and fuller of expression. By the end of the week you could hardly tell old Breckinridge Helm had had a second stroke.

Except for one thing. He didn't know where he was.

"Goddamn it, I want to go home!" he'd say, fifty-four times a day. And he'd pound his right fist into his left palm, feebly, in the same gesture Mary Preston had used as we sat outside in the car. "I'm sick and tired of this goddamn hospital. I want to go home. If I have to be sick I'll be sick in my own bed. I want to go home right now!"

Why he didn't work himself into a heart attack or another stroke I'll never know.

"But, Grandfather, you are home," the different grandchildren would tell him, time and again, and so would Miss Kittinger and Charlotte. "You *are* right in your own bed, in your own room."

"Do you think I'm a goddamn fool?" old Breckinridge Helm would explode. "Do you think I don't know my own room? I'm in a goddamn hospital, and I don't like it and I want to go home."

Most of them gave up trying to convince him after a while, even Charlotte. They just ignored him the best they could. After all, there wasn't a thing in this world they could do. He *was* at home. But Emily, more patient than the rest, never stopped trying.

"Look around you, Grandfather," she'd urge. "Look over there at your wardrobe. That's your own wardrobe, in your very own room at home. Don't you recognize it? Nobody else has a wardrobe like that."

Certainly nobody did. It was easily the ugliest black walnut wardrobe in the world.

"No! Do you think I'm a goddamn idiot?" old Breckinridge would roar. "That's not my wardrobe. This isn't my room. I'm in a goddamn hospital and I've had enough of it and I damn well want to go home."

It was depressing and somehow a little frightening. If Mr. Helm had been entirely out of his mind it wouldn't really have seemed so bad. But to have him normal on every other subject, recognize every name and face he'd ever heard or seen, discuss the news in the *Courier-Journal* as well as anybody could, and still not know where he was, was practically uncanny.

Of course it didn't upset Charlotte and me the way it did the grandchildren. When you've lived as long as we have you've heard of such cases again and again. And of course Miss Kittinger, specializing in paralytic nursing, didn't let it bother her at all. But it got on the grandchildren's nerves.

Dr. Jordan explained it to them, rather condescendingly, but clearly enough.

It seems that when you have a stroke, a little blood clot forms—or a big blood clot, as the case may be. A clot on the brain. There's nothing much to be done for it in the way of medical treatment; all the doctor can do is keep the patient quiet and hope that the clot will either dissolve or move on. When a paralyzed person shows signs of improvement it means the clot is doing one of those two things.

"The way the patient is affected depends on the location of the clot,"

Dr. Jordan explained precisely. "For instance, suppose the memory suffers. We may assume a clot on that portion of the brain which controls recollection. Or suppose the patient finds himself unable to talk. In that case the clot has occurred in the speech area."

"Then Grandfather's clot is on the part of the brain that tells him where he is," Martina said.

Dr. Jordan bowed to her. "Exactly, Mrs. Greer."

"And nowhere else?"

"Nowhere else as far as I have been able to determine," Dr. Jordan said. "Mr. Helm's mind seems perfectly clear except on the one point."

Breck Helm asked, "But his judgment isn't good, is it? I mean, he can't reason the way he used to, can he, or make up his mind?"

If you've ever seen the wind make a ripple over a field of corn or a quiet pond, you've seen something like what went over the Helm grandchildren's faces. They were all thinking about the same thing—the new will, all typed now and put away carefully in Mr. Fownes's safe, ready for Breckinridge Helm to sign.

Dr. Jordan waited a minute before he answered. He put the tips of his fingers together and looked all around the circle of faces, slowly. Then he said, "I'm not entirely sure I understand what you mean, Captain Helm. Do you mean, 'Is Mr. Helm able to transact business of any importance? Would he, for instance, be considered competent to draw up such a thing as a will?'"

"Well—yes," Breck Helm said, startled. The doctor had certainly hit the nail on the head; he knew it, too, and smiled a pussycat smile.

"Then I am afraid you are asking me something outside my province, Captain Helm," Dr. Jordan said smoothly. "Only a lawyer could tell you whether such a document could be successfully probated. And of course he could only give you his opinion, at best. However." Dr. Jordan put his finger tips together again, irritating me almost beyond endurance. He also cleared his throat. "It has been my observation—unless the testator has been previously declared incompetent, of course—that the jury is inclined to give him the benefit of the doubt."

He said goodbye then all around, took his hat from Emily and went out.

"Well!" Mary Preston said. "It looks to me as if we'd better have Grandfather declared incompetent."

"*Mary Preston!*" Charlotte said, really shocked.

John Todd Brown said teasingly—and he didn't sound the least bit shocked, "You have such a nice, delicate way of putting things, my dear."

"She really does," Mary Preston's brother agreed grimly.

Martina Greer said, "Perhaps there is a nicer way of saying it. But didn't it have to be said?"

"Well, really, Martina!" Charlotte was outraged. "Your Grandfather Helm is no more incompetent than you are." Her eyes flashed. "I don't know what you children are thinking of."

"Well, Aunt Charlotte, I for one am thinking of Holliday Hall," Breck Helm said quietly. I looked at him in real surprise. Because he had such beautiful manners and such beautiful self-control, and because he was Charlotte's favorite, I'd somehow credited him with being a good deal different from that young primitive Mary Preston, even if they did look alike. But now while he was standing up to Charlotte, I could see his grandfather in him too. Underneath that quiet manner young Breck Helm was hard as nails.

He went on talking. "Grandfather all our lives has intended for us to inherit his money. Maybe he got mad at one or the other of us from time to time. That was all right. But you notice he never changed his will. Until he had these strokes—and these clots of blood pressing against his brain—he never even called his lawyer."

"But he talked about it, Breck. Before he ever had a stroke at all."

Martina Greer said, looking at Charlotte rather hard, "We know that, Cousin Charlotte. I was just wondering how *you* did."

Charlotte flushed but didn't say anything.

"Aunt Charlotte," Breck said, "I'm going to lay all my cards on the table. I hope it won't hurt you. I value your good opinion, as you know. But I value Holliday Hall too."

He drew a deep breath.

"It's my honest belief," Breck Helm said slowly, "that Grandfather is as competent to make a will as I am."

"Breck!" came sharply from Mary Preston and John Todd Brown. Martina said something under her breath that sounded like, "You talk too much, young man." Emily Craig didn't say anything at all, but her eyes flashed at him and the expression on her face reminded me of the day in Charlotte's living room when, with the other heirs, she'd watched Mr. Fownes go up the steps.

Martina's husband had turned his face away. I couldn't see it. But some kind of ejaculation escaped him too, harsh and sharp.

Breck held up his hand to hush them all, the way a clergyman does when he's giving a benediction, and the same kind of silence fell.

"I *think* Grandfather is competent," Breck Helm said again. "But I don't *know*. He certainly does have *something* the matter with his mind; he doesn't know where he is. And if he has one thing the matter with his mind he may have something else the matter, too. I don't know much about this blood clot business. And I don't see any special reason to go into it. I don't see any reason why I should give up Holliday Hall, either. Coming back to Holliday Hall is all I've thought about these last few months. It's all that's kept me going— Well, skip that. What I mean is this: I don't want to wait till Grandfather makes another will and dies, and then let a jury give him the benefit of the doubt. I want to give myself the benefit of the doubt. Now."

"By having Grandfather declared incompetent. Now."

John Todd Brown stated it as a fact. His eyes were glittering. He got across the room in two steps and kissed Mary Preston, good and hard. I thought he was celebrating rather too soon, but Mary Preston seemed to like it.

Martina said, "But is it that simple, actually? What do you have to do to get a person declared incompetent? Does anybody know?"

"I do!" It was like the crack of a whip, in a voice I'd never heard before. It certainly wasn't the voice meek little Emily used on ordinary occasions. I never was so surprised in my life.

Breck Helm smiled and nodded at her encouragingly, as if he were the chairman of a meeting. "That's swell, Emily. Go on and tell us."

Emily went on, sounding more like herself, "Well, first you get two doctors to come and see him, together. The one who's been taking care of him right along, usually, and then another one. It's better to talk to the new doctor first, and sort of prepare his mind. Then you file a petition in the circuit court and ask for a hearing to determine competency."

I couldn't help wondering where sheltered little Emily, eighteen years old, had got all this.

"Then the court serves a summons on the two doctors the family has picked out, and maybe the family, and the servants, and just anybody that's seen the patient a lot and knows his condition," Emily went on glibly. "And everybody goes to court and they empanel a jury. You have to have a lawyer go with you so he can object to questions."

"What questions?"

"Well, maybe the commonwealth's attorney will try to make you say something you don't want to say."

"I don't see why he would. What difference does it make to him?" Mary Preston wanted to know.

"Well, I don't know," Emily admitted, confused. "But anyway, you answer all the questions your lawyer doesn't object to, and then they instruct the jury, and the jury deliberates and brings in a verdict. And if they say he's incompetent the judge appoints a committee for him, to manage all his affairs in his place and stead."

That last was certainly a quotation.

"Well, who would be on the committee? All of us?" asked Breck.

"Oh, *no*, Breck," Emily said importantly. "A committee is only one person. You'd probably be the one."

"I never heard of a committee with just one person on it," Martina said doubtfully.

John Todd Brown said, laughing right out loud, "Well, that's how it is, though, Martina. Emily's taken expert legal advice from a rising young man that's going right on up or he'll know the reason why. A young man, I may add, who has every reason to interest himself in the fortunes of our family."

Emily's face got a slow dark red.

"Hush up, Johnny," Mary Preston said. "It's a good thing somebody had sense enough to find out about it. And I expect Sergeant Morgan is a right good lawyer."

It took me a minute to think where I'd heard of Sergeant Morgan before. Then I remembered he was the one who'd called Emily four different times, the morning after old Mr. Helm had his stroke.

"Does he know Kentucky law, though, I wonder?" Breck said thoughtfully. "Did he look it up, Emily? Maybe it's not the same here as it is in his state."

Emily said, nodding, "He looked it up. All that I told you, that's Kentucky law."

"It was kind of your Sergeant Morgan to go to so much trouble, Emily, and I'm sure we all appreciate it," Martina said smoothly, while her brother laughed and Mary Preston said, "Johnny, hush up!" again. "It's too bad we can't have him handle the case. But I suppose since he's in the Army we'll have to get somebody else."

"John Ewing would be good," Breck said thoughtfully.

Mary Preston frowned at him. "He's too young. Do you think Cousin Henry Powell would touch it with a ten-foot pole?"

"My dear children—" Charlotte said.

If I had known what an effective speech Charlotte was going to make I would have cut her off. I honestly didn't think she had it in her. Of all the shocks I got that afternoon—and I got plenty, beginning with Johnny Brown's kissing Mary Preston like that, right in front of everybody, and ending with meek little Emily's speaking up and telling them how they could get their grandfather declared incompetent—nothing set me back on my heels harder than that speech that Charlotte began, "My dear children—" Without mincing matters in any way, shape, or form, she told them how it was.

"And furthermore, let me tell you this," Charlotte said in conclusion.

She was shaking her forefinger at them by this time, and her Edwardian fringe was fairly bouncing up and down. "You children are going to have to get a mighty good lawyer if you take this case to court. A lot better lawyer than young John Ewing or old Henry Powell. Because *I'm* going to be in court, and I'm going to testify. And you talk about seeing the doctor first, to sort of prepare his mind. You can't see the doctor soon enough. *I*," Charlotte said magnificently, "am going to see the doctor before you do. *All* the doctors."

The Helm grandchildren still just sat there with their mouths slightly open. So was mine, I'm afraid.

Charlotte said in a quieter tone, breaking the silence herself, "You can't win your case in court, children. I just won't let you. But I hope you won't let it go to court. I hope you'll come to your senses first. And I believe you will."

There's something to be said for long skirts, in moments of stress at least. Not that Charlotte's are long enough to touch the ground, but she swept out as if they did. Under cover of her exit I melted unobtrusively through the red velvet portieres, something, of course, that I should have done long before. But my mind was only just beginning to work. Oh, Charlotte, Charlotte, I was saying to myself. You don't know what you've done. Maybe I do read too many murder books, the way you say. But you read too few. Why couldn't you have let it go by? Because they'll never try to get him declared incompetent now. They know they'd never have a chance against you in court, not if you're half as good on the witness stand as you were just then. And they know you meant what you said. But you shouldn't have said it, Charlotte. Of course, I know exactly how you felt. I felt the same way. It was awful to think of that poor old man railroaded into an institution, when probably he's as sane as you and I.

But at least he'd have been alive.

CHAPTER NINE

My first thought had been for Mr. Helm; but right on the heels of it, and making me forget all about anybody else, came my second thought, and that was for Julia Tyler. The case that had seemed like such an interesting little problem, viewed from the bosom of my family in Annapolis, didn't seem so attractive now, or even safe. I was too close to it for comfort. I was living in a house where the plot I'd so often read in books, the old moth-eaten plot about a rich man murdered before he could change his will, was going to come true.

Sometimes I felt a little silly, locking my door at night and taking the other precautions I knew Anne and Dick would want me to. But I kept on just the same. Charlotte made a great show of ignoring everything; but tacitly she approved, I think. It was Thelma, who brought our breakfast trays up every morning, that thought I was a harmless eccentric because I always had to get out of bed to let her in.

This morning, though, it was Mary Preston who brought my tray. Thelma, it seemed, was cleaning up the mess she'd made dropping Charlotte's on the second-floor landing.

"That child!" Mary Preston said maturely. "She breaks something just about every day. But she's the best cleaner I believe we've ever had—moves even the heavy furniture when she vacuums, and gets down in the corners on her hands and knees. There aren't many of them these days that get down on their hands and knees. Thelma doesn't miss a thing."

I had an almost immediate demonstration of the fact. Thelma came knocking on my door while Mary Preston was downstairs getting another tray for Charlotte, and announced she'd found a wedding ring in the vacuum and had brought it for Miss Mary Preston to see.

"A wedding ring? Well, that was fortunate, wasn't it?" I asked, pouring my second cup of coffee. "Sit down in that little chair, Thelma. Miss Mary Preston will be back in just a minute."

I could have sent her down the front stairs to overtake Mary Preston, of course. But needless to say I didn't even consider it.

Mary Preston arranged Charlotte's tray deliberately on the bed table while Thelma told her about the ring. She said, "Yes, I think I know who lost it. One of the ladies that was here yesterday. Thank you very much, Thelma. You were a good girl. Do you think my aqua sweater would look nice on you?"

Thelma, grinning from ear to ear, thought it would. She departed perfectly happy again, after obvious disappointment when Mary Preston took the ring. She'd hoped it would be hers to keep, and if what Charlotte says she suspects is true, there's nobody that could use a wedding ring to more advantage.

Mary Preston looked at the door until it shut, and then at me. "Miss Julia, if I told you something would you promise not to tell? Cross your heart? Not even Aunt Charlotte?"

We both looked across at Charlotte, dead to the world in the other bed. It's fantastic what she can sleep through.

"Last night after you went upstairs," Mary Preston said, "Emily was looking for something she'd lost. She just about tore the house up. She wouldn't tell me what it was; she just said, 'Something.' But I knew it was something little, because she kept looking in places where nothing big would go."

Emily! I was too flabbergasted to say anything.

"I've been afraid of something like this," Mary Preston said grimly.

I hazarded, "Is it that Sergeant Morgan? The one Johnny was teasing her about? Tell me about him."

"Well, there isn't much to tell, Miss Julia," Mary Preston answered, a little reluctantly, I thought. I remembered that she hadn't seemed to want to talk about him before, either. "He's just a sergeant Emily met at the USO. She's had some dates with him since. He comes from some little town up in Indiana, I think, and he used to be a lawyer. That's all."

"Is he nice?"

Mary Preston said, frowning, "He's all right, I reckon. But he's not as nice as Emily. You see, I've practically brought Emily up, Miss Julia"—she was three years older—"and she *is* sweet and I didn't want her to marry just anybody."

I picked up the platinum wedding ring again and looked inside. There wasn't a mark in it. It was brand-new, obviously, and unless I was much mistaken it had come from one of those stores where they sell matched bridal pairs, as they call them, on the instalment plan. It had diamonds all the way around, each one sprouting out of the heart of an orange blossom. Emily Post wouldn't have thought much of it, probably, but I expect it looked like the end of the rainbow to poor little Emily Craig.

"It just couldn't belong to anybody else," Mary Preston said, still with the, frown. "Breck wouldn't buy a thing like that for Janie and she wouldn't wear it. She just about lives in riding breeches. Besides, they're going to wait till after the war."

"Of course some visitor *could* have dropped it," I suggested halfheartedly.

Mary Preston shook her head and got up to leave. "You should have seen Emily looking under carpets."

"Well, keep me posted. Mary Preston," I said, and Mary Preston promised she would.

The morning Thelma found the ring was the same one that Miss Kittinger, Johnny to the contrary notwithstanding, up and left. Mr. Helm was well enough to swear at her and holler at her now, and he did, and nobody blamed her for going. But as far as Charlotte and I were concerned she couldn't have left at a worse time. We'd been planning to leave the next day ourselves—the plasterers had finally finished Charlotte's ceiling—and it didn't seem very nice, as long as we could be a help to Mary Preston and Emily. We weren't either of us good at anything like real nursing, but we'd sat by the hour with old Mr. Helm.

"But nevertheless we're going," Charlotte told me firmly. "I'm going to get you out of this house, Julia. I think you're perfectly ridiculous to be scared—and don't think I haven't seen you locking that door every night, waiting till you think I've gone to sleep and then sneaking out of bed. Nothing's going to hurt *you*. Or anybody," Charlotte said, whistling to keep up her courage. "But as long as you *are* scared, Julia, we'll go back to the Puritan tomorrow, just as we planned."

I said with dignity, "I am not scared, Charlotte. I've just been locking the door because if Dick Travers ever found out I hadn't he'd have a fit and never let me out of his sight again." Charlotte's smile goaded me on: "And just to show you I'm not scared, I'll leave it unlocked tonight. I'll even put the key on the outside, so you'll *know*." I crossed the room and did it defiantly, there and then.

Maybe that was why, in spite of my big talk to Charlotte, I was so long getting to sleep. I was still wide-awake, and it was nearly midnight, when the crash came outside.

It was muffled, because of the thick walls and the heavy walnut door. But it was sharp and loud enough to scare me nearly out of my mind. I sat bolt upright in bed, and I could tell by the way the ribbon on my nightgown kept moving and tickling me that I was shaking all over.

Charlotte, across the room from me in the other big walnut bed, slept on like a log. A happy little noise, not exactly a snore, came from her parted lips. It was the only sound I could hear, whatever other sounds there may have been outside.

A tremendous annoyance with Charlotte swept over me, blotting out fear and everything else. Otherwise I couldn't have got out of my bed and across the room to hers. I shook her a good deal harder than I needed to, I'm afraid.

"Crash? Why, no, Julia, I didn't hear any crash," Charlotte said. "Was it something out in the hall? Didn't you look to see?"

I said with fine sarcasm, "Look to see? My dear Charlotte, this is a house there's been a murder in. Maybe I do read too many books about murder, but at least they've taught me what not to do. You don't go out in halls to investigate noises in the middle of the night. That's what some fool character does in every book, and he always gets knocked in the head."

"Knocked in the head? Really, Julia!" Charlotte said. "And as for the noise you think you heard, maybe you'd dropped off to sleep before you knew it. Maybe you were having a nightmare. But if you *did* hear it,"

Charlotte said hastily, noticing my face, "it probably wasn't a thing but Johnny coming home. Sometimes he drinks a little more than he should, you know. He might knock a vase off the table, or even stumble and fall."

"Charlotte, where are you going?"

Charlotte said, moving towards the door, "Well, Julia, *somebody* has to put your mind at rest. I'm going to see about it myself, of course." She laid her hand on the doorknob and turned it. At least turn it was what she tried to do.

The door was locked. Locked on the outside.

After half an hour or so we went back to bed. There wasn't a bell to ring and the speaking-tube arrangement they had instead had been broken in that room for years, Charlotte said. Of course we could have screamed out the window, but neither of us is quite the type. There was nothing for it but wait till morning. But we left the desk light burning, and before we turned off the others I took a good solid walnut side chair and wedged it firmly under the knob of the door. And this time Charlotte didn't say a word.

At seven-thirty next morning I'd stood it as long as I could. Emily was always awake at that hour, I knew, so she was the one I called, standing against the door and banging on it as hard as I could.

It took Emily a mighty long time to come. Her hands were slow and fumbling when they finally unlocked the door, and when between us we got it open, she stood there swaying back and forth as if she were going to fall. I was scared to death at the way she looked. Then I looked beyond her into the hall.

The hall was, otherwise, empty. There was no sign of the broken vase Charlotte had suggested, and certainly none of my friend John Todd Brown, either drunk or sober. The only thing out of the ordinary was old Mr. Helm's bedroom door. He liked it tightly closed, night and day. This time it was standing wide.

And I could look inside, and old Mr. Helm was dead.

Perhaps it was because I'd looked on two other cases of violent death, back in Annapolis, that I could feel as calm as I did at first. But I don't think so. I think it was because you rather expect people to die in bed especially old, sick people like Mr. Helm—and finding them so is never the shock it might be otherwise. Even if it's been a horrible death.

This had been a horrible death. I had to make myself look at the face on the pillows, that had been so handsome and arrogant and sure the first time I saw it. It wasn't anymore. His smile was a caricature of the one he'd worn in lifetime—*risus sardonicus*, they call it after death— with the bluish lips drawn up to show his teeth, and his eyes staring horribly, and his body—

I could hear Charlotte Buckner's voice as plainly as if she'd been in the room. ". . . his body all twisted as if he'd died in agony, and the sheets and covers halfway off the bed every which way, and the medicine glass knocked off the bedside table...."

I was beginning to lose control. I looked at the bedside table in panic, and Mr. Helm's medicine glass was still there. That part hadn't repeated itself. But everything else was the same that Charlotte had told me about Gus's murder. Even the glass itself, that in Gus's case had been lying on its side on the floor, and in this case was standing neatly upright on the little table. Even the glass was the same in its essential particular. There was some kind of whitish deposit in the bottom, and halfway up the inside surface was faintly etched and scarred.

I didn't touch anything. I had no temptation to. I got out of the room as fast and as impulsively as I'd gone in. I hardly noticed Emily, by this time lying on the floor in a dead faint. Certainly I hadn't heard her fall. I passed her right by and pounded hard on young Breckinridge Helm's door.

"Your grandfather—" I told him. I couldn't say anymore.

"Wait a minute, Miss Julia," Breck Helm said without surprise. He'd come to the door in just the bottom half of his pajamas, and he was back and picked up a blue and black striped dressing gown and put it on. Then he took me by the elbow and we went down the hall to old Mr. Helm's room. But I let him go in alone.

As if I were walking in my sleep, I got some water for poor little Emily, while Breck was calling the doctor and the police. After that I waked Charlotte, and then he and she waked everybody else, while I sat in my room and stared off into space. I didn't even think. I hardly heard the noise of feet on the stairs, and Charlotte talking to Dr. Jordan and another unattractive young man, Lieutenant Bates, from the police. Charlotte had to come all the way into the room and put her hand on my shoulder, the way I have to do with her when she's asleep.

We joined Martina and Dr. Greer and the girls outside old Breckinridge's door. The doctor and police, of course, went on in. The rest of us just sat in silence, listening to the unpleasant noises coming out of Johnny Brown's room. I hear those same sounds every morning in Rossville, when poor Mrs. Upchurch, my next-door neighbor, is trying to get her husband so he can go down to the office. Finally Breck and Johnny Brown came on out. Johnny sank down in a chair, took one look around the circle of his relatives and me, and dropped his head in his hands.

"Is everybody here?" Lieutenant Bates asked suddenly behind me, making me jump. I hadn't heard him come out. He moved like a cat. "You, up there!" Lieutenant Bates went on in a bellow, making me jump again. "What are you afraid of? Come on down."

We all turned. I think we'd all forgotten about the servants. There they were, the four of them, scared to death and not making a sound, huddled together at the top of the stairs that led to the attic floor. It was a narrow little enclosed flight without a railing—a regular firetrap, as Lieutenant Bates said later. But it was pretty typical of the service stairs architects used to plan for the big houses. The only unusual thing about it was the fact that something white and glistening had been spilled on it, almost at the top.

It looked like confectioner's sugar, but sugar doesn't come in glass bottles like the one that was lying in fragments in the middle of this mess. And it doesn't sparkle in the sun.

"I don't believe they *can* come down, Lieutenant Bates," I took it on myself to say. "There's broken glass, and something white spilled on the stairs."

Lieutenant Bates hadn't seen it. He went over then and looked. He took his time about it, and I couldn't make out the expression on his face when finally he straightened up and spoke to the little group at the head of the stairs.

"Who spilled this stuff?"

Nobody said anything, but the new butler—I never could remember his name—gave my friend Thelma a little push that brought her to the front.

Lieutenant Bates said sternly, "You. What's your name? . . . All right. Are you the one spilled this white powder on the stairs?"

"Yes—yes, sir," Thelma said. Her pert little yellow face had an unhealthy tinge, as if she'd gone through a long spell of sickness.

"When'd you do it?"

"Last—last night," Thelma said. "I was fixing to clean it up before anybody saw it today. But last night I come in late—and I was so tired—"

"I'm not bawling you out for messing up the steps, girl," Lieutenant Bates said. His voice was almost kind. He seemed pleased, though what about I didn't at the moment see. "It's not my business how you clean up this house. What I want to know is, did you spill this stuff going up to bed, and were you the last one in?"

"Yes, sir, she was," the butler said with dignity. He gave her what's called a dirty look. "Thelma keeps late hours, yes, sir. The rest of us was all in bed and sound asleep last night, when Thelma comes in and drops some glass bottle or something on the stairs, making enough noise to wake the—"

To wake the dead, he'd almost said.

"What time?"

Thelma said defensively, "It wasn't but half-past eleven. Some people around here goes to bed with the chickens."

"So you came in at half-past eleven," Lieutenant Bates said musingly. "You went upstairs and dropped this jar of white stuff and spilled it, and woke these others up. And you can prove it by all of them." He looked at the other three servants, and three black heads nodded in unison. "And the powder says nobody's been down these stairs since. There's not that first footprint. Any other way to get down from your floor to this one?"

The servants said, "No, sir," together, like a well-trained chorus.

Lieutenant Bates said, "Well, then. You've got an alibi for this murder, the way the old ladies have. Somebody killed old Mr. Helm, all right, between half-past two and six. But it wasn't any of you."

He turned his back on them and looked in turn at Martina and her husband, at Breck Helm in his striped dressing gown, and Johnny Brown with his head in his hands, and Mary Preston sitting protectively on the arm of poor little Emily's chair.

"Well, boys and girls," Lieutenant Bates said, "here we are again."

CHAPTER TEN

The first thing I'd noticed about Lieutenant Bates was that he was an unpleasant young man. The next was that he was slipshod. Not that I wasn't delighted to have, with Charlotte, an alibi for the time of old Mr. Helm's murder. But I thought he accepted our tale about being locked in much too unquestioningly, in his eagerness to narrow the suspects down to the six grandchildren he'd suspected before and was obviously out to get this time.

Aside from refusing flatly to let us move back home, he was polite enough to Charlotte and me. But the way he went about interviewing the others made my blood boil. Not knowing much about detectives outside of books—knowing exactly one of them, that is, in the actual flesh—I'd concluded they were all about like my friend Lieutenant Ben Kramer, who'd been to law school and served in the FBI. I couldn't imagine Ben Kramer's yelling at people the way this Bates did, and I certainly couldn't imagine anybody's talking the way he did to poor little Emily Craig.

"Well, what would you expect?" Charlotte said, wearily, when I mentioned it to her. "He thinks Emily killed her grandfather. He thought she killed Gus, too. It made him wild to think he couldn't prove anything on her."

"Emily!" I said with scorn.

Charlotte nodded. "I know. It sounds crazy. Of course, he didn't know Emily. He just knew she was the last one who admitted seeing Gus alive, and then she did give him some medicine, and she was the one that found the body."

"But she didn't have a motive."

"None of them did. At least, Lieutenant Bates couldn't find any," Charlotte said.

We looked at each other.

I said slowly, "I'm beginning to think the motive was the same as it was for killing old Mr. Helm. Money."

Charlotte was puzzled. "But Gus didn't have any money."

"He was in a position to influence somebody that did, though," I countered, thinking fast. "Suppose Gus was the one who found out about the 'bad, bad thing' one of the grandchildren did, and told Mr. Helm. Wouldn't that be a motive for murdering him?"

"Well, yes," Charlotte agreed. "But it was a good while before he died that Gus told me all that, Julia."

"That doesn't make any difference." I was warming to my theory, which I hadn't thought so much of myself when I started out. "Maybe the murderer didn't find out about it for a while, and— Oh, I'm sorry, Charlotte. I shouldn't have said that. I didn't mean to make you cry."

Charlotte said, dabbing at her eyes, "There's no reason why you shouldn't have, Julia. It *was* a murder—both of them were—and whoever did it was a murderer. No matter—who it is. It's just that they've been such sweet children. All of them. I just can't seem to get it through my head."

If there was anything helpful or appropriate for me to say I couldn't think of it.

"I never did really think it was a tramp, Julia. You saw that right away. But," Charlotte went on pitifully, rolling her handkerchief into a wet little ball, "I still don't know which one it could have been. My mind just goes round and round, Julia, and I can't think about anything else, and I don't know which way to turn—"

I said, feeling rather ashamed of myself, "Well, I couldn't be much help, but— Maybe if you just talked about it, Charlotte."

"Maybe so," Charlotte said docilely, putting her handkerchief away. "Dr. Moffat always tells us that. 'A burden shared is a burden shed.' But we've *been* talking about it, haven't we? I don't know how you mean."

"Well, you have to approach it psychologically. That's what Ben says," I answered briskly. Then of course, remembering when I saw Charlotte's blank expression that she'd never heard of him, I had to take time out, as Dick calls it, to explain to her about Lieutenant Ben Kramer of the Baltimore Police Department, and how he'd been kind enough to undertake my criminal education.

"Ben says just the same thing Hercule Poirot does. He says Hercule Poirot is perfectly sound." I could see at this point that poor Charlotte had never heard of Poirot either, but I wasn't going to stop again. It didn't matter. "You have to find a subject that fits into the crime psychologically. For instance, if you have a victim who's been hit with an axe time and time again when once would have been enough, you want to look for a suspect with a violent, revengeful kind of temper."

Charlotte shuddered.

"And if you find a case of poisoning you usually think of a woman. Poison is a woman's kind of weapon. Lots of women couldn't possibly bring themselves to stab somebody, or strangle him, or anything like that; but they don't mind putting arsenic in his food any more than they'd mind putting in vanilla."

I don't believe Charlotte would ever really enjoy a murder case, even if the people involved were perfect strangers and not her nearest and dearest. She shuddered again.

"I don't mean it's always women that murder by poison, or strong men by axes, but Ben says it's a fairly good rule of thumb," I pursued. "Sometimes you'll find a weak-looking little woman using the axe. But in that case she's likely to be a strong *character*. And when a man picks out poison to murder with it's usually because there's a weak, sneaky, cowardly, feminine streak in him, no matter how big and strong he *looks*."

"In other words, you can't just go by appearances," Charlotte said. "You have to look deeper."

"That's it. You have to look all the way down, Ben says. And I don't believe this Lieutenant Bates is doing it, Charlotte. That's why he's picked on poor little Emily Craig."

Charlotte said, with an air of feeling her way, "I suppose he thinks Emily's just the kind of timid, put-upon little soul that would think of poison. But actually—"

"Actually," I nodded, thinking of the same thing Charlotte was, "Emily's a different person underneath. Out of all those bright, quick, up-and-coming young people it was timid little Emily who spoke up and who'd been smart enough to find out how they could keep their grandfather from signing a new will."

"Well, I wouldn't call it smart, Julia," Charlotte said reprovingly. "I think it was a mighty ugly thing to do."

I agreed impatiently. "Of course it was. But don't sidetrack me, Charlotte, and keep the ethics out of it. It was smart, too. Emily acts usually as if she couldn't say boo to a goose, but in an emergency she might be the coolest one in the house."

"Well, she is, except for Mary Preston," Charlotte agreed. "Mary Preston is wonderful in an emergency. She just takes charge of things like a general. And of course she overshadows Emily—always has. But if Mary Preston isn't there, or if *she's* the one that's hurt—I remember the time she fell downstairs last summer and lit on her head. Emily was right there, cool as a cucumber, bossing the job."

"Then you don't think Emily would have picked out poison?"

"No, I don't," Charlotte said firmly. "Nor Mary Preston, either. Mary Preston would have taken the poker and hit him over the head."

I thought she expressed that very well. I agreed with her.

"However," I said thoughtfully, "Mary Preston wants to be a doctor. Maybe she's been reading some pharmacopeial books and got interested in poisons. Mary Preston could plan a murder, all right, and take her own sweet time. She wouldn't have to depend on just losing her temper and grabbing up the first thing she saw."

"Well, really, Julia," Charlotte reproved me. "I don't think that was a very nice thing to say. I thought you liked Mary Preston."

"I don't think it was any worse than your saying she would have taken the poker and hit her grandfather over the head," I said reasonably. "I'm just trying to be objective, Charlotte. I do like Mary Preston. Why else would I have put up with that little varmint Blockbuster all that time?"

Blockbuster wasn't my problem any longer, thank goodness, now that Mr. Helm was dead. It's an ill wind. Mary Preston had full charge and responsibility of him now, and it was only force of habit that kept me worrying about the furniture across the street, where he was still visiting the janitor.

"Well, I don't think Mary Preston would fool around with anything like poison," Charlotte said, mollified. "What about Martina?"

I said slowly, "Well, of course I don't know Martina as well as you do. She may be as different underneath as Emily Craig is. She may have a heart of gold, and tell stories to children, and like to stay home and knit. It isn't fair to judge her just because she looks like Beatrice Cenci. But she does. And I bet she'd really enjoy a good artistic poisoning."

"Why, Julia!" Charlotte said, shocked. But she didn't mind the way she would have if I'd said it about Mary Preston or Emily. I thought Charlotte made quite a bit of distinction between the Brown children, Johnny and Martina, and the grandchildren of her old friend Emily Powell. It seemed to me that if Mr. Helm himself could treat them all alike, just as though they were all his own blood kin, it wouldn't have hurt Charlotte to let the Browns call her aunt too, instead of merely cousin. It wasn't as if they weren't nice and attractive. Martina was always perfectly charming—though Beatrice Cenci was that way too, I understand—and as for that young Johnny Brown, Charlotte wouldn't have been human or female, for all her seventy years, if she had been impervious to *him*.

"Johnny would be a good poisoner, too," I reflected. "I mean, I think he'd always choose a polite, good-natured kind of crime. I can't imagine his losing his temper and banging somebody over the head."

"I can't either. But I don't think there's anything very polite or good-natured about poisoning a person, Julia." Charlotte took a dignified tone. "And anyway, I can't think Johnny would have poisoned his grandfather. He's too sweet a boy in the first place, and in the second place he goes out of his way to avoid anything the least bit unpleasant. And for all your talk about polite, good-natured crimes, Julia, you must admit that poisoning your grandfather is an unpleasant thing to do."

I choked back laughter, for which Charlotte would never have forgiven me and I wouldn't blame her. "Well, then, that just leaves Breck to talk about," I said.

Charlotte rose right up, the way a mother bear is supposed to when somebody threatens her cub. "Breck's out of the question."

"Nobody's out of the question in a murder case, Charlotte," I said firmly, quoting Ben Kramer. "We've discussed all the other grandchildren, and it's only fair for us to discuss Breck too."

"But none of the grandchildren did it!" Charlotte answered triumphantly, like a flash.

I said wearily, "Now, Charlotte, don't start that tramp business again. The doors were *locked*. And of course the servants were here, but that white powder didn't have any footprints in it, remember. They *couldn't* have done it. Goodness knows I believe in keeping up a front as much as you do, but you can keep a front up only just so long. And now that time's gone by. I don't say it was your precious Breck that murdered his grandfather, but *one* of Mr. Helm's grandchildren did."

"Then you're overlooking the logical person, Julia," Charlotte told me with quiet triumph. "I've been thinking as we've talked along. What about Dr. Greer? He had the same chance they had to do it. He had a motive. He had the poison—right under his bed," Charlotte said impressively, as if that made it worse. "And—he isn't blood kin to any of us, Julia." She paused for effect, and then let loose her bombshell. "He doesn't even come from Kentucky."

We went down to dinner on that.

At least, I started down. We were almost at the bottom of the stairs when I sneezed—I'd been trying to catch cold all day long—and, reaching for my handkerchief, discovered that I didn't have the sign of one.

"Send one of the boys," Charlotte urged; but I went back myself, sneezing all the way.

I got two handkerchiefs out of my box. Then I stopped with the handkerchiefs in mid-air, the same way I had with my brush the time before. I was hearing the same footsteps again. Somebody was walking again in the room where Gus had died.

I don't know where my sudden access of courage came from, but I crossed the brightly lighted hall and went up the servants' stair. It was light, too; in fact it was a bulb at the top of the servants' stair that was giving what light there was in the hall. Gus's door—I could see it straight in front of me—was closed. But when I sneezed again, in spite of all that I could do, it opened wide.

The room was dark. I could feel rather than see somebody looking down at me as I stood there in the light of the bare electric bulb. I didn't move. I couldn't have. And then the light snapped out, and somebody slipped down past me, not touching me, on the stairs.

I got down three flights myself then, in less time than it takes to tell it. I was breathless when I got to the dining room door, but something made me pull myself up. I went in more like a lady.

Breck Helm got up and came over and settled me in my chair. I had a chance to look around the circle then. Mary Preston was at the head of the table, all the rest of them in their usual places. Everybody looked placid and unhurried, and everybody's soup plate was empty halfway down.

CHAPTER ELEVEN

"The laboratory report has just come in, Miss Helm," Lieutenant Bates said, coming in himself. Mary Preston and I were in the hall, sorting the cards that had come on the funeral flowers. There were mountains of flowers, but not, anymore, enough visitors to speak of.

Mary Preston said, "Yes?"

"Your grandfather died of sodium fluoride poisoning, Miss Helm.

Does that surprise you?"

"I didn't know what my grandfather died of, Lieutenant Bates," Mary Preston answered him steadily.

"Oh, yeah?" Lieutenant Bates said, and passed on.

That was the way he interviewed. He got the story, though.

It had been Mary Preston's turn to stay with her grandfather the evening before he died. She stayed with him till nine o'clock and saw him settled for the night, giving him the amytal capsule he always had and then adjusting the speaking-tube by the bed, so that from then on Breck could hear their grandfather in his room if he wanted anything. Then she got dressed and went out to dance with—I was glad to hear—Bill Howard from Fort Knox.

Mary Preston said that, on account of the curfew, she'd got in early. There wasn't any place to go. She said it was just five minutes after one when she turned out her light. According to Mary Preston, she'd let herself in with her own key and gone straight upstairs to bed. But it would have been a natural thing for her to look in on her sick grandfather, and there was nobody to prove her statement that she hadn't.

Emily said she hadn't looked in on him either. Emily was out that evening too. She'd had a date with her Sergeant Morgan, and they'd gone to the movies and then driven in Emily's car out to Churchill Downs. Churchill Downs is pretty deserted now, this first year they haven't had a spring race meeting. I *would* come to Louisville for the only May since 1875 they haven't run a Kentucky Derby. It does seem a shame. The day one of Charlotte's friends was kind enough to drive me out and show me the track—which of course is one of the sights of Louisville, even without horses—I felt downright depressed. It certainly was a lonesome place.

But maybe that was what Emily and her sergeant wanted. Anyway, they were mighty late getting home from there—at least Lieutenant Bates thought they were. Neither one of them would say the time. They both just "hadn't noticed". Nobody had seen Emily let herself in at home, and as Sergeant Morgan was on a three-day pass from Fort Knox and registered at the Henry Clay Hotel, there wasn't anyone to check up on him either. Desk clerks have too much to do in wartime, like everybody else.

John Todd Brown had got home at half-past eight that night, having eaten dinner downtown. He worked in his room all the rest of the evening—some soap-flakes campaign for his advertising agency in New York—and drank a good deal harder than he worked. The last time he remembered looking at the clock it was twenty minutes to twelve. Sometime after that he passed out cold, he said, and didn't wake up until Breck applied cold water and coffee next morning, after Mr. Helm's body was found.

The fact that Johnny Brown was still fully dressed that morning, lying face down across the bed, did seem to prove his story of getting drunk and passing out. He undoubtedly had. But of course there wasn't anything to substantiate his story that he hadn't poisoned his grandfather first.

Martina and Dr. Greer had been out playing bridge. One of Martina's old friends had asked them out to her house in the Highlands. They'd got back between half-past eleven and twelve, and up to then they could alibi each other. But from that time on they couldn't. Martina and her husband, as *Courier-Journal* readers were titivated to learn next morning, occupied separate bedrooms.

Martina's story was different from the others only insofar as she admitted going to Mr. Helm's room in the night. She said that after she'd gone to her own room and got ready for bed she decided she'd look in on her grandfather. It was about half-past twelve, she said, when she opened his door, saw that he was sleeping quietly, and went back to her own room.

Breck had been out at Holliday Hall all day. He got home before nine, in time to relieve Mary Preston as arranged, went to his room and stayed there the rest of the night. He got to bed early, he said, and before and after he didn't hear a sound from his grandfather's room.

"Are you a sound sleeper, Captain Helm?" Lieutenant Bates wanted to know, and Breck admitted that he was. "I always sleep like a log."

I was glad to hear it. I'd been afraid that Breck Helm, nervous and keyed up as he undoubtedly was under his quiet manner, had more than a touch of what they call flying fatigue. Insomnia is usually a part of it, I understand. But if he could sleep like a log there was nothing to worry about.

"Then would you have heard Mr. Helm if he'd needed you in the middle of the night?" Lieutenant Bates pursued acidly.

"Maybe not."

"And that didn't bother you, Captain Helm?"

Breck spread out his hands. "Look, Lieutenant. Somebody sat up with my grandfather every night while he was really sick. Even after he got all right again—except for his leg and not knowing where he was—one of us stayed with him in the daytime, too. Every minute. But when he took that sedative at nine o'clock he went to sleep, and I mean sleep. He didn't need anybody in the room with him, or to sit up all night. If he had, we would have done it. You can't accuse us of neglecting my grandfather, Lieutenant."

"Yes, I do," Lieutenant Bates said. "That ant powder that little nig spilled on the servants' stairs, and was too lazy to clean up, alibis all four of the help. And the old ladies alibi each other. That leaves just you six. Mr. Helm was murdered by one of his grandchildren."

"But which one, Lieutenant?" Breck persisted, still softly and politely.

"Don't you know which one?"

Lieutenant Bates exploded. "I'll find out which one, Captain Helm. Don't you worry about that."

Breck said placidly, "That'll be nice. And find out who killed Gus too, why don't you, while you're at it?"

I didn't feel I knew Breck Helm well enough to lecture him myself. But I spoke to Charlotte. "Charlotte, really, somebody ought to talk to him about it," I said earnestly. "That's no way to act around the police. If Breck antagonizes Lieutenant Bates—well, there's no telling what could happen."

"Breck doesn't like Lieutenant Bates," Charlotte said complacently, as if that explained everything and excused it all.

I gave her up and tried Mary Preston.

"Can't you get Breck to be a little more—well, cooperative, Mary Preston?" I urged. "It's none of my business, of course, but when an innocent person is talking to the police he ought to watch his p's and q's."

"So ought a guilty person, I should think," Mary Preston said.

I said impatiently, "There's no use in just putting your worst foot forward. I don't believe Breck killed your Grandfather Helm and I don't want the police to think he did."

"I don't believe he did either," Mary Preston agreed. "But it doesn't matter what the police think, Miss Julia."

"That's what you think," I said inelegantly, in Dick's idiom. "My dear child, that Lieutenant Bates is out for blood, in case you don't know it. He's got no idea of letting this turn out to be one of Louisville's unsolved crimes—or Gus's murder, either. He means to get a conviction."

"He can't get one, though," Mary Preston said, almost indifferently.

I counted silently to ten. "It means a lot to him to get a conviction. Maybe he doesn't care much about abstract justice; I don't think he does. But he cares about his reputation and his promotions."

"You mean he'd frame Breck?" For the first time, Mary Preston did look a little anxious.

"Well, maybe not," I said cautiously. I didn't really think Lieutenant Bates would do a thing like that, but it was an idea worth keeping in Mary Preston's mind. Anything to make her stop opening her mouth and putting her foot in it, as Dick says.

"You see, we have a lot of money now," Mary Preston said matter-of-factly. She certainly didn't have the instincts of a lady, Charlotte's family tree to the contrary notwithstanding. I never have heard anybody, in any walk of life or before or since, pop out with worse things than that child did. "All of us have a lot of money. And we're all going to stick together. And if we do, the police probably won't convict anybody of killing Grandfather. Not anybody, ever."

I just looked at her with my mouth open.

"You see, it's like this, Miss Julia," Mary Preston said kindly. "There're six of us, counting Martina's husband, and we all have to stick together because we're kin. Nice people always do that. It's just trash that talk about their relatives out in public, and don't do everything they can for them when they need it. At least that's what Aunt Charlotte always said. She always told us you could tell nice people by the way the families stuck together and kept their mouths shut and their heads up."

Charlotte's admirable teachings had certainly backfired, I thought. I looked with something like horror at that little Mary Preston, so pretty and sweet and smart and—as she hadn't hesitated to point out herself—so rich. She had everything there was to have in this world—and no more moral sense than a canary bird.

"If we won't give evidence against each other—and we won't—" Mary Preston went on, "and there aren't any fingerprints on the glass but Grandfather's and no circumstantial evidence of weight"—that was plainly a quotation from somebody, and I wondered who—"why, we don't see how any of us can be convicted, Miss Julia. Do you?"

"Well, you'd better consult a lawyer," I said feebly.

Mary Preston said, "Oh, we have. We've talked to Cousin Henry and John Ewing and Sergeant Morgan, all three, and a man named Selden Lowry is on his way from New York. They say he's about the biggest criminal lawyer there is."

"He is," I said weakly. Even I had heard of Selden Lowry.

"So, you see, there's nothing to worry about," Mary Preston finished, and she really didn't seem to think there was. "It's going to be all right."

Well, there wasn't any use telling that child about her duty to society. But I think Charlotte should have. I said instead, making the best recovery I could, "Mary Preston, there's one thing maybe you haven't thought of. Suppose you do all stick together, and not a single one of you is convicted of these murders. If no one person is convicted you'll all be convicted. Don't you see what I mean? People will talk about you all your lives. And you may not think now that you'll mind it, but you will. It'll be hard on every one of you—and on other people, too. It'll be hard on your children, and on the people you marry. And maybe you won't even get to marry the ones you'd like to. Breck's Janie, for instance, might not want him if he were under suspicion for murder."

"Oh, yes, Janie would," Mary Preston said. But she was frowning a little, thoughtfully, and I really thought my sermon had done some good.

"Well, you think that over, Mary Preston," I said, and left.

I was curious to see Selden Lowry, who certainly was a very famous criminal lawyer, so I was glad when, as things turned out, Charlotte and I were the ones that met him at the airport. Charlotte knew him. It seemed his first wife had been a Louisville girl, and that, in Charlotte's mind, went a long way toward making up for the facts that, though brilliant, Selden Lowry wasn't just the most scrupulous lawyer on earth and there was talk about him personally, too. But he won his cases. Charlotte thought the children had been mighty smart to retain him.

On the way out to the airport I told Charlotte about the children's plan. Somebody needed to, I thought. They hadn't exactly been taking her into their confidence, not since she'd told them off, as Dick calls it, about their grandfather's mind.

Charlotte looked mighty old and tired when I'd finished. "Julia, I just don't know what to do. You're right. Every word you said to Mary Preston was just right. And yet—well, I just don't know what else they can *do*."

"The murderer could confess," I suggested dryly.

"Suppose the murderer is Mary Preston—not that I think it is," Charlotte hastened to say. "Can you imagine her confessing? Or Martina? Or Johnny? Or—"

"Or any of them, really," I said. "I see your point, Charlotte. Well, assuming the murderer doesn't confess—And I must say that I for one would be ashamed to do a murder and then confess unless I actually had to."

Charlotte said mildly, "Really, Julia."

"So unless one of them gives evidence against another—and Mary Preston says they've talked it over and decided they won't—and anyway I don't think they know anything—" I pursued, thinking out loud. "I'm pretty sure Mary Preston doesn't know a thing."

"I am too."

"And I don't have a doubt in the world that Johnny was drunk all night. And Breck— Well, Charlotte, what have I said now?" For

Charlotte was getting out her handkerchief.

"Breck—!" Charlotte faltered, and wept.

I said the only thing I could think of. "Charlotte, did he do it?"

"No!"

"Then what are you crying about?" I demanded, a little sharply, I'm afraid.

Charlotte said after a minute, putting her handkerchief away and speaking in a perfectly composed voice, "Because Breck knows who did it, Julia. And he ought to tell, and he won't. No, he didn't see the murderer. He heard him, in Breckinridge's room."

I must have looked my surprise. Those walls are inches thick, and anyway, Breck's room was way across the hall.

"You know Breck told that policeman he slept like a log," Charlotte went on. "But that was a story, Julia. He hasn't been sleeping well at all. He should have had this leave a long time ago. They say the Army takes such good care of their fliers, but I don't think they do. Anyway," Charlotte said, "sometime in the middle of the night he heard somebody say— He said it sounded like somebody right by his own bed, but of course later he realized he'd been hearing through the speaking-tube from Breckinridge's room. Don't you remember? Mary Preston opened it up, she said, when she put her grandfather to sleep at nine o'clock."

"But what did he hear, Charlotte?" I asked impatiently.

Charlotte said, "This voice whispered, 'Wake up, Grandfather. Wake up, Grandfather. Wake up and take your medicine.' And Breck was half asleep himself or he would have realized Breckinridge wasn't supposed to take any medicine in the middle of the night. And— This sounds awful, Julia, but of course he couldn't know. He just went back to sleep."

CHAPTER TWELVE

I'd never gone to a coroner's inquest before and I hope I never have to go again. I definitely don't like the sick feeling I got when the sheriff—or somebody from his office, anyway—handed me my summons to be a witness. I didn't like having my picture taken when Charlotte and I went up the steps. And I certainly didn't like the coroner— Well, you might say I just didn't like anything about inquests.

They aren't the kind of thing that get nicer with practice, either. I could tell that from the expression on Charlotte's set face, and Mary Preston's air of defiance and Emily's shrinking one, and the way Breck Helm's jaw stuck out about an inch farther than usual. They weren't enjoying their second experience any more than they had their first. Martina and John Todd Brown didn't seem to mind, but they're both the kind that go dry-eyed to the gallows—though it's the electric chair in Kentucky, I understand. As for Dr. Greer, I forgot to notice him. He was the kind of man—I've said this before—that you keep forgetting about, which it seems to me is about the worst affliction a person can have. I'd rather be the ugliest man on earth, and have people notice and remember me for that at least, than not have them notice or remember me at all.

"Now, Julia," Charlotte said, the way she always does when I talk like that.

"Well, I would," I maintained. "And it's a good thing I feel that way, considering this picture of me in the *Courier-Journal*. Just look at that thing, Charlotte! It's memorable, all right."

Charlotte said soothingly, "You can't expect to take a good picture with the camera stuck right up in your face and the cameraman yelling at you. Those reporters! I must say, Julia, they weren't as polite as they were last time."

"Neither was the coroner."

"Oh, this wasn't the same man I told you about before," Charlotte said. "He was really *very* nice. He acted as if it had been a death in his own family. The man that asked the questions this time was just a deputy, or whatever they call them. The regular coroner is sick."

"Well, I'm glad to hear it," I said. "I mean, I'm glad to hear the taxpayers didn't elect a man like that Riley. The only person he was really nice to was Dr. Jordan, and I don't like *him*."

Dr. Jordan had been the first one to take the chair. First of all, he had to what they call qualify himself as an expert witness—tell what medical school he graduated from, and so on. Then the real questions began.

"When did you last visit your patient, Dr. Jordan?"

Dr. Jordan put the tips of his fingers together the way he had that day in the Helm front hall, and it irritated me just as much this time. "I last saw him—alive, that is—on the afternoon of May the third. Friday."

"Exactly," the coroner said. I keep calling him coroner, but it's more convenient. "And what was his condition then?"

"Mr. Helm's condition was good," Dr. Jordan said. "He was in relatively good spirits, his heart seemed strong, and on examining him I found a slight but none the less very encouraging improvement in the muscles of his left leg."

"May we take it that you thought Mr. Helm was on the road to recovery, doctor?"

"I hoped so, yes, sir," Dr. Jordan said.

"And did you pass this good news on to the people who would naturally be most interested—that is, to Mr. Helm's family?" asked the coroner. Nasty sarcastic thing.

"I told Mrs. Greer and Captain Helm. They were the only ones I saw when I came out," Dr. Jordan said.

I could see from Selden Lowry's face that if this had been a regular trial he would have been on his feet objecting to having that question answered. But it was only an inquiry and nobody was accused of anything, and anyway it was the coroner's court, with no judge set over him. Apparently he could go up all the suggestive little by-paths he wanted to.

"Exactly," the coroner said again. That word ought to be put on his tombstone when the time comes; and I didn't care if it came soon. "Now will you tell us about the next visit you made to the Helm home, doctor, after Mr. Helm was found dead?"

You could feel the people in the courtroom getting tenser, even if you were sitting up in front the way I was and couldn't look around to see.

Dr. Jordan said, with pauses for effect, "Captain Helm called me the next morning—May the fourth, that is—about seven-fifteen. He said his grandfather was dead, and asked if I wasn't supposed to come even so. I said I was." Dr. Jordan took his glasses off and put them on again. "I asked Captain Helm if he was positive his grandfather was dead and not in coma. He said he was. When I reached the house I realized, of course, why Captain Helm could be so sure."

Everybody in the room seemed to let his breath out at once, and the coroner said, "Yes, doctor?"

"Mr. Helm had obviously been poisoned," Dr. Jordan said. "Of course, it was not possible for me to determine just which poison had been employed. To a certainty, that is. But from the convulsed condition of the body and features, the etching of a glass which stood on a table beside the bed, and the fact that I had recently—ah—observed another case of sodium fluoride poisoning, I felt reasonably sure that had been the means employed."

"Did you perform an autopsy on the body, Dr. Jordan?" Dr. Jordan said he hadn't, that the medical examiner did that.

"Exactly," said the coroner, who had known it right along, of course. "I have his statement here. Since he is not able to be in court this morning I will read it aloud, and then pass it to the members of the jury." He read aloud, Dr. Jordan listening smugly from the witness chair. The statement described the "simple test"—it didn't sound very simple to me—that had established the presence of sodium fluoride in old Breckinridge Helm's body, and went on to say that was what he had died of, beyond the shadow of doubt.

I got all worked up over the American judicial system while the jury was examining that paper. At least half of them didn't know what it was all about. The little scrubby one on the end couldn't even read, as far as I could see, and the others weren't getting any too much out of what they read. I've seen that blank look too many times in the course of teaching forty years; I certainly ought to recognize it. There weren't but three men on the whole jury who looked smart enough to weigh evidence and make reasonable deductions from it. But when you just go out the door and collect a lot of street-corner loafers, the way they do for juries in coroner's and police courts, well, what can you expect?

"Just a few more questions, Dr. Jordan," the coroner was saying. "This sodium fluoride. Is it a common poison?"

"Not one of the *most* common poisons, no, sir," Dr. Jordan said. "But sodium fluoride is a popular insecticide, in use in a great many homes. It's also used commercially for disinfecting fermenting apparatus in breweries and distilleries, and in making paste and mucilages. I believe it is also a preservative of wood. Medically, we sometimes use sodium fluoride in the treatment of certain skin diseases or wounds. It was formerly prescribed for internal use as an antiperiodic, but I believe that has fallen entirely into disuse. Similarly, its internal use in the treatment of dental caries has not as yet entirely been established."

I didn't like the man, but he did seem to know what he was talking about.

"One more question, doctor," the coroner said respectfully. "Is there any difference to speak of between, say, sodium fluoride used as insecticide and sodium fluoride used to treat skin diseases?"

"No difference that an autopsy would show, no, sir," Dr. Jordan answered definitely. "Of course, the fluoride used medicinally is chemically pure, whereas the type sold commercially for ant poison is only eighty or ninety per cent pure. The inert ingredients that make up the other ten or twenty per cent are, of course, not under consideration in body analysis."

The coroner thanked him then and he stepped down, I think, to everybody's relief. Dr. Jordan was a splendid witness, undoubtedly, but a bit pedantic for the general taste.

"Miss Emily Craig!"

Emily got up and made her way to the witness chair—and just barely made it, too. You could see she was scared to death. She was trembling a little, and she kept biting her lips. The lipstick had come off in splotches. She looked so young and defenseless, in her childish dark blue dress with the white collar, that I didn't see how the coroner could help feeling sorry for her.

He could, though.

Emily was sworn in first, and gave her name and told where she lived.

"Describe your movements on the morning of May the second, Miss Craig."

"I woke up at seven o'clock when my alarm went off. We didn't have a nurse for Grandfather and I always got up early and gave him his bath," Emily said. Her voice was almost inaudible at first, but it got a little better as she went along. She looked at the jury after a minute, too, when Selden Lowry motioned that she should. But even after she took her eyes off her lawyer's face you could tell she was still reciting her lesson back to him. It didn't make a good impression, to put it mildly.

"I heard Miss Julia Tyler calling me and banging on her door. She was locked in. But when I got as far as her room I could see inside Grandfather's room, right across the hall. I—I forgot about her and went in."

"Go on, Miss Craig."

"Well, he—Grandfather was dead," Emily said. She stopped again, biting her lips.

"Describe what you saw, please."

"I saw what Dr. Jordan has described already," Emily said with an unexpected flicker of spirit. "Grandfather looked as if he'd died in some kind of convulsion. There was a glass on the table by the bed, just as Dr. Jordan told you. There wasn't anything in it, but the bottom half was all scratched and whitish, and I thought right away it must have been half full of—something strong."

"Had you ever seen a glass in that condition before?"

Emily bowed her head.

"Answer the question, please, Miss Craig."

"Yes, sir, I had," Emily said.

"Where?"

"In our house. In Gus's room. The morning after Gus had died."

"I believe you made that discovery also, Miss Craig?" Emily said she had. Her voice was so low again the coroner had to ask her to speak up.

"And then what did you do?"

Emily said, like a child, "I ran. I ran across the hall, and Miss Tyler was still pounding on her door and calling me. I managed to get it open—the key was in the lock—and then I reckon I fainted. My cousin—Miss Helm—was taking care of me when I woke up. And then the doctor came, but I was all right by then. The rest of them were all in the hall—the family, I mean. And I could see the servants at the top of the fourth-floor stairs. Grandfather's room is on the third, you know. But none of them came down. The police were inside with—Grandfather. We all just sat and waited for them to come out. That's all."

"Not quite all, Miss Craig," the coroner said smoothly. "Suppose we go back to your statement that, on discovering Mr. Helm's body, you ran, and afterwards fainted in the hall. Why did you run, Miss Craig?"

"Why did I run?" Emily repeated it blankly after him, and I for one agreed with her. Why on earth wouldn't she run?

"Exactly, Miss Craig," the coroner said, and waited.

"Why, I ran because I was scared," Emily said. "Naturally I was scared. And shocked. And, well—scared."

"Exactly," the coroner said again, looking like the cat that swallowed the canary. "And surprised, Miss Craig? Were you surprised to find your grandfather dead?"

I could see Selden Lowry's handsome, unpleasant face getting darker by the minute. Beside him, Mary Preston was mad as she could be too, her back as straight as a poker and her white-gloved hands tightening on the arms of her chair as if she wished they were Mr. Riley's neck. One of the nicest things about Mary Preston, I thought, was the way she was always on Emily's side.

"Why, yes, sir," Emily was saying. "Of course I was surprised."

The coroner said sternly, "Let me remind you, Miss Craig, that you are on your oath."

"Yes, sir."

"You have sworn to tell the truth, the whole truth, and nothing but the truth, so help you God."

Emily bowed her head.

"Do you think the jury will be inclined to believe your testimony if it can be shown that in any part of it you have failed to tell the truth?"

"Why, no, sir," Emily said, bewildered. "But I did tell the truth. Everything happened just the way I said it did. I woke up at seven o'clock, and then I heard Miss Tyer calling, 'Emily! Emily!' and pounding on the door. And when I went to see about *her* I could see into Grandfather's room. And he was dead. And I was scared and ran, and after I let Miss Tyler out I must have fainted. And then the others came, and the doctor, and we sat down and waited in the hall."

"Exactly," the coroner said. I can't describe the nasty way he said it.

"And I suppose your name is Emily Craig, too?"

Well, I'd been expecting it, subconsciously at least. So had Mary Preston; I could tell by the way her shoulders suddenly sagged.

But Emily straightened right up. She was full of surprises, that child. I'd expected her to crumple and cry right there on the witness stand, now that the coroner had—obviously—turned up the fact of her marriage to Sergeant Morgan. Instead, she really told him off, as Dick says.

"Certainly my name is Emily Craig," the child said, looking him straight in the eye. "I was born named that, Mr. Riley, and it's my own name that nobody can take away from me, and it'll be my name as long as I live, no matter how many people I marry."

Judging from the sound, everybody in the courtroom gasped. Everybody, that is, but Mary Preston and me, and Selden Lowry. He was sitting there with his arms folded and his clever, dissipated face as black as your hat.

"I reckon I'm what they used to call a Lucy Stoner," Emily went on, and she certainly did sound as strong-minded as Miss Stone in her palmiest days. "That's why when you asked me, I said I was Emily Craig. And it was the truth as I see it." For just a minute she looked exactly like her grandfather, sardonic and sure of herself, with a little smile on her face. "But if you're going to go around digging up marriage licenses, Mr. Riley, and go by what they say, I reckon I'm Emily Brown."

Emily Morgan, my mind was saying at the same time, and for a minute I couldn't believe my ears. Emily Brown! But then Emily was looking out past the obnoxious Riley, over the group of startled white faces and way to the back of the room. Her own face was just as calm as you please, and she was saying calmly, "Emily Craig Brown. Is that what you want me to say, Mr. Riley? Mrs. John Todd Brown."

CHAPTER THIRTEEN

Well, after that bombshell, nobody paid much more attention to testimony. Breck Helm got up on the witness stand and told how I got him out of bed, and from then on just as Emily had told the story. Martina Greer followed him as witness, she and Hattie Carnegie. I'd never seen anybody whose looks and clothes I admired more. Ordinarily the jury would have agreed with me, but this time they didn't pay very much attention to her. Nor to Mary Preston either, pretty as she was in her black suit and white blouse that weren't mourning and yet just right. Poor little Mary Preston, I couldn't help thinking of what she'd said that day when she told me they'd all decided to stick together. Mary Preston said, quoting Charlotte, that you could always tell nice people by the way they kept their mouths shut and their heads up. Poor child, she was white as a sheet and looked as if somebody had kicked her in the stomach, but Charlotte should have been proud of her.

The shock seemed to wear off almost everybody in between Breck Helm's testimony and John Todd Brown's. Not that Johnny Brown had anything very interesting to say, any more than the rest of them had. But naturally, after what Emily had popped out with, everybody in the room was sitting on the chair edge to hear him. You would have thought he was making revelations too, instead of just telling the same story over again.

They certainly were telling the same story, all of them. Selden Lowry had done his work well. Not so much as a single detail of the accounts varied, and Riley couldn't shake them no matter how hard he tried.

When he got to Dr. Greer, though, he began to talk about the poison again. No wonder, when Dr. Greer had enough of it under his bed to kill everybody on West Ormsby Street.

The coroner said dryly, after bringing out that fact, "Perhaps, Dr. Greer, you'd better explain to the jury how this quantity of sodium fluoride happened to be in your possession."

"I'll be glad to," Dr. Greer said. He shifted his position in the witness chair so the full glare of the sun struck his balding head instead of his quiet, commonplace face—animated now for the first time since I'd known him. What a man for Martina Brown to have married, I thought again, the way I always did.

Dr. Greer began, in a lecturing kind of a voice, "The sodium fluoride is in my possession because I am using it for dental research. I am a practicing dentist in Cincinnati, though my residence is just across the river in Shelton, Kentucky." He went on to say where he'd gone for his DDS and how long he'd been practicing. Seven years. "In March and April, 1944, I did some special study which I considered in the line of postgraduate work, even though it wasn't done academically," Dr. Greer went on. "I spent those months in or near the town of Hereford, Texas, and also at the headquarters of the Texas State Board of Health, Austin. As you know, some of the most important and interesting research in the country is being done there now."

"Suppose you tell the jury something about that, Dr. Greer," said the coroner, meaning of course that he'd never heard of it himself.

Dr. Greer did—and how, as Dick says. But it was too late then to stop him.

"Hereford, Texas, is located in Deaf Smith County in that part of the state known as the Panhandle. It is a level, high plains country, nearly four thousand feet elevation, with more than its share of sunshine hours and freedom from dust and smoke pollution. The topsoil is a dark, sandy loam, twelve or more inches deep on a clay known as *caliche*. This clay shows in analysis 71% to 88% assimilable calcium carbonate. Calcium is also highly present in the water supply, which is uniform and typical for both urban and rural areas. I believe it is 45 ppm, and the pH ranges from 7.5 to 7.7. The pH is, of course, the hydrogen ion concentration, or degree of acidity or alkalinity. There is also a very high proportion of magnesium in these waters—67 ppm—and fluoride is present to the extent of 2.2 to 2.7 ppm."

Dr. Greer drew a deep breath and went on before the coroner could stop him. He was having the time of his life.

"For a number of years the dental profession has credited assimilable calcium with the building of strong, healthy teeth. Pregnant women, and others who for physiological reasons have a calcium deficiency, are encouraged to take it regularly in tablet form. And of course all persons, young children in particular, are urged to drink plenty of milk, which is high in calcium lactate."

The jurors' eyes were definitely beginning to glaze.

"However," Dr. Greer said, "while we have recognized and still do recognize the value of calcium in tooth building, we have to face the fact that it is by no means a full solution. We know too many cases of people who dislike milk and never drink it, and who do not otherwise especially have calcium in their diet, who nevertheless have excellent teeth. Similarly, there are persons with very bad teeth who have drunk the optimum quantity of milk all their lives."

"That's very interesting, Dr. Greer," the coroner said, getting a word in edgewise. That was all he did get, though; Dr. Greer took him right up.

"Indeed it is, Mr. Riley. There isn't a one of us who shouldn't be interested in the splendid work they're doing down there in Texas. Dental caries—tooth decay," he explained condescendingly—"may not be a relatively serious disease, but it's almost universal and it's certainly a very unpleasant thing to have."

"It certainly is," Mr. Riley said. "Now, doctor—"

"Calcium alone does not prevent tooth decay. Neither does phosphorus nor Vitamin D. They are probably all valuable. But the essential factor—at least, that is what some of us believe now—is sodium fluoride."

With the introduction of these magic words Dr. Greer really was off to the races, as Dick says. His eyes shone, he sat forward on the edge of his chair, and his words came fairly tumbling out. The coroner didn't have a chance.

"Sodium fluoride is naturally present in the Deaf Smith County water to such an extent that serious mottling occurs. By mottling I mean an unattractive permanent marking of the enamel. But persons whose enamel has already been formed—persons over the age of seven or eight years, that is—are not subject to this disfiguration. And they are not subject to tooth decay."

"Not at all, Doc?" It came unexpectedly from one of the jurors, and of course we all turned. Dr. Greer said, "In forty-three native-born, continuously resident people examined in Deaf Smith County as a test, not one single carious tooth or filled tooth was found."

The interested juror was leaning forward in his chair, his face split in an ingratiating smile that revealed some unattractive black stumps. "Is this Deaf Smith County a pretty nice place to live, Doc?"

Everybody laughed and then stopped as suddenly, remembering this was a murder inquest.

"Yes, it's a very pleasant place," Dr. Greer answered, smiling. "But it would soon be very unpleasantly crowded if all the people troubled with tooth decay started to move down. Nor is that necessary. It's possible now to get the proper quantity of fluoride—not too much fluoride, as the Deaf Smith County people have—any place you live.

"There are three present ways of administering fluoride in the approved ratio," Dr. Greer went on happily. "One way is in drinking water, one part to one million parts of water, which is sufficient to prevent tooth decay but not enough to mottle the enamel. Second, it may be administered by means of bonemeal or bone flour capsules, which are rich in fluoride and other valuable elements. Third, it is possible to apply a concentrated solution directly to the teeth in the form of paste or mouthwash. Dentists in various parts of the country have conducted interesting experiments in one or the other of these methods. But as far as I know," Dr. Greer said modestly, "I am the only dentist who is conducting experiments in all three fields at once. I am giving bone flour capsules to one group of my patients and concentrated fluoride mouthwash to another group, and I am about to institute an experiment in community health which involves expertly controlled fluoride in the water supply. Which brings me to the matter of the large quantity of sodium fluoride you mention as being in my possession."

"Exactly," said the coroner, with a thankful sigh.

"Just before my wife and I were called to Louisville by her

grandfather's condition," Dr. Greer said, "I was able to persuade the town authorities in Shelton, the place in which I live, to try sodium fluoride in the water for the next ten years. I offered them my services free as part-time public health dentist, promising to conduct a careful survey over that period of time. After considerable discussion—perhaps some of you gentlemen will remember the storm that was raised years ago, when chlorine was introduced into your Louisville water—the matter was, as I have said, agreed on. I was authorized to order a supply of chemically pure sodium fluoride for the Shelton Water Plant."

"And are we to understand this is the fluoride in your possession now?"

"Yes, sir. And perhaps I should explain that it was sent here by mistake. It should have been sent to me in Shelton, of course," Dr. Greer said. "But when I wrote ordering the fluoride I used stationery with Mr. Helm's Louisville address on it. I did say in the body of the letter that I wanted the fluoride shipped to my permanent address in Shelton, but it was a very natural mistake for the shipping clerk to make."

"Exactly," the coroner said. "Now tell the jury how much fluoride you have on hand, if you please."

Dr. Greer said, rather reluctantly, I thought, though I couldn't see why, "I have eleven or twelve screw-top five-pound bottles."

"Don't you know exactly, doctor? Is it eleven, or is it twelve? Don't you know how many bottles you ordered? If not"—and it seemed to me that Riley's tone of voice wasn't far from a threat—"of course it will be easy to check back."

"Of course," Dr. Greer repeated, without expression.

"What company did you order from?"

"Eimer and Amend, in New York," answered Martina's husband, clearing his throat. "But I remember now, Mr. Riley. I ordered twelve."

It sounded funny for him to be forgetful about his number of bottles, when he'd been so positive about hard-to-remember things like how thick the topsoil was in Deaf Smith County, and the 67 ppm and pH, whatever they were.

"Have you used any of this material for any purpose whatsoever?"

Dr. Greer said he hadn't, faintly.

"Have you given or sold any of it to another person?"

"No, sir."

"Then you have the twelve five-pound bottles still intact?"

Dr. Greer said, so faintly this time that I on the second row from the front could hardly hear him, "No, sir. One of the bottles is gone. Somebody took it—I don't know when. I missed it the day before Mr.

Helm was killed."

Well, I don't know why such a wave of excitement should have gone around the courtroom when he said that. It seemed pretty obvious to me that Mr. Helm couldn't have been poisoned with Dr. Greer's sodium fluoride if it was all still under Dr. Greer's bed.

"No, sir, I had no reason to suspect any special person of taking it," Dr. Greer was saying when the wave died down. "At first I thought some member of the household might have known it was an insecticide, and wanted a little for that purpose. But my wife thought not."

"Oh, you discussed the theft with your wife, did you?" The coroner seemed to take a sinister pleasure in hearing that. I certainly didn't see why Dr. Greer shouldn't have mentioned it to Martina.

"Why, yes, sir," Dr. Greer was answering, as if he didn't either. He'd entirely recovered his poise. "My wife pointed out that there was plenty of sodium fluoride downstairs. Mary Preston—Miss Helm, that is— had bought some quite a while before.

The coroner called Mary Preston back to the stand then.

"Yes, sir, I buy it every year," Mary Preston said. "It's the best thing we've ever used for ants. And we get ants in our kitchen every spring that's the least bit damp. Nasty little red ants, all over everything. It's an old house, and the kitchen's in the basement, and we can't seem to keep them out."

The coroner said carefully, "So you are in the habit of buying sodium fluoride, Miss Helm. You are aware it is a deadly poison?"

"Yes, sir. It says so on the outside. But we don't have any children at our house, and we didn't have any dogs and cats until I got my puppy, so I never saw anything to be afraid of. And when I brought the puppy home I took him straight upstairs and shut him in my room until the servants had cleaned all the powder up. I told them they'd just have to go back to using coffee grounds, even if they weren't so good."

Mary Preston made a fine witness, it seemed to me. She said yes sir and no sir to the coroner as naturally as if he'd been that kind of person, and she seemed to be telling the truth freely and fully. At least it seemed that way to me. But the coroner knew something I didn't.

"Why did you give a jar of fluoride to your brother, Miss Helm?"

"Why, because he had ants out at his house too," Mary Preston's answer to that came promptly, even though you could see she'd been taken by surprise. "Out at Holliday Hall. They're just about to take the place."

"Did you afterwards regret giving Captain Helm the fluoride, Miss Helm?" The coroner's voice was like the best kind of silk that you can't get anymore.

"Why, no, sir," Mary Preston said.

"But you went out and bought some more?"

"No, sir."

"No?"

"I didn't buy any more ant poison, no, sir," Mary Preston said firmly, looking him straight in the eye. "I don't know where you got the idea I did, but it isn't so."

The coroner said then, after a long and very nasty pause, that he was much obliged to her and that would be all. "Call Mrs. Nettie Thompson," he said to the clerk. "That will be all, Miss Helm. You may step down."

But Mary Preston just sat there in the witness chair as if she hadn't heard him either time. One of her hands was clenched around the arm of the chair. The other had gone up to her mouth, and the glove on it wasn't a great deal whiter than she was.

CHAPTER FOURTEEN

Mrs. Thompson had her teeth in. That was the first thing I noticed, when I realized from her address she was the Mrs. Thompson Charlotte had spoken of. For the rest, she was a neatly dressed, middle-aged, middle-class woman, with round blue eyes behind rimless glasses, and black bobbed hair. I say "bobbed" advisedly; that's what Mrs. Thompson, greatly daring, had done to it circa 1926, and she hadn't changed the style since. It still showed just the tips of her ears on both sides, slanted over her forehead toward her right eye, and was shingled way up high in the back. It was a lot more out of style than Charlotte's Edwardian fringe.

"Oh, yes, sir," Mrs. Thompson was saying, after the preliminaries. "Of course I know Miss Helm. I've lived two doors away from her ever since she was just a little thing." She beamed nervously in Mary Preston's direction. "Yes, sir, I'd recognize her anywhere, I should think."

"Please tell the jury what happened on the morning of April the fifth, Mrs. Thompson."

"Well, that morning I had some business to do down on Market Street," Mrs. Thompson said, looking around defiantly. Market Street, Charlotte says, isn't just the nicest part of town. "I certainly don't go to pawnshops as a general rule, and neither do the people I rent my apartments to. I made my home over into apartments, after Mr. Thompson was taken. I'm just as particular about who I rent to as I would be about who I'd invite for a visit, and before the war I wouldn't take a soul that couldn't prove they were permanent, and didn't have any cats or dogs or children, and didn't promise to keep the radio turned down low."

Mrs. Thompson was having about as good a time as Dr. Greer had had.

"But this little thing sort of got under my skin, so to speak," Mrs. Thompson went on. "Not much more than a child herself, and then those two cute little children, and determined to follow her husband around just as long as he was on this side, even though she didn't have a cent in the world but her allotment. So I rented her my third floor back. *Without* the first month in advance."

She and her audience sighed together.

"Well, I soon found out *he* was no good," Mrs. Thompson said darkly. "Everything he needed furnished him out there at Fort Knox, and thirty-two dollars a month just to spend for laundry and insurance and little things. Plenty—just a plenty—if he didn't gamble or drink." She shook her head sadly. "But every month it was the same. He got his hands on more of that allotment than she did. And when they finally sent him out to Fort Sill, Oklahoma, and she came down to tell me they were going, she was three months behind with her rent."

There was a moment of silent sympathy.

"She felt awful bad about it," Mrs. Thompson resumed. "But there wasn't anything she could do. The Red Cross said they'd send her and the children back where they came from, but they wouldn't do anything about her back bills, and her folks weren't able to help her either, she said. And she was—sick herself"—Mrs. Thompson hurried on, her face bright pink—"and couldn't go to work and pay me back. She felt so bad about it I felt real sorry for her. And she said she knew her things weren't worth so much but she'd feel better if I took them. There was a little chip diamond she got when she graduated from high school, and one of those turquoise bracelets, and then the big silver cup his captain gave the baby after they named it for him. My, I certainly did hate to take them!"

But not enough, I said to myself nastily. I could see Charlotte eying the lady rather coldly too.

"Well, of course the things were no good to me," Mrs. Thompson went on. "She told me the name of a pawnshop down on Market Street where they'd buy things outright, if that was what you wanted. So that morning you're talking about I took the cup and the jewelry and went down there."

"That was the morning of April fifth?"

"Yes, sir."

"Please tell the jury what happened."

"Well, while I was waiting to transact my business," Mrs. Thompson said, "I noticed this girl the man I was waiting for was talking to. She had her back to me, but she looked familiar, and when she turned around I saw it was Mary Preston Helm. At least I thought it was."

The coroner said, frowning a little, "You have testified that you are well acquainted with Miss Helm, Mrs. Thompson, and would recognize her anywhere. Will you explain yourself to the jury?"

"Well, it was just that I never saw her before with her hair up," Mrs. Thompson explained, a little flustered at having her testimony quoted back at her. "It made quite a difference. And she had on dark glasses—real dark, so you couldn't tell what color her eyes were—and a dress I hadn't seen before."

"Go on, please."

"Well, I started to speak to her," Mrs. Thompson said. "And then, well, I don't know why you feel so funny in a pawnshop, but you do. And I was there on perfectly respectable business, and I certainly hope I'm known to be a respectable woman, no matter where I go. But I didn't speak to her, somehow. I turned my back and pretended I was looking at some jewelry in the showcase."

"And then?" the coroner prompted her.

"Then I went on and did my business I'd come to do and started back home. I thought I'd seen the last of Mary Preston, because she'd had time to get way ahead of me, even if she was walking. But when I came out of the pawnshop I saw her standing on the next street corner. She was talking to a soldier."

"Did you know who that was, Mrs. Thompson?"

Mrs. Thompson visibly hesitated. "Well, no, sir. I wouldn't like to say. I thought for a minute I recognized him, but I couldn't see his face. And then he touched his cap to her and started down the street, and Mary Preston went in the Taylor Drug Store they'd been standing in front of."

"And what did you do, Mrs. Thompson?"

Mrs. Thompson said complacently, "Well, my better nature asserted itself. I was kind of ashamed of the way I'd acted in the pawnshop, not speaking. And I thought, 'Well, here Mary Preston and I both are, a long way from home, and we'll probably both go back to West Ormsby on the same car, and any minute she's likely to turn around and see me, and she'll think it's funny if I don't speak. It's my *duty* to speak,' I said to myself. I didn't want the child to think I'd turned against her because of the way people were talking. About Gus being murdered, I mean. I'd always liked her and Emily both, and of course I'm an old friend of the whole family, living just two doors away from them all these years."

I couldn't resist looking over at Charlotte, who was looking down her nose.

"So I went in the drugstore and stood by the magazine rack while she—made her purchase," Mrs. Thompson said, and stopped abruptly and breathlessly.

"Exactly," the coroner agreed—purred—while the jury leaned forward and I'm afraid I did too. "Did you overhear her conversation with the clerk? . . . Then will you please repeat it to the jury?"

Mrs. Thompson said slowly and rather unhappily, I thought, "She said, 'I want a can of sodium fluoride ant poison, please,' and he said, 'Twenty-five or fifty-nine cent size? The fifty-nine is two full pounds and a very good value, special this week.' But she said no, the twenty-five-cent size would be plenty. She said—"

"Yes, Mrs. Thompson?"

"Well, she sort of laughed a little," Mrs. Thompson said reluctantly. "And she said, 'I've used this stuff before. A little goes a long way.'"

I don't know how to describe the sound that went up from that roomful of people. It was mixed up out of a lot of human emotions. So was poor Charlotte's face, when I looked across at her, and then on to Selden Lowry's and Emily's and young Breck Helm's. John Todd Brown and his sister Martina and Dr. Greer weren't visible—their faces, that is—from where I sat. But I had a clear view of Mary Preston, and I wished I could wipe that terrible little sarcastic smile off her mouth. It wasn't doing her a bit of good with the people who were looking at her too and who didn't know, as I did, how sweet and generous and affectionate she could be.

"Then she paid for it and started out of the store," Mrs. Thompson was going on. "And when she got close to me I put out my hand, like this, and I said, 'Why, hello, Mary Preston! What are you doing way down here? Visiting some of your Junior League kiddies?'" Mrs. Thompson took a deep breath. "And she looked down at my hand—this way—and answered me in a kind of Yankee voice. 'I'm afraid you've mistaken me for somebody you know,' she said. 'I don't know *you*.' And she sort of bowed and smiled like a stranger and went on out."

The coroner said, into the silence that followed that, "Will you tell the jury what effect this incident had on your opinion, Mrs. Thompson? Your opinion about the young lady's identity, that is. Did you still think it was Miss Helm?"

Mrs. Thompson didn't answer for quite a long time. When she did I think everybody in the room, even those of us who didn't like what she was saying, could tell she was being honest and really trying to be fair.

"I just didn't know what to think, Mr. Riley," Mrs. Thompson said. "You see, right that minute—right when it happened, when I still thought it was Mary Preston I was speaking to—I'd just gotten through doing a silly thing myself. Turning my back in that pawnshop so nobody I knew would recognize me. And I thought, 'Well, Mary Preston's ashamed of going to the pawnshop too. She feels just the way I did.' And I thought it was kind of childish of her to think she could fool me, right face to face, just because she had her hair up on her head and dark glasses and put on a Yankee accent. But I didn't blame her for trying. At least, that's the way I felt about it at the time.

"But I don't think Mary Preston Helm would do anything real bad," Mrs. Thompson went on firmly. "And I certainly don't believe she put on any disguise and went out and bought ant poison so she could kill poor Mr. Helm. I thought at the time it was Mary Preston I saw, and I still say the girl I did see looked enough like her to be her twin sister. But I think now I could have been mistaken."

Well, it was a nice try, as Dick says, and the family appreciated it. Even Charlotte smiled at Mrs. Thompson cordially as she got down from the witness chair, and poor little Mary Preston looked as if she were resolving never to laugh at her again, no matter with what startling effect the teeth were produced from that capacious dress front. But nobody felt that it had done much good. Even I, fond as I'd got of Mary Preston, could see it was most unlikely that a girl "enough like her to be her twin sister" and wearing disguising dark glasses, had gone into that Taylor Drug Store for sodium fluoride.

There wasn't any very interesting testimony after that. Charlotte and I were called, and told how we'd been locked in, and I corroborated, briefly, Emily's story about finding the body. Mr. Riley seemed more interested in my reactions to Emily's fainting spell—he tried to make me say it mightn't have been real, but of course I wouldn't—and when I'd noticed the white powder spilled on the stairs.

The white powder was sodium fluoride, Thelma testified—which we already knew. Anyway, there was so much sodium fluoride in this case—in both the victims' medicine glasses, and in the kitchen, and out at Holliday Hall, and in big five-pound jars under Dr. Greer's bed—that it would have been a shock if the spilled white powder had proved to be something else.

Thelma told about how she'd spilled it on the stairs the night before old Mr. Helm's murder, going up to bed. She hadn't meant to steal, indeed she hadn't, she told the jury. She was scared to death and her eyes were so wide open in her flat little yellow face that the backs of her eyeballs nearly showed. But she thought if Miss Mary Preston wouldn't let them use it in the kitchen anymore, on account of the new puppy's being in and out, she wouldn't mind her taking it home to her sister. Thelma's sister, apparently like everybody else in Louisville this damp season after the big March flood, was bothered with ants and water bugs. So Thelma had just put the jar of ant poison aside, and that was what she'd been carrying upstairs, because she was packing to visit her sister for the week end. And she'd meant to clean it all up, indeed she had, next morning before anybody saw it. But she'd overslept. Nobody in the house had an alarm clock but Miss Emily, and couldn't get one. She was sorry, Thelma said fervently.

"Well, you needn't be. You'd better be glad," the coroner told her, in the jocular, patronizing tone white people who aren't socially very sure of themselves use when they're talking to colored people. "That little layer of ant poison may have saved your neck, Thelma. Be sure you clean up after yourself better next time, hear? But be glad you didn't this once."

"Yes, *sir*, I sho' *will*," Thelma said, showing her teeth and eyeballs widely as she got out of the witness chair.

She was the last witness to be called, and then the coroner instructed the jury. I was a little nervous about the jury, not because there was any evidence to point conclusively to any one suspect, but because the jury looked so dull I wouldn't have put anything past them. When they came back with the verdict, though, it was "Murder by person or persons unknown."

Selden Lowry walked out of the courtroom with Charlotte and me, and in a minute or two Johnny Brown caught up with us.

He said cheerfully, "Well, Mr. Lowry, that turned out pretty well, don't you think? And there the matter will hang."

"There the lot of you will hang, for all I care, young man," Mr. Lowry answered grimly. He was mad as fire. "It's one thing not to tell a judge and jury everything you know. It's another thing not to tell your lawyer. How do you expect me to protect your interests and advise you properly when you spring these little surprises on me in court? I suppose you merely forgot to mention the fact you'd married Miss Craig, and likewise it slipped Miss Helm's mind that she'd disguised herself so she wouldn't fool a tenyear-old child and gone out to buy a new supply of poison."

"Well, yes, sir, I reckon it did." Johnny was completely unabashed and cheerful. "At least, I can't answer for Mary Preston; I hadn't heard about that poison buying episode myself. Maybe it did just slip her mind. But it certainly never would have occurred to me to tell you I'd married my little cousin Emily. Married Emily!"

And I could hardly believe my ears but he laughed out loud.

We were all three pretty much stunned, I think, but Charlotte finally found her voice. "John Todd Brown, you listen to me," she was beginning in no uncertain terms, when Johnny laughed again. The thought flashed through my mind that he must be drunk. But even drunk he'd always been so polite to Charlotte.

"I'm sorry, Cousin Charlotte. Some other time," he said now. "I've got to run if I'm going to ride with Mary Preston."

Not with Emily. With Mary Preston.

We could see him throwing open the door of Mary Preston's blue coupe halfway down the block, and then lost sight of him while the rest of us—including Emily, who either hadn't seen or didn't mind—piled into the old ark that had been Mr. Helm's pride and joy, but that Breck wouldn't be caught driving much longer, if I knew anything about young people. Mary Preston's blue car was a long way ahead of us most of the trip home, but after we got on Fourth Street they had a lot of bad luck with the traffic lights and we had some good luck, and finally there wasn't but one other car between us and them. They had to stop at the corner of Fourth and Ormsby for still another light, and through the back window of the blue coupe we could watch John Todd Brown kissing Mary Preston, the same uninhibited way I'd seen before.

But he was married now, and Mary Preston knew it. Married to Mary Preston's own cousin, whom she seemed so fond of and always took charge of and stood up for. I wasn't any too surprised at Johnny Brown, but really, I must say, I was surprised at *her*.

CHAPTER FIFTEEN

Charlotte and Breck made the arrangements for old Breckinridge Helm's funeral. They had it in the red stone house he'd lived and died in, which was an ideal spot for a funeral and not much else, and then at Cave Hill Cemetery. Poor Dr. Moffat, I thought, watching the raw early-May wind flutter his surplice. No wonder his voice fluttered too, with all that money for Grace and St. Peter's gone forever. Some of the social workers looked pretty sad as well, and of course the servants, who'd only been with the Helms a month or less, cried like old family retainers, the facile, flattering way all colored people can. I wish I could do it. There was only one person who seemed to me really sincerely, unselfishly sorry, though, and that was Charlotte, who wept quietly at the head of the grave.

The Helm grandchildren didn't cry, not even Emily. But they were all there, of course, and their conduct left nothing to be desired. The three girls all wore black suits or dresses and the two civilians black bands around their left sleeves. Breck Helm stood by Charlotte at the head of the grave with his own head bowed down the whole time, as if the weight of sorrow were too much for him.

Or maybe it wasn't the weight of sorrow but the weight of something else.

Young Jane Shelby and I stood together a little at one side, as behooved two people almost in the family circle but not quite. I liked Janie. I'd thought I would, because usually the people who care about horses are pretty nice people, and Mary Preston had said Janie just about lived in riding breeches. She'd look best in riding breeches, I thought, watching her sideways. But she looked mighty nice and sweet in her inexpensive little grey suit, even though she didn't have Mary Preston's figure or Martina's air of high fashion. She wasn't as pretty as my Anne, either, but she looked enough like her, in the same brown-eyed, brown-haired, clear-skinned way, to make me very much on Janie's side. I didn't like what the Helm grandchildren were letting her in for, as Dick calls it. She was too nice a girl to spend her life married to a man under suspicion of murder.

Or to a murderer, of course.

After the funeral Mr. Fownes went back to the house with the family and read them the will. I've never known that to be done before, though of course it happens all the time in books. I suppose it hadn't happened before in my experience because I never knew any other very rich people. Most of the people I know in Virginia don't have much money, and when they make their wills they just usually keep them in their desks or their sewing baskets, which are plenty safe enough.

I didn't go to hear the will read, of course, but Charlotte did, because Mr. Fownes had notified her she was in it. Old Breckinridge Helm had left her a silver tea service that had been in the Murray family originally but that the Helms had got by marriage. It was a handsome, massive thing, and Charlotte was as pleased as if she'd had some place to put it. She kept saying tearfully how wonderful it was of Breckinridge to have thought about her. I didn't think there was anything so wonderful about it, after all the attention and affection she'd given his grandchildren all their lives. It was the least he could do to leave her something.

There were a number of other relatively small bequests: a few annuities—though not to Gus and Martha, who'd still been with Charlotte when this will was made—a scholarship to the University of Louisville, and a stained-glass altar piece to Grace and St. Peter's

Church. Emily Powell Helm's diamond engagement ring was to go to her namesake Emily Powell Craig, and Breck was to get a gold-headed cane that had been his great-great-grandfather's. I could imagine how pleased he'd be with that. All the rest of the estate, both real and personal, was to be divided equally among the three real and the two step-grandchildren.

Even with the inheritance tax taken out, Mr. Fownes told them, there'd be between six and seven million dollars to be divided.

"Well, I'm glad for Dr. Greer that he can stop practicing now and devote all his time to research, the way you say he wants to," I said, when Charlotte got back and told me about the will. "And Mary Preston can be a doctor now, and Breck can keep Holliday Hall—"

"Oh, that reminds me, Julia," Charlotte said, I thought a little hurriedly. "Breck asked me if I thought you'd like to see Holliday Hall. He and Janie are going out there tomorrow and spend the day—he has to see the farmer about some things, and Janie's refinishing the parlor furniture. She's taken a great fancy to you, Julia. Why don't you go? You can take a lunch and have a nice day."

"I'd like to see the place, certainly," I said. "But wouldn't they rather go by themselves?"

"Evidently not, or they wouldn't have asked you. They didn't have to," Charlotte answered sensibly. Even Charlotte, with her long skirts and her curled grey bang, knows that the day of chaperons is over.

So I did go. Afterwards, after what happened, I never could make up my mind whether I was sorry or glad.

They took me all over Holliday Hall, Janie and Breck. Janie was about as proud of it as he was. It wasn't a show place, really; nobody famous had ever lived there and it wasn't any architectural wonder. It was just a gentleman's country house, built by slave labor about 1830, I should judge, out of bricks made on the place. You could still see the big hole in the ground where they'd dug the clay. "It would be a nice place for a swimming pool, wouldn't it?" Janie said. "Maybe someday—"

Breck told her firmly, "Not until we get a lot of other things first. We can't patch up those stables to last many more years, and we'll have to build a track, of course."

They'd both forgotten about the money, bless their hearts. Then you could see them remembering all of a sudden that Breck's grandfather had died and left him well over a million dollars, and they could do anything they wanted with Holliday Hall—swimming pool, track, and brand-new stables full of the best horseflesh in Kentucky. Breck and Janie looked at each other with a wild surmise, but they didn't say anything, probably on account of me.

I said something about it myself, later, when Breck had gone off to see the tenant farmer and Janie and I were alone in the big white-walled parlor with its rolled-up rugs and the beautiful gilt window cornices that looked funny without curtains hanging down from them. Janie had spread newspapers and was down on the floor using varnish remover on a carved walnut side chair. The child certainly had put in a lot of work on that parlor furniture; she'd got the two sofas and eight of the ten matching chairs down to the natural wood, and if she'd left even a trace of stickiness in those deep-carved roses my eyes weren't sharp enough to see it. It was a professional-looking job, and I told her so.

"But, Janie, aren't you ruining your hands? I've never used that stuff, but I've heard people say it took the skin right off."

"It *is* strong. My hands feel funny for a long time after I've used it," Janie said, spreading them out. "But it's the stain that really makes them look awful."

"Oh, are you going to use stain?"

Janie attacked one of the walnut roses with an old toothbrush dipped in the varnish remover. "I always use a little stain, right before the linseed oil and wax. I don't like that light, new-looking finish you get if you just sand things and go on. But I certainly will have a dark finish on my hands after I've stained two sofas and ten chairs and a piano."

"My dear child, you won't be able to go anywhere," I said. "And neither would Breck, if he did it for you. Why don't you see that old Mr. Brown, Janie? He's doing a beautiful job on Charlotte's bureau where Blockbuster chewed it. Of course he's high, but—"

"But we can afford him now—now that Mr. Helm is murdered and Breck has a million dollars," Janie said rather bitterly. "No, Miss Julia, I don't think we've got any business touching that money till everything's—settled." She didn't mean just the estate. "Do you, now, really?"

"Well, but, Janie, that may take a long time," I said neutrally, and Janie stuck out her chin.

"I don't care how long it takes. I think we ought to wait. And anyway," Janie said, achieving lightness with an effort, "I want to brag to my grandchildren about how I did all these things myself. I'll let Breck put on the linseed oil, because it always makes me sick to smell it, but that's absolutely all. Don't you think my grandchildren will be impressed—and maybe mind me better?"

"I'm sure they will," I said, liking Janie more than ever.

It was a nice day—one of the few nice ones we'd had, after that too-early spring spell the month before—and really warmer outdoors than in. There wasn't any dining room furniture anyway, so we had our lunch under a big beech tree in the neglected garden. Everything was nice. The Helm cook had a real talent for frying chicken—I suppose Mary Preston had cut it up for her first—and Charlotte had contributed one of her chocolate cakes. She made one every time they came out to spend the day, Janie said, because it was Breck's favorite and he certainly hadn't got much cake out where he'd been, flying those mountains between China and India.

"I don't see where she gets the sugar," I said. But as soon as I said it I realized Charlotte had probably gone without sugar from the time Breck went into service, saving all she could get hold of against the day he'd be back home. She would do a good deal more for that boy than drink her coffee black; I was glad I could give her an alibi for the time of old Mr. Helm's murder.

I'd never been able to see before why Charlotte was so wild and crazy about Breck Helm, who to my way of thinking wasn't half as attractive as young Johnny. I conceded his dark good looks and his nice manners, and I didn't doubt he'd been a big help to his grandfather in the factory and was a good air force officer now. He'd just never seemed to me outstanding among the other attractive, good-looking young people in that family. That day at Holliday Hall, though, I was ready to agree with Charlotte about him. Nobody could have been nicer. He was a changed person, really, with the strain all smoothed out of his face and voice, and his hands perfectly steady, and his laugh, that I'd never heard even once before, coming every few minutes. If Holliday Hall always had such a good effect on him it certainly would have been a shame to sell it.

Janie was nervous, though. She kept her end up, as Dick says, as well as anybody could have done it, laughing and talking and eating more chicken and chocolate cake than would have been considered ladylike in my young days. But toward the end of the meal she was uneasy underneath. I could see it even if Breck couldn't. I thought, of course, it was on account of old Mr. Helm's murder, the implications and consequences of which were enough to upset any prospective in-law.

Breck was reaching for his third piece of cake when Janie said his name quietly. Just his name, but his hand stopped in mid-air. Janie needn't ever worry about her grandchildren's not minding her; they'd mind her, all right.

"I didn't say anything before because I thought maybe I'd imagined it," Janie went on evenly, without raising her voice. "But for the last ten or fifteen minutes I've been seeing something move back of that hedge. It wasn't the wind. There wasn't any wind blowing. And now it's stopped, and I'm sure I just heard somebody in the house. Listen!"

She held up her hand.

Across the stretch of uncut lawn between us and the library windows there was utter silence for a minute or two. But then it came again, the noise Janie had heard. Somebody was in the house, all right. The sound he was making was the sound of metal sliding along metal, and he was making it slowly, carefully, and doubtless unavoidably.

I couldn't identify it, but Breck did. He said briefly, looking at Janie, "The door of the safe. You stay here."

"You be careful," Janie answered as briefly. She seemed less worried than I felt as we watched him making his way to the house. But I was thankful to see he'd taken something out of a back pocket and had it in his hand. I knew officers carried them on duty but I didn't know they had them all the time.

"Miss Julia, I'm going in through the dining room window," Janie said. "There's a closet between it and the library, where the safe is, that opens both ways. Probably he won't need me, but—"

"But we'll both go, just in case." I expect I read too many shilling shockers, as I understand they call them in England, but it honestly never occurred to me that at sixty-eight I'd probably serve better if I'd only stand and wait. The idea began to dawn on me, though, when I essayed the dining room window. It was quite high up off the ground, and Janie had to hoist me. The dining room didn't have any furniture in it, as I've said, or any rug, and our footsteps made a shockingly loud hollow sound, careful as we tried to be. Janie took her shoes off and left them on the window sill, but I carried mine into the closet with me. With those heavy metal arch supports built in they wouldn't make bad weapons, and anyway they were all the weapons I had.

The closet was a big one, with shelves at each end and a door, as Janie had said, into each of the rooms it lay between. The doors were thick mahogany and we couldn't hear a thing until Janie got down and put her ear to the crack underneath, and I took my place at the big empty keyhole.

". . . out of here," Breck Helm was saying. "Are you crazy? Of all the times to come—"

"I had to come when I could," somebody else said reasonably. It didn't sound like the way a burglar would talk to the master of the house, but then the voice didn't sound like a burglar's either. But I didn't recognize it at first.

"Well, you see it isn't here," Breck said. "Would I be likely to leave it in an empty house in a safe with a broken dial? So you'd better be starting back. Fast."

"You wouldn't like to give it to me first?" the voice asked, delicately mocking. And this time I recognized it. It was Martina Greer's voice.

I couldn't believe it. Martina Greer sneaking into Holliday Hall and trying to steal something out of the safe. Martina of all people.

I took my ear away from the keyhole then and put my left eye there instead. That way I couldn't hear a thing they said, and I could see that they were still talking; but I could see them facing each other, Breck so dark and handsome and tired-looking, with his face white as a sheet and the little bluish pistol dangling from his fingers, and Martina in her black suit with the big silver bracelet and earrings, and a calm, superior little smile on her beautifully rouged mouth.

It was like a scene from one of those plays that run about a week.

I took my eye away from the keyhole as Martina turned to go, and put my left ear back. But it was too late. I'd missed everything else, whatever it was. Martina just said, "Well, goodbye," and Breck didn't say anything at all.

We waited until we heard a car start in the distance, really way off. Then I tied the laces of my shoes, and Janie got hers off the dining room window sill and slipped them on. Through the window we could see Breck heading back to the place he'd left us.

"Quick, out through the parlor," Janie said. She hustled me across the hall and across the parlor to its garden door. The garden at Holliday Hall is a big half-circuit affair, touching the back and sides of the house. Naturally, on account of the house, you can't see one end of the crescent from the other. We strolled along the garden path to meet Breck, just as if we'd merely gone to see the other end of the garden and hadn't been in the house at all. It wasn't that we didn't intend to tell him we'd listened in the dining room closet. It was just that for a while it's natural to go on doing things in a devious way, after a tour of taking off your shoes and snooping through keyholes.

But we didn't get a chance to tell him.

"Well, show's over," Breck called out instead, as soon as he saw Janie and me. "Nothing to worry about, but I'm glad you heard him, Janie—"

"Him?" I said stupidly. It just came out. I couldn't help it.

"It was a little colored boy, ten or twelve years old," Breck said. "I don't know who he was. Somebody'd told him we had a safe behind the map in the library, and I reckon he thought it was full of gold and silver. You can't much blame the kid."

Janie and I were still just staring at him. He probably thought we were still scared.

"But I gave him a good talking-to," Breck Helm said easily, reassuringly. "I don't think he'll be back again."

CHAPTER SIXTEEN

Lieutenant Arthur Bates had set up temporary office in the library of the Helm house. It was a good room for conducting a murder investigation, just as the house as a whole had been a good, suitable place for conducting a funeral. Old Breckinridge Helm—or whoever was guilty of decorating that house—had been crazy on the subject of red. The library had a red carpet and curtains too, a lurid, murderous shade of red, and ugly leather chairs and a big black walnut desk that made even Lieutenant Bates look insignificant behind it. But I don't believe he knew that.

Before the funeral, when old Mr. Helm's body had been lying in state across the hall, he'd shown a certain amount of decency. But after the funeral he went from bad to worse.

Mary Preston said between her teeth, coming out of the library into the hall where I was waiting my turn with Lieutenant Bates, "That man! Somebody ought to murder *him!*"

"Maybe somebody will," I answered, and went on in without waiting to see how she took that. I'd given up, now that they had Mr. Lowry to advise them, all effort to teach any of the children caution.

"Good morning, Miss Tyler. Sit down," Lieutenant Bates said. It didn't seem to occur to him to get up himself. I sat down.

"What do you think of that girl?" he asked me, just like that.

"Why—I think she's a very nice girl," I said, flabbergasted. I'd never been around a detective like this one. "I like her."

Lieutenant Bates said, very unprofessionally, I thought, "Well, I don't. And I sure would like to know what it is she's trying to hide. What is it, Miss Tyler?"

"I'm sure I don't know," I said. "I don't think she knows who murdered her grandfather, if that's what you mean. And I certainly don't think she did it herself."

"Why not?"

I didn't like the way he said it, especially when I didn't have a logical answer ready. "I just don't think so."

"Well, I don't know but what I do," Lieutenant Bates said. "Now, look, Miss Tyler. As far as I can see you're the only person knows about this case that isn't trying to pull the wool over my eyes. Your friend Mrs. Buckner is. She won't come out and tell a downright story, as she calls it, but she certainly don't mind leading me around by Robin Hood's barn. All I can get out of her is that old Mr. Helm was hard to get along with and his grandchildren were all high-spirited."

"Well, that's true," I said.

Lieutenant Bates said, "As far as it goes, I expect it is. But you've got to admit there's a little more to it than that, Miss Tyler, with old Mr. Helm laying out in his little marble house in Cave Hill."

I did admit it.

"Well, then," Lieutenant Bates went on, "suppose you break down and tell me what you know about this ring."

"This ring" was just his way of talking. There wasn't a ring in sight. But naturally my mind flashed instantly to the showy little platinum and diamond circle that Emily still didn't wear, though I happened to know that Mary Preston had put it on her bureau. I said, a good deal too promptly and positively, "Not a thing."

"How do you know you don't, Miss Tyler?" Lieutenant Bates asked with quiet triumph. "I didn't even say what ring I meant." He didn't add, "Aha, now I've got you," but he certainly looked that way. It brought out the worst in me.

"I certainly *don't* know what ring you mean, Lieutenant Bates," I heard myself saying. "I just don't know anything about *any* ring."

"Oh, yes, I think you do, Miss Tyler," the nasty thing said, and sat back and sneered the way they don't even do in the movies anymore. I was good and mad by that time. I don't approve of telling stories any more than Charlotte Buckner does, and this Bates had fairly made me pop out with one. And, perversely, I resented his practically calling me a liar because of it. It was no way to conduct a murder investigation, it seemed to me. It wasn't necessary. I'd seen a murder investigation conducted before and I knew.

I haven't lost my temper in a good many years but this time I was right on the ragged edge. I sat there just simmering. But then I saw Lieutenant Bates was watching me, and I realized all at once that blow my top, as Dick calls it, was exactly what he wanted me to do. It was the Bates technique, apparently, to make people mad and then note down what they'd blurt out. I didn't doubt he'd got a good deal of his information from things Mary Preston and some of the others had said in anger.

Well, he wouldn't get anything out of *me*.

"Did you find a ring under Mr. Helm's body, Lieutenant?" I asked, as pleasantly as I could. I'd just read about a case like that, in one of Mignon Eberhart's books. "If you'd like to describe it to me maybe I can identify it. But otherwise I'm afraid I can't help you. Much," I couldn't help adding, though the last thing I wanted was to sound sarcastic, "as I'd like to do it."

Arthur Bates looked at me for fully a minute then, and I looked at him right back. I could have kept it up as long as he could. He said finally, "No, we didn't find a ring under Mr. Helm's body. We can't find it anywhere. That's just the trouble."

"Well, if you could describe it," I said patiently.

"It's a diamond solitaire, Miss Tyler. Tiffany setting," Lieutenant Bates told me, with elaborate courtesy. "Size of stone about two carats, pure blue-white. And round. The setting's yellow gold. It was right in style in 1893. From all I can hear about it it was just like everybody else's engagement ring then, except the stone was bigger."

Engagement ring! "Well, I never saw it or heard of it," I said, this time with perfect truth.

"You've heard of it if Mrs. Buckner told you about the old man's will," Lieutenant Bates corrected me, and waited.

I said carefully, "Do you mean this is the ring he willed to Emily Craig? Her grandmother's engagement ring?"

"It sure is," Lieutenant Bates said, watching me. "Where is it, Miss Tyler?"

I was more bewildered than mad. I couldn't imagine what he was driving at. "Where is it? Why, I suppose it's in a deposit box at some bank. Unless the executors have already turned it over to Emily Craig."

"The executors can't find it, I tell you," Lieutenant Bates said with elaborate patience and not too much politeness this time. "They've gone through Mr. Helm's box at the First National, and it isn't there, and it isn't in the safe in his bedroom, where it always stayed."

"I didn't know he had a safe in his bedroom," I said, for want of something better to say. There were too many safes in this murder, it seemed to me.

"Behind the picture of the old dame in the white cap," Lieutenant Bates told me kindly. "He kept some money in there, like to pay the servants and all. Convenient. And then some of this old family jewelry too. Don't ask me why he did *that*. Nobody ever wore it. Why he didn't take it down to the First National, when he had a box and all— This ring that's missing, now, must have been worth two-three thousand dollars in any man's money."

"Is anything else missing?" I asked.

"Well, money, if there was any in there. Probably not so much. We've traced the ring to Mr. Brown," Lieutenant Bates said casually, "and there the trail ends."

"To Mr. *Brown?*"

Bates nodded. "Mr. Brown. And Mr. Brown isn't talking. He won't say he got it out of the pawnshop any more than your friend Miss Helm'll say she put it in."

I said rather desperately, "Lieutenant Bates, I don't know why you're telling me all this, but if you're going to I'd like to get it straight. Is it your contention that Mary Preston Helm stole this ring out of her grandfather's safe and pawned it, and that John Todd Brown went down later and got it out? Can you prove that?"

"If we could prove it we'd arrest that Helm girl for murder so fast it would make your head swim," Lieutenant Bates said grimly. "All we need is the ring. The Jew at the pawnshop can identify it positively, he says. And he's already identified Mr. Brown positively, as a man that came in and redeemed a diamond ring. And that Mrs. Thompson's identification of the Helm girl is good enough for me, and will be for any murder jury."

I couldn't help shuddering.

"Now, I believe you know where that ring is, Miss Tyler. You or Mrs. Buckner. Or maybe both of you," Lieutenant Bates said, and waited.

He'd be waiting yet, as far as I was concerned, except that the dinner gong boomed just then. Maybe it reminded him that he was hungry himself; I can't imagine his caring whether or not he made me late. Anyhow, he said I could go.

Lieutenant Bates didn't eat with us, fortunately. I was glad he hadn't read some of the murder books I had, in which the police detective did as a matter of course, whether he was asked or not. So there was just the family and Charlotte and me, and old Breckinridge Helm's empty chair.

It was at the very end of the meal—a rather silent, uncomfortable one, as so many of our meals were now—that Emily said she wanted to make a speech.

We all just sat and looked at her. She had on her pale blue dress again, and it made her look about twelve years old, not eighteen as she actually was. And she was shaking all over. But her voice when she went on to talk wasn't the quavery little one she'd made her announcement in, but the one we'd heard that day she spoke up and told them how to get their grandfather adjudged insane.

"This can't go on," Emily said, and then in the stronger voice, "This can't go on. It's awful. I can't stand it. I thought I could, when we were all talking about how we'd stick together. But it's so *long*."

"Now, Emily, it isn't really long, you know," somebody said reasonably. I think it was Johnny Brown. I wasn't taking my eyes off Emily's grim little face.

"It is too long! It's seemed like a thousand years already. To me," Emily said. "But that isn't what I mean. I mean there isn't any end to it. It'll be like this all our lives. I can't stand it. And it isn't fair. I think the murderer ought to confess."

You could have cut the silence with a knife.

Finally Martina said, "It would be hard on you if the murderer confessed, though, Emily, wouldn't it? A member of your family—"

"Yes, it would," Emily said. "I'd hate to have people saying one of my cousins was a murderer. But this way they're talking about *all* my cousins, Martina. And they'll never get tired of it. Don't you see? Somebody will always be saying that maybe you did it—or Mary Preston—or one of the boys—or *me*."

"Ah, well, now we come to it," Johnny Brown said, in not the nicest tone in the world. It tried to be light and fooled nobody. "That's what you're really worried about, isn't it, my dear? What people are saying about *you*. What Lieutenant Bates thinks—"

Mary Preston cut in. "Johnny, that's crazy. Everybody knows Lieutenant Bates is a fool. Nobody else thinks Emily did it. She *is* thinking about all of us—not just herself. And she's right, too. It *is* hard to take. Harder than I thought it would be. Do you realize how many callers we've had in this house since Grandfather's funeral? Just exactly two. Mr. Fownes. Janie's mother. And both of them felt they simply had to come."

Dr. Greer said, his voice like dry ice, "So you're backing out too, Mary Preston?"

"I am *not!*" Mary Preston said, her eyes flashing. "I promised, didn't I? And I can take it, Robert Greer, just as well as you or anybody else can. I just said it was hard, and it is. I feel sorry for Emily. She's younger than the rest of us are."

Breck Helm was the only one of the lot who hadn't spoken. He spoke now, his voice as hard as nails. "I'd feel a lot sorrier for Emily if I thought she was speaking her own mind, and not an outsider's."

"I am speaking my own mind!" Emily flashed. "And I'll say what I think again, Breck Helm. I think the murderer ought to confess and let the rest of us go free."

It must have been fully five minutes that the silence lasted. It felt like an hour. And finally it was only Charlotte that broke it—Charlotte pushing back her chair and speaking in a dead kind of voice to the flush-faced girl at the head of the table. "I think I've stayed too long already, Mary Preston. If you'll excuse us, Julia and I had better go upstairs."

I murmured too, and struggled to my own feet.

Breck Helm was at the door before we were, holding aside the awful red velvet portiere. He said, as if nothing had happened, "Don't forget, Miss Julia. Tomorrow morning at ten."

I looked at him stupidly.

"Your appointment with the dentist. Don't you remember, Miss Julia? I'll take you down there at ten, and afterwards I'll pick you up again and you and Aunt Charlotte are going to have lunch with me."

Rather incredibly, we did—as if that scene at the dinner table had never happened at all. The dentist didn't keep me long this time, or hurt me much, and Charlotte read old *National Geographies* in the waiting room, and Breck was right on time picking us up.

Asked where we'd like to have our lunch, Charlotte thought it would be nice to go to the Plantation Room in the Seelbach Hotel.

"Well, Aunt Charlotte, you're coming right along," Breck said. "That's a bar."

Charlotte, flushing, admitted that she knew it. "I've been there before. But the bar part is up front. Of course, it does smell bad all over. Like— well, like a bar. But I want Julia to see the little steamboat coming round the bend. It's a cyclorama—diorama—panorama—"

Unfortunately neither of us could help her out.

"Well, anyway. You see this little white house all lit up, Julia—of course it's a big plantation house really, but you're supposed to be looking at it from way off. White columns, and big trees with Spanish moss, the kind they have way down South, and slaves dancing around in the moonlight having a good time. And then this old-time steamboat starts coming round the bend, with all *its* lights on, too, and passes the house. And then the lights go out, and the sun starts coming up, and all the same things happen again in daylight."

But as things turned out we didn't give the house and the steamboat our full attention long. Breck ordered, and our nice lunch came almost right away, and then he ignored his and put his elbows on the table and began to talk.

"Aunt Charlotte—Miss Julia—I want you to help me out. I'm worried about Emily."

"Emily?" we said together.

"Something is going to happen to Emily," Breck Helm said. "I've got to get her out of that house. If I don't do it right away—well, not to put too fine a point on it, Emily's going to be murdered."

"Not Emily!"

"But, Breck, why—"

Breck told us, "Emily did a mighty dangerous thing last night. That agreement we made—whether we should have made it or not—

Anyway, it's all that lets the murderer feel—safe. He's gone too far now to go back. And if he has to do it he'll kill again."

"He?"

Breck moved his head impatiently. "Or she. I don't know who it is, Aunt Charlotte. I've got my own ideas. I reckon we all do. But when Emily said what she did about thinking the murderer ought to confess, well, she certainly was looking right at the same person that *I've* got in mind."

"I didn't notice," I murmured, chagrined. It was perfectly apparent Breck had no idea of telling us.

"And what did he do—the one she was looking at?—or she do?" Charlotte wanted to know.

Breck Helm said, "Nothing. We all sort of discussed it a little more, after you left; but of course the murderer didn't confess, and nobody would come right out and side with Emily's point of view. And finally we just dropped it, I reckon. All but Emily. You know how Emily is, Aunt Charlotte. Stubborn! Even if there's nobody putting her up to it—and I think in this case somebody is—she doesn't tend to give in."

Charlotte nodded.

"So if the murderer has the sense God gave geese," Breck Helm finished wearily, "he'll put her out of the way."

The little steamboat floated down the river in the moonlight, past the miniature plantation house with its clean white columns and happy slaves, and disappeared from view. The lights in the house had gone out and the sun was coming up before any of us spoke again.

"What I wish you'd do, Aunt Charlotte," Breck Helm said, "is let Emily stay over in your apartment for a while. Wouldn't that work? They say it's easier to hide a person right under the police's nose than it is anywhere else. You've got some canned stuff in the kitchenette, haven't you. And Miss Julia could take her some other things, maybe, in that bag she carries her needlepoint in."

Charlotte said, frowning, "She could stay there if it weren't for the lights. But she wouldn't want to go to bed as soon as it got dark every night, and light does show through the chinks in those Venetian blinds. The—the murderer could see it right from your house."

"And another thing, Breck," I said hastily, "Mary Preston has been doing all our errands. She's just insisted; Charlotte and I haven't been over there at all. She'd think it was mighty funny if we stopped sending her now."

"Oh, well, it wouldn't matter if just Mary Preston knew about Emily," Charlotte said.

Sometimes I really do despair of Charlotte.

"I don't think it would matter either, Aunt Charlotte," Breck Helm told her gently. "But just to be on the safe side—after all, this may be a matter of Emily's life, you know. It isn't a little thing."

"Just to be on the safe side, not one of you should know," I said pointedly. "Excuse me for saying so, Breck, especially when I'm sitting right here eating your bread and salt. And these sweetbreads are mighty good, too. But my main objection to hiding Emily in Charlotte's apartment is that *somebody* knows about it before we even start. You. And I don't really think you did these murders—but then, again, sometimes I think you did."

"What makes you think that, Miss Julia?" Breck asked mildly, while Charlotte said, "*Julia!*" in tones of outrage.

"Well, the main time I thought so was after Charlotte told me about your hearing your grandfather's murderer in the night," I said frankly. Recklessly, too. I didn't think about its being reckless till afterward, but of course if Breck really were the murderer I was doing quite as dangerous a thing as Emily had done. "I've got a friend who's a police lieutenant, Breck, and he says people who commit crimes have quite an urge to confess them. Usually they give way to it either fully or not at all. But sometimes when they don't have any idea of confession they still feel they have to get *something* off their chests. So they tell some part of the crime, but of course they twist it around so they won't give themselves away. For instance, suppose you really had killed your grandfather. You wouldn't for anything tell your Aunt Charlotte or anybody else that you did, but it might take a load off your mind—part of a load, anyway—if you pretended you'd heard somebody else saying what *you'd* actually said, and if you repeated the words over again: 'Wake up, Grandfather. Wake up, Grandfather. Wake up and take your—'"

The reason I faltered off then without finishing was that I suddenly realized Breck Helm was looking at me hard; and that was when I began to feel a little scared, though of course not really.

CHAPTER SEVENTEEN

I don't know how I happened to think of Mrs. Thompson as a person who might let Emily hide in her house. I reckon it was a case of the short horse soon curried. There were so few people I really knew in Louisville, outside the family we were visiting, that I came very soon to the end of my list of possibilities.

Of course I didn't really know Mrs. Thompson either, in a way. I'd

NO POCKETS IN SHROUDS

called on her, with Charlotte, a day or two after the inquest. Charlotte wanted to show the family's appreciation of the way Mrs. Thompson had spoken up for Mary Preston on the witness stand. Except for that she was a perfect stranger to me. But I'd formed an opinion of her, of course, from the call and from the way she'd testified at the inquest; and three o'clock of the afternoon we'd lunched with Breck found me knocking on Mrs. Thompson's door.

The door had glass side lights curtained with some thin white material that you could see through mistily if you stood close enough. I stood close enough, I'm ashamed to say. And I was duly rewarded by the sight that had so fascinated Mary Preston as a little girl, that she'd kept running away from home to see. Mrs. Thompson came leisurely along the hall till she was abreast of the carved oak hatrack; then without changing her pace, she put her hand into the bosom of her dress, the place where ladies of my dear mother's generation used to carry love letters or a pressed red rose. And then with one swift, clean, efficient movement Mrs. Thompson's hand flashed to her mouth. It was hanging nonchalantly by her side again when she opened the door.

"Well, bless your heart, I'd be glad to take her," Mrs. Thompson said when I'd explained my errand. "I always liked Emily. I think you're right, Miss Tyler. She ought to be away for a while. And I never have rented my third floor back. Those children I had wrote and drew pictures just all over the walls, and I wanted to have it papered again before I rented it out. You get a better class of renter if you have things nice. But the paperhanger just hasn't come, and he *hasn't* come, and so there the place is empty—one big room furnished, and a nice little kitchenette and bath—everything she'd need. And she'd be welcome to it, poor child. But there's just one thing."

I waited politely for her to tell me what it was.

"Well, I wouldn't want to get myself in trouble with the police," Mrs. Thompson said frankly. "Harboring a fugitive from justice—wouldn't I be doing that? I've been a law-abiding woman all my life, Miss Tyler, and a church member, and no matter how much money there is in it for me, well, I just can't take the risk."

Money hadn't been mentioned; I hadn't even thought about that part of it myself. But of course it readily explained Mrs. Thompson's eager open-heartedness about poor little Emily, which subconsciously I'd been finding hard to reconcile with the story she'd told about that other poor little girl, the one whose jewelry and whose baby's cup she'd sold.

I said, smiling at Mrs. Thompson as cordially as I could, "Of course you can't risk getting into trouble. But Emily isn't a fugitive from justice, Mrs. Thompson. She isn't charged with any crime. She's just being questioned by the police, like all the others. And I think she isn't supposed to leave the state, but of course she wouldn't be doing that. It's no more against the law for her to come over to your house and stay than it is for her to go out to Jane Shelby's and eat lunch."

Mrs. Thompson thought that over and appeared to be convinced. She nodded her head several times.

"I think it would be a good idea for Emily to leave Lieutenant Bates a note," I pursued. "And one for the family, of course. Don't you? She could say she was tired and nervous and going for a visit and a little rest. She could say she'd told the police everything she knew about her grandfather's murder, anyway, and now the doctor said she needed to rest."

"He won't like that. Putting it on him," Mrs. Thompson said.

"Dr. Jordan? Well, I don't care if he doesn't," I said comfortably. "He did say she'd be sick if she didn't get some rest. She's taken this harder than any of them, in a way. I'll be very happy to think of her here with you, Mrs. Thompson. I know you'll take good care of her."

"I certainly will," Mrs. Thompson said, beaming. "I'll treat her just the way I'd treat my own child."

If your own child had plenty of money, I added to myself.

"And I'll bring in everything she needs to eat and amuse herself with, so she won't have to go out even in the hall," Mrs. Thompson resumed. "And I won't let a soul so much as suspicion she's in this house, not even— Well, what about that, Miss Tyler? What about her own husband? Seems as if he ought to know."

I said grimly, "Over my dead body. The idea is to get her away from *all* danger, Mrs. Thompson, and that means *everybody*. I don't think John Todd Brown did it—"

"Oh, my, neither do I."

"But just in case he *is* the murderer—well, we can't be too careful, Mrs. Thompson. Husband or no husband, he's under suspicion from the police, just like everybody else."

"Well, I certainly can't get used to *him* being Emily's husband," Mrs. Thompson said, musing. "If it had been Mary Preston, now—he's always been crazy about her. I never did know why those two didn't marry. Not that he was what you'd call the marrying type. But she was the one that broke it off."

I nodded. "Mrs. Buckner was telling me."

"But Emily—!" Mrs. Thompson said. "I declare, Miss Tyler, if I hadn't heard it said right out in court I just wouldn't believe it. It just don't ring true."

Her words came back to me next afternoon.

We'd got Emily over to Mrs. Thompson's, bag and baggage, the night before. Nobody in any of Mr. Oppenheim's books, I flatter myself, could have managed it more neatly and expeditiously than Charlotte and I did. Emily simply packed the clothes and toilet articles she needed in the big cardboard box her new suit had come in, remarked to Martina that she was taking it back to have the hemline changed, and walked out of the house with it, no questions asked. She was sure nobody saw her, she said, when she cached the box behind Mrs. Thompson's japonica bush. Then she went on downtown by streetcar, went to the picture show and ate her dinner, and then as soon as it was dark she walked back home, retrieved her baggage out of the shrubbery, and went in Mrs. Thompson's side door. It was as if, Lieutenant Bates said, the earth had opened up and swallowed her.

He would have liked to say that somebody had murdered Emily too, and that she hadn't voluntarily disappeared by any means. But there was Emily's polite little note to him, saying that she was tired and nervous and the doctor had said she ought to rest, so she was going to pay a visit to an old friend. She wouldn't leave Kentucky, she said, and she'd watch the papers and come back if the police really seemed to need her, even though her rest cure wasn't over. But, meantime, she'd told them everything and helped them every way she could.

It really put Lieutenant Bates on his left ear, as Dick says.

Then there was the note that Emily left on the breakfast table for the family. I was there when they found it the next morning; Charlotte and I, wide-eyed and innocent as Ethel Barrymore would have looked in similar circumstances, had been called in to participate in the search and panic that followed the news Emily hadn't slept in her bed. I watched them all as they read Emily's letter through—Martina and Dr. Greer, Mary Preston, Breck, and John Todd Brown. Naturally I watched Johnny Brown the hardest—or maybe it was Breck, my current suspect. But nobody batted an eye.

I felt mighty sorry for Charlotte, watching them too.

Those two were all the notes I'd advised Emily to send—standing over her and dictating them nearly word for word. Emily might be independent and efficient when she had to be, but she leaned every chance she could. So I was naturally surprised, and exasperated too, to find out she'd written a third note, on her own responsibility, and addressed that one to me.

I'd never before seen the stocky, black-eyed young soldier that brought it. But of course I remembered my conversations with Mary Preston, and then, too, I'd talked with Sergeant Morgan myself, over the telephone the morning after Mr. Helm's second stroke.

"Virgil Morgan," the young man said, standing in the middle of the drawing room floor. "I've heard Emily talk about you a lot, Miss Tyler. She said to come and see you and give you this note."

I took it, after a pause, and asked the young man to sit down. I didn't have any idea why he should be coming to call on me. And why Emily, safely and—if I knew Emily—permanently married now to her cousin Johnny Brown, was still seeing and sending notes by Sergeant Virgil Morgan, I couldn't for the life of me tell.

When I finished reading the note my confusion was complete.

> "Dear Miss Julia," Emily had written. "I know you don't want me to tell anybody where I'm going, and I haven't. But I'd feel a lot better if you would keep in touch with my husband while I'm gone, and let him know how I'm getting along, and maybe bring me some messages from him. So I'm asking him to come to see you as soon as I get away. I've been wanting you to meet him anyway. I think you'll like him. I do."

I read, "Lovingly, Emily," and then folded up the childish little note and looked at the young man who'd brought it, hard. I felt rather sorry for him as I did. He seemed like a nice, upstanding boy, and he was really mixed up in a mess.

"Well, Sergeant?" I said. "So you're Emily's husband. Suppose you begin by telling me about *that*. How many husbands has Emily got?"

Virgil Morgan laughed nervously. "She hasn't got but one, Miss Tyler. Me. It's very simple."

"Not so far," I said dryly.

"Well, it's like this," Virgil Morgan said. "You see, marriage is a contract between persons. The names don't matter. Lots of people, for various reasons, marry under names that aren't their own. It's nothing very serious, unless there's attempt to defraud. One of the commonest reasons—among people who don't know much law"—I can't describe the pity in his voice as he said that—"is thinking they won't have any trouble getting a divorce when the time comes. But they find out different. They're married just as tight and fast as if they'd married under their right names. Because marriage is a contract between *persons*, as I've said. And this marriage was a contract between Emily and me. So we're married. But—"

"But you put her cousin's name on the marriage license, instead of your own," I said. "Why was that, Sergeant Morgan?"

"Well, we wanted to keep it quiet," Sergeant Morgan said. "We went way over to Mount Sterling to get married, but Emily's family was rich, and then all that publicity about old Gus's murder—and it's pretty hard to keep those things quiet anyway. But Emily was determined to try—she was scared to death of her grandfather—and I certainly didn't want *my* folks to hear about it at that point. They read the papers like anybody else, and I didn't want them getting prejudiced against Emily before they ever saw her. So we thought we'd fix it so if it did come out there wouldn't be any serious harm done. Old Mr. Helm didn't have any objection to Emily's marrying. He just wouldn't have let her marry me."

"Why not?"

"Well, to tell you the truth, Miss Tyler, I do not rightly know," Sergeant Morgan told me, slowly and with intense seriousness. "Of course I'm not rich like Emily's folks. But I'm a master sergeant—I make as much as a commissioned officer does, considering I don't have to buy my own uniforms. And when I go back to Marcy, Indiana, after the war, I've got a nice law practice waiting for me. My partner's keeping things together while I'm gone. Oh, I could support Emily, all right. It wasn't that."

I waited.

"And I don't drink, or anything. I don't even smoke. Maybe it was because my folks weren't society people," Sergeant Morgan said, difficultly. "They're not, of course. But there aren't any finer people living, Miss Tyler, than my mother and dad. And my Aunt Etta, that helped bring me up. And anyway I don't understand this society business. It's screwy—how people get that way."

"Well, yes, it is," I admitted.

"You take this girl Breck Helm's going to marry, after the war," Sergeant Morgan said. "Old Mr. Helm was tickled to death with *her*. Of course, she's a nice little thing, but what else has she got on the ball? Never went any farther than high school"—if there's anything more withering than the scorn of the new-educated I don't know what it is—"and her mother rents out rooms, and Janie helps her, and then holds down a part-time job at the riding academy. Schooling horses. Can you feature that? The first time I saw her she'd just been thrown off a horse and had manure all over her pants. Manure!"

"Well, she's a direct descendant of the first governor of Kentucky," I offered mildly.

"Yes, and who was he?" Sergeant Morgan took me up. He answered himself. "His family weren't any more society people than mine are. I looked him up in the *Dictionary of American Biography*. He married a society girl—"

"The way you've done. Maybe you'll be governor of Indiana someday," I said.

Sergeant Morgan didn't smile. "I just don't get it, Miss Tyler. They've got a warped way of looking at things, it seems to me. Pleased as Punch, everybody is, when Mary Preston has dates with this Jim Alexander—"

"I never heard of that one," I said.

"Well, she has dates with a lot of different ones. But Jim Alexander's folks make their money out of whisky, Miss Tyler. He works for their distillery himself. Boy, you ought to hear my mother and Aunt Etta on where the people go that make whisky. The devil's traffic, Aunt Etta calls it. And tainted money."

"Well—" I said.

"Aunt Etta's not going to be just crazy about Emily's folks being in the tobacco business, either," Sergeant Morgan said frankly. "She says she can't think that's much better. And I certainly hope Emily never tells her about poor Mr. Throckmorton, the way she did me."

"Mr. Throckmorton?" The name had a vaguely familiar sound.

"The one the poor girl followed around. I thought Mrs. Buckner'd probably told you, Miss Tyler. Emily said it was one of the great Louisville tales."

"She did." I remembered it finally. Charlotte said her mother had often seen this woman on the street. Dressed all in black; Crazy Ellen, the Louisville people called her. It seems she was a local girl who'd got involved with a man a good many steps above her socially—this Mr. Throckmorton. He done her wrong, as Dick says, and wouldn't marry her, and it more or less affected her brain. Anyway, she got neatly back at him. Heavily veiled, always dressed in her dead-black clothes, she followed him every place he went for the rest of his life. She'd walk about a block behind, perfectly quiet and well behaved, so there wasn't a thing the police could do about it. She didn't annoy Mr. Throckmorton any way. It was just that she was always there. If Mr. Throckmorton went into his club, she'd wait for him outside. When he woke up every morning and looked out his bedroom window, there she was, watching the house. When he started downtown to the office he had only to look behind him, any time, and there she'd be, her usual block away. It was awful for him, Charlotte said. One time he was so desperate he got on a boat and went to Cuba. He thought she surely wouldn't follow him there. But when he looked out of the hotel window there she was in her black dress and veil, sitting on a bench in the little park across the street.

"What happened finally?" I'd asked Charlotte, and Charlotte had said vaguely that she believed he'd shot himself. Maybe not. She couldn't quite remember how her mother had told the story. It was all a long time ago—but, of course, part of the Louisville tradition.

"And Emily was sorry for *him*," Sergeant Morgan said. "Can you feature that, Miss Tyler? 'Poor Mr. Throckmorton!' Never a thought for the poor *girl*—and all because she was what they call 'common' and Mr. Throckmorton was 'nice'. Nice!"

I said defensively, "She was just repeating it the way somebody'd told it to *her*, Sergeant Morgan. There isn't a nicer, sweeter, kinder little girl anywhere than Emily Craig."

"Well, I guess I know that." Sergeant Morgan agreed with me instantly, softening. I was glad to see he didn't even admit the possibility—I couldn't forget about it, myself—that Emily might also have killed her grandfather and Gus. "She's a fine little girl, Miss Tyler. I know people are going to think it's Emily's money I care about. Her family think that now. But I give you my word, Miss Tyler, the minute I saw Emily that night at the USO, before I knew who she was or whether she had a cent, I said to myself, 'Virgil Morgan, there she is.'"

He really meant it. "Well, I hope you'll be very happy," I said.

Sergeant Morgan told me, frowning terrifically between the eyebrows, "We'll be happy if I can get this murder straightened out. I won't let Emily go through life under a cloud, Miss Tyler. So the murderer won't confess. Well, that's all right. I'm working on this case, Miss Tyler. I've got one or two little items that look to me *pret-ty* good—"

"Emily's been letting you in to hunt around," I said. I felt considerably relieved. But then, when my friend didn't go on to say, "Yes, I've been the one walking over your head in Gus's room. I was the one that passed you on the stairs," I didn't feel too good again.

Virgil Morgan went on guardedly, "There's one more thing I'm looking for. I think I'll find it in Mr. Helm's old room. I've *got* to find it and hang it on the murderer before—"

"Before what?"

"The murderer hangs it on me," Virgil Morgan said.

CHAPTER EIGHTEEN

Emily Craig's disappearance caused such a furor that Charlotte and I were scared. Big screaming headlines splashed across the front pages of the *Times* and the *Courier-Journal*, and Lieutenant Bates stalking around muttering like a character in Shakespeare, and all of us questioned and cross-questioned from morning till night. There hadn't been so much fuss in Louisville, Charlotte said, since the big kidnapping a few years ago.

Charlotte stood perfectly firm, I'm glad to say. I'd been a little nervous about her. But apparently Lieutenant Bates brought out the worst in her just as he did in me, and she had no idea of giving him any satisfaction. She kept saying, "I don't know anything about it," over and over again, without batting an eyelash.

We had planned to slip over and see Emily about once a day, one or the other of us, but when there was such excitement and publicity we were afraid to take the risk. It was three evenings later that Charlotte, taking the bull boldly by the horns, told Mary Preston in Lieutenant Bates's hearing that we were going over to Mrs. Thompson's to play bridge.

Johnny Brown said amusedly, "You and Mrs. Thompson are certainly getting thick, Cousin Charlotte, after all these years. How'd you happen to change your mind about her?"

We could have killed him, of course. Except for his saying that, Lieutenant Bates would have thought Charlotte and Mrs. Thompson had played bridge together for years.

"Well, really, Johnny, I never formed an opinion of Mrs. Thompson before," Charlotte told him, with dignity. "I didn't know her. That's one disadvantage about a city—you so seldom get to know the neighbors well. I'm sure we overlook a great many nice people that way. It's just when something happens that you really get acquainted. I thought it was my duty to call on Mrs. Thompson and express my appreciation, after she spoke so nicely about Mary Preston at the inquest. This family needs all the loyal friends it can get, it seems to me."

"It sure does," Lieutenant Bates said, quite gratuitously. Nobody was talking to him.

Bridge had just been Charlotte's excuse, but as things turned out we really did play bridge, Emily and Mrs. Thompson and Charlotte and I, and had three very nice rubbers. Emily loved to play, and had missed it, she said. She'd read and done jigsaw puzzles until she never wanted to see a puzzle or a book again.

"What you really need is a feather and a drop of molasses," I told her absent-mindedly, adding up the score.

Emily said suddenly, looking over my shoulder, "Miss Julia, isn't that funny! I scored the same for those last three games—just exactly the same—as I did in three straight games last Christmas Eve, when we were playing in Grandfather's room."

"You don't mean to say you remember your scores from way last Christmas Eve!" I said.

Charlotte told me, nodding her head complacently, "Yes, Emily's got a wonderful memory for cards, Julia. She remembers just how they fell and everything. I expect she remembers every single card she played that time."

Emily disclaimed that, flushing and actually embarrassed. "Oh, no, indeed, Aunt Charlotte! It's just sometimes I remember pretty well. And I wouldn't have remembered those scores at all—but I just happened to keep that Christmas Eve tally because it was such a pretty one. Two little kittens out in the snow. I've been using it for a bookmark ever since; it was in a book I brought over here to read. See?"

She took it out of *The King's General* and passed it around. Charlotte and Mrs. Thompson admired it fulsomely, but personally I never care much for coy pictures of animals dressed up in human beings' mufflers and mittens, however much they may need them while out making snowballs.

But I was suddenly interested in something else I saw. Down in one corner on the other side, quite away from the rows of penciled figures that made up the bridge score, there were five figures more, written down so lightly that I could hardly see. 14-10-23-3-1. I wouldn't have thought anything of them if Emily hadn't been talking on. Babbling, a person who didn't like her would have said.

"I got those tallies to give away for Christmas, but then Grandfather got sick and liked for us to play a lot in his room, so he wouldn't be alone, and W. K. Stewart was sold out and I couldn't get any others," Emily was saying. "Usually we had to cut in, because there were six of us even when Grandfather just watched. But that night there were only four of us playing, except for just a little while. Grandfather was worrying about the servants' Christmas presents, and Mary Preston and Martina were helping him fix the little envelopes—he always gave them money—and get the money out of the safe after Gus came and opened it."

It was just as she said "out of the safe" that I noticed those five little figures penciled so lightly down in the corner of the tally card: 14-10-23-3-1. They might not mean a thing. I told myself sternly that they probably didn't. I told myself that only the very worst kind of a fool would jump to conclusions.

But my heart was racing.

Those figures looked mightily like the combination of a safe. The safe that Gus had been called to open, under old Mr. Helm's eye—though the room was full of his grandchildren. Evidently Mr. Helm hadn't wanted to give any one of them the combination. But some one of them had wanted to know it anyway; and when Gus came, and swung aside the Jouett portrait that Lieutenant Bates called the old dame in the white cap, and twisted the dial this way and that, that one person had watched him and written the numbers down, quietly and unobtrusively, on the corner of the tally card.

I didn't actually know any of it, of course, but I would have bet my last cent.

And then he—or she—had come back some time later and opened the safe and taken out a ring. The diamond engagement ring that Mary Preston had pawned and Johnny had redeemed and Lieutenant Bates had been so sure Charlotte or I knew about.

". . . arrest that Helm girl for murder so fast it would make your head swim," I could hear Lieutenant Bates saying grimly. "All we need is the ring." And he hadn't explained the connection, and I didn't necessarily accept its existence myself. But assuming that he was right, that taking this ring out of old Mr. Helm's bedroom safe was related to old Mr. Helm's murder, I had only to find out who jotted down those figures—

"Whose writing is this on the tally, Emily?" I asked, too abruptly. I saw Charlotte looking at me. I went on fast, "They're such nice neat little figures. Most tallies look like hen tracks."

"Why, I don't know, Miss Julia," Emily said. "I don't remember who was keeping score."

"But you know the writing," I persisted. Not only Charlotte but Mrs. Thompson was looking at me queerly now, but I couldn't help it.

Emily said, with the flawless courtesy that doesn't even raise its eyebrows in the face of importunate questioning, "No, I'm sorry, Miss Julia. Of course I'd know it if it were *writing*—not just figures off by themselves. But I think figures are hard to tell apart."

They are, of course. But they can be checked.

"Well, it's fortunate that they're on the other side from the kittens, isn't it?" I said desperately. "Such an adorable picture. Some child would love it. I wonder if you could use something else for a bookmark, Emily, and let me borrow this to show to a little sick girl I know? She'd think it was wonderful—the two little kittens out making snowballs, in their little red mufflers and stocking caps—"

I needn't talk about Emily's babbling. I was the one that was doing it this time, like an idiot, and Emily was the one acting like a lady of poise, putting me at my ease and then tactfully changing the subject.

"Why, of course, Miss Julia. Please give it to her to keep. I've had it all winter—and anyway Mrs. Thompson has plenty of kittens that I can look at. Did you notice this one with the cute little cactus for a tail?"

Charlotte, winning my undying gratitude, burst into praise of this spotted china monstrosity, and went on to admire Mrs. Thompson's extensive collection of cacti, mother-in-law's tongue, and other unpleasant little plants, all potted in china animals from the ten-cent store. I hastily put the kitten tally in my bag, under cover of Charlotte's social graces. I avoided her eyes—Charlotte who was quite aware I didn't know a single little girl, sick or well, in the city of Louisville.

But I still thought I'd made a fool of myself in a good cause.

"Well, there's good news in the evening paper, isn't there?" Mrs. Thompson said then, relieving Charlotte. "Not that I usually attend the Derby myself. But it don't seem like Louisville not to have the Derby run every year."

Charlotte agreed. "It's bad enough not to have it in May. If the ban had just gone off a little sooner— But I think they've done mighty well, and worked mighty fast and hard, to have it set now for so early in June."

"Do you expect to attend, Mrs. Buckner?"

"Oh, my, no. No, of course not," Charlotte answered, to my surprise. Charlotte had been carrying on about there being no Derby as if Adolf Hitler had fixed it to insult her personally, and here she was telling Mrs. Thompson that she never went, she hadn't gone to a Derby in years. "I'd rather keep my memories of it from my younger days, Mrs. Thompson. It was all so different then. Of course it's still enjoyable for the young people, and visitors like Julia—Julia, you certainly will have to go. The Derby's an experience you really shouldn't miss, if you've never seen one. But in my time—"

"Oh, Aunt Charlotte, I don't see how it could ever have been lovelier than it is now," Emily said softly, her eyes shining—and wistful, I'm afraid. Sergeant Morgan probably didn't approve of going to horse races. "The way the horses come stepping out— They're so beautiful, Miss Julia. Like different colored satin. And then they line up at the post, and there's always one that rears and won't stand still. And then it's time for them to start, and the band plays My Old Kentucky Home—and usually the sun *is* shining bright—and everybody gets up, and it's so beautiful you want to cry."

"I'll definitely be there, my dear," I said.

Mrs. Thompson contributed, "It's a long race, Miss Tyler—what they *call* a long race. A mile and a quarter. But it's over in just a minute. Before you know it they're putting that big wreath of roses around the winner's neck. It's a great big thing; it hangs way down. And, my, he looks so proud! He lifts his feet up high—"

"Oh, yes. That part. That part doesn't change," Charlotte said. "But it's all so commercialized now, Julia. And a Kentucky horse hardly ever wins. Oh, maybe it was foaled in Kentucky—there's nothing like our limestone anywhere else. But it always belongs to some New York banker or some woman that makes cold cream or candy bars. And the boxes and the clubhouse are simply full of people you *do not* know. I don't mean the strangers. It's always nice to have visitors come to town. But people that live right here in Louisville—women smoking cigarettes with their juleps, and big loud men that call the waiters by their first names."

I didn't know what else they'd call them by, but I let that pass.

"Well, wait until Breck has his stock farm going, Aunt Charlotte," Emily said. "You'll see another Kentucky horse win the Derby yet."

"I understand we're going to see a wedding in that quarter soon, too," Mrs. Thompson said coyly. "Little Jane Shelby—I remember so well when she used to come over and play with Mary Preston. They spent the whole afternoon with me once. Good as gold; they both just sat and watched me all the time."

I met Charlotte's eyes for the first time since my fumbling efforts to get the kitten tally, and we both of us nearly choked.

I said hastily, "I hope Breck and Janie will have a big wedding, and remember to ask me. I suppose you'll be matron of honor, Emily? That would make up a little for your not having a big church wedding of your own."

We could mention that freely now, for Emily had broken down and told Mrs. Thompson all about Mrs. John Todd Brown's being Mrs. Virgil Morgan, really, and Mrs. Thompson thought the whole thing was just too romantic and sweet. I sort of thought so myself, by this time. I liked Sergeant Morgan. His views weren't altogether mine, but I like people who have the courage of their convictions.

Charlotte, though, still folded her lips and looked forbidding when the sergeant's name was mentioned. She folded them now, for Emily simply loved to talk about him—poor child, you couldn't blame her, after keeping her marriage secret all that time—and my opening was all the excuse she asked. She favored us with Virgil's views on big weddings now—theatrical, extravagant, practically sacrilegious—and threw in Virgil's opinion that the Episcopal Church might as well be Roman Catholic for all the difference he could see. So they wouldn't have had a big wedding even in the natural course of events. Virgil's father would probably have married them, he being a minister of the Primitive Baptist Church.

Emily had quite a time explaining the Primitive Baptists to Charlotte, who apparently had thought they were all primitive.

"And Virgil says I should tithe my check. My first allotment check came the day before I left home," Emily said, getting her bag and pulling it out to show us proudly. "I hadn't seen my new name written out before—not by anybody else, I mean. Doesn't it look wonderful?"

Mrs. Thompson and I agreed that it looked wonderful. The check was made out to Mrs. Emily C. Morgan, and it was for a hundred and thirty-five dollars, and somewhere else it said "George V. Morgan, M-Sgt." with a great long serial number. Charlotte's eyes fastened on that.

"Is George his real name?"

"Well, it's his first name, Aunt Charlotte," Emily said. "He's never used it; he's been called Virgil all his life. But in the Army, you know, they make you use the first name."

How well did I know it, I may say without going into past history.

"Well, George is always a nice name," Charlotte said kindly. "I expect you'll both be so used to it by the time the war's over you'll want to go on using that. George V. Morgan. Mrs. George V. Morgan. It sounds very nice, my dear."

"I like Virgil. Everybody is named George," Emily said stubbornly.

"Oh, but on the other hand—" Charlotte began, and did stop before she said, "*Nobody* is named Virgil." Which is true, of course. Much as I admire the great Publius Virgilius Maro, having taught his works for forty years, I must admit it is not his readers who name their children after him. But I liked this particular namesake, and I didn't like the way Charlotte Buckner was already trying to push him around, as Dick says.

Obviously there was going to be grim war between Charlotte and the Primitive Baptists, but I thought it could very well be postponed awhile.

I got up to go.

I really was tired, as I told Emily and Mrs. Thompson. I was tired the way you are when you've gone through a spasm of intellectual effort and then relaxed. Not that my conversational by-product about the kitten tally had sounded intellectual, but actually I'd put everything I had into finding out about those figures and getting them in my possession, and ever since then I'd felt exhausted and let-down and very far from happy.

I'd got more deeply involved in this murder case than I'd ever meant to be. I'd got fond of the people, too, who had been only names in a newspaper when I first came to Louisville. Emily and Johnny and Breck and Mary Preston—I was devoted to them all. I liked Dr. Greer, too, as far as I'd been able to get acquainted with him. And of course

Martina, though her type always rubs me the wrong way and—perhaps through my own fault—I didn't know her very well either, had always been extra nice to me and I liked her too.

It made me feel pretty miserable to think that the little square of cardboard in my pocketbook, with the simpering mittened kittens on one side and the rows of figures and the faint little extra figures on the other, might be the means of sending one of them to the electric chair.

When Charlotte and I got home that night and Lieutenant Bates was waiting for us in the hall, I felt it was the last straw. I just couldn't stand it. But fortunately he wasn't, either, in an interviewing mood. He was very brief and businesslike this time. He said in place of "Good evening" that he wanted to speak to both Charlotte and me alone, and that he'd take me first.

For a minute after Charlotte had gone into the dining room and closed the door, Lieutenant Bates sternly said nothing at all. He held up something instead. It was a little velvet box, old, worn red velvet, open to show a yellowed white-satin lining inside. The firm's name of Kendrick, the famous old Louisville jeweler that Charlotte's "nice people" still go to, was on the lining in gold. Against that background, a beautiful Tiffany-set big diamond gleamed, as they say in some of the books I read, like a baleful eye.

"No, I don't recognize it. I never saw it before," I said with perfect truth. "But it's old Mrs. Helm's engagement ring, isn't it, that Mr. Helm willed to Emily Craig?"

Lieutenant Bates nodded, watching me. "It came by special delivery mail after you left, Miss Tyler. Wiped clean. Wrapped up in some secondhand paper and string that came from Baynham's Shoe Store. The address was cut out of the Louisville *Times* article last night—Lt. Arthur Bates, Louisville police—and glued to the outside. No way to trace it that I can see."

"It's beautiful," I said. "Could I see it up close?"

I don't usually care much about diamonds, but this one—quite aside from whatever its role in the murders of Gus and Mr. Helm—was the biggest and bluest I'd ever seen.

Lieutenant Bates handed it over.

I don't know what kind of a nose he had that he hadn't noticed the smell. I noticed it the minute I got the little box in my hands. But maybe he had and it just didn't mean anything to him. It didn't at first to me. But then my mind went back to the day we'd spent at Holliday Hall, Breck Helm and Janie and I, and Janie down on the floor scrubbing the parlor furniture with a toothbrush and saying, "I'll let Breck put on the oil. The smell of it always makes me sick."

It made me feel a little sick, too, to realize that the person who'd handled that red velvet ring box had been using linseed oil.

"All we need is the ring," Lieutenant Bates had said.

Here it was. Here was the tally in my handbag, with—I hadn't enough doubt to mention—the combination to the safe. We were close to the end of the trail.

CHAPTER NINETEEN

What I should have done—and I knew it perfectly well—was turn the tally card with the figures over to Lieutenant Bates. If I hadn't disliked him so I would have done just that. My impulses are naturally on the side of law and order. But I couldn't forget the rude, ugly way he'd talked to poor little Emily Craig. And he was so stupid, too. How did I know he wouldn't laugh at my poor little piece of evidence, and not bother to test it out?

Checking the tally card numbers myself, though, presented difficulties. The door to old Mr. Helm's room was still locked, and Lieutenant Bates had the key.

I have plenty of interest in detecting crime, but none of the skills that would help me do it. I couldn't have picked a lock to save my life. As for taking a wax impression of the keyhole, the way they do in books when they want an extra key made, I hadn't the slightest notion how to go about that either.

There was only one thing for it that I could see.

"Sergeant Morgan," I said next day—he'd come to see me again about Emily—"you told me you'd been investigating in old Mr. Helm's room, didn't you, as well as Gus's? Well, how did you get in? Because the police have had it locked up ever since he—died."

Sergeant Morgan said, looking at me a little queerly, "I had a key made, Miss Tyler. You take a wax impression—" He laughed nervously. "It sounds bad, doesn't it? But I just had to get in."

"I know. I have to too. I wonder, Sergeant," I said hurriedly, not meeting his eyes, "if I could borrow your key? Just for ten minutes or so? Lieutenant Bates isn't here right now—"

Sergeant Morgan said, slowly, "I'm sorry, Miss Tyler. I don't have that key with me. Maybe another time—"

"It's important."

"It's dangerous, too, Miss Tyler," Sergeant Morgan said. "Why don't you let me do it for you—whatever it is? I've got in that room before; I'm not afraid to go again. But, for you, it's running a risk."

"Oh, I'd lock the door on the inside," I said.

"Even so." Sergeant Morgan's voice was grave. "It isn't that I'm trying to pump you, Miss Tyler, or anything. Though naturally I'd like to know." His Primitive-Baptist mouth relaxed briefly in a smile. "I'd just like to do your—errand—for you, in case there should be some trouble. You've been nice to Emily—she thinks a lot of you."

I nearly weakened. After all, if he didn't mind doing it—and I certainly didn't want to get myself (Dick's words came back to me, bothering my conscience) hurt, or even scared—

But I was afraid to trust him. Sergeant Morgan, I mean. It wasn't as if this were a book. In a book the author never lets the murderer turn out to be a person who hasn't appeared, and qualified as a minor suspect at least, quite early in the action. It isn't considered fair to the reader. But since it wasn't a book, I couldn't help remembering that all I knew about this Sergeant Morgan was what he and Emily had told me; that she'd been letting him into the house at night—the nights of the murders, for all I knew; that, married to Emily, he had the same money motive the rest of them had; and that at least one person—the murderer, *he* said—considered him a possibility to pin the murders on.

I said firmly, "I'd still rather do it myself, sergeant. I appreciate your offering, but—you know how it is. I'm in this, and I'd like to see it through."

"Well. All right," Sergeant Morgan said. He seemed to make up his mind. "I'll get you the key, Miss Tyler. When were you thinking about going in?"

"As soon as I can." I thought fast. "Could you get it to me this afternoon, sergeant? In an envelope—special delivery? Then right after dinner I could excuse myself and go upstairs—"

"You'll have it in time," Sergeant Morgan promised, getting up to go. "And maybe it won't be so risky for you after all, Miss Tyler. Good luck."

We shook hands solemnly. I'm afraid he found mine cold.

The key was cold against my skin, hidden under my dress like Mrs. Thompson's teeth, when Charlotte and I went down to dinner. At least I hoped it was hidden, but it was so big—to fit that inch-and-a-half keyhole—that I couldn't help feeling somebody could see the outline through my clothes. But nobody did, of course, and nobody seemed to think it was funny when after dinner I said I had a letter to write and went upstairs.

Mr. Helm's room was dark, pitch dark. The shades had been pulled down and the heavy draperies drawn across them, right after Mr.

Helm had died. Judging from the musty smell in the room, they hadn't been opened since.

I didn't want to turn on the chandelier, even so. Fortunately I had a good flashlight, which I never travel without. I circled the room with it—empty fireplace; the black walnut wardrobe Emily had tried so hard to make Mr. Helm recognize; desk; bookcase; big stripped walnut bed. Finally the Jouett portrait of Eliza Allen Breckinridge, the one Lieutenant Bates called the old dame in the white cap. I put my hand on the gilded frame and swung it out.

Fourteen. The first of the numbers written lightly on my tally card. I laid it down on the table in front of me. Ten, then. Back around to twenty-three. The other way, to three. And then finally to one, the last number on the card.

The safe door came open in my hand.

My sigh was so loud I scared myself. It was too loud. I realized then I couldn't have made it alone. I whirled.

Behind me, leaning over the back of a carved walnut love seat, was a stocky, black-eyed, uniformed young man.

"Too bad, Miss Tyler," Virgil Morgan said. "Don't you want to break down and tell me what you expected to find?"

I couldn't possibly have said a word.

"I could have told you that safe was empty. Emily was here when they opened it, after her grandfather died," Sergeant Morgan went on. "They had a safe expert out, because nobody else—after Gus was killed too—was supposed to know the combination." He was looking at me pretty hard. "And the police and the executors, between them, took everything away. Left the safe as bare as you found it just now."

I still couldn't say a word. I was shaking from head to foot.

"How did I get in here?" Sergeant Morgan went on with a little smile. "There's nothing to be scared about, Miss Tyler. I'm sorry I startled you, but I was afraid to have you come in here by yourself. So I had another key made this afternoon—they'll make 'em while you wait—and beat you in."

I had found my voice. I said, trying not to sound sarcastic, "To take care of me, you say?"

"To take care of you," Sergeant Morgan answered, nodding. "You see, every time I've been in this room, Miss Tyler—and I've tried to be extra quiet and careful, you can imagine, and the walls and doors are thick—but every time I've been here somebody's heard me. The person I believe is the murderer, but that I can't prove it on. Yet."

"How do you know he's heard you?" I added, the way Charlotte had that day in the Plantation Room, "—or she?"

Virgil Morgan said, with a little smile, "Let's just say 'he', Miss Tyler. Because he's opened the door and come in, is how I know. Opened it with another key."

"Still another key?" To save my life—and that was exactly what it might amount to, I realized—I couldn't keep the sarcasm out of my voice this time.

Virgil Morgan nodded. "With another key. That part's easy enough, Miss Tyler. It's how he heard me that bothers me. I was always so careful—and there aren't any hot air registers around, or anything like that—"

But there was. I remembered it in a flash. For the first time I felt a little confidence in Sergeant Morgan's bona fides, his not too plausible story of why he'd tracked me down. Maybe he wasn't the murderer after all. I still wanted to get out of that locked room, but— "There's the communication system, Sergeant," I said. "See that little speaking thing—like a telephone mouthpiece—on the wall right by the bed?"

I was edging toward the hall door while he looked. "Oh, that old thing," Sergeant Morgan said. "It doesn't work, Miss Tyler. I've seen the one in Emily's room. She says it hasn't worked for years. They just never bothered to take it out, because it would spoil the plaster."

"It does work too! Maybe not in Emily's room. It's out of fix in my room too. But in here, and in at least one other room that I know of— probably all the rest— Don't you remember Mary Preston said the last thing she did, the night her grandfather was killed, was adjust his speaking-tube so Breck could hear him in his room?"

Sergeant Morgan's black eyes were bright and glittering as coal. "I hadn't heard about that. Breck, huh? Well—"

"But probably he wasn't the only one, sergeant," I went on, trying to be fair. "Because otherwise she wouldn't have had to make any adjustment—if it worked in Breck's room only, I mean. They'd simply leave it set. You look at that little row of buttons right under the mouthpiece. They're all marked—"

I was across the room like a flash while Sergeant Morgan did. Maybe he wasn't the murderer after all, but just to be on the safe side I was getting out of there. Unfortunately, having read in too many murder books how keys left in locks could be turned from the outside, I'd taken mine out of the hole when I locked myself in. I had to fumble for it now. My hands were like ice. Before I could tell one end of it from the other Sergeant Morgan was turning round.

"Stay right where you are, Miss Tyler. Keep behind that door." Virgil Morgan's voice was like steel. The edge of the beam from my flashlight, which I'd left on the table under the portrait safe, caught the glint of steel in his hand. "I think," Virgil Morgan said, "our friend the murderer is coming in."

I heard it myself then.

Somebody was standing outside the door, fumbling to fit another key into the hole.

The person who stood then in the doorway was the last one in the world I expected to see. My knees felt as if they wouldn't hold me up much longer. And my heart was beating an eccentric rhythm, way up, apparently, in my throat.

"Well, Miss Julia, this *is* a surprise!" the murderer said. It was the murderer, all right. Somehow, all of a sudden, I knew. "I'm getting used to meeting the sergeant here—I see he's brought a pistol along this time. But *you*—well, I'm surprised."

"You're surprised, all right," Virgil Morgan said grimly, behind his gun. "You're caught this time, my friend. And this time you're not getting off scot-free."

The murderer laughed gently. "Caught because I investigate a noise in an unused room and find an outsider with a gun? I'm not speaking of Miss Julia here—I suppose it isn't really actionable for a guest in our house to look around a bit. Perhaps a little unconventional—"

I said, flushing in spite of myself, "I'll be glad to tell you what I've been looking for, too. I was looking to see if the numbers on the tally you used last Christmas Eve were the combination of this safe—that you wrote down while your grandfather was telling Gus—"

The murderer said in a whisper, after a long pause, "The tally? What tally?"

"The tally that's lying right over on that table right now," I said firmly. There was no longer the slightest doubt in my mind. "Certainly, look at it if you want to. Just don't bother to touch it, please. There are plenty of your fingerprints on it now. And of course it's in your handwriting, too."

I didn't actually know that last, of course.

Sergeant Morgan said grimly, behind his gun, "It's what they call evidence, in case you wouldn't know."

"The kind of thing *you've* been hunting for, Sergeant." The murderer nodded. "But not much by itself—and you've not been too successful adding to it, would you say? I've been able to keep a pretty good check on you, haven't I? Through the speaking-tube."

"Pretty good," Sergeant Morgan said. "But not quite good enough, my friend. What would you say if I told you I did have something to add?"

The murderer said kindly, "I'd be interested, of course. By all means,

Sergeant. Tell me what it is."

"Suppose I show you instead," Sergeant Morgan said. Without lowering the pistol in his right hand, he put his left hand into a side pocket and pulled out two letters. I couldn't, of course, read them from where I stood, even after he spread them out. But I could see that one was long and closely written, covering both sides of a big sheet of paper, and that the other looked like a letter somebody had started to write and then discarded, after he'd made a big blot on the page. They didn't mean anything to me, but to the murderer they did.

There was the longest silence I ever want to live through again.

Sergeant Morgan broke it. He said, almost gently, "And now, don't you have something to tell *me?*"

"I've got a lot to tell you, Sergeant. Or somebody," the murderer agreed. "And I reckon you and Miss Julia deserve it. After all, you beat me to finding that stuff. I've turned this house upside down— Well! Shall we all sit down? Miss Julia, wouldn't you rather have this chair?" Incredibly, as if it had been a party, we all sat down.

The murderer began whimsically, "No interruptions, please. I'll try to do this right. This is my confession that I murdered Gus Johnson on March 30 and Breckinridge Helm senior on May 4, 1945 . . ."

The voice went on. The pistol in Sergeant Morgan's hand did not move.

CHAPTER TWENTY

The murderer said, "Of course, the money meant a lot to us. We all had pretty definite ideas about the kind of life we wanted to have. I know I did—and I felt I was entitled to it. After all, I'd been brought up to expect my share. I didn't see why I should stand by and see myself virtually cut out of Grandfather's will.

"He shouldn't have tried to change it, after he'd told us all our lives the money was coming to us. He brought his murder on himself. And so did Gus—he brought *his* murder on himself, too. He shouldn't have interfered.

"I'd always had a pretty healthy respect for Gus; he was always getting me in trouble with Grandfather, ever since he worked here— telling him things. He thought it was his duty to report anything we did. So generally I kept out of his way. But that last time, the time he caught me going through this safe, I laughed in his face. I thought I could afford to. It was just a few days after Grandfather had the first stroke. He'd rallied from it, but he'd had a heart attack just that morning, and the doctor and the nurse and everybody expected him to die. I knew Gus wouldn't dare tell Grandfather anything upsetting until he got a good deal better—and I was pretty sure he wasn't going to.

"But he did get better. He was so much better within the next few days that I thought I'd better have it out with Gus.

"I had no intention of killing him. Believe that, won't you? I went to see him in his room—he was in bed with a cold—and we talked. I pointed out in my best manner"—again, that best manner was very much to the fore—"that an old man in Grandfather's condition, subject to heart attacks and now to paralytic strokes too, ought not to be bothered with disagreeable things. No matter how true they were. He just couldn't stand any shocks. 'How would you feel,' I, said, 'if you were so busy getting some little thing off your conscience that you made him have another stroke?'

"Gus agreed with me. He said it not only could happen, it *had* happened. Grandfather'd had his first stroke, Gus said, right in the middle of writing a letter about my misdeeds. He was so mad he worked himself up, Gus said, and brought it on.

"So he and I made a bargain. He wouldn't tell Grandfather about the bedroom safe—not even if he got well. And I," the murderer said, with a charming smile, "I, for my part, promised I'd turn over a new leaf and never let my foot—or my hand—slip again."

It wasn't the first time, I gathered, that promise had been made.

"I went down to the kitchen to make Gus a hot toddy before he went to sleep. He really was sick, you know." The murderer laughed. "Poor old man, he always said when he was well that whisky was an abomination in the sight of the Lord, but he called it medicine when he was sick. We used to tease him about that, but he never could see the joke.

"While I was down in the kitchen getting the toddy things, I was thinking, of course, about the bargain we'd made. I had a pretty good idea I might not keep my part of it any too well, and of course Gus wasn't perfect either—for all that holier-than-thou stuff. Someday— especially if he knew I hadn't done my part—there was a good chance he'd spill the beans.

"That was when I happened to see the jar of ant poison on the kitchen shelf.

"I didn't put any in his toddy, but he always took a glass of water after his medicine—to wash the taste out of his mouth, I always thought, so he wouldn't get to liking it. I'd held the water glass—like a fool—for Gus to drink out of, so of course I had to wipe it off. I should have planted his fingerprints on it after that, but I had to get out. Fast. It was pretty bad." The murderer wasn't laughing now. You could see that it had been—pretty bad. It was a minute or two before the tale went on. "Poor old Gus, he'd irritated all of us ever since he'd been with the family, moralizing and criticizing and carrying tales to Grandfather; but he was a faithful, well-meaning old soul. Honestly, I wouldn't have touched him—but I couldn't see any other way. I felt awful."

There was another pause.

"I felt bad about poor little Emily, too, when the police decided it was murder and started suspecting her. Of course they hadn't the evidence for anything to come of it, but it was pretty unpleasant for her meantime. I tried to shield her," the murderer said, over Emily's husband's snort, "and do everything I could for her, to make up.

"Well, when I washed the things I'd used for the hot toddy, down in the kitchen, I thought I was washing my hands of murder too. They say you don't mind doing them, after the first one. But that isn't true. I never expected to kill again as long as I lived.

"But Grandfather kept getting better and better, and one day he arranged to get us all out of the house and Mr. Fownes came and they drafted a new will.

"I went to my grandfather's room that night, and if the walls hadn't been so thick we'd have waked everybody in the house. I yelled at him and he yelled at me. I was nearly out of my mind. You see, I thought that will was already signed. Until you took that telephone message, Miss Julia, the next day— I didn't know till then Mr. Fownes had only made a draft. I thought everything was all over—all my plans. I thought I hadn't anything to lose if I told my grandfather a few things, and I did. And he told me a few—and then I really did lose my head. I asked him if he knew what happened to people that got in my way. He'd done it once, I said, but that wouldn't happen again. I asked him if he thought Gus Johnson had really died a natural death.

"I never saw anybody have a stroke before. He opened his mouth to say something, and then one side of it twitched up into a grin—"

We waited in silence again.

"I went back to my room then, and after a while one my cousins happened to go into Grandfather's room and gave the alarm.

"I thought I was set then, that he couldn't possibly get over the second stroke. But he did, with the exception of not remembering where he was. He remembered what I'd said to him that night, all right. I could see it in his eyes every time he looked at me.

"Still, I didn't want to kill my grandfather. I hated him, of course— more than the others did. I had more reason. But I'd had enough of killing. I'm not a killer, Miss Julia. I was delighted when we hit on what seemed like a good way out. If we could get my grandfather declared incompetent, our money would be safe from his signing a new will, and my secret about Gus would be safe too. Grandfather might talk, but nobody would pay any attention to him after the law said *non compos mentis*.

"It was a good idea—we appreciated it, Sergeant!—but it fell through. And then there was only one thing left to do.

"There wasn't any more sodium fluoride used in the kitchen, on account of the new puppy. That little fool Thelma had hidden some of it away, but I didn't know that. Anyway, there was enough of the pure stuff—jar after jar, under one of the beds upstairs—to poison half of Louisville. And a little goes a long way—as I knew from using it before. But I had to grab a whole jar, because I thought I heard somebody coming. Later, of course, I had to throw it and most of the fluoride in it away. Dropped it into a ditch in Bourbon County, if you're interested in knowing where. I put the little fluoride I did keep in a bath salts jar in your bathroom, Miss Julia. Of course, that was before you moved across the street. You never knew."

No, I never knew. Charlotte and I just thought somebody had left the top off the Harriet Hubbard Ayer Pink Clover, so the crystals had lost all their strength.

"Well, then I had to steal some back from *you*. And one night that seemed like a good time to do it I emptied it into a medicine glass. I took it into Grandfather's room in the dark. He was sound asleep, sleeping under sedative. I had a hard time getting him awake. I had to say over and over again, 'Wake up, Grandfather. Wake up, Grandfather. Wake up and take your medicine.' But finally he waked up —just half awake—and did."

There was no pause afterward this time, as there had been after the account of Gus's death. The murderer said in parentheses, seeing something, evidently, in my face, "I hated *him*, you know," and went on.

"Most of my dear family, of course, have suspected me right along—the ones that knew that. I'm not a killer or anything like it. I've put up with a lot from Grandfather. We all have, all our lives, on account of the money. But any time in the last three years—

"Well, it was a nice idea, all of us sticking together and not giving evidence, so nobody could be arrested now or later. But of course it wouldn't have worked. It was the same thing I came up against when I got to thinking about Gus, just before my eye lighted on that ant poison. Gus honestly intended not to tell anything; but he was human, just as my family were. Someday, sooner or later, people talk."

I nodded agreement. They mostly do.

"Of course, I couldn't wipe out my family the way I disposed of Gus," the murderer went on, reasonably. "In the first place, I didn't want them to die. I'm very fond of them all! And in the second place, if all the other suspects had got killed off and only I was left, even Lieutenant Bates could have figured it out.

"So it seemed better to let the case be solved. And right there, Sergeant, was where I made my mistake." I must have looked as puzzled as I felt, because the murderer, after bowing elaborately to Virgil Morgan, turned to me. "I picked him for the scapegoat, Miss Julia. I hated to do it, of course—Emily's husband. But he was the person I was most afraid of—talking, I mean. Not that he actually knew anything, or could get much out of Emily. But right from the first he was opposed to the idea of letting the murders stay unsolved. He said just as you did that if none of us was convicted we'd all be convicted, and we'd suffer for it the rest of our lives. He said right out he didn't want that for Emily. It was all right for him to feel that way, of course. Naturally I could see his point. But as time went on I could see he wasn't going to leave it there.

"I had to try to pin it on him. There wasn't anybody else. There weren't any servants in the house the night of the first murder, and they had an alibi the second time. And I locked the door so you two would be out of it. Of course, the sergeant wasn't here himself, either night. But he couldn't deny that Emily had let him in lots of *other* nights—too many people had seen him. Half the family, and some of the servants."

"Not Gus," Sergeant Morgan said.

The murderer agreed. "No, not Gus. It wasn't till after Gus was killed that you and Emily married, and she began letting you in. But Gus had bawled you out more than once before that, for getting Emily home too late—or what Gus thought was too late. He didn't approve of late hours."

"He didn't approve of *me*," Virgil Morgan said wryly.

"No, he didn't. The last time he threatened him with Grandfather, Miss Julia—said he'd have Grandfather forbid Emily's having dates with him anymore. I've got the letter the sergeant wrote Emily the morning after that—worrying about the possibility the old man really would tell Grandfather about 'last night.' I thought if I produced that letter to the police—it wasn't too conclusive, but Bates really needed to save his face—and in the meantime planted a few selected items on him, such as that diamond ring—"

"But you couldn't find the diamond ring," I said.

"No, I couldn't. I certainly did try—almost as hard as I tried to find that other stuff." The murderer's gesture took in Sergeant Morgan's spread-out letters and my tally card. "But the worst mistake I made was underestimating my man, Miss Julia. He was just too smart for me."

I thought the pistol in Sergeant Morgan's hand wavered a little, for the first time, at that ingenious compliment. The murderer thought so too—I could tell. But again the murderer had misjudged the man; and so had I.

Sergeant Morgan said dryly, "Thanks. But I hope you weren't expecting anything in return for that. Because you're not going to get it."

"I wasn't expecting to get it." But the murderer was rather white. "Of course, I'm Emily's cousin—"

"I'm Emily's husband. That didn't bother *you*."

"Well, not very long," the murderer said, and actually smiled. "But look at it this way, Sergeant. Turn me over to the police and it's not going to be any fun for anybody. Me or you or Emily—anybody. Whereas if you and Miss Julia would just be kind enough to go out in the hall and shut this door behind you—"

"You mean it's two stories down to the street?" Sergeant Morgan asked bluntly.

"I mean I've got something better than that in my pocket, Sergeant," the murderer said gently. "You haven't given me much chance to get it out. And even if you had, I don't have any sharpshooter's medals on *my* chest; you surely would have got me first. But given some privacy and a good close range—say an inch or two—I believe I could save the Commonwealth of Kentucky the expense of a trial."

I shuddered violently. I couldn't help it. I said, getting up blindly, "Sergeant—"

Sergeant Morgan didn't hesitate but a minute more. "Okay, Miss Tyler. Out you go. Take your tally card with you, and hang on to it. It's evidence. We'll need it, unless—you wouldn't like to write your confession down, would you? Just a few lines—no use going into detail."

"No, no use going into detail," the murderer said, softly. "Yes, that would be better, Sergeant."

"Take your hand away from that pocket," Sergeant Morgan said violently. "I'll give you something to write with when the time comes. I'll have that pistol first. Face the wall and lean on your hands. Well, Miss Tyler? I thought I told you to leave."

"There's something I want to know," I said unsteadily. "Why did you hate him? I mean, why you more than the rest? Because the rest of them had just as much money to gain— And Charlotte said you were the one, out of all the rest, that got out of doing unpleasant things—"

"Well, there was one pretty special reason, Miss Julia," the murderer said. I never saw an uglier look come over a person's face. "Three years ago—the invitations were already out and the presents coming in— I don't doubt Cousin Charlotte's told you. And Grandfather broke it up. Blackmailed me—and lied to her, Miss Julia. If he'd only told the truth—she could have taken that. He knew she could have. So he lied. And so he's dead. And now—"

"Out of here, Miss Tyler," Sergeant Morgan said again. I reckon I did get out. Certainly I was in the hall—how much later was it?—with Charlotte holding her smelling salts bottle under my nose till I waved her away. Lieutenant Bates and two of his policemen were coming up the stairs, faster than I'd ever seen them move, and down in the kitchen I could hear the servants wailing together, the way they always do. Martina Greer was crumpled up like a child on the parlor sofa, crying as if her heart would break, and Mary Preston was locked in her room upstairs, and John Todd Brown was dead.

CHAPTER TWENTY-ONE

"I can't get over it. I just *cannot* get over it," I kept saying to Charlotte. "Why, the first thing I noticed about that boy was his eyes—how blue they were and how steady. They made you like him and trust him right away. I remember I said so at the time."

"Yes, I remember you did," Charlotte said dryly. "And I didn't contradict you. But actually, Julia, nobody that knew Johnny ever trusted him at all. I don't mean about stealing the company's money. I didn't know about that. But there were little things—"

Breck had told us that about the company's money. He and Janie had come to dinner that evening—we were back in the apartment across the street—with Emily and Sergeant Morgan. Not a party, of course, Charlotte said. But the young Morgans were leaving for California in the morning, and really, as Charlotte told them, nobody had had a chance to get acquainted with him at all.

Mercifully, as things turned out, there wasn't much chance for it even then. It was only once in a while that Charlotte got in some personal question at "George", as she persisted in calling him. It would have made a cat laugh to hear Emily pointedly calling him "Virgil", immediately thereafter, every time.

Much as we'd have been interested in Sergeant Morgan's past

experiences and future prospects, ordinarily, we were all much too full of the murder to stay off that subject long. There were lots of little things that needed to be cleared up in our minds, and then it seemed to make Breck, at least—Breck was the one that knew the most about it—feel better to talk it out.

He said, when I asked him, "Oh, always, Miss Julia. As far back as I can remember. Johnny was—well, you know what Johnny was like. Swell in lots of ways. The best disposition in the world. And the best company. But you couldn't depend on him. I felt pretty sick when he and Mary Preston got engaged, I can tell you that."

"The good Lord was mighty kind to us there, Breck," Charlotte told him solemnly. "I never knew what really happened to break it off."

"Well, Mary Preston didn't know either, poor kid," Breck said. "I didn't want to tell her about Johnny's getting caught embezzling from the Helm Tobacco Company. Nobody knew except the advertising manager, that Johnny worked under, and Grandfather and me; and we wanted to stop it there. Mary Preston wasn't but eighteen—I was afraid she couldn't keep her mouth shut. I've found out since. She can."

We all nodded. She certainly could.

"So Grandfather packed Johnny off to New York," Breck Helm went on. A little muscle underneath his jaw twitched back and forth. "Threatened him with Eddyville if he didn't go—and wouldn't let him talk to Mary Preston first. Or later." He said, shaking his head, "He just told Mary Preston there was a good and sufficient reason she and Johnny shouldn't marry. I didn't agree with the way Grandfather handled that."

"I'm surprised she took his word for it," I said.

Breck said, "Well, Aunt Elizabeth—she lived at our house, you know, for a while after she left Johnny's father. Gosh, was she beautiful! Like Martina, only more so. Well, Aunt Elizabeth died of paresis, Miss Julia. Not to put too fine a point on it. Mary Preston knew all that—and overheard plenty of other things about Johnny's father, in her time. Grandfather just let her draw her own conclusions. They were wrong, but they did the work. And then when Johnny didn't write—" Charlotte said, "Elizabeth really did have to leave Johnny's father, Julia. Martin Brown was—well, I told you she'd made an unfortunate marriage, but it was worse than that. He was—awful. The Browns are one of the very nicest families in Kentucky; but, well, these things sometimes happen."

I nodded agreement, avoiding Sergeant Morgan's eyes.

"Johnny did all right in his new job," Breck resumed. "He really was good at advertising, you know. His copy had—well, everything that he did." Breck's eyes swept the circle of our faces to see if we knew what he meant, and we did. "But he got in with an expensive set, and he lived their way. And he just didn't have the money to keep it up. New York is heaven if you've got plenty, he told me once—oh, a long time ago. And hell on earth if you have to count your change. I asked him why he didn't get a job somewhere else. But he said he could manage there till Grandfather died. He said he'd found the place he liked to live, and seen the way he wanted to live, and, by God, he intended to stay the course. I beg your pardon, Aunt Charlotte, Miss Julia."

"This is where I come in," Virgil Morgan said, clearing his throat. "Brown got in trouble again—the way you'd expect him to. He padded his expense accounts the whole three years he was with that New York firm; that was one way he 'managed.' And finally he got caught. His employer was—kinder than he deserved. I guess Brown really was a good advertising man, as Breck says. Anyway, he told him that if he'd make the money good within two months, and of course give up his job, he wouldn't prosecute him for theft. That was a pretty generous offer, I think."

"Johnny was—Johnny," Charlotte said. "Even a man that he'd stolen from—"

Sergeant Morgan nodded. "I know. I liked him myself, at first. Well, anyway, Brown sits down and writes a letter to old Mr. Helm. He didn't know where else to turn, and it was quite a lot of money—between twelve and fifteen hundred dollars. He asked Mr. Helm to make it good, and he promised *he'd* be good from then on out and—lots of things. It was quite a letter. It would have taken most anybody in; but not old Mr. Helm, this time. He'd had enough. He told Gus so, and Gus begged him to take time to think it over. He did think it over. But he'd had enough. And on the twenty-third of March he sat down and wrote Johnny Brown a letter and told him so, and told him he was going to change his will."

Breck said, "So that's how Johnny knew."

"No, it wasn't," Sergeant Morgan contradicted. "He knew from something Gus said. That letter was never sent. It was never finished. That's the letter old Mr. Helm was writing when he had his first stroke. You can see right where it happened. Three or four words that you can't read at all—maybe they aren't really words—and then a long, wavery line, and then a blot."

"Oh, then you saw it, George?" Charlotte asked, while Emily, unable to get a "Virgil" in edgewise, gave her what Dick calls a dirty look.

"I certainly did see it, Mrs. Buckner," George Virgil Morgan said with pride. "I found it. I found them both. It took me a good long time, because I didn't have much chance to look—just occasional weekend nights, when Emily'd let me in. I found it finally in old Mr. Helm's room. Inside a book, where Gus had put it in a hurry before he called the doctor."

"You spent your time in Gus's room, too," I said. I could still shudder, remembering the night he'd passed me on the stairs. "And I saw a light up there—it was the night I came—"

"Well, I guess it was Brown that time, Miss Tyler," Sergeant Morgan said. "Sometimes he was the one. And sometimes both of us. One time I met him coming out of Gus's room, just when I was going in. We got used to running into each other later, but— It gave us both a turn, I can tell you that. Well, it was that night I began to suspect that he was the murderer, and he got it through *his* head that I was going to make him trouble and he'd better dispose of *me*."

"I think most of *us* thought it was Johnny, too," Emily said. "But we couldn't be sure. Something else would point to another person, and then we'd be all up in the air again."

Breck said firmly, "Not me. There never was any real doubt in my mind. Not after Johnny admitted pawning that ring. He said he'd asked Gus for money first, and Gus had refused to get it out of the safe. He would refuse, of course. Johnny knew Gus better than that. I told him he was a fool even to ask."

A goddamned bloody fool. I remembered.

"I wish you'd begin at the beginning about that ring, Breck," I said. "It seems to me it's been hopping around all over the place, all through this murder case, and practically everybody involved has had it in his hands."

"Well, not quite, Miss Julia," Breck Helm said. "To begin at the beginning—we all knew the ring was in Grandfather's safe—along with some other old family stuff. It was just Johnny's bad luck that he happened to take the one piece of jewelry that Grandfather mentioned in his will."

"When did he take it?" Charlotte asked, and Breck said, "The first chance he got, Aunt Charlotte. A few days after we were all called home. He offered to sit in Grandfather's room while the nurse ate dinner with the rest of us. We didn't think anything of it at the time. But Gus just happened to go back upstairs to see how Grandfather was, and he caught Johnny going through the safe. They must have had quite a scene."

"Yes. Well. We can skip that part," Charlotte said, hurriedly.

"Well, it was four or five days after Gus's death that Johnny got around to pawning the ring. He was practically unable to do unpleasant things, you know. Not unless he just had to. You take that business of his asking Gus to open the safe *for* him," Breck Helm said parenthetically, "when he knew the combination himself. Had known it ever since Christmas Eve. Well, anyway. He put this off as long as he could—pawning the ring, I mean. And when he couldn't put it off any longer—he had to get the money to the man in New York by a certain date—he got my little sister to do his dirty work for him."

Breck Helm's jaw set grimly; underneath it, the little muscle was twitching back and forth again.

"He told Mary Preston it was his own grandmother's ring, and she believed him. She believed everything he ever told her. Grandfather may have broken that engagement up, but Mary Preston still thought Johnny was the sun, moon, and stars," Breck went on somberly, in the same words that I remembered Charlotte's using. "I hope she'll get over it now. Well, anyway, Johnny told her a well-dressed woman always got more at the pawnshops than a man did, and of course she was glad to do it for him. Mary Preston would have done anything for Johnny. Anything in this world."

Again I recognized Charlotte's very words.

"Whose idea was it about the disguise? Hers or Johnny's?" I asked.

"Johnny's. He knew he was putting her in a dangerous position, if she didn't. But of course Mary Preston thought it would be fun to dress up. She was pleased as a kid when she happened to meet Virgil Morgan on the corner after she came out of that pawnshop, and stopped and asked him the way to the car line and he didn't recognize her."

"Well, I didn't know Mary Preston very well then. I'd only seen her a few times," Sergeant Morgan said apologetically.

"Mrs. Thompson knew her right away."

"Yes, but that was what upset Mary Preston so on the witness stand," Breck said. "She thought she'd finally fooled Mrs. Thompson too. And then she didn't think the police would call her. Mrs. Thompson must have gone home and talked, I reckon."

"About seeing a girl enough like Mary Preston to be her twin sister. Naturally," I nodded. "Well, Breck, what about her buying that sodium fluoride on that same trip? Why did she want it, and what possessed her to do a dangerous thing like that?"

"Well, she didn't think it was dangerous, Miss Julia." Breck Helm answered my last question first. "She'd just got through talking to Virgil Morgan, remember, without his recognizing her. She thought she was pretty good, and there wasn't a chance in the world that drug clerk would know her again, without her dark glasses and with her hair the other way."

"But why did she buy the fluoride?"

"Just to use on ants," Breck answered simply. "She'd given me all the stuff she had, to take out to Holliday Hall. And then she needed some more to use in her own kitchen. All this was before she got that pup, of course. But by that time Gus was dead, and it didn't seem quite the thing for—any of us to go out and buy. It was just when she found out how well her wonderful disguise had worked on Virgil Morgan, and happened to be standing right in front of a drugstore, that she thought she might as well."

"Breck, I asked you about the ring, and then I got you off the track myself," I said. "Please go on about that. Why did Johnny redeem it himself, and where did he get the money to?"

Breck said grimly, "Because I made him. Because I gave him the money. I haven't had much chance to spend it, out where I've been. I drove that young man down to the pawnshop myself, and waited in the car till he came out. And then I took that ring in charge. Aunt Charlotte very kindly kept it for me a few days, till I could hide it out at Holliday Hall—"

"*Charlotte?*"

"Right on this finger," Charlotte said complacently, spreading out her left hand. Her wide gold band was on the wedding finger, as usual, together with her three Tiffany-set diamond solitaires—her own, her mother's, and her mother-in-law's engagement rings. "Lieutenant Bates suspected I had it, somehow, but I flourished it right in front of his face and he didn't know. Nobody did. I just simply put Mama's ring in a safe place, and wore Emily's for a few days instead. They were just about alike."

They were. As Lieutenant Bates had said, Emily Powell Helm's ring was about like everybody's engagement ring, back in those days.

"And then I took it out to Holliday Hall and hid it inside the piano. Not in that old broken wall safe, of course. But Martina—Martina was like Mary Preston; she'd do anything for Johnny—was dumb enough to come out looking for it there. It was the day we had lunch, Miss Julia, Janie—remember? I told you it was a little colored boy we heard."

Janie and I nodded, looking at each other without saying anything. Janie, in fact, hadn't said a word since we started to talk about Johnny Brown. But she was looking mighty young and happy, bless her heart—happier than I'd ever seen her.

"At first I thought Johnny just wanted that ring back because of the money value," Breck went on. "When I finally got it through my head he wanted to plant it on Virgil Morgan, as evidence along with the other items he mentioned in his—confession, I thought it was safer to send it to the police. So I did."

It was as simple as that.

"It's a wonder you didn't get your own sister arrested, sending it to the police," I told him severely. "Lieutenant Bates said himself that ring was the only thing he needed. He'd switched suspicion from Emily to Mary Preston, by that time. If Emily hadn't disappeared—"

"I got away just in time to keep from being scared to death, anyway," Emily said. "We thought it was so kind of Johnny to let us use his name and promise to keep it quiet, when Virgil and I married. But afterwards, when I was pretty sure he was the murderer, and thought about his having that hold—"

"There's one thing I didn't understand at the time, and don't yet," Janie said suddenly. "Why did Dr. Greer get so upset, and testify he didn't remember whether he had eleven bottles of poison or twelve? He wasn't mixed up in it at all."

Breck told her simply, "He was just scared, Janie. He was under a strain, and he's naturally a weak person. Maybe that's why Martina married him. I certainly never could think of any other reason. But Martina is strong. Maybe she enjoys holding her husband up. The way she always held up her brother."

"Well, I don't want to have to hold *my* husband up," Emily said. "I want him to hold me up."

I said, shaking my head at her, "I think you'll always stand on your own two feet, my dear, from what I've seen. And your husband will stand on his."

As if he'd been waiting for a signal, Sergeant Morgan stood promptly on his own two feet. "That reminds me, Miss Tyler. Emily and I had better be going. Our train leaves at half-past eight, and I want Emily to get a good night's sleep. It'll be the last until she gets to San Francisco."

"Oh, my dear child!" Charlotte looked more tragic than she had all evening. "Couldn't you get a reservation? Can't you wait for one?"

Emily shook her head, blinking her blond eyelashes so fast you could hardly see them. "Oh, no, Aunt Charlotte. I *want* to go in the day coach. I want to be with Virgil every single minute until he sails. Maybe— maybe it'll be as long as two months."

Charlotte repressed a shudder as Sergeant Morgan put his arm around Emily and pulled her over against his ugly mustard-colored sleeve. But I thought it was rather nice, and certainly Emily did. I said hastily, to cover up for Charlotte, "That's fine," though usually I don't approve of wives following soldiers all around the country. It's the officers' wives in Pullmans that make non-commissioned officers have to sit up in day coaches, and the non-commissioned officers' wives, like Emily, who make common soldiers stand in the aisles.

"Well, my dear, I was in San Francisco on my own honeymoon," Charlotte contributed then, sighing heavily. "Your Uncle Tom took me around the world, you know. I'll never forget those cable cars. I was scared to death. And Gump's showrooms. And you must be sure to stay at the Palace Hotel."

Emily smiled. "We'll stay at the Palace Hotel on our *golden* wedding trip, Aunt Charlotte. I'm afraid it would be too expensive for us this time. You see," Emily went on, as the million and a half she'd inherited from Mr. Helm hung unmentioned in the air, "until the war is over, anyway, we're going to live on what Virgil makes."

"And probably after that," Sergeant Morgan said firmly. "Can you imagine it, Mrs. Buckner?—this girl thought I'd married her for her money. It wasn't just her family thought I was interested in that. *She* did. That's why she was knocking herself out trying to get her grandfather adjudged incompetent, or anything so he couldn't sign that new will. Because she thought *I* wanted his money. Can you feature that?"

Emily squirmed slightly. "Well, most people do like a lot of money." Including your whole family, my dear, I thought silently. It was the root of all your evil. Not just Johnny. Mary Preston. Breck. Martina and Dr. Greer. You, too, probably, after the first flush of young love has worn off. "And you know how it always was, Aunt Charlotte," Emily went on. "I know it isn't the kind of thing you say right out. But Mary Preston always had so *many* dates—and I'm not beautiful the way she is—"

Sergeant Morgan told her firmly, in the tone of one instructing a backward child, "Of course you're not beautiful the way Mary Preston is. Mary Preston has blue eyes, and yours are mostly grey. And Mary Preston's hair is black, and you've got golden hair—"

It wasn't golden at all, just plain, ordinary blond. But even Charlotte softened at that, and she was reaching for her handkerchief by the time the four young people had finished saying good night and got outside the door. Charlotte is perfectly the type that always cries at weddings, and this was the next best thing.

"It's a happy ending after all, isn't it, Julia?" Charlotte asked then, wiping tears.

"Yes, indeed," I said, as enthusiastically as I could. Nice sweet little Emily with her shrinking manner and her pale eyelashes wasn't my idea of a heroine. "Not quite what I'd expected, though, Charlotte," I couldn't help adding. "I was hoping Mary Preston and that nice young

Captain Howard—"

Charlotte shook her head. "Mary Preston'll go on and study medicine now, Julia. Breck was telling me. And she doesn't think she'll ever have a happy ending, now that Johnny's gone." "Gone" was certainly a nice way of putting it, I thought. "But life goes on," Charlotte went on herself, as if she'd just discovered it, "and the war in Europe's over, and Breck and Janie have decided to be married, too, and the Derby comes this Saturday, after all."

"Yes, after all," I said.

THE END

Made in the USA
Middletown, DE
04 May 2025